The Collected Supernatural and Weird Fiction of R. H. Benson

The Collected Supernatural and Weird Fiction of R. H. Benson

One Novel 'The Necromancers' and Twenty-Eight Tales of the Strange and Unusual

R. H. Benson

LEONAUR

*The Collected
Supernatural and Weird
Fiction of
R. H. Benson*
One Novel 'The Necromancers' and Twenty-Eight Tales of the Strange and Unusual
by R. H. Benson

FIRST EDITION

Leonaur is an imprint of Oakpast Ltd

Copyright in this form © 2019 Oakpast Ltd

ISBN: 978-1-78282-792-4 (hardcover)
ISBN: 978-1-78282-793-1 (softcover)

http://www.leonaur.com

Publisher's Notes

Contents

Prologue

"I maintain," said *Monsignor* with a brisk air of aggressiveness, and holding his pipe a moment from his mouth, "I maintain that agnosticism is the only reasonable position in these matters. Your common agnostic is no agnostic at all; he is the most dogmatic of sectarians. He declares that such things do not happen, or that they can be explained always on a materialistic basis. Now, your Catholic—"

Father Bianchi bristled and rolled his black eyes fiercely. If he had had a moustache he would have twirled it.

We were sitting in the upstairs *sala* of the presbytery attached to the Canadian Church of S. Filippo in Rome. It had been a large, comfortless room, stone floored, stone walled, and plaster ceilinged, but it had been made possible by numerous rugs, a number of armchairs, and an English fireplace. Above, in the cold plaster, dingy, flesh-coloured gods and nymphs attempted to lounge on cotton clouds with studied ease, looking down dispiritedly upon seven priests and myself, a layman, who sat in a shallow semicircle round the red logs. In 1871 the house had fallen into secular hands, whence issued the gods and nymphs, but in 1897 the Church had come by her own again, and had not yet banished Olympus. There was no need to annihilate the conquered.

In the centre sat the Father Rector, a placid old man, and round about him were the rest of us—Monsignor Maxwell, a French priest, an English, an Italian, a Canadian, a German, and myself. This was five years ago. I do not know where these people are now—one I think is in heaven, two I should suppose in purgatory, four on earth. In spite of my feelings toward Padre Bianchi, I should assign him to purgatory. He made a good death two years later in the Naples epidemic.

We had begun at supper by discussing modem miracles. The second nocturn had furnished the text to the mouth of *Monsignor*, and we had passed on by natural channels to levitation, table-turning, family curses, ghosts, and banshees. The Italian was sceptical and scornful. Such things, in his opinion, did not take place; he excepted only the incidents recorded in the lives of the saints. I did not mind his

7

scepticism (that, after all, injures no one but the sceptic), but scorn and contumely is another matter, and I was glad that Canon Maxwell had taken him in hand, for that priest has a shrewd and acrid tongue, and wears purple, besides, round his person and on his buttons, so he speaks with authority.

"You have some tale, then, no doubt, *Monsignor?*" sneered the Italian.

The Englishman smiled with tight lips.

"Everyone has," he said briefly. "Even you, Padre Bianchi, if you will but tell it."

The other shook his head indulgently.

"I will swear," he said, "that none here has such a tale at first hand."

It was Father Meuron's turn to bristle. "But yes!" he exclaimed.

Canon Maxwell drew on his pipe a moment or two and regarded the fire.

"I have a proposition to make," he said. "Father Bianchi is right. I have one tale, and Father Meuron has another. With the Father Rector's permission, we will tell our tales, one each night. On Sunday two or three of us are supping at the French College, so that shall be a holiday, and by Monday night these other gentlemen will no doubt have remembered experiences—even Father Bianchi, I believe. And Mr. Benson shall write them all down, if he wishes to, and make an honest penny or two, if he can get any publisher to take the book."

I hastened to express my approval of the scheme.

The Father Rector moved in his chair.

"That will be very amusing, *Monsignor.* I am entirely in favour of it, though I doubt my own capacity. I propose that Canon Maxwell takes the chair."

"Then I understand that all will contribute one story," said *Monsignor* briskly, "on those terms—?"

There was a chorus of assent.

"One moment, *Monsignor,*" interrupted Father Brent; "would it not be worthwhile to have a short discussion first as to the whole affair? I must confess that my own ideas are not clear."

"Well," said *Monsignor* shortly, "on what point?"

The younger priest mused a moment.

"It is like this," he said; "half at least of the stories one hears have no point—no reason. Take the ordinary haunted-house tale or the appearances at the time of death. Now, what is the good of all that? They tell us nothing; they don't generally ask for prayers. It is just a white woman wringing her hands, or a groaning or something. At the best one only finds a skeleton behind the panelling. Now, my story, if I tell it, has absolutely no point at all."

"No point?" said *Monsignor,* "you mean that you don't understand the point, or that no one does; is that it?"

"Well, yes; but there is more, too. How do you square these things with purgatory? How can spirits go wandering about, and be so futile at the end of it, too? Then why is everything so vague? Why don't they give us a hint? I'm not wanting precise information, but a kind of hint of the way things go. Then the whole thing is mixed up with such childish nonsense. Look at the spiritualists, and the tambourine business, and table-rapping. Either those things are true, even if they're diabolical—and in that case people in the spiritual world seem considerably sillier even than people in this—or they're not true; and in that case the whole thing is so fraudulent that it seems useless to inquire. Do you see my point?"

"I see about twenty," said *Monsignor,* "and it would take all night to answer them. But let me take two. Firstly, I am entirely willing to allow that half the stories one hears are fraudulent or hysterical—I'm quite ready to allow that. But it seems to me that there remain a good many others; and if one doesn't accept those to some extent, I don't know what becomes of the value of human evidence. Now, one of your points, I take it, is that even these seem generally quite pointless and useless; is that it?"

"More or less," said Father Brent.

"Well, first I would say this: It seems perfectly clear that these other stories aren't sent to help our faith, or anything like that. I don't believe that for one instant. We have got all we need in the Catholic Church, and the moral witness, and the rest. But what I don't understand in your position is this: What earthly right have you got to think that they're sent just for your benefit?"

The other demurred.

"I don't," he said; "but I suppose they're sent for somebody's benefit."

"Somebody still on earth, you mean?"

"Well—yes."

Monsignor leaned forward.

"My dear Father, how very provincial you are—if I may say so! Here is this exceedingly small earth, certainly with a very fair number of people living on it, but absolutely a mere fraction of the number of intelligences that are in existence. And all about us—since we must use that phrase—is a spiritual world compared with which the present generation is as a family of ants in the middle of London. Things happen; this spiritual world is crammed full of energy and movement and affairs. . . . We know practically nothing of it all, except those few main principles which are called the Catholic Faith—nothing else. What conceivable right have we to demand that the little glimpses that we seem to get sometimes of the spiritual world are given to us for our benefit or information?"

"Then why are they given?"

Monsignor made a disdainful sound with closed lips.

"My dear Father, a boy drops a piece of orange peel into the middle of the ants' nest one day. The ants summon a council at once and sit on it. They discuss the lesson that is to be learned from the orange peel; they come to the conclusion that Buckingham Palace must be built entirely of orange peel, and that the reason why it was sent to them was that they were to learn that great and important lesson."

Father Brent sat up suddenly.

"My dear *Monsignor*, you seem to me to strike at the root of Revelation. If we aren't to deduce things from supernatural incidents, why should we believe in our religion?" *Monsignor* lifted a hand.

"Next day there is slid into the ants' nest a box divided into compartments, containing exactly that which the ants need for the winter—food and so forth. The ants hold another Parliament. Two-thirds of them who have determined in the last hour or two to reject the Buckingham-Palace-orange-peel theory reject this, too. All is fortuitous, they say. The orange peel was; therefore, the box is."

Father Brent relapsed, smiling.

"That is all right," he said; "I was a fool."

"One-third," continued the Canon severely, "come to the not unreasonable conclusion' that a box which shows such evident signs of intelligence, and of knowledge and care for their circumstances, proceeds from an Intelligence which wishes them well. But there is a further schism. Half of those who accept Revelation remain agnostic about most other things, and say frankly that they don't know—especially as regards the orange peel. The other half rages on about the orange peel; some are inclined to think that there was no orange peel—it was no more than an hallucination; others think that there is some remarkable lesson to be learned from it, and these differ evidently as to what the lesson is. Others, again, regard it unintelligently and say to one another, 'Look, a piece of orange peel! How very beautiful and important!'"

I laughed softly to myself. *Monsignor* spoke with such earnestness. I would like him to be my advocate if I ever get into trouble.

"Now, my dear Father," he went on, "I take up the first position of those who accept Revelation, and I acknowledge the fact of the orange peel; but really nothing more. My religion teaches me that there is a spiritual world of indefinite size; and that things not only may, but must, go on there which have nothing particular to do with me. Every now and then I get a glimpse of some of these things—an orange pip at the very least. But I don't immediately demand an explanation. It probably isn't deliberately meant for me at all. It has something to do with affairs of which I know nothing, and which manage to get on quite well without me."

Father Brent, still smiling, protested once more.

"Very ingenious, *Monsignor*; but then why does it happen to happen to you?"

"I have not the slightest idea, any more than I have the slightest idea why Providence made me break a tooth this morning. I accept the fact; I believe that somehow it works into the scheme. But I do not for that reason desire to understand it. . . . And as for purgatory—well, I ask you, what in the world do we know about purgatory except that there is such a thing, and that the souls of the faithful detained there are assisted by our suffrages? What conceivable possibility is there that we should understand the details of its management? My dear Father, no one in this world has a greater respect for, or confidence in, dogmatic theology than myself; in fact, I may say that it is the only thing which I do have confidence in. But I respect the limits which it itself has laid down."

"Then you are an agnostic as regards everything but the Faith?"

"Certainly I am. Well, possibly, except mathematics, too. And so is every wise man. I have my ideas of, and I make guesses sometimes; but I really do not think that they have any value."

There was silence a moment.

"Then there is this, too," he continued; "it really is important to remember that the spiritual world exists in another mode from that in which the material world exists. That is where the ant simile breaks down. It is more as if an ant went to the Royal Academy. . . . . Of course, in the Faith we have an adequate and guaranteed translation of the supernatural into the natural and *vice versa;* and in these ghost stories, or whatever we call them, we have a certain sort of translation, too. The real thing, whatever it is, expresses itself in material terms, more or less. But in these we have no sort of guarantee that the translation is adequate, or that we are adequate to understand it. We can try, of course; but we really don't know. Therefore, it seems to me that in all ghost stories the best thing is to hear it, to satisfy ourselves that the evidence is good or bad—and then to hold our tongues. We don't want elaborate commentaries on what may be, after all, an utterly corrupt text."

"But some of them do support the Faith," put in Father Brent.

"So much the better, then. But it is much safer not to lean your weight on them. You never can tell. Now, with the Faith you can."

There was another silence.

Then the rector stood up, smiling.

"Night prayers, reverend Fathers," he said.

Monsignor Maxwell's Tale

I was still thinking over the canon's remarks as I came up into the *sala* on the following evening. They seemed to me eminently sensible; or, in other words, they exactly represented what I had always held myself, though I had never so expressed them even to my own mind.

I felt some interest, therefore, in the question as to the class to which *Monsignor's* own story would be found to belong—whether to that which contains merely a series of phenomena or to that which appeared to corroborate the Christian Religion.

The rest of the company, with two or three strangers, were already in their places when I arrived, and *Monsignor* was enthroned in the centre chair, staring with a preoccupied look at the blazing fire. The rector was on his right.

The conversation died away at last; there was a shifting of attitudes. Then the canon looked at his watch, bending his sleek grey head sideways.

"We have twenty minutes," he said in his terse way. Then he crossed his buckled feet and began without any preliminary comment.

"This happened to me in England. Naturally I shall not mention where it took place, nor how long ago. I knew a man, a Catholic from birth, of a remarkable faith and piety. He had tried his vocation in religion again and again, for he seemed a born Religious, but his health had always broken down, and he had finally married. He had been told by his director that his vocation was evidently to live in the world and as a layman. Whether I agree or disagree with the latter part of his advice is not to the point, but there was no question as to the former part of it. The man's health simply could not stand it. But he led a most mortified and interior life with his wife in his London house, with a servant or two to look after them, and was present daily at mass at the church that I served then. His wife, too, was a very exceptional woman, utterly devoted to her husband, and I may say that I never paid them a visit without being very much the better for it.

"Now, he had a brother, a solicitor in a town in the north, also a Catholic, of course, whom I never saw, but who enters very materially into the story. We will call the brothers, if you please, Mr. James and Mr. Herbert, though I need not say that these were not their names.

"One morning after mass Mr. James came to me in the sacristy and said he wished to have a word with me, so I took him through into the presbytery and up into my own room. I could see that something was very much the matter with him.

"He took a letter out and gave it to me to read. It was from his brother, Mr. Herbert, and contained very sad news indeed—nothing else, in fact, than an announcement of his intention to secede from the Church. There was a story of a marriage difficulty, too, as there so often is in such cases. He had fallen in love with a woman of strong agnostic convictions, and nothing would induce her to marry him unless he conformed to her religion, such as it was. But, to do Mr. Herbert justice, I could see that there was a real loss of faith as well. There were two or three sheets filled with arguments that I could see were real to the man—or statements, perhaps, rather than arguments—against the Incarnation and the inspiration of the Scriptures and the authority of the Church, and so on, and I must confess that they were not mere clap-trap. The woman was plainly capable and shrewd, and had been talking to him, and both his heart and his head were seriously entangled.

"Well, I handed the letter back to Mr. James, and said what I could—recommended a book or two, promised to get him prayers, and so on, but the man waved it aside.

"'Yes, yes, Father,' he said; 'I know, and I thank you, but I must do more than that. You don't know what this means to me. I got the letter yesterday at midday, and I may say that I have done nothing but pray since, and this morning at mass I saw a light; at least, I think so, and I want your advice.'

"He was terribly excited, his eyes were bright and the lines in his face deeper than I had ever seen them, for he was only just entering middle age, and the papers shook in his hands. I did my best to quiet him, but it was no good. All his tranquillity, which had been one of his most striking virtues, was gone, and I could see that his whole being was rent.

"'You don't know what this means to me,' he said again. 'There is only one thing to be done. I must offer myself for him.'

"Well, I didn't understand him at first, but we talked a little, and at last I found that the idea of mystical substitution had seized on his mind. He was persuaded that he must make an offering of himself to God, and ask to be allowed to bear the temptation instead of his brother. Of course, we know that that is one of the claims of the Contemplative, but, to tell the truth, I had never come across it before in my own experience.

"Well, he didn't want my opinion upon the doctrine, and, indeed, I was glad he didn't, for I knew nothing about it myself; but he wanted to know if I thought him justified in running the risk—for he seemed to take it as a matter of course that I believed it.

"'Am I strong enough, Father?' he asked. 'Can I bear it? I cannot imagine my losing my faith,' and a smile just flickered on his mouth and vanished again in trembling; 'but—but God knows how weak I am.'

"Well, I reassured him on that point, at any rate, and told him that so far as his faith was concerned I considered it robust enough. To tell the truth, I suppose I was a little careless, because—because"—and *Monsignor* shifted a little in his chair and looked around—"well it was all so bewildering.

"Well, he soon went after that, saying that he would tell his wife, and imploring me to get prayers for him in his struggle, and I was left alone to think it over.

"For the next day or two he appeared at mass as usual, and just waited for me one morning to tell me that he had made the offering of himself before God. Then I had to go into the country on some business or other and was away from Monday to Saturday.

"Now, to tell the truth, I did not think of him very much; I was harassed and bothered myself about my business, and scarcely did more than just mention his name at the altar, and I am ashamed to say I completely forgot to get prayers elsewhere for his brother or himself, and I was entirely unprepared for what was waiting for me when I reached home on the Saturday evening."

Monsignor paused a moment or two. He was evidently speaking with a certain difficulty. His brisk, business-like way of talking had just a tinge of feeling in it which it generally lacked, and he moved in his chair now and then with something almost like nervousness. The other priests were silent. The young Englishman was bending forward in the firelight with his chin on his hands, and old Father Stein had sat back in his chair very quiet and was shading his face from the candlelight.

"My housekeeper heard my key in the lock of the front door," went on Canon Maxwell, "and was waiting for me in the hall. She told me that Mr. James' wife had sent round four times for me that afternoon, saying she must have me at once on my return, and that any delay might be fatal. But it was not a case for the Last Sacraments, apparently. I was astonished by such phrases, but they were evidently word for word what she had said, for my housekeeper apologised for repeating them.

"'There is something terribly the matter, Father,' she said; 'the last time the servant was crying, and said that her master was out of his mind.'

"Well, I ran into church and told my penitents there that they must wait, or go to my colleague, and that I had had a sick call and did not know how long I should be away; and then I ran straight out of the church and down to the house, which was three or four streets off. (You must forgive my telling you this story with so many details; but somehow it is the only way I can do it; it is all as vivid and clear as if it had happened last week.) . . .

"It was a November evening; all the lamps were lit as I passed out of the thoroughfare down the side road where his house was; here the pavements were empty, and I ran again as fast as I could down the street and up the steps that led to his front door. Even as I stood there out of breath I knew that something was seriously wrong.

"Down in the kitchen below, as I could see plainly through the lighted windows, the Irish cook had been kneeling with her face hidden on the table; and she was now staring up at me with her eyes red and her hair disordered as the peal of the bell died away. Then she was out in the area almost screaming:

"'Oh, God bless you, Father!' and then the door opened and I was in the hall.

"'Where is he?' I asked the maid, all panting with my run; and she told me, 'In his study,' and then I was up at the door in a moment, knocking, and then, without waiting, I went in.

"It was one of those little back rooms that you see sometimes in London houses, just at the top of the stairs that lead down to the servants' quarters. There was a little garden at the back of the house and a side street beyond that. The curtains over the window had not been drawn, and a lamp shone into the room from the lane outside. But I did not understand that at the time. I was only aware that the room was dark, except for a pale light that lay across the floor and wall and on the door that I closed behind me.

"But the horror of the room was beyond anything that I have ever felt. It—it"—*Monsignor* hesitated—"it was almost physical, and yet I knew it was not, but it was the sense of some extraordinary influence, spiritual and on the point of—" He stopped again. "You must forgive me," he said, "but I can put it in no way but this—it seemed on the point of expressing itself visibly or tangibly; at any rate, I felt my hair rise slowly as I stood there, and then I leaned back against the door and groped for the handle."

Old Father Stein nodded gravely.

"I know, I know," he said in his heavy voice; "it was so with me at Benares."

"It was so dark at first," went on *Monsignor*, "that I could see nothing but the outlines of the furniture. There was the writing table, and so on, immediately on my left, the fireplace beyond it in the left-hand wall, a tall bureau beside the window opposite me. Then I felt my hand seized and gripped in the dark, and I looked down, horribly startled, and saw that his wife had been kneeling at his *prie-dieu* on the right, and had turned and clutched my hand as she saw me in the light of the street lamp, but she said nothing, and her silence was the worst of all.

"I looked again round the room and then suddenly gasped and, I must confess, nearly screamed, because quite close to me the man sat and stared up at me. I had been confused as I came in, and I believe now that I only had not seen him, because I had taken the dark outline of his body and the whiteness of his face to be a little side-table with papers upon it that often stood by his writing-place.

"Well, however that was, here was the man quite close to me, sitting bolt upright, with the lamplight falling on that deadly face, all lined as it was, with patches of dark beneath those awful, bright eyes."

Monsignor stopped again, and I could see that the hand on his chair arm twitched sharply once or twice.

"Well, two or three times, I should think, I opened my mouth to speak, and I have never known before or since what it was literally not to be able to do it. It was as if a hand gripped my throat each time. I suppose it was a kind of hysterical contraction of the muscles. I understood then why the wife could not speak. The only emotion I was conscious of was an insane desire to get out of the room and the house, away from that terrifying silence and oppressiveness; and, under God, I believe that the one thing that kept me there was that frightful grip on my fingers, that tightened as if the wife read my thoughts even as the desire surged up.

"I stood there, I suppose, half a minute more before I moved or spoke, and then I made a little motion, and drew my fingers out of hers, and made the sign of the cross, and even then, I dared not speak. But the face remained still in that tense quietness and the bright, sunken eyes never flinched or stirred.

"Then I dropped on my knees; and at last with really an extraordinary effort, as if I was breaking something, I managed to speak and say a prayer or two—the *Our Father* and the *Hail, Mary*; I could remember nothing else. Then I glanced at him quickly, and he had not stirred, but was watching me with a kind of bitter indifference—that is all I can say of it. I

went on with the creed, finished it, said Amen, and then one loud, harsh bark of laughter broke from him, and—and—I could swear that something else laughed, too."

A sharp exclamation broke from Father Brent, and a kind of sigh from the French priest as *Monsignor* suddenly sat up and struck his hand on his knee at his last word, and my own heart leaped and stood still, while my nerves jangled like struck wires.

"There, there," said the rector; "our nerves are out of order; be kind to us, *Monsignor*."

He shook his head.

"But I must tell you," he said, "though I hardly know what words to use. . . . This other laughter was not like his. I could not swear that—that there was a vibration of sound. It might have been interior, but it was there; it was objective and external to me. . . . Only I was absolutely convinced that there was laughter, neither mine, nor the man's, nor his wife's. There; that is all I can say of it."

He paused a moment.

"Well," he went on, "we got him; upstairs at last, and on his bed. I tell you it was a very odd relief to get out of the room downstairs.

He had not slept, his wife whispered to me as we went up, for four nights—not since the Monday, in fact, and had scarcely eaten, either. There was no time to hear more, for he turned round as he walked up and looked at us as we held him, and there was no more talking with that face before us. And there we sat beside him in his bedroom—he lay quiet with closed eyes—and I did not dare to leave him till three or four in the morning, when I was nearly dead with weariness. His wife made me go then, and promised to send again if there was any change.

"Well, during the sung mass, at which I was not officiating, the message came, and I was back at his house directly. There had been a change; he was now willing to talk. He looked ghastly, but his wife told me that she thought he had slept an hour or two after I had left.

"Well, we talked, and I found that the man's faith was gone—or perhaps it is safer to say completely obscured. I scarcely know how to express it, but it was as if he had practically no conception of what I was talking about.

"'I believed it once,' he said; 'yes, I am sure I did, but I can't imagine why or how.'"

"'Then what is all this trouble of mind about?' I asked.

"'Why,' he said, 'why, if it is not true, what is left?'

"I didn't quite see what he meant, and asked him.

"'You,' he said, and just touched me with his finger; 'you and I,' and he touched himself, 'and—and—all this,' and he tapped the table, 'and—all that,' and he flung his arm out toward the window and the chimney-pots and the bustling thoroughfare. 'All of it—all of it—what does it all mean; what is the good of it?'

"It was a piteous thing to see his face, the blackness and the misery of his despair at an empty, meaningless world and a self that could do nothing but writhe and cry in the dark.

"You see the whole thing for him stood or fell by God, lived and moved in Him; now God was gone, and what was left?

"Well, of course I reminded him of his offering of himself to God for his brother. God had accepted it, I told him; and he just laughed miserably in my face.

"'Do you think Herbert suffered like this?' he asked.

"Well, I was tired and bewildered, and this seemed to me an answer. Of course, you all see the explanation."

"The other suffered less because his faith was less," put in Father Brent instantly.

"Exactly," said *Monsignor*. "Well, I am ashamed to say I didn't see

18

that, at least not clearly enough to put it to him; but I did point out that it was of the very essence of his contract that he should suffer severely in the very manner in which he was suffering, and that the coincidence was remarkable; and, further, that the fact that he was in such distress showed that God was something to him after all. I don't know even then that I accepted the whole thing as being quite real. But what else could I say? . . . Well, he smiled again at that.

"'Have you never regretted a happy dream?' he said.

"Well, I am wearying you," said *Monsignor*, looking at his watch, "but I am just at the end. I went to that man every day for, I suppose, two or three hours for five or six weeks, and it seemed practically useless. I had never realised before so completely that faith was a gift which can be given or withdrawn; that it is something infused into us, not produced by us. Finally, the man died of congestion of the brain."

"Good Lord!" said a voice.

"Yes," said Canon Maxwell, blowing down his pipe, "those—those were my sentiments."

"*Monsignor!* Do you mean he died without faith?"

"Father Jenks, I gave him the sacraments. He asked for them. I did not press too many questions; I thought it best to leave well alone."

"And the brother?"

"Oh, the brother—Mr. Herbert—was at the funeral, and informed me that the marriage was broken off, and I never heard of his apostasy. And there was one other person who contributed to the interest of the whole affair, and that was the wife."

"What happened to her?"

"She became a Poor Clare. She told me that self-immolation was the only possible act for her after what she had seen and known." There was a long silence.

"Well, well, well," said Father Bianchi.

Father Meuron's Tale

Father Meuron was very voluble at supper on the Saturday. He exclaimed; he threw out his hands; his bright black eyes shone above his rosy cheeks, and his hair appeared to stand more on end than I had ever known it.

He sat at the further side of the horse-shoe table from myself, and I was able to remark on his gaiety to the English priest who sat beside me without fear of being overheard.

Father Brent smiled.

"He is drunk with *la gloire*," he said. "He is to tell the story tonight. *N.B.* This explained everything.

I did not look forward, however, to his recital. I was confident that it would be full of tinsel and swooning maidens who ended their days in convents under Father Meuron's spiritual direction; and when we came upstairs I found a shadowy corner, a little back from the semi-circle, where I could fall asleep if I wished without provoking remark.

In fact, I was totally unprepared for the character of his narrative.

When we had all taken our places, and *Monsignor's* pipe was properly alight, and himself at full length in his deck chair, the Frenchman began. He told his story in his own language; but I am venturing to render it in English as nearly as I am able.

"My contribution to the histories," he began, seated in his upright armchair in the centre of the circle, a little turned away from me— "my contribution to the histories which these good priests are to recite is an affair of exorcism. That is a matter with which we who live in Europe are not familiar in these days. It would seem, I suppose, that grace has a certain power, accumulating through the centuries, of saturating even physical objects with its force. However, men may rebel, yet the sacrifices offered and the prayers poured out have a faculty of holding Satan in check and preventing his more formidable manifestations.

"Even in my own poor country at this hour, in spite of widespread apostasy, in spite even of the deliberate worship of Satan, yet grace is in the air; and it is seldom indeed that a priest has to deal with a case of possession. In your respectable England, too, it is the same; the simple piety of Protestants has kept alive to some extent the force of the Gospel. Here in this country of Italy it is somewhat different. The old powers have survived the Christian assault, and while they cannot live in Holy Rome, there are corners where they do so."

From my place I saw Padre Bianchi turn a furtive eye upon the speaker, and I thought I read in it an unwilling assent.

"However," went on the Frenchman with a superb dimissory gesture, "my recital does not concern this continent, but the little island of La Souffrière. These circumstances are other than here. It was a stronghold of darkness when I was there in 1891. Grace, while laying hold of men's hearts, had not yet penetrated the lower creation. Do you understand me? There were many holy persons whom I knew, who frequented the Sacraments and lived devoutly, but there were many of another manner. The ancient rites survived secretly among the negroes, and darkness—how shall I say it?—dimness made itself visible.

"However, to our history."

The priest resettled himself in his chair and laid his fingers together like precious instruments. He was enjoying himself vastly, and I could see that he was preparing himself for a revelation.

"It was in 1891," he repeated, "that I went there with another of our Fathers to the mission-house. I will not trouble you, gentlemen, with recounting the tale of our arrival, nor of the months that followed it, except perhaps to tell you that I was astonished by much that I saw. Never until that time had I seen the power of the Sacraments so evident. In civilized lands, as I have suggested to you, the air is charged with grace. Each is no more than a wave in the deep sea. He who is without God's favour is not without His grace at each breath he draws. There are churches, religions, pious persons about him; there are centuries of prayers behind him. The very buildings he enters, as M. Huysmann has explained to us, are browned by prayer.

"Though a wicked child, he is yet in his father's house: and the return from death to life is not such a crossing of the abyss, after all. But there in La Souffrière all is either divine or Satanic, black or white, Christian or devilish. One stands, as it were, on the seashore to watch the breakers of grace, and each is a miracle. I tell you I have seen holy Catechumens foam at the mouth and roll their eyes in pain, as the saving water fell on them, and that which was within went out. As the Gospel relates, '*Spiritus conturbavit ilium: et elisus in terram, volutabatur spumans.*' (The spirit troubled him, and he fell to the ground, in convulsions.)

Father Meuron paused again.

I was interested to hear this corroboration of evidence that had come before me on other occasions. More than one missionary had told me the same thing; and I had found in their tales a parallel to those related by the first preachers of the Christian religion in the early days of the Church.

"I was incredulous at first," continued the priest, "until I saw these things for myself. An old father of our mission rebuked me for it. 'You are an ignorant fellow,' he said; 'your airs are still of the seminary.' And what he said was just, my friends.

"On one Monday morning as we met for our council I could see that this old priest had somewhat to say. M. Lasserre was his name. He kept very silent until the little businesses had been accomplished, and then he turned to the Father Rector.

"'*Monseigneur* has written,' he said, 'and given me the necessary, permission for the matter you know, my father. And he bids me take another priest with me. I ask that Father Meuron may accompany me. He needs a lesson, this zealous young missionary.'

"The Father Rector smiled at me as I sat astonished, and nodded at Father Lasserre to give permission.

"'Father Lasserre will explain all to you,' he said as he stood up for the prayer.

"The good priest explained all to me as the Father Rector had directed."

N.B. It appeared that there was a matter of exorcism on hand. A woman who lived with her mother and husband had been affected by the devil, Father Lasserre said. She was a Catechumen, and had been devout for several months, and all seemed well until this—this assault had been made on her soul. Father Lasserre had visited the woman and examined her, and had made his report to the Bishop, asking permission to exorcise the creature, and it was this permission that had been sent on that morning.

"I did not venture to tell the priest that he was mistaken and that the affair was one of epilepsy. I had studied a little in books for my medical training, and all that I heard now seemed to confirm me in the diagnosis. There were the symptoms, easy to read. What would you have?"—the priest again made his little gesture—"I knew more in my youth than all the Fathers of the Church. Their affairs of devils were nothing but an affection of the brain—dreams and fancies! And if the exorcisms had appeared to be of direct service, it was from the effect of the solemnity upon the mind. It was no more." He laughed with a fierce irony.

"You know it all, gentlemen!"

I had lost all desire to sleep now. The French priest was more interesting than I had thought. His elaborateness seemed dissipated; his voice trembled a little as he arraigned his own conceit, and I began to wonder how his change of mind had been wrought.

"We set out that afternoon," he continued. "The woman lived on the further side of the island, perhaps a couple of hours' travel, for it was rough going; and as we went up over the path Father Lasserre told me more.

"It seemed that the woman blasphemed. (The subconscious self, said I to myself, as M. Charcot has explained. It is her old habit reasserting itself.)

"She foamed and rolled her eyes. (An affection of the brain, said I.)

"She feared holy water; they dared not throw it on her, her struggles were so fierce. (Because she has been taught to fear it, said I.)

"And so, the good father talked, eyeing me now and again, and I smiled in my heart, knowing that he was a simple old fellow who had not studied the new books.

"She was quieter after sunset, he told me, and would take a little food then. Her fits came on her for the most part at midday. And I smiled again at that. Why it should be so I knew. The heat affected her. She would be quieter, science would tell us, when evening fell. If it were the power of Satan that held her she would surely rage more in the darkness than in the light. The Scriptures tell us so.

"I said something of this to Father Lasserre, as if it were a question, and he looked at me.

"'Perhaps, brother,' he said, 'she is more at ease in the darkness and fears the light, and that she is quieter therefore when the sun sets.'

"Again, I smiled to myself. What piety, said I, and what foolishness!

"The house where the three lived stood apart from any others. It was an old shed into which they had moved a week before, for the neighbours could no longer bear the woman's screaming. And we came to it towards a sunset.

"It was a heavy evening, dull and thick, and as we pushed down the path I saw the smoking mountain high on the left hand between the tangled trees. There was a great silence round us, and no wind, and every leaf against the rosy sky was as if cut of steel.

"We saw the roof below us presently, and a little smoke escaped from a hole, for there was no chimney.

"'We will sit here a little, brother,' said my friend. 'We will not enter till sunset.'

"And he took out his office book and began to say his *Matins* and *Lauds*, sitting on a fallen tree-trunk by the side of the path.

"All was very silent about us. I suffered terrible distractions, for I was a young man and excited; and though I knew it was no more than epilepsy that I was to see, yet epilepsy is not a good sight to regard. But I was finishing the first *nocturn* when I saw that Father Lasserre was looking off his book.

"We were sitting thirty yards from the roof of the hut, which was built in a scoop of the ground, so that the roof was level with the ground on which we sat. Below it was a little open space, flat, perhaps twenty yards across, and below that yet further was the wood again, and far over that was the smoke of the village against the sea. There was the mouth of a well with a bucket beside it; and by this was standing a man, a negro, very upright, with a vessel in his hand.

"This fellow turned as I looked, and saw us there, and he dropped the vessel, and I could see his white teeth. Father Lasserre stood up and laid his finger on his lips, nodded once or twice, pointed to the west, where the sun was just above the horizon, and the fellow nodded to us again and stooped for his vessel.

"He filled it from the bucket and went back into the house.

"I looked at Father Lasserre and he looked at me.

"'In five minutes,' he said; 'that is the husband. Did you not see his wounds?'

"I had seen no more than his teeth, I said, and my friend nodded again and proceeded to finish his *nocturn.*"

Again, Father Meuron paused dramatically. His ruddy face seemed a little pale in the candle-light, and yet he had told us nothing yet that could account for his apparent horror. Plainly, something was coming soon.

The rector leaned bade to me and whispered behind his hand in reference to what the Frenchman had related a few minutes before, that no priest was allowed to use exorcism without the special leave of the bishop. I nodded and thanked him.

Father Meuron flashed his eyes dreadfully round the circle, clasped his hands and continued:

"When the sun showed only a red rim above the sea we went down to the house. The path ran on high ground to the roof and then dipped down the edge of the cutting past the window to the front of the shed.

"I looked through this window sideways as I went after Father Lasserre, who was carrying his bag with the book and the holy water, but I could see nothing but the light of the fire. And there was no sound. That was terrible to me!

"The door was closed as we came to it, and as Father Lasserre lifted his hand to knock there was a howl of a beast from within.

"He knocked and looked at me.

"'It is but epilepsy!' he said, and his lips wrinkled as he said it."

The priest stopped again, and smiled ironically at us all. Then he clasped his hands beneath his chin like a man in terror.

"I will not tell you all that I saw," he went on, "when the candle was lighted and set on the table, but only a little. You would not dream well, my friends—as I did not that night.

"But the woman sat in a corner by the fireplace, bound with cords by her arms to the back of the chair and her feet to the legs of it.

"Gentlemen, she was like no woman at all. . . . The howl of a wolf came from her lips, but there were words in the howl. At first, I could not understand till she began in French, and then I understood. My God!

"The foam dripped from her mouth like water, and her eyes—but there! I began to shake when I saw them until the holy water was spilled on the floor, and I set it down on the table by the candle. There was a plate of meat on the table, roasted mutton, I think, and a loaf of bread beside it. Remember that, gentlemen—that mutton and bread! And as I stood there I told myself, like making acts of faith, that it was but epilepsy, or at the most madness.

"My friends, it is probable that few of you know the form of exorcism. It is neither in the Ritual or the Pontifical, and I cannot remember it all myself. But it began thus

The Frenchman sprang up and stood with his back to the fire, with his face in the shadow.

"Father Lasserre was here where I stand, in his cotta and stole, and I beside him. There where my chair stands was the square table, as near as that, with the bread and meat and the holy water and the candle. Beyond the table was the woman; her husband stood beside her on the left hand, and the old mother was there"—he flung out a hand to the right, "on the floor telling her beads and weeping—but weeping.

"When the Father was ready and had said a word to the others, he signed to me to lift the holy water again—she was quiet at the moment—and then he sprinkled her.

"As he lifted his hand she raised her eyes, and there was a look in them of terror, as if at a blow, and as the drops fell she leaped forward in the chair, and the chair leaped with her. Her husband was at her and dragged the chair back. But my God! it was terrible to see him; his teeth shone as if he smiled, but the tears ran down his face.

"Then she moaned like a child in pain. It was as if the holy water burned her; she lifted her face to her man as if she begged him to wipe off the drops.

"And all the while I still told myself that it was the terror of her mind only at the holy water—that it could not be that she was possessed by Satan—it was but madness—madness and epilepsy!

25

"Father Lasserre went on with the prayers, and I said Amen, and there was a psalm—*Deus in nomine tuo salvum me fac* (God save me in your name)—and then came the first bidding to the unclean spirit to go out, in the name of the Mysteries of the Incarnation and Passion.

"Gentlemen, I swear to you that something happened then, but I do not know what. A confusion fell on me and a kind of darkness. I saw nothing—it was as if I were dead."

The priest lifted a shaking hand to wipe off the sweat from his forehead. There was a profound silence in the room. I looked once at *Monsignor*, and he was holding his pipe an inch off his mouth, and his lips were slack and open as he stared.

"Then when I knew where I was, Father Lasserre was reading out of the Gospels; how Our Lord gave authority to his Church to cast out unclean spirits, and all this while his voice never trembled."

"And the woman?" said a voice hoarsely from Father Brent's chair.

"Ah! the woman! My God! I do not know. I did not look at her. I stared at the plate on the table; but at least she was not crying out now.

"When the Scripture was finished Father Lasserre gave me the book.

"'Bah, Father!' he said; 'it is but epilepsy, is it not?'

"Then he beckoned me, and I went with him, holding the book till we were within a yard of the woman. But I could not hold the book still, it shook, it shook—"

Father Meuron thrust out his hand. "It shook like that, gentlemen.

"He took the book from me, sharply and angrily. 'Go back, sir,' he said, and he thrust the book into the husband's hand.

"'There,' he said.

"I went back behind the table and leaned on it.

"Then Father Lasserre—my God! the courage of this man!—he set his hands on the woman's head. She writhed up her teeth to bite, but he was too strong for her, and then he cried out from the book the second bidding to the unclean spirit.

"'*Ecce crucem Domini!* Behold the Cross of the Lord! Flee ye adverse hosts! The lion of the tribe of Judah hath prevailed!'

"Gentlemen"—the Frenchman flung out his hands—"I who stand here tell you that something happened. God knows what. I only know this, that as the woman cried out and scrambled with her feet on the floor, the flame of the candle became smoke-coloured for one instant. I told myself it was the dust of her struggling and her foul breath. . . . Yes, gentlemen, as you tell yourselves now. . . . Bah! it is but epilepsy, is it not so, sir?"

The old rector leaned forward with a deprecating hand, but the Frenchman glared and gesticulated; there was a murmur from the room, and the old priest leaned back again and propped his head on his hand.

"Then there was a prayer. I heard *Oremus*, but I did not dare to look at the woman. I fixed my eyes so on the bread and meat; it was the one clean thing in that terrible room. I whispered to myself, 'Bread and mutton, bread and mutton.' I thought of the refectory at home—anything. You understand me, gentlemen—anything familiar to quiet myself.

"Then there was the third exorcism. . . ."

I saw the Frenchman's hands rise and fall, clenched, and his teeth close on his lip to stay its trembling. He swallowed in his throat once or twice. Then he went on in a very low, hissing voice.

"Gentlemen, I swear to you by God Almighty that this was what I saw. I kept my eyes on the bread and meat. It lay there beneath my eyes, and yet I saw, too, the good Father Lasserre lean forward to the woman again, and heard him begin, '*Exorcizo te* . . .'

"And then this happened—this happened . . .

"The bread and the meat corrupted themselves to worms before my eyes . . ."

Father Meuron dashed forward, turned round and dropped into his chair as the two English priests on either side sprang to their feet.

In a few minutes he was able to tell us that all had ended well; that the woman had been presently found in her right mind, after an incident or two that I will take leave to omit; and that the apparent paroxysm of nature that had accompanied the words of the third exorcism had passed away as suddenly as it had come.

Then we went to night-prayers and fortified ourselves against the dark.

Father Brent's Tale

It was universally voted on Monday that the Englishman should follow Father Meuron, and we looked with some satisfaction on his wholesome face and steady blue eyes as he took up his tale after supper.

"Mine is a very poor story," he began, "after the one we heard on Saturday and, what is worse, there is no explanation that I have ever heard that seemed to me adequate. Perhaps someone will supply one

27

this evening. I feel very much like the ant in London whom *Monsignor* has such sympathy with."

He drew at his cigarette, smiling, and we settled ourselves down with looks of resolute science on our features. I at least was conscious of wishing to wear one.

"After my ordination to the sub-diaconate I was in England for the summer, and went down to stay with a friend on the Fal at the beginning of October.

"My friend's house stood on a spot of land running out into the estuary; there was a beech wood behind it and on either side. There was a small embankment on which the building actually stood, of which the sea-wall ran straight down on to the rocks, so that at high tide the water came half way up the stone-work. There was a large smoking-room looking the same way and a little paved path separated its windows from the low wall.

"We had a series of very warm days when I was there, and after dinner we would sit outside in the dark and listen to the water lapping below. There was another house on the further side of the river about half a mile away, and we could see its lights sometimes. About three miles upstream—that is, on our right—lay Truro; and Falmouth, as far as I remember, about four miles to the left. But we were entirely cut off from our neighbours by the beechwoods all round us, and, except for the house opposite, might have been clean out of civilization."

Father Brent tossed away his cigarette and lit another.

He seemed a very sensible person, I thought, unlike the excitable Frenchman, and his manner of speaking was serene and practical.

"My friend was a widower," he went on, "but had one boy, about eleven years old, who, I remember, was to go to school after Christmas. I asked Franklyn, my friend, why Jack had not gone before, and he told me, as parents will, that he was a peculiarly sensitive boy, a little hysterical at times and very nervous, but he was less so than he used to be, and probably, his father said, if he was allowed time, school would be the best thing for him. Up to the present, however, he had shrunk from sending him.

"'He has extraordinary fancies,' he said, 'and thinks he sees things. The other day—' and then Jack came in, and he stopped, and I clean forgot to ask him afterward what he was going to say.

"Now, if anyone here has ever been to Cornwall they will know what a queer county it is. It is cram full of legends and so on. Everyone who has ever been there seems to have left their mark. You get the Phoenicians in goodness knows what century; they came there for tin, and some of the mines still in work are supposed to have been opened by them. Cornish cream, too, seems to have been brought there by them, for I need not tell you, perhaps, that the stuff is originally Cornish and not Devon. Then Solomon, some think, sent ships there, though personally I believe that is nonsense; but you get some curious names—Marazion, for instance, which means the bitterness of Zion. That has made some believe that the Cornish are the lost tribes. Then you get a connection with both Ireland and Brittany in names, language, and beliefs, and so on. I could go on forever. They still talk of 'going to England' when they cross the border into Devonshire.

"Then the people are very odd—real Celts—with a genius for religion and the supernatural generally. They believe in pixies; they have got a hundred saints and holy wells and holy trees that no one else has ever heard of. They have the most astonishing old churches. There is one convent—at Lanherne, I think—where the Blessed Sacrament has remained with its light burning right up to the present. And lastly, all the people are furious Wesleyans.

"So, the whole place is a confusion of history, of a sort of palimpsest, as the Father Rector here would tell us. A cross you find in the moor may be pagan, or Catholic, or Anglican, or most likely all three together. And that is what makes an explanation of what I am going to tell you such a difficult thing.

"I did not know much about this when I went there on October 3rd, but Franklyn told me a lot, and he took me about to one or two places here and there—to Truro to see the new cathedral, to Perranzabuloe, where there is an old mystery theatre and a church in the sands, and so on. And one day we rowed down to Falmouth.

"The Fal is a lovely place when the tide is in. You find the odd combination of seaweed and beech trees growing almost together. The trees stand with their roots in saltish water, and the creeks run right up into the woods. But it is terrible when the tide is out—great sheets of mud, with wreckage sticking up, and draggled weed, and mussels, and so on.

"About the end of my first week it was high tide after dinner, and we sat out on the terrace looking across the water. We could hear it lapping below, and the moon was just coming up behind the house. I tossed over my cigarette end and heard it fizz in the water, and then I put out my hand to the box for another. There wasn't one, and Franklyn said he would go indoors to find some. He thought he had some

Nestors in his bedroom.

"So, Franklyn went in and I was left alone.

"It was perfectly quiet; there was not a ripple on the water, which was about eight feet below me, as I got up from my chair and sat on the low wall. There was a sort of glimmer on the water from the moon behind, and I could see a yellow streak clean across the surface from the house opposite among the black woods. It was as warm as summer, too."

Father Brent threw his cigarette away and sat a little forward in his chair. I began to feel more interested. He was plainly interested himself, for he clasped his hands round a knee and gave a quick look into our faces. Then he looked back again at the fire as he went on.

"Then across the streak of yellow light, and where the moon glimmered, I saw a kind of black line moving. It was coming toward me, and there seemed to be a sort of disturbance behind. I stood up and waited, wondering what it was. I could hear Franklyn pulling out a drawer in the bedroom overhead, but everything else was deadly still.

"As I stood it came nearer swiftly; it was just a high ripple in the water, and a moment later the flat surface below heaved up, and I could hear it lapping and splashing on the face of the wall.

"It was exactly as if some big ship had gone up the estuary. I strained my eyes out, but there was nothing to be seen. There was the glimmer of the moon on the water, the house lights burning half a mile away, and the black woods beyond. There was a beach, rocks, and shingle on my right, curving along toward a place called Meopas; and I could hear the wave hiss and clatter all along it as it went upstream.

"Then I sat down again.

"I cannot say I was exactly frightened; but I was very much puzzled. It surely could not be a tidal wave; there was certainly no ship; it could not be anything swimming, for the wave was like the wave of a really large vessel.

"In a minute or two Franklyn came down with the Nestors, and I told him. He laughed at me. He said it must have been a breeze, or the turn of the tide, or something. Then he said he had been in to look for Jack, and had found him in a sort of nightmare, tossing and moaning; he had not wakened him, he said, but just touched him and said a word or two, and the boy had turned over and gone to sleep.

"But I would not let him change the subject. I persisted it had been a really big wash of some kind.

"He stared at me.

"'Take a cigarette,' he said; 'I found them at last under a hat.'

"But I went on at him. It had made an impression on me, and I was a little uncomfortable.

"'It is bosh,' he said; 'but we will go and see if you like. The wall will be wet if there was a big wave.'

"He fetched a lantern, and we went down the steps that led round the side of the embankment into the water. I went first, until my feet were on the last step above the water. He carried the lantern.

"Then I heard him exclaim.

"'You are standing in a pool,' he said.

"I looked down and saw that it was so; the steps, three of them, at least, were shining with water in the light of the lantern.

"I put out my hand for the lantern, held on to a ring by my left hand, and leaned out as far as I could, looking at the face of the wall. It was wet and dripping for at least four feet above the mark of the high tide.

"I told him, and he came down and looked, too, and then we went up again to the house.

"We neither of us said very much more that evening. The only suggestion that Franklyn could make was that it must have been a very odd kind of tidal wave. For myself, I knew nothing about tidal waves; but I gathered from his tone that this certainly could not have been one.

"We sat about half an hour more, but there was no sound again.

"When we went up to bed we peeped into Jack's room. He was lying perfectly quiet on his right side, turned away from the window, which was open, but there was a little frown, I thought, on his forehead, and his eyes seemed screwed up."

The priest stopped again.

We were all very quiet. The story was not exciting, but it was distinctly interesting, and I could see the others were puzzled. Perhaps what impressed us most was the very matter-of-fact tone in which the story was told.

The rector put in a word during the silence.

"How do you know it was not a tidal wave?" he asked.

"It may have been, Father," said the young priest; "but that is not the end."

He filled his lungs with smoke, blew it out, and went on.

"Nothing whatever happened of any interest for the next day or two, except that Franklyn asked a boatman at Meopas whether he had

31

heard anything of a wave on the Monday night. The man looked at us and shook his head, still looking at us oddly.

"'I was in bed early,' he said.

"On the Thursday afternoon Franklyn got a note asking him to dine in Truro, to meet someone who had come down from town. I told him to go, of course, and he went off in his dog-cart about half-past six.

"Jack and I dined together at half-past seven, and I may say we made friends. He was less shy when his father was away. I think Franklyn laughed at him a little too much, hoping to cure him of his fancies.

"The boy told me some of them, though, that night. I don't remember any of them particularly, but I do remember the general effect, and I was really impressed by the sort of insight he seemed to have into things. He said some curious things about trees and their characters. Perhaps you remember Macdonald's *Phantastes*. It was rather like that. He was fond of beeches, I gathered, and thought himself safe in them; he liked to climb them and to think the house was surrounded by them. And there was a lot of things like that he said. I remember, too, that he hated cypresses and cats and the twilight.

"'But I am not afraid of the dark,' he said. 'I like the dark as much as the light, and I always sleep with my windows open and no curtains.'"

Monsignor Maxwell nodded abruptly. I could see he was watching.

"I know," he said—"I knew another child like that."

"Well," went on Father Brent, "the boy said goodnight and went to bed about nine. I sat in the smoking-room a bit, for it had turned a little cold, and about ten stepped out on to the terrace.

"It was perfectly still and cloudy. I forget whether there was a moon. At any rate, I did not see it. There was just the black gulf of water, with the line of light across it from the house opposite. Then I went indoors and shut the windows.

"I read again for a while, and finished my book. I had said my office, so I looked about for another novel. Then I remembered there had been one I wanted to read in Franklyn's room overhead, so I took a candle and went up. Jack's room was over the smoking-room, and his father's was beyond it on the right, and there was a door between them. Both faced the front, remember.

"Franklyn's room had three windows, two looking on to the river and one upstream toward Truro, over the beach I spoke of before. I went in there, and saw that the door was open between the two rooms, so I slipped off my shoes for fear of disturbing the boy and went across to the book-shelf that stood between the two front windows. All three windows were open. Franklyn was mad about fresh air.

"I was bending down to look at the backs of the books, and had my finger on the one I wanted when I heard a kind of moan from the boy's room.

"I stood up, startled, and it came again. Why, he had had a nightmare only three days before, I remembered. As I stood there wondering whether it would be kind to wake him, I heard another sound.

"It was a noise that came through the side window that looked up the beach, and it was the noise of a breaking wave."

The priest made a momentary pause, and as he flicked the end of his cigarette I saw his fingers tremble very slightly.

"I didn't hesitate then, but went straight into the room next door, and as I went across the floor heard the boy moaning and tossing. It was pitch dark, and I could see nothing. I was thinking that tidal waves don't come downstream. Then my knee struck the edge of the bed.

"'Jack,' I said, 'Jack.'

"There was a rustle from the bed-clothes, and (I should have thought) long before he could have awakened I heard his feet on the floor, and then felt him brush past me. Then I saw him outlined against the pale window, with his hands on the glass over his head. Then I was by him, taking care not to touch him.

"All this took about five seconds, I suppose, from the time when I heard the wave on the beach. I stared out now over the boy's head, but there was nothing in the world to be seen but the black water and the glimmer of the light across it.

"Jack was perfectly silent, but I could see that he was watching. He didn't seem to know I was there.

"Then I whispered to him rather sharply.

"'What is it, Jack? What do you see?'

"He said nothing, and I repeated my question.

"Then he answered, almost as if talking to himself.

"'Ships,' he said; 'three ships.'

"Now I swear there was nothing there. I thought it was a nightmare.

"'Nonsense,' I said; 'how can you see them? It's too dark.'

"'A light in each,' he said; 'in the bows—blazing!'

"As he said it I saw his head turning slowly to the left as if he was following them. Then there came the sound of the wave breaking on the stone-work just below the windows.

"'Are you frightened?' I said suddenly.

"'Yes,' said the boy.

"'Why?'

"'I don't know.'

"Then I saw his hands come down from the window and cover his face, and he began to moan again.

"'Come back to bed,' I said; but I daren't touch him. I could see he was sleep walking.

"Then he turned, went straight across the room, still making an odd sound, and I heard him climb into bed.

"I covered him up and went out."

Father Brent stopped again. He had rather a curious look in his face, and I saw that his cigarette had gone out. None of us spoke or moved.

Then he went on again abruptly.

"Well, you know, I didn't know I was frightened exactly until I came out on to the landing. There was a tall glass there on the right hand of the staircase, and just as I came opposite I thought I heard the hiss of the wave again, and I nearly screamed. It was only the wheels of Franklyn's dog-cart coming up the drive, but as I looked in the glass I saw that my face was like paper. . . . We had a long talk about the Phoenicians that evening. Franklyn looked them out in the *Encyclopaedia*; but there was nothing particularly interesting.

"Well, that's all. Give me a match, Father. This beastly thing's gone out. It's a *spaghetti*."

We had no theories to suggest. *Monsignor* alone was temerarious enough to remark that the story was an excellent illustration of his own views.

The Father Rector's Tale

The Father-Rector of San Filippo was an old man, a Canadian by birth, who had been educated in England, but he had worked in many parts of the world since receiving the priesthood nearly fifty years ago, and for my part I certainly expected that he would have many experiences to relate.

At first, however, he entirely refused to tell a story. He said he had had an uneventful life, that he could not compete with the tales he had heard. But persuasion proved too strong, and on going in to see him on another matter one morning I found him at his tin despatch-box with a diary in his hand.

"I have found something that I think may do," he said, "if no one else has promised for this evening. It is really the only thing approaching the preternatural I have ever experienced."

I congratulated him and ourselves; and the same evening after supper he told his story, with the diary beside him, to which he referred now and then. (I shall omit his irrelevancies, of which there were a good many.)

"This happened to me," he said, "nearly thirty years ago. I had been twenty years a priest, and was working in a town mission in the south of England. I made the acquaintance of a Catholic family who had a large country house about ten miles away. They were not very fervent people, but they had a chapel in the house, where I would say mass sometimes on Sundays, when I could get away from my own church on Saturday night.

"On one of these occasions I met for the first time an artist, whose name you would all know if I mentioned it, but it will be convenient to call him Mr. Farquharson. He made an extremely unpleasant impression on me, and yet there was no reason for it that I could see. He was a big man, palish, with curling brown hair. He was always very well dressed, with a suspicion of scent about him; he talked extremely wittily and would say the most surprising things that were at once brilliant and dangerous; and yet in his talk he never transgressed good manners. In fact, he was very cordial always to me; he seemed to go out of his way to be courteous and friendly, and yet I could not bear the fellow. However, I tried to conceal that, and with some success, as you will see.

"I was astonished that he asked me no questions about our beliefs or practices. Such people generally do, you know; and they profess to admire our worship and its dignity. In the evening he played and sang magnificently—very touching and pathetic songs, as a rule.

"On the following morning he attended mass, but I did not think much of that. Guests generally do, I have found, in Catholic houses. Then I went off in the afternoon back to my mission.

"I suppose it was six weeks before I met him again, and then it was at the same place. My hostess gave me tea alone, for I arrived late, and as we sat in the hall, told me that Mr. Farquharson was there again. Then she added, to my surprise, that he had expressed a great liking for me, and had come down from town partly with the hope of meeting me. She went on talking about him for a while; told me that three of his pictures had been taken again by the French Salon, and at last told me that he had been baptised and educated as a Catholic, but had for many years ceased to practise his religion. She had only learned this recently.

"Well, that explained a good deal; and I was a good deal taken aback. I did not quite know how to act. But she talked on about him a little, and I became sorry for the man and determined that I would make no difference in my behaviour toward him. From what she said, I gathered that it might be in my power to win him back. He had everything against him, she told me.

"Now, let me tell you a word about his pictures. I had seen them here and there, as well as reproductions of them, as all the world had at that time, and they were very remarkable. They were on extraordinarily simple and innocent subjects, and often religious—a child going to first Communion; a knight riding on a lonely road; a boy warming his hands at the fire; a woman praying. There was not a line or a colour in them that anyone could dislike, and yet—yet they were corrupt. I know nothing about art; but it needed no art to see that these were corrupt. I did not understand it then, and I do not now; but—well, there it is. I cannot describe their effect on me; but I know that many others felt the same, and I believe that kind of painting is not uncommon in the French school."

The priest paused a moment.

"As I went down the long passage to the smoking-room I declare that I was not thinking of this side of the man. I was only wondering whether I could do anything, but the moment I came in and found him standing alone on the hearth-rug all this leaped back into my mind.

"His personality was exactly like his own pictures. There was nothing that one could point to in his face and say that it revealed his character. It did not. It was a cleanshaven, clever face, strong and artistic; his hand as he took mine was firm and slender and strong, too. And yet—yet my flesh crept at him. It seemed to me he was a kind of devil.

"Again, I did my utmost to hide all this as we sat and talked that evening till the dressing gong rang; and again, I succeeded, but it was a sore effort. Once when he put his hand on my arm I nearly jerked it off, so great was the horror it gave me.

"I did not sit near him at dinner; there were several people dining there that night, but our host was unwell and went to bed early, and this man and myself, after he had played and sung an hour or so in the drawing-room, talked till late in the smoking-room, and all the while the horror grew; I have never felt anything like it. I am generally fairly placid; but it was all I could do to keep quiet. I even wondered once or twice whether it was not my duty to tell him plainly what I felt, to—to—well, really, this sounds absurd—but to curse him as an unclean and corrupt creature who had lost faith and grace and everything, and was on the very brink of eternal fire." The old man's voice rang with emotion. I had never seen him so much moved, and was astonished at his vehemence.

"Well, thank God, I did not!

"At last it came out that I knew about his having been a Catholic. I did not tell him where I had learned it, but perhaps he suspected. Of course, though, I might have learned it in a hundred ways.

"He seemed very much surprised—not at my knowing, but at my treating him as I had. It seemed that he had met with unpleasantness more than once at the hands of priests who knew.

"Well, to cut it short, before I went away next day he asked me to call upon him some time at his house in London, and he asked me in such a way that I knew he meant it."

The priest stopped and referred to his diary. Then he went on.

"It was in the following May, six months later, that I fulfilled my promise.

"It may have been association, and what I suspected of the man, but the house almost terrified me by its beauty and its simplicity and its air of corruption. And yet there was nothing to account for it. There was not a picture in it, as far as I could see, that had anything in it to which even a priest could object. There was a long gallery leading from the front door, floored, ceiled, and walled with oak in little panels, with pictures in each along the two sides, chiefly, I should suppose now, of that same French school of which I have spoken. There was an exquisite crucifix at the end, and yet, in some strange way, even that seemed to be tainted. I felt, I suppose, in the manner that Father Stein described to us when he mentioned Benares; and yet there, I have heard, the pictures and carving correspond with the sensation, and here they did not.

"He received me in his studio at the end of the passage. There was a great painting on an easel, on which he was working, a painting of Our Lady going to the well at Nazareth—most exquisite and yet terrible. I could hardly keep my eyes off it. It was nearly finished, he told me. And there was his grand piano against the wall.

"Well, we sat and talked; and before I left that evening I knew everything. He did not tell me in confession, and the story became notorious after his death five years later; but yet I can tell you no more now than that all I had felt about him was justified by what I heard. Part of what the world did not hear would not have seemed important to any but a priest; it was just the history of his own soul, apart from his deeds, the history of his wanton contempt of light and warnings. And I heard more besides, too, that I cannot bear to think of even now."

The priest stooped again; and I could see his lips were trembling with emotion. We were all very quiet ourselves; the effect on my mind, at least, was extraordinary. Presently he went on:

"Before I left I persuaded him to go to confession. The man had not really lost faith for a moment, so far as I could gather. I learned from details that I cannot even hint at that he had known it all to be true, pitilessly clear in his worst moments. Grace had been prevailing especially of late, and he was sick of his life. Of course, he had tried to stifle conscience, but by the mercy of God he had failed. I cannot imagine why, except that there is no end to the loving kindness of God; but I have known many souls, not half so evil as his, lose their faith and their whole spiritual sense beyond all human hope of recovery."

The priest stopped again, turned over several pages of his diary, and as he did so I saw him stop once or twice and read silently to himself, his lips moving.

"I must miss out a great deal here. He did not come to confession to me, but to a Carthusian, after a retreat. I need not go into all the details of that, so far as I knew them, and I will skip another six months.

"During that time, I wrote to him more than once, and just got a line or two back. Then I was ordered abroad, and when we touched at Brindisi I received a letter from him."

The priest lifted his diary again near his eyes.

"Here is one sentence," he said; "listen.

"'I know I am forgiven; but the punishment is driving me mad. What would you say if you knew all! I cannot write it. I wonder if we shall meet again. I wonder what you would say.'

"There was more that I cannot read; but it offers no explanation of this sentence. I wrote, of course, at once, and said I would be home in four months, and asked for an explanation. I did not hear again, though I wrote three or four times; and after three or four months in Malta I went back to England.

"My first visit was to Mr, Farquharson, when I had written to prepare him for my coming."

The old man stopped again, and I could see he was finding it more and more difficult to speak. He looked at the diary again once or twice, but I could see that it was only to give himself time to recover. Then he lowered it once more, leaned his elbow on the chair arm and his head on his hand, and went on in a slow voice full of effort.

"The first change was in the gallery; its pictures were all gone, and in their place hung others—engravings and portraits of no interest or beauty that I could see. The crucifix was gone, and in its place stood another very simple and common—a plaster figure on a black cross. It was all very commonplace—such a room as you might see in any house. The man took me through as before, but instead of opening the studio door as I expected, turned up the stairs on the right, and I followed. He stopped at a little door at the end of a short passage, tapped, and threw it open. He announced my name and I went in."

He paused once more.

"There was a Japanese screen in front of me, and I went round it, wondering what I should find. I caught a sight of a simple, commonplace room with a window looking out on my left, and then I saw an old man sitting in a high chair over the fire, on which boiled a saucepan, warming his hands, with a rug over his knees. His face was turned to me, but it was that of a stranger.

"There was a table between us, and I stood hesitating, on the point of apologising, and the old man looked at me, smiling.

"'You do not know me,' he said.

"Then I saw he bore an odd sort of resemblance to Mr. Farquharson; and I supposed it was his father. That would account for the mistake, too, I thought in a moment. My letter must have been delivered to him instead.

"'I came to see Mr. Farquharson,' I said. 'I beg your pardon if—' Then he interrupted me. Well, you will guess—this was the man I had come to see.

"It took a minute or two before I could realise it. I swear to you that the man looked not ten, nor twenty, nor thirty, but fifty years older.

"I went and took his hand and sat down, but I could not say a word. Then he told me his story; and as he told it I watched him. I looked at his face; it had been full and generous in its lines, now the skin was drawn tightly over his cheeks and great square jaw. His hair, so much of it as escaped under his stuff cap, was snow white and like silk. His hands, stretched over the fire, were gnarled and veined and tremulous. And all this had come to him in less than one year.

"Well, this was his story: His health had failed abruptly within a month of my last sight of him. He had noticed weakness coming on soon after his reconciliation, and the failure of his powers had increased like lightning.

"I will tell you what first flashed into my mind—that it was merely a sudden, unprecedented breakdown that had first given room for grace to reassert itself, and had then normally gone forward. The life he had led—well, you understand.

"Then he told me a few more facts that soon put that thought out of my head. All his artistic powers had gone, too. He gave me an example.

"'Look round this room,' he said in his old man's voice, 'and tell me frankly what you think of it—the pictures, the furniture.'

"I did so, and was astonished at their ugliness. There were a couple of hideous oleographs on the wall opposite the window; perhaps you know them—of the tombs of our Lord and His Blessed Mother, with yellow candlesticks standing upon them. There were green baize curtains by the windows; an Axminster carpet of vivid colours on the floor; a mahogany table in the centre with a breviary upon it and a portfolio open. It was the kind of a room that you might find in twenty houses in a row on the outskirts of a colliery town.

"I supposed, of course, that he had furnished his room like this out of a morbid kind of mortification, and I hinted this to him.

"He smiled again, but he looked puzzled.

"'No,' he said; 'indeed not. Then you do think them ugly, too? Well, well; it is that I do not care. Will you believe me when I tell you that? There is no asceticism in the matter. Those pictures seem to me as good as any others. I have sold the others.'

"'But you know they are not good,' I said.

"'My friends tell me so, and I remember I used to think so once, too. But that has all gone. Besides, I like them.'

"He turned in his chair and opened the portfolio that lay by him.

"'Look,' he said, and pushed it over to me, watching my face as I took it.

"It was full of sheets of paper scrawled with such pictures as a stupid child might draw. There was not the faintest trace of any power in them. Here is one of them that he gave me." (He drew out a paper from his diary and held it up.) "I will show it you presently.

"As I looked at them it suddenly struck me that all this was an

40

elaborate pose. I suppose I showed the thought in the way I glanced up at him. At any rate, he knew it. He smiled again pitifully.

"'No,' he said; 'it is not a pose. I have posed for forty years, but I have forgotten how to do it now. It does not seem to me worthwhile, either.'

"'Are you happy?' I asked.

"'Oh, I suppose so,' he said.

"I sat there bewildered.

"'And music?' I said.

"He made a little gesture with his old hands.

"'Tell Jackson to let you see the piano in the studio,' he said, 'as you go downstairs. And you might look at the picture of Our Lady at Nazareth at the same time. You will see how I tried to go on with it. My friends tell me it is all wrong, and asked me to stop. I supposed they knew, so I have stopped.'

"Well, we talked a while, and I learned how all was with him. He believed with his whole being, and that was all. He received the sacraments once a week, and he was happy in a subdued kind of way. There was no ecstasy of happiness; there was no torment from the imagination, such as is usual in these cases of conversion. He had suffered agonies at first from the loss of his powers, as he realised that his natural perceptions were gone, and it was then that he had written to me."

The rector stopped again a moment, fingering the paper.

"I saw his doctor, of course, and—"

Monsignor broke in. I noticed that he had been listening intently.

"The piano and the picture," he said.

"Ah, yes. Well, the piano was just a box of strings; many of the notes were broken, and the other wires were hopelessly out of tune. They were broken, the man told me, within a week or two of his master's change of life. He spoke quite frankly to me. Mr. Farquharson had tried to play, it seemed, and could scarcely play a right note, and in a passion of anger it was supposed he had smashed the notes with his fists. And the picture—well, it was a miserable sight. There was a tawdry sort of crown, ill drawn and ill coloured, on her head, and a terrible sort of cherub was painted all across the sky. Someone else, it seemed, had tried to paint these out, which increased the confusion.

"The doctor told me it was softening of the brain. I asked him honestly to tell me whether he had ever come across such a case before, and he confessed he had not.

"It took me a week or two, and another conversation with Mr.

Farquharson, before I understood what it all meant. It was not natural, the doctor assured me, and it could scarcely be that Almighty God had arbitrarily inflicted such a punishment. And then I thought I understood, as no doubt you have all done before this."

The old priest's voice had an air of finality in his last sentence, and he handed the scrap of paper to Father Bianchi, who sat beside him.

"One moment, Father," I said; "I do not understand at all."

The priest turned to me, and his eyes were full of tears.

"Why, this is my reading of it," he said; "the man had been one mass of corruption, body, mind, and soul. Every power of his had been nurtured on evil for thirty years. Then he made his effort and the evil was withdrawn, and—and—well, he fell to pieces. The only thing that was alive in him was the life of grace. There was nothing else to live. He died, too, three months later, tolerably happy, I think."

As I pondered this the paper was handed to me, and I looked at it in bewildered silence. It was a head grotesque in its feebleness and lack of art. There was a crown of thorns about it, and an inscription in a child's handwriting below:

Deus in virtute tua salvum me fac! (God has the power to save me!)

Then my own eyes were full of tears, too.

Father Girdlestone's Tale

"I have found another *raconteur* for this evening," said *Monsignor* as he came in to dinner on the following day, "but he cannot be here till late."

The rector looked up questioningly.

"Yes, I know," said *Monsignor* unfolding his napkin. "But it is a long story; it will take at least two nights; but—but it is a beauty, reverend Fathers."

We murmured appreciatively.

"I heard him tell it twenty years ago," proceeded the priest. "I was a boy then. . . . I had a bad night after it, I remember. But the first part is rather dull."

The appreciative murmur was even louder. "Well, then, is that settled?"

We assented.

The entrance of Father Girdlestone that evening was somewhat dramatic. We were all talking briskly together in our wide semicircle when Father Brent uttered an exclamation. The talk died, and I, turning from my corner, saw a very little old man standing behind the rector's chair, motionless and smiling. He was one of the smallest men, not actually deformed, I have ever seen; small and very delicate looking. His white, silky hair was thin on his head, but abundant over his ears; his face was like thin ivory, transparent and exquisitely carved; his eyes so overhung that I could see nothing of them but two patches of shadow with a diamond in each. And there he stood, as if materialised from air, beneath the folds of his ample Roman cloak.

"I beg your pardon, reverend Fathers," he said, and his voice was as delicate as his complexion. "I tapped, but no one seemed to hear me."

The rector bustled up from his chair.

"My dear Father," he began; but *Monsignor* interrupted.

"A most appropriate entry, Father Girdlestone," he said. "You could not have made a more effective beginning." He waved his hand—"Father Girdlestone," he said, introducing us. "And this is the Father Rector."

We were all standing up by now, looking at this tranquil little old man, and we bowed and murmured deferentially. There was something very dignified about this priest.

Then chairs were re-sorted. I got my own again, moving it against the wall, watching him as with almost foreign manners he bowed this way and that before seating himself in the centre. Then we all sat down; and after a word or two of talk he began.

"I understand from my friend, Monsignor Maxwell," he said, "that you gentlemen would like to hear my story. I am very willing indeed to tell it. No possible harm can follow from it, and, perhaps, even good may be the result, if ever anyone who shall hear it is afflicted with the same visitation. But it is a long story, gentlemen, and I am an old man and shall no doubt make it longer."

He was reassured, I think, by our faces, and without further apology he began his tale.

"My first and only curacy," he said, "was in the town of Cardiff. I was sent there after my ordination, four years before the re-establishment of the hierarchy in England; and the year after our bishops were given us I was sent to found a mission inland. Now, gentlemen, I shall not tell you where that was, though no doubt you will be able to find out if you desire to do so. It will be enough now to describe to you the circumstances and the place.

"It was a little colliery village to which I went—we will call it Abergwyll. There was a number of Irish Catholics there, who are, as you know, the most devout persons on the face of the earth. They begged

43

very hard for a priest, and I expect, gentlemen, there was collusion in the matter. The bishop's chaplain had Irish blood in his veins."

He smiled pleasantly.

"At least, there I was sent, with a stipend of £40 and a letter of commendation and permission to beg. My parishioners set at my disposal a four-roomed house standing at the outskirts of the village, removed, I should say, forty yards from any other house. Behind my house was open country—a kind of moor—stretching over hill and dale to the mountains of Brecon. The colliery itself stood on the further side of the village and beneath, it, half a mile away. Of the four rooms, I used one as a chapel on the ground floor; that at the back was the kitchen. I slept over the kitchen, and used as my sitting-room and sacristy that over the chapel.

"I will not detain you with my first experiences. They were most edifying. I have never seen such devotion and fervour. My own devotion was sensibly increased by all that I heard and saw. The shepherd in this case, at least, was taught many lessons by his sheep.

"Now, the first ambition of every young priest who is worthy of the name is to build a great church to God's glory. Even I had this ambition. I had not a great deal of work to do—in fact, I may say that there was really nothing to do except to say mass and office and to conduct evening devotions, as I did every night in the chapel; and that little chapel, gentlemen, was full every night.

"Much of the day, therefore, I spent in walking and dreaming. In the morning, as summer came on, I was accustomed to take my office-book out with me and to go over the moor, perhaps three hundred yards away, to a little ravine where a stream went down into the valley. There I would sit in the shade of a rock, listening to the voice of the water and saying my prayers. When I had done I would lie on my back, looking up at the rock and the sky, and dreaming—well, as every young priest dreams.

"I do not know when it was that I first understood what God intended me to do. I began by thinking of a great town where my church should stand—Cardiff, or perhaps Newport. I even arranged its architecture; it was to be a primitive Roman basilica, large and plain, with a great apse with a Christ in glory frescoed there. On His right were to be the redeemed, on His left the lost—no, more than that, with a pair of great angels behind the throne. That, gentlemen, without text or comment, has always seemed to me the greatest sermon on earth."

He paused and looked round at us an instant.

"Well, gentlemen, you know what daydreaming is. I even occupied my time—I, with £40 a year and twenty colliery parishioners—in drawing designs for my church. And then suddenly on a summer's day a new thought came to me, and something else with it.

"I was lying on my back on the short grass, looking up at the rock against the sky, when the thought came to me that here my basilica should stand. The rock should be levelled, I thought, to a platform. The foundations should be blasted out, and here my church should stand, alone on the moor, to witness that the demands of God's glory were dominant and sovereign. . . . Yes, gentlemen, most unpractical and fantastic. . . .

"I sat up at the thought. It came to me as a revelation. In that instant I no more doubted that it should be accomplished than that God reigned. I looked below me at the stream. Yes; I saw it all; there the stream should dash and chatter; all about me were the solemn moors; and here on the rock behind me should stand my basilica, and the Blessed Sacrament within it.

"I was just about to turn to look at my rock again when something happened."

The old man stopped dead.

"Now, gentlemen, I do not know if I can make this plain to you. What happened to me happened only interiorly; but it was as real as a thunderclap or a vision. It was this: It was an absolute conviction that something was looking at me from over the top of the rock behind.

"My first thought was that I had heard a sound. Then simultaneously the horn blew from the colliery a mile away, and—and"—he hesitated—"I was aware that this external sound was on a different plane. I do not know how to make that plain to you; but it was as when one's imagination is full of some remembered melody and a real sound breaks upon it. The horn ceased and there was silence again. Then after a moment my interior experience ceased, too, as abruptly as it had begun.

"All that time, three or four seconds, at least, I had sat still and rigid without turning my head. I must describe to you as well as I can my sensations during those seconds. You must forgive me for being verbose about it.

"Those who have attained to Saint Teresa's Prayer of Quiet tell us that it is a new world into which they consciously penetrate—a world with objects, sounds and all the rest—but that these are almost incommunicable even to the brain of the percipient. No adequate image or analogy can be found for those intentions; still less can they be expressed in words. I suppose that this is an illustration of the truth that the Kingdom of Heaven is within us. . . .

"Well, gentlemen, I was aware during those seconds that I was in that state that I had, as it were, slipped through the crust of the world of sense and even of intellectual thought. What I perceived of a person watching me was not on this plane at all. It was not One who in any sense had a human existence, who had ever had one, or ever would. It did not in the least resemble, therefore, an apparition of the dead. But the perception of this was gradual, as also of the nature of the visitation, of which I shall speak in a moment. At first there was only the act of the entrance into my neighbourhood, as of one entering a room; then gradually, although with great speed, I perceived the nature of the visitation and the character of the visitant.

"And again, that sound, if I may call it so, was not that of a material object; it was not a cry or a word or a movement. Yet it was in some way the expression of a personality. Shall we say"—he stopped again—"well, do you know what the sound of a flame is? There is not exactly a vibration—not a note—not a roar nor a—nor anything. Well, I do not think I can express it more clearly than by saying that that is the nearest analogy I can name in the world of sense. It was as the note of a vivid and intense personality, and it continued during that period and died noiselessly at the end like a sudden singing in the ears.

"Now, I have taken the sense of hearing as the one which best expresses my experience; but it was not really hearing any more than seeing or tasting or feeling. It seemed to me that if it was true, as scientists tell us, that we have but one common sense expressing itself in five ways, that common sense was indirectly affected in this intense and piercing way only beneath its own plane, if I may say so.

"And one thing more. Although this presence seemed to bring on me a kind of paralysis, so that I did not move or even objectively think, yet beneath, my soul was aware of a repulsion and a hatred that I am entirely unable to describe. As God is Absolute Goodness and Love, so this presence affected me with precisely the opposite instinct. . . . There, I must leave it at that. I must just ask you to take my word for it that there was present to me during those few seconds a kind of distilled quintessence of all that Is not God, under the aspect of a person, and of a person, as I have said, quite apart from human existence."

The priest's quiet little voice, speaking now even lower than when he began, yet perfectly articulate and unmoved, ceased, and I leaned back in my chair, drawing a long breath. Again, I will speak only for myself, and say that he had seemed to be putting into words for the first time in my experience something which I had never undergone and which yet I recognized as simply true. I doubted it no more than if he had described a walk he had taken in Rome.

He looked round at the motionless faces; then he lifted one knee on to the other and began to nurse it.

"Well, gentlemen, it would be about ten minutes, I suppose, before I stood up. I looked over my shoulder before that, yet knowing I should see nothing; and, indeed, there was nothing to see but the old rock and the sky and the silhouette of the grasses against it. I continued to sit there, because I felt too tired to move. It was a kind of complete languor that took possession of me. I had no actual fear now; I knew that the thing, whatever it was, had withdrawn itself—it had whisked, if I may say so, out of my range as swift as a lizard who knows himself observed. I knew perfectly well that it would approach more cautiously if it should ever approach me again, but that for the present I need not fear.

"There was another curious detail, too. I had—and have now—no reflex horror when I think of it. You see that it had not taken place before my senses; not even, indeed, before my intellect or my conscious powers. It was completely in the transcendent sphere, and, therefore—at least I can only suppose that this is the reason—therefore when the door was shut and I was returned to my human existence, I had no associations or even direct memory of the horror. I knew that it had taken place, but my objective imagination was not tarnished by it. Later it was different; but I shall come to that presently. There was the languor, taking its rise, I suppose, in the very essence of my being where I had experienced and resisted the assault, and this languor communicated itself to my mind, just as weariness of mind communicates itself to the body. Then, after a little rest, I got up and went home. It was curious also that after dining the languor had risen even higher; I felt intolerably tired, and slept dreamlessly in my chair the whole afternoon.

"That, then, gentlemen, was the beginning of my visitation. It was only the beginning, and to some degree differed from its continuation. It seemed to me later when I looked back upon it that the personality had changed its assault somewhat, that at first it had rushed upon me unthinking, impelled by its own passion, and that afterward it laid siege with skill and deliberation. . . . But are you sure, gentlemen, that I am not boring you with all this?"

Monsignor answered for us. I noticed that he cleared his throat slightly before speaking.

"No, no, Father. . . . Please go on."

The old priest paused a moment as if to recollect himself, then still nursing his knee, he began again in his quiet little voice.

"I do not know exactly how long it was before I began to understand my danger; but I think the thought first occurred to me one day during my meditation. Soon after my ordination I had read Mme. Guyon's book on prayer in order to understand exactly what it was that had been condemned in Quietism, and I suppose it had affected me to some extent. It is indeed a very subtle book and extremely beautiful. At any rate, I had long been accustomed to close my meditation with what she calls the 'awful silence' in the Presence of God. I do not think that, normally speaking, there is any harm in this; on the contrary, for active-minded people in danger of intellectualism I think it a very useful exercise. Well, it was one day I should think within a fortnight of my experience by the rock that I first understood that for me there was danger. I was in my little chapel before the Blessed Sacrament. Everything was quite quiet; the men were at work and the women in their houses; it was a hot, sunny morning, I remember, breathlessly still. I had finished my formal meditation and was sitting back in my chair.

"You all know, gentlemen, of course, the way in which one can approach the Silence before God. Of course, the simplest can do it if they will take pains."

Monsignor Maxwell interrupted, still in that slightly strained voice in which he had spoken just now.

"Please describe it," he said.

The priest looked up deprecatingly.

"Well, then, first I had withdrawn myself from the world of sense. That takes, as you know, sometimes several minutes; it is necessary to sink down in thought in such a manner that sounds no longer distract the attention, even though they may be heard and even considered and reflected upon. Then the second step is to leave behind all intellectual considerations and images, and that, too, sometimes is troublesome, especially if the mind is naturally active. Well, this day I found an extraordinary ease in both the acts."

Father Brent leaned forward.

"May I interrupt, Father? But I am not sure that I understand."

The old man pursed his lips. Then he glanced up at the rest of us almost apologetically.

"Well, it is this, my dear Father. . . . How can I put it? . . . It is the introversion of the soul. Instead of considering this object or that, either by looking upon it or reflecting upon it, the soul turns inward. There are the two distinct planes on which many men, especially those who pay little or no attention to the soul, live continually. Either they continually seek distractions—they cannot be devout except in company or before an image—or else—as, indeed, many do who have even the gift of recollection—they dwell entirely upon considerations and mental images. Now the true introversion is beneath all this. The soul sinks, turning inward upon itself . . . there are no actual considerations at all; these become in their turn as much distractions to the energy of the soul as external objects to the energy of the mind. . . . Is that clearer, my dear Father?"

It was all said with a kind of patient and apologetic simplicity. Father Brent nodded pensively two or three times, and dropped his chin again upon his hand. The old priest went on.

"Well, gentlemen, as I said just now, on this morning I came into the Silence without an effort. First the sensible world dropped away; I heard a woman open and shut her door fifty yards away down the street, but it was no more than a sound. Then almost immediately the world of images and considerations went past me and vanished, and I found myself in perfect stillness.

"For an instant it seemed to me that all was well. There was that strange tranquillity all about me. . . . I cannot put it into words except by saying, as all do who practise that method, that it is a living tranquillity full of a very vital energy. This is not, of course, that to which contemplatives penetrate; St. John of the Cross makes that very plain; it is no more than that in which we ought always to live. It is that Kingdom of God within of which our Blessed Lord tells us, but it is not the Palace itself. . . . However, as I have said, when one has but learned the way there—and the difficulty of doing so lies only in its extreme and singular simplicity—when one has learned the way there it is full of pleasure and consolation.

"I remained there, as my manner was, drawing a long breath or two, as one is obliged to do. I do not know why—and at first all seemed well. There was that peace about me which may be described under the image of any one of the five senses. I prefer to speak of it now as under the image of light—a very radiant, mellow light full of warmth and sweetness. There was, too, just at first, that sense of profound abasement and adoration which is so familiar. . . . As I said, gentlemen, I do not, of course, for an instant pretend to the gift of pure contemplation; that is something far beyond.

"Then all in instant that sense of adoration vanished.

"Now, it was not that I had risen back again to meditation; there were no images before my attention, no reflections of any formulated kind. It was still the pure perception, and yet all sense of adoration and of God's majesty was gone. The light and the peace were there still, but—but not God. . . .

"Then I perceived, if I may say so, that something was on the point of disclosure. It was as if something was about to manifest itself. I perceived that the light was not as it had been. It was like that strange, vivid sunlight that we see sometimes when a heavy cloud is overhead. That is the only way in which I can express it. It is for that reason that I called it *light* rather than sound or touch. For an instant still I hesitated. The thought of what had happened to me by the rock never came to my mind, and with inconceivable swiftness the process passed on. To use an auditory metaphor for a moment it was like the change of an orchestra. The minor note steals in; a light passes over the character of the sound, and simultaneously the volume increases, the chords expand, tearing the heart with them, and the listener perceives that a moment later the climax will break in thunder."

He had raised his voice a little by now; his eyes glanced this way and that, though still without a trace of self-consciousness. Then again, his voice dropped.

"Well, gentlemen, before that final moment came I had remembered; the vision of the rock and the chatter of the stream was before me sharp as a landscape under lightning. . . . I do not know what I did, but I was aware of making a kind of terrified effort. My soul sprang up as a diver who chokes under water, and in an instant the whole thing was gone. Then I became aware that my eyes were open and that I was standing up. I was still terrified by the suddenness of the experience, and stood there, saying something aloud to Our Lord in the Tabernacle. Then I heard the door open behind me.

"'Did you cry out, Father?' said Bridget. 'Why, Mother of Mercy'

"I felt myself beginning to sway on my feet. Well, gentlemen, I need not trouble you with all that. The truth was that Bridget, who was washing up my breakfast things in the kitchen, heard me cry out. She told me afterward that when she saw my face she thought that I was dying. . . . I sat down a little then, and she fetched me something, and presently I was able to walk out.

"Well, gentlemen, that is enough for this evening."

He stopped abruptly.

We got up and went to night-prayers.

******

"Well, so far," began Father Girdlestone on the following evening—"so far you see two things had happened to me. First there seems to have been a kind of unpremeditated assault that affected my body, mind, and soul. That was the attack by the rock. Then he began to lay siege more deliberately, and attacked me in my meditation, in what I may call the innermost chamber, that anteroom of the transcendent world. Now, I have to tell you of his next assault."

There was a rustle of expectation as we settled ourselves to listen. I had found on questioning the others in the morning that they were in the same attitude as myself, impressed, but not convinced—indeed, strangely impressed by the extreme subtlety of the experience related to us. Yet there had been no proof, no tangible evidence, such as we are accustomed to demand, that the incidents had been anything more than subjective. At the same time there had been something remarkable in the priest's assurance as well as in the precise particularity of his narrative. It seemed now, however, from what he said, that perhaps we were to have more materialistic elements presented to us.

"The result, of course," continued Father Girdlestone, "of the attack upon my soul was that I became terrified at the thought of any further act of introversion. It seemed to me on reflection that I had probably overstrained my faculties a little and that I had better be more distinctly meditative in devotion.

"I fetched down, therefore, from my shelves a copy of the *Spiritual Exercises*, and set to work. I began with a carefully objective act of the Presence of God, dwelling chiefly upon the Blessed Sacrament, and then pursued carefully the lines laid down. Two or three times every day, I should say, I was tempted to fall back upon the Prayer of Quiet, and each time I resisted it. It was a kind of frightened fascination that I felt for it. It was as if it had been a cupboard where something terrible lurked in silence and darkness, ready to tear me if I opened the door. Of course, I should have opened it boldly; any priest of experience would have told me so at once; but I did not fully understand what

51

was wrong. The result was as you shall hear.

"All went well for several days. I meditated with care, making the prescribed considerations—the preludes, the pictures, and all the rest, observing to go straight from the intellectual act to the voluntary. I became soothed and content again. Then, without any warning, the new assault was made. It came about in this fashion:

"I was meditating upon the Particular Judgment, and had formed the picture as vividly as possible of my soul before the Judge. I saw the wounds and the stains on one side, the ineffably piercing grace and holiness on the other. I saw the reproach in the Judge's face. I seized my soul by the neck, as it were, and crushed it down in humility and penitence. And then suddenly it seemed to me that my hold relaxed, and all faded. Now this assault came to me in intellectual form, yet I cannot remember the arguments. It began, if I may say so, as a blot upon the subject of my meditation, effacing the image of my Judge and of myself, and it spread with inconceivable swiftness over the whole of my faith. ..."

The priest paused, smiling steadily at the fire.

"How shall I put it?" he said. . . . "Well, in a word, it was intellectual doubt of the whole thing. A kind of cloud of infidelity seemed to envelop me. I beat against it, but it passed on, thick and black. There seemed to me no person behind it; it was the very negation of Personality that surrounded me. 'After all,' it seemed to say to me, yet without words or intellect, you understand—'after all, this is a pretty picture, but where is the proof? What shadow of a proof is there that the whole thing is not a dream? If there were objective proof, how could any man doubt?

If there is not objective proof, what reason have you to trust in religion at all—far more, to sacrifice your life to it? . . . Death, too, what is that but the resolving of the elements that issue in what you call the soul? And when the elements resolve the soul disperses.' . . . And so on, and so on. You know it, gentlemen. . . . It suggested horrible things against Our Lord when I turned to the Tabernacle. And then, on a sudden, as it had done in the deeper plane, it spread upward to an intolerable climax. I began to see myself as a dying spark in a burning-out world, and there was no escape, for there was nothing but empty space about me—no God, no heaven, not even a devil to hint at life in some form at least after death. I looked during those seconds into the gulf of annihilation. . . . I cried out in my heart that I would sooner live in hell than die there . . . and the vision, if I may call it so, of ultimate eternal blackness cleared every instant before my intellect until it was imminent upon me as a demonstrable certainty; and then, once more, before that loomed out as actually intellectually certain, I struggled and stood up, saying something aloud, the name of God, I think, while the sweat poured down my face.

"It passed then—at least, in its acuteness. There was the little domed tabernacle before me with its white curtains, and the altar-cards and the gilt candlesticks, and a woman went past the window in clogs, and I heard a bird twitter beneath the eaves, and it was all, for a while, natural and peaceful again."

The priest stopped.

"Now, gentlemen," he said very slowly, "intellectual difficulties have occurred to most people, I imagine. How should it not be so? If religion were small enough for our intellects it could not be great enough for our soul's requirements. But this was not just that fleeting transient obscurity that we call intellectual difficulty. It was to ordinary darkness what substance is to imagination, what a visible concrete scene is to a fancy, what life is to dreaming. I know I cannot express what I mean; but I want you to take it on my word that this visitation in the realm of the intellect was a solid blackness, compared with which all other difficulties that I have ever heard of or experienced are as a mere lowering of intellectual lights. It was paralleled only by my experience in introversion. That, too, had not been an emotional withdrawal, or a spiritual dryness, as we commonly use those words.

"It had been a solid, unutterably heavy burden—real beyond description. . . . And further, I want you to consider my dilemma. I had been routed in my soul and dared not take refuge there; I had been overwhelmed, too, in my intellect, and even when the first misery had passed it seemed to me that the arguments against the Faith were stronger than those for it. I did not dare to pit one against the other. A heavy deposit had been left upon my understanding. I did not dare to sit down and argue; I did not dare to run for refuge to the Silence of God. I was driven out into the sole thing that was left—the world of sense."

Again, he stopped, still with that tranquil smile. I hardly understood him, though I think I saw very dimly what he had called his dilemma. Yet I did not understand what he meant by the "world of sense."

After a little pause he went on.

"To the world of sense," he repeated. "It seemed to me now that this was all that was left. I determined then and there to drop my meditation and to confine myself to mass, office and rosary. I would say the words with my lips, quickly and steadily, keeping my mind fixed upon them rather than upon their meaning, and I would trust that presently the clouds would pass.

"Well, gentlemen, for about two months I continued this. The misery I suffered is simply indescribable. You can imagine all the suggestions I made to myself when I was off my guard. I told myself that I was a coward and a sham—that I had lost my faith and that I continued to act as a priest! What was especially hard to bear was the devotion of my parishioners. As I knelt in front saying the rosary and they responded I could hear the thrill of conviction in every word they uttered. Oh, those Irish! The things they said to me sometimes were like swords for pain . . . the masses they asked me to say . . !

"I went to a priest at a distance once or twice and told him the bare outline—not as I have told it to you. He laughed at me, kindly, of course. He told me that it was the effect of loneliness, while I knew that at the best it was the work of One who bore me continual company now and who was stronger than I. He told me that all young priests had to win the victory in some form or other; that every priest thought his own case the most desperate. . . . Yet I knew from every word that he said that he did not understand, and that I could never make him understand. Yet, somehow, I set my teeth; I told God that I was willing to bear this dereliction for as long as He willed—so paradoxical and mysterious is the gift of Faith—if He would but save my soul, and at last, in a kind of defiance, I began to look once more at my designs for the church I was to build.

"You see, gentlemen, what I meant by taking refuge in the world of sense. I deliberately contemplated never daring to face God again interiorly, or even my own soul. I would do my duty as a priest; I would say my mass and office; I would preach strictly what the Church enjoined; I would live and die like that, with my teeth set. Better God beaten and denied than all the world beside in prosperity!"

For the first time in the whole of his narrative Father Girdlestone's voice trembled a little. He passed his thin old hand over his mouth once or twice, shifted his position and began again.

"It was on the first of October that I took down my plans again. I had not looked at them for two months; I had not the heart to do so.

"Now let me describe to you exactly the room in which I sat, and the other necessary circumstances.

"In the centre of my room stood my table, with two windows on my left, the fire in front, and the door behind me to the right. The windows were hung with serge curtains. I had no carpet, but a little mat only beneath my table and another before the fire.

"It was in the beginning of October—to be accurate, the third of the month—that this thing happened that I am about to tell you.

"I awoke early that morning, said my mass as usual, with attention and care, but no sensible devotion, and after my thanksgiving sat down to breakfast. It was then that I first had any uneasiness.

"I was breakfasting at my table, and beyond me, in front and to the right, stood a large basket-chair. I was reading some book or other, and can honestly say that nothing was further from my mind than my experiences in the summer. Remember, during two months nothing had happened—nothing, at least, beyond that intolerable intellectual darkness. Then the basket-chair suddenly clicked in the way in which they do half an hour after one has sat in them. It distracted my attention for an instant—it was just enough for that; no more. I went on with my book.

"Then it clicked again three or four times, and I looked up, rather annoyed. . . . Well, to be brief, this went on and on. After breakfast, when Bridget came to fetch the tray, I asked whether she had touched the chair that morning. She told me No. All this time, remember, no thought of anything odd had entered my head. I supposed it was the damp and said so.

"Well, she was still in the room. I went out to fetch my breviary from the chapel, and as I set foot on the stairs, leaving the door open behind me, I heard her, as I thought, come out after me with the tray and follow me, three or four steps behind, all down the staircase. I had no more doubt of that than of the fact that I myself was going downstairs. At the turn of the stairs I did not even look behind. By the sounds—not clear footfalls, you understand, but a kind of shuffling and breathing, and still more by the consciousness that there she was—I judged she was in a hurry, as she often was. At the foot of the stairs I turned to say something, and as I began to turn I will swear that I saw a figure out of the corner of my eye; but when I looked it was simply not there. There was nothing there. . . . Do you understand, gentlemen? Nothing at all.

"I called up to her, and heard her come across the floor. Then she looked over the banister.

"'Did you come out of the room just now?' I said.

"'No, your reverence.'

"Well, I made my theory, of course. It was to the effect that she had moved in the room as I came out; that I therefore thought she was following me, and that the rest was simply self-suggestion.

"I got my breviary and came out. As I came into the little lobby again there occurred to the impression that someone was there, waiting in the corner. I looked round me; there was nothing, and I went upstairs.

"Gentlemen, do you know that nervous condition when one feels there is someone in the room? It is generally dissipated by ten minutes' conversation. Well, I was in that condition all the morning. But there was more than that.

"It was not only that sense of someone there; there were sounds now and then, very faint, but absolutely distinct, coming from all quarters—sounds so minute and unimportant in themselves that I might have heard them a hundred times without giving them another thought if they had not been accompanied by that sense of a presence with me. They were of all kinds. Once or twice a piece of woodwork somewhere in the room clicked, as my basket-chair had done—a sharp, minute rap, such as one hears in damp weather. Once the door became unlatched and slid very softly with the sound of a hush over a piece of matting that lay there. I got up and shut the door again, looking, I must confess, for an instant on to the landing, and as I came back to my chair that clicked twice.

"Gentlemen, I know this sounds absurd. You will be saying, as I said, that I was simply in a nervous condition. Very well, perhaps I was; but please wait. Once, as I sat in my chair drawn sideways near the fireplace, a very slight movement caught my eye. I turned sharply; it was no more than the fringe of the mat under the table lifting in the draught. As I looked it ceased.

"Well, my nerves got worse and worse. I stared every now and then round the room. There was nothing to be seen but the boards, the mats, the familiar furniture, the black and white crucifix over the mantle-shelf, my few books, and the vestment-chest near the door. There were the curtains, too, hanging at the windows. That was all. It was a cloudy October day, and rained a little about half-past twelve. I remember starting suddenly as a gust came and dashed the drops against the glass.

"At about a quarter to one Bridget came in to lay dinner. . . . I am ashamed to say it, but I was extraordinarily relieved when I heard her open the downstairs door. She came in, you remember, three or four

56

times a day to see after me; otherwise I was alone in the house.

"When she came into the room I looked up at her. . . . She smiled at me, and then it seemed to me that her face took on it rather an odd expression. She stopped smiling, and before she set down the tablecloth and knives she looked round the room rather curiously, I thought.

"'Well, Bridget,' I said, 'what is it?'

"There was just a moment before she answered.

"'It is nothing, your reverence,' she said.

"Then she laid dinner. I dined, reading all the while, and she brought in the dishes one by one. I am afraid I hurried rather over dinner. I made up my mind to go out for a long walk; there was something else in my mind, too—well, I may as well tell you; it seemed to me that I should rather like to be out of the house before she was. Yes; it was cowardly; but remember that all this while I was telling myself that I had an attack of the nerves, and that I had better not be alone except in the fresh air.

"Well, nothing at all happened that afternoon. It seemed to me as I went over the moors that all sense of haunting had ceased; I noticed first consciously that it had gone soon after leaving the outskirts of the village; I was entirely happy and serene.

"As I came back into sight of the village at dusk and saw the lights shining over the hill the uneasiness came on me again. It struck me vividly for the first time that a night spent alone in that house would be slightly uncomfortable. By this time, of course, too, the possibility of a connection between my present state and my previous experiences had occurred to my mind; but I had striven to resist this idea as merely one more nervous suggestion.

"My uneasiness grew greater still as I came up the street. I am ashamed to say that I stopped to talk three or four times to my parishioners simply out of that unaccountably strong terror of my own house. I noticed, too, across the street that a face peeped from Bridget's window and drew back on seeing me. A moment later her door opened and she came out.

"I did not turn or wait for her, but as I reached my door I was conscious of a very distinct relief that she was behind me, and as I went in she came immediately after me.

"'I am very sorry, Father,' she said, 'I haven't your tea ready yet.'

"I told her to bring it as soon as she could, and went slowly upstairs with the horror deepening at every step. I knew perfectly well now why she had waited; it was that she did not like to enter the empty house alone. . . .Yet I did not feel that I could ask her what it was she feared. That would be a kind of surrender on my part—an allowing to myself that there was something to fear, and you must remember that I still was trying to tell myself that it was all nerves."

The rector leaned forward.

"I am very sorry, Father Girdlestone," he said softly, "but it is past time for night-prayers." He paused. "But may we make an exception tonight and hear the rest afterward?"

The old man stood up and motioned with a little smile toward the chapel gallery.

★★★★★★

"As I went forward into the room," began the old man again as soon as we had taken our seats in silence, "I knew beyond doubt that I was accompanied. I heard Bridget moving about downstairs, but it was as sound heard through the roar of a train. There went with me something resembling a loud noise—interior, you understand, yet on the brink of manifestation in the world of sense; or you may call it a blackness, or a vast weight, as heavy as heaven and earth, and it was all centred round a personality. It was of such a nature that I should have been surprised at nothing. It appeared to me that all that I looked upon—the serge curtains, my table, my chair, the glow of the fire on the hearth, and the glimmer on the bare boards—all these were but as melting shreds and rays hanging upon some monstrous reality. They were there, they were just in existence, but they were as accidents without substance.

"I do not know if there were definite sounds or not, or even definite appearances, beyond the normal, material sounds and sights. There may have been, but I do not think so.

"I went across the room, walking, it seemed to me, on nothingness. My body was still in sensible relations with matter, but it seemed to me that I was not. I found my chair and sat down in it to wait. I was nerveless now, sunk in a kind of despair that I cannot hope to make plain to you. I imagine that a lost soul on the edge of death must be in that state.

"I looked almost vacantly round the room once or twice; but there was nothing. I understood without consideration what was happening, and the general course of events. It was all one, I perceived now. That which had started up at the rock, which had invaded first the innermost chamber of my soul, and then the intellectual plane, and

58

had established itself there, had now taken its frail step forward, and was claiming the world of sense as well. I felt entirely powerless. You will wonder why I did not go downstairs to the Blessed Sacrament. I do not know, but it was impossible. Here was the battlefield, I knew very well.

"I perceived something else, too. It was the reason of the assaults. I did not fully understand it, but I knew that the object was to drive me from the place—to make the village and the neighbourhood detestable to me. I knew that I could escape by going away, yet it was not exactly a temptation. I had no interior desire to escape. It was merely a question as to which force would prevail in my soul—that which impelled me away and grace which held me there. I was as a passive dummy between them....

"I do not know how long it was before Bridget pushed open the door. I saw her with the tray come across the room and set it down upon my table. Then I saw her looking at me.

"'Bridget,' I said, 'I shall want no supper tonight. And tell the people that I am unwell and that there will be no night-prayers. There will be mass, I hope, as usual in the morning.'

"I said those words, I believe; but the voice was not as my own. It was as if another spoke. I saw her looking at me across the dusk with an extraordinary terror in her face.

"'Come away, Father,' she whispered.

"I shook my head.

"'Come away,' she whispered again. 'This is not a good house to be in.'

"I said nothing.

"'Shall I fetch Father Donovan to you, Father,' she whispered, 'or the doctor?'

"'Fetch no one,' I said to her. 'Tell no one. Ask for prayers, if you will. Go and leave me to myself, Bridget.'

"I think I understood even then what the struggle was she was going through. I do not know if she perceived all that I perceived, but even from her face, without her words, I knew that she was conscious of something. Yet she did not like to leave me alone. She stood perfectly still, looking first at me, then slowly round the room, then back at me again. And as she looked the dusk fell veil on veil.

"Then something happened, I do not know what; I never questioned her afterward, but she was gone. I heard her stumbling and moaning down the stairs. An instant later the street door opened and banged, and I was left alone.

"I cannot tell you what I felt. I knew only that the crisis was come, and that the result was out of my hands. I closed my eyes, I think, and lay right back in my chair. It was as if I were submitting myself to an operation; I wondered vaguely as to what shape it would take.

"All about the room I felt the force gathering. There was no oscillation, no vibration, but a steady, continuous stream concentrating itself within the four walls. With this the sense of the central personality grew every moment more and more intense and vivid. It seemed to me as if I were some tiny, conscious speck of matter in the midst of a life whose vastness and malignance was beyond conception. At times it was this; at other times it was as if I looked within and saw a space full of some indescribable blackness—a space of such a nature that I could not tell whether it was as tiny as a pinhole or as vast as infinity. It was spaceless space, sheer emptiness, but with an emptiness that was a horror, and it was within me.

"Yet it was not simple spirit—it was not the correlative of matter. It was rather spirit in the very throes of manifestation in matter. . . .

"Sometimes then I attended to this; sometimes I lay with every sense at full stretch—at a tenseness that seemed impossible, directed outward. I cannot tell even now whether the room was poised in deathly silence or in an indescribable clamour and roar of tongues. It was one or the other, or it was both at once.

"Or, to take the sense of sight. . . . Although my eyes were closed, every detail of the room was before me. Sometimes I saw it as rigid as a man at grips with death, in a kind of pallor—the table, the dying fire, the uncurtained windows—all in the pallor—the very names of the books visible—all, as it were, striving to hold themselves in material being under the stress of some enormous destructive force with which they were charged—as rigid and as silent and as significant as an electric wire—and as full of power. Or at times all seemed to me to have gone, simply to have dissolved into nothingness, as a breath fades on a window—to retain but a phantom of themselves. . . .

"Well, well . . . words are very useless, gentlemen; . . . they are poor things—"

The old priest paused a moment, leaning forward in his chair with his thin, veined hands together. For myself I cannot say what I felt. I seemed to be in somewhat of the same state as that which he was describing; all my senses, too, were stretched to the full by the intensity of my attention. Yet the narrator seemed little affected; he leaned and looked peacefully into the fire, and I caught the glint of light on his deep eyes.

Then he leaned back and went on.

"Now you must picture to yourselves, gentlemen, that this state grew steadily in its energy. I did not know before—and I can scarcely believe it now—that human nature could bear so much. Yet I seemed to myself to be observing my strained faculties from a plane apart from them. It was as the owner of a besieged castle might stand on a keep and watch the figures of his men staring out over the battlements at a sight he could not see. There were my eyes looking, my ears listening, even the touch of my fingers on the chair-arms questioning what it was that they held; and there was I—my very self—far within waiting for communications.

"I suppose that I knew there was no escape. I could not descend into the sphere of reason, for another Power held the keys; I could not sink again to the inner Presence of God, for that chamber, too, was occupied; there was this last stand to be made—the world of sense. If that was lost, all was lost; and I could not lift a finger to help. And, as I said, the strain grew greater each instant, as the opening swell of an organ waxes with a long, steady crescendo to its final roar. . . .

"I do not know at exactly what point I understood the assault, but it became known to me presently that what was intended was to merge the world of sense, so far as I was concerned, into this mighty essence of evil—to burst through, or, rather, to transcend the material. Then I knew I should be wholly lost. I remember, too, that I perceived soon after this that this was what the world calls madness . . . and I understood at this moment as never before how that process consummates itself. It begins, as mine did, with the carrying of the inner life by storm; that may come about by deliberate acquiescence in sin. I should suppose that it always does in some degree. Then the intellect is attacked—it may only be in one point—a 'delusion' it is called, and with many persons regarded only as eccentric—the process goes no further. But when the triumph is complete the world of sense, too, is lost, and the man raves. I knew at that time for absolute fact that this is the process. The 'delusions' of the mad are not non-existent—they are glimpses, horrible or foul or fantastic, of that strange world that we take so quietly for granted, that at this moment and at every moment is perpetually about us, foaming out its waters in lust or violence or mad irresponsible blasphemy against the Most High.

"Well, I saw that this was what threatened, yet I could not move a finger. No thought of flight entered my mind. All had gone too far by now. . . .

"Then, gentlemen, the climax came."

Again, the old priest was silent.

I heard *Monsignor's* pipe drop with a clatter, and my nerves thrilled like a struck harp. He made no movement to pick it up. He stared only at the old man.

Then the quiet voice went on.

"This was the climax, gentlemen. . . . The intensity swelled and swelled; . . . each moment I thought must be the last—the utmost effort of hell. Then with a crash the full close sounded; and through the rending tear, through the veil of matter that whirled away and was gone, I caught one swift glimpse of all that lay beneath. It was not through one sense that I perceived it; it was through perception pure and simple. . . . Well, how can I say it? It was this. . . .

"I perceived two vast forces pressed one against the other, as silent and as rigid as . . . as the glass of a diver's helmet against the huge, incumbent, glittering water. It is a wretched simile. . . . Let us say that the appearance was as the meeting of fire and water without mist or tumult. The forces were absolutely opposed, absolutely alien, yet absolutely one in the plane of being. They could meet as the created and uncreated could not—as flesh and spirit cannot. They met, level, coincident, each rigid to breaking point—each full of an energy to which there is no parallel in this world.

"It seemed to me that all had waited for this. The enemy had been permitted to enter the gate; and at the instant of his triumph the fire of God was upon him, locked in the embrace of utter repulsion. . . .

"And it was given to me to watch that, gentlemen. . . . On the edge of what the world labels as madness, at the very instant that I hung balanced on that line, I saw that endless war of spirit and spirit, which has been waging since Michael drove Satan from heaven—that ceaseless, writhing conflict in which all that is not for God is against Him, seeking to dethrone and annihilate Him who gave it being. Ah, words . . . words . . . but I saw it . . . !"

There was a dead silence in the room. The priest drew one breath.

"Then I saw no more. I was in my chair as before, holding the arms; and the room round me stole back into being—through the pallor of a phantom to the dusk of earthly twilight; and I perceived that my eyes were dosed and not open.

"There then I stayed, knowing that the war still waged beneath, yet fainter every moment as the tide crawled back, contesting inch by inch, rolled back by that remorseless power. Twice or three times I heard the murmur of sound in the room; the serge curtains swayed. I could hear them. I heard the door vibrating softly; then once more the quiet silence was there, and I heard the ashes slip by their weight from grate to fender. Nature at least was itself again. Then once more, as into my intellect, the light stole back, and I knew that God reigned and that His Son was Incarnate, crucified and risen by many irrefragable proofs, round the house I could hear the murmuring of voices, and saw through closed eyelids of utter repose the glimmer of lanterns on the ceiling.

"Within myself, too, I watched the roar of evil; I drew breath after breath, deep and life-giving, as far down within the secret chambers of my soul the foul filth ebbed and sank, and that spring raising into life everlasting, of which our Saviour spoke, welled up in its stead, filling every cranny and corner of my soul with that strange sweetness, so sweet and so dear that we forget it as the very air we breathe.

"The murmur of conflict was infinitely far away; and it seemed to me that once more I went down, down, in that introversion of which I spoke just now, seeing all clear and sweet about me, down into the Presence of the Lord who rules heaven and earth at His will. Then a door closed, deep, deep below, and I knew that the enemy was gone. . . .

"Well, gentlemen," said the priest after a pause, leaning back, "that is really the story. But there are a few details to add.

"When the men that Bridget had fetched came upstairs they found me asleep, but they told me afterward there were streaks of foam at the corners of my mouth. Yet she was not gone three minutes.

"I never spoke a word to them of what happened. They knew quite enough for laymen. . . . We had night-prayers as usual that evening. I said the *Visita quasumus Domine* at the end. . . .

"I slept like a child, and I said a mass of thanksgiving next day."

Father Brent broke the silence that followed. His voice seemed strange.

"And the church, Father?"

The old priest smiled at him full.

"You have guessed it," he said. "Yes, the church was built thirty years later. It is a *basilica*, as I said; it presents Our Lord in glory in an apse. It stands, curiously enough, on the rock; but it is in the middle of a huge colliery town, and—well, I may as well say it—there is a grated tribune above the high altar at one side through which a convent of

Poor Clares can assist at the holy sacrifice. Poor Clares!

"I ceased to wonder at the assault as soon as the convent was built."

He stood up, smiling.

Father Bianchi's Tale

Father Bianchi, as the days went on, seemed a little less dogmatic on the theory that miracles (except, of course, those of the saints) did not happen. He was warned by Monsignor Maxwell that his turn was approaching to contribute a story, and suddenly at supper announced that he would prefer to get it over at once that evening.

"But I have nothing to tell," he cried, expostulating with hands and shoulders, "nothing to tell but the nonsense of an old peasant-woman."

When we had taken our places upstairs, and the Italian had again apologised and remonstrated with raised eyebrows, he began at last, and I noticed that he spoke with a seriousness that I should not have expected.

"When I was first a priest," he said, "I was in the south of Italy, and said my first mass in a church in the hills. The village was called Arripezza."

"Is that true?" said *Monsignor* suddenly, smiling.

The Italian grinned brilliantly. "Well, no," he said, "but it is near enough, and I swear to you that the rest is true. It was a village in the hills, ten miles from Naples. They have many strange beliefs there; it is like Father Brent's Cornwall. All along the coast, as you know, they set lights in the windows on one night of the year, because they relate that our Lady once came walking on the water with her divine Child, and found none to give her shelter. Well, this village that we will call Arripezza was not on the coast. It was inland, but it had its own super-stitions to compensate it—superstitions cursed by the Church.

"I knew little of all this when I went there. I had been in the semi-nary until then.

"The *parroco* was an old man, but old! He could say mass some-times on Sundays and feasts, but that was all, and I went to help him. There were many at my first mass as the custom is, and they all came up to kiss my hands when it was done.

"When I came back from the sacristy again there was an old wom-an waiting for me, who told me that her name was Giovannina. I had seen her before as she kissed my hands. She was as old as the *parroco* himself—I cannot tell how old—yellow and wrinkled as a monkey.

"She put five *loie* into my hands.

"'Five masses, Father,' she said, 'for a soul in purgatory.'

"'And the name?'

"'That does not matter,' she said. 'And will you say them, my Father, at the altar of S. Espedito?'

"I took the money and went off, and as I went down the church, I saw her looking after me, as if she wished to speak, but she made no sign, and I went home; and I had a dozen other masses to say, some for my friends, and a couple that the *parroco* gave me, and those, therefore, I began to say first. When I had said the fifth of the twelve, Giovannina waited for me again at the door of the sacristy. I could see that she was troubled.

"'Have you not said them, my Father?' she asked. 'He is here still.'

"I did not notice what she said, except the question, and I said no; I had had others to say first. She blinked at me with her old eyes a moment, and I was going on, but she stopped me again.

"'Ah! Say them at once, my Father,' she said; 'he is waiting.'

"Then I remembered what she had said before and I was angry.

"'Waiting!' I said; 'and so are thousands of poor souls.'

"'Ah, but he is so patient,' she said; 'he has waited so long.'

"I said something sharp, I forget what, but the *parroco* had told me not to hang about and talk nonsense to women, and I was going on, but she took me by the arm.

"'Have you not seen him too, my Father?' she said.

"'I looked at her, thinking she was mad, but she held me by the arm and blinked up at me, and seemed in her senses. I told her to tell me what she meant, but she would not. At last I promised to say the masses at once. The next morning, I began the masses, and said four of them, and at each the old woman was there close to me, for I said them at the altar of S. Espedito that was in the nave, as she had asked me, and I had a great devotion to him as well, and she was always at her chair just outside the altar-rails. I scarcely saw her, of course, for I was a young priest and had been taught not to lift my eyes when I turned round, but on the fourth day I looked at her at the *Orate fratres* and she was staring not at me or the altar, but at the corner on the left. I looked there when I turned, but there was nothing but the glass case with the silver hearts in it to S. Espedito.

"That was on a Friday, and in the evening, I went to the church again to hear confessions, and when I was done, the old woman was there again.

"'They are nearly done, my Father?' she said, 'and you will finish them tomorrow?'

"I told her Yes; but she made me promise that whatever happened I would do so.

"Then she went on, 'Then I will tell you, my Father, what I would not before. I do not know the man's name, but I see him each day during mass at that altar. He is in the corner. I have seen him there ever since the church was built.'

"Well, I knew she was mad then, but I was curious about it, and asked her to describe him to me; and she did so. I expected a man in a sheet or in flames or something of the kind, but it was not so. She described to me a man in a dress she did not know—a tunic to the knees, bareheaded, with a short sword in his hand. Well, then I saw what she meant, she was thinking of S. Espedito himself. He was a Roman soldier, you remember, gentlemen?

"'And a *curiass?*' I said. 'A steel breastplate and helmet?'

"Then she surprised me.

"'Why, no, Father; he has nothing on his head or breast, and there is a bull beside him.'

"Well, gentlemen, I was taken aback by that. I did not know what to say."

Monsignor leant swiftly forward.

"Mithras," he said abruptly.

The Italian smiled.

"*Monsignor* knows everything," he said.

Then I broke in, because I was more interested than I knew.

"Tell me, *Monsignor*, what was Mithras?"

The priest explained shortly. It was an Eastern worship, extraordinarily pure, introduced into Italy a little after the beginning of the Christian era. Mithras was a god, filling a position not unlike that of the Second Person of the Blessed Trinity: He offered a perpetual sacrifice, and through that sacrifice souls were enabled to rise from earthly things to heavenly, if they relied upon it and accompanied that faith by works of discipline and prayer.

"I beg your pardon, Father Bianchi," he ended.

The Italian smiled again.

"Yes, *Monsignor*," he said, "I know that now, but I did not know it for many years afterwards, and I know something else now that I did not know then. Well, to return.

"I told my old woman that she was dreaming, that it could not be so, that there was no room for a bull in the corner, that it was a picture of S. Espedito that she was thinking of.

"'And why did you not get the masses said before?' I asked.

"She smiled rather slyly at me then.

"'I did get five said once before,' she said, 'in Naples, but they did him no good. And when once again I told the *parroco* here, he told me to be off; he would not say them.'

"And she had waited for a young priest, it seemed, and had determined not to tell him the story till the masses were said, and had saved up her money meanwhile.

"Well, I went home, and got to talking with the old priest, and led him on, so that he thought that he had introduced the subject, and presently he told me that when the foundation of the church had been laid forty years before, they had found an old cave in the hill, with heathen things in it. He knew no more than that about it, but he told me to fetch a bit of pottery from a cupboard, and showed it me, and there was just the tail of a bull upon it, and an eagle."

Monsignor leaned forward again.

"Just so," he said, "and the bull was lying down?"

The Italian nodded, and was silent.

We all looked at him. It seemed a tame ending, I thought. Then Father Brent put our thoughts into words.

"That is not all?" he said.

Father Bianchi looked at him sharply, and at all of us, but said nothing.

"Ah! that is not all," said the other again persistently.

"Bah!" cried the Italian suddenly. "It was not all, if you will have it so. But the rest is madness, as mad as Giovannina herself. What I saw, I saw because she made me expect it. It was nothing but the shadow, or the light in the glass case."

A perceptible thrill ran through us all. The abrupt change from contempt to seriousness was very startling.

"Tell us, Father," said the English priest; "we shall think no worse of you for it If it was only the shadow, what harm is there in telling it?"

"Indeed, you must finish," went on *Monsignor*; "it is in the contract."

The Italian looked round again, frowned, smiled and laughed uneasily.

"I have told it to no one till today," he said, "but you shall hear it. But it was only the shadow—you understand that?"

A chorus, obviously insincere, broke out from the room.

"It was only the shadow, Padre Bianchi." Again, the priest laughed shortly; then the smile faded, and he went on.

"I went down early the next morning, before dawn, and I made my meditation before the Blessed Sacrament; but I could not help looking across once or twice at the corner by S. Espedito's altar; it was too dark to see anything clearly; but I could make out the silver hearts in the glass case. When I had finished Giovannina came in.

"I could not help stopping by her chair as I went to rest.

"'Is there anything there?' I asked.

"She shook her head at me.

"'He is never there till mass begins,' she said.

"The sacristy door that opens out of doors was set wide as I came past it in my vestments; and the dawn was coming up across the hills, all purple."

Monsignor murmured something, and the priest stopped.

"I beg your pardon," said *Monsignor*, "but that was the time the sacrifice of Mithras was offered."

"When I came out into the church," went on the priest, "it was all grey in the light of the dawn, but the chapels were still dark. I went up the steps, not daring to look in the corner, and set the vessels down. As I was spreading the corporal the server came up and lighted the candles. And still I dared not look. I turned by the right and came down, and stood waiting till he knelt beside me.

"Then I found I could not begin. I knew what folly it was, but I was terribly frightened. I heard the server whisper, *In nomine Patris* . . .

"Then I shut my eyes tight, and began.

"Well, by the time I had finished the preparation, I felt certain that something was watching me from the corner. I told myself, as I tell myself now," snapped the Italian fiercely—"I told myself it was but what the woman had told me. And then at last I opened my eyes to go up the steps, but I kept them down, and only saw the dark corner out of the side of my eyes.

"Then I kissed the altar and began.

"Well, it was not until the Epistle that I understood that I should have to face the corner at the reading of the Gospel; but by then I do not think I could have faced it directly, even if I had wished.

"So, when I was saying the *Munda cor* in the centre, I thought of a plan, and as I went to read the Gospel I put my left hand over my eyes, as if I were in pain, and read the Gospel like that. And so, all through the mass I went on; I always dropped my eyes when I had to turn that way at all, and I finished everything and gave the blessing.

"As I gave it, I looked at the old woman, and she was kneeling there, staring across at the corner; so, I knew that she was still dreaming she saw something.

"Then I went to read the last Gospel."

The priest was plainly speaking with great difficulty; he passed his hands over his lips once or twice. We were all quiet.

"Well, gentlemen, courage came to me then; and as I signed the altar I looked straight into the corner."

He stopped again, and began resolutely once more; but his voice rang with hysteria. "Well, gentlemen, you understand that my head was full of it now, and that the corner was dark, and that the shadows were very odd."

"Yes, yes, Padre Bianchi," said *Monsignor* easily, "and what did the shadows look like?"

The Italian gripped the arms of the chair, and screamed his answer.

"I will not tell you, I will not tell you. It was but the shadow. My God, why have I told you the tale at all?"

Father Jenks' Tale

I have not yet had occasion to describe Father Jenks, the Ontario priest; partly, I think, because he had not previously distinguished himself by anything but silence, and partly because he was so true to his type that I had scarcely noticed even that.

It was not until the following evening, when he was seated in the central chair of the group, that I really observed him sufficiently to take in his characteristics with any definiteness and to see how wholly he was American. He was clean-shaven, with a heavy mouth, square jaw, and an air of something that I must call dullness, relieved only by a spark of alertness in each of his eyes, as he leaned back and began his story. He spoke deliberately, in an even voice, and as he spoke looked steadily a little above the fire; his hands lay together on his right knee, which was crossed over his left, and I noticed a large, elastic-sided boot cocked toward the warmth. I knew that he had passed a great part of his early life in England, and I was not surprised to observe that he spoke with hardly a trace of American accent or phraseology.

"I, too, am a man of one story," he said, "and I dare say you may think it not worth the telling. But it impressed me."

He looked round with heavy, amused eyes as if to apologize.

"It was when I was in England, in the eighties. I was in the

Cotswolds. You know them, perhaps?"

Again, he looked round. Monsignor Maxwell jerked the ash off his cigarette impatiently. This American's air of leisure was a little tiresome.

"I lived in a cottage," went on the other, "at the edge of Minchester, not two hundred yards from the old church. My own schism shop, as the parson called it once or twice in the local paper, was a tin building behind my house; it was not beautiful. It was a kind of outlandish stranger beside the church, and the parson made the most of that. I never was able to understand."

He broke off again and pressed his lips in a reminiscent smile.

"Now, all that part of the Cotswolds is like a table; it is flat at the top, with steep sides sloping down into the valleys. The great houses stand mostly half way down these slopes. It is too windy on the top for their trees and gardens. The Dominicans have a house a few miles from Minchester up one of the opposite hills; and I would go over there to my confession on Saturdays and stay an hour or two over tea, talking to one of them. It was there that I heard the tale of the house I am going to speak about.

"This was a house that stood not two miles from my own village— a great place, built half way down one of the slopes. It had been a Benedictine house once, though there was little enough of that part left; most of it was red brick with twisted chimneys; but on the lawn that sloped down toward the wood and the stream at the bottom of the valley there was the west arch of the nave still standing, with the doorway beneath and a couple of chapels on either side. Mrs.— er—Arbuthnot we will call her, if you please—had laid it out with a rockery beneath; and once I saw her from the hill behind drinking tea with her friends in one of the chapels.

"Then the dining-room, I heard from the Dominicans, had been the abbot's chapel. This, too, was what they told me. The house had been shut up for forty years and had a bad name. It had once been a farm, but things had happened there—the sons had died, a famous horse bred there had broken its neck somehow on the lawn. Then another family had taken it from the owner, and the only son of the lot, too, had died; and then folks began to talk about a curse; and the oldest inhabitant was trotted out as usual to make mischief and gossip; and the end was, the house was shut up.

"Then the owner had built on to it. He pulled down a bit more of the ruins, meaning to live in it himself, and then his son went up.

70

The Canadian smiled with one corner of his mouth.

"This is what I heard from the Dominicans, you know."

Father Brent looked up swiftly.

"They are right, though," he said. "I know the house and others like it."

"Yes, Father," said the other priest; "your island has its points."

He recrossed his legs and drew out his pipe and pouch.

"Well, as this priest says, there are other houses like it. Otherwise I could scarcely tell this tale. It's too ancient and feudal to happen in my country."

He paused so long to fill his pipe that Father Maxwell sighed aloud.

"Yes, *Monsignor*," said the priest without looking up, "I am going on immediately."

He put his pipe into the corner of his mouth, took out his matches and went on.

"Well, Mrs. Arbuthnot had taken the house a year before I came to Minchester. She was what the Dominicans called a frivolous woman; but I called her real solid before the end. What they meant was that she had parties down there, and tea in the chapel, and a dresser with blue plates where the altar used to stand in the abbot's place, and a vestment for her fire-screen, and all that; and a couple of chestnuts that she used to drive about the country with, and a groom in boots, and a couple of fellows with powdered hair to help her in and out.

"Well, I saw all that at a garden-party she gave, and I must say we got on very well. I had seen her before once or twice out of my window on Sunday morning going along with a morocco prayer-book with a cross on it, and a bonnet on the back of her head. Then I showed her round the old church one day with some visitors of hers, and she left a card on me next day.

"On the day of the garden-party I saw the house, and the blue china and the rest, and she asked me what I thought of it all, and I said it was very nice; and she asked me whether I thought it wrong, with a sort of cackle; and I told her she had better follow her own religious principles and let me follow mine, and not have any exchanges. She told me then I was a sensible man, and called up her son to introduce us. He was a fellow of twenty or so, a bright lad, up at Oxford. He was just engaged to be married, too—that was why they had the party— and when I saw his girl, too, I thought things looked pretty unwhole- some for the old curse, and I think I said so to the lady. She thought me more sensible than ever after that, and I heard her telling another old body what I had said."

The Canadian paused again to strike a match, and I saw the corners of his mouth twitching either with the effort to draw or with amusement; I scarcely knew which. When the pipe was well alight he went on.

"It was on the last Sunday of September that year that I heard the young man was ill, and that the marriage was put off. I remember it well, partly because they were having a high time at the church, decorating it all for Michaelmas, which was next day, with the parson pretending it was for Harvest Festival, as they always do. I had seen the pumpkins go in the day before, and wondered where they put them all. I went up to the churchyard after mass to have a look, and was nearly knocked down by the parson. I began to say something or other, but he ran past me, through from the vicarage, with his coat-tails flying and his man after him. But I stopped the man, and got out of him that Archie was ill, and that the parson was sent for.

"Well, then I went back home and sat down."

The priest drew upon his pipe in silence a moment or two.

I felt rather impressed. His airy manner of talking was shot now with a kind of seriousness, and I wondered what was coming next.

He went on almost immediately.

"I heard a bit more as the day wore on.

One of my people stayed after catechism to tell me that the young man was worse, that a doctor had come from Stroud, and another wired for from London.

"Well, I waited. I thought I knew what would happen. I thought I had seen a bit more in the old lady than the Dominicans had seen, but what I was going to say to her I knew no more than the dead.

"Then that night as I was going to bed—I had just said *Matins* and *Lauds* for Michaelmas day—the message came.

"I was halfway upstairs when I heard a knocking at the door, and I went down again and opened it. There stood one of the fellows I had seen on the box of the carriage, and he was out of breath with running. He had a lantern in his hand, because there was a thick mist that night up from the valley.

"He gave me the lady's compliments, and would I step down? Master Archie was ill. That was all."

"Well, in a minute we were off into the thick of the mist. I took nothing with me but my stole, for it was not a proper side call. We said little or nothing to each other. He just told me that Master Archie had been taken ill about ten o'clock, quite suddenly. He didn't know what it was."

The priest paused again for a moment. Then he went on almost apologetically. "You know how it is, gentlemen, when something runs in your head. It may be a tune or a sentence. And I don't know if you've noticed how strong it is sometimes when you have something on your mind.

"Well, what ran in my head was a bit of the office I had just said. It was this. I have never forgotten it since:

"*Stetit Angelus juxta oram templi habens thuribulum aureum in manu sua.*" (Angel stood at the edge of the Temple, having gold in her hand.)

He said it again, and then added:

"It comes frequently in the office, you remember. It was very natural to remember it.

"Well, in half an hour we were at the top of the hill above the house. I think there must have been a moon, because we could see the mist round us like smoke, but nothing of the house, not even the lights in the top floors below us. It was all white and misty.

"Then we started down through the iron gate and the plantation. I could have lost my way again and again but for the fellow with me, and still we saw nothing of the house till we were close to it on one side; and then I looked up and saw a window like a great yellow door overhead.

"We came round to the front of the house, and there was a carriage there drawn up, with the lamps smoking in the mist, and as we came up I saw that the horses were steaming and blowing. The driver had just brought the London doctor from Stroud and was waiting for orders, I suppose."

The Canadian paused again.

I was more interested than ever. His descriptions had become queerly particular, and I wondered why. I did not understand yet. The rest, too, were very quiet.

"We went in through the hall past the stuffed bear that held the calling cards and all that, you know, and then turned in to the left to the big dining-room that had been the abbot's chapel. Some fool had left the window open. I suppose they were too flurried to think of it. At any rate, the mist had got in, and made the gas-jets overhead look high up like great stars.

"There was a door open upstairs somewhere, and I could hear whispering.

73

"Well, we went up the staircase that opened on one side below the gallery, that they had put up above the eastern end. The footpad was still there, you know, below the gallery, and the sideboard stood there.

"We came out on to the gallery presently, and my man stopped.

"Then someone came out with Mrs. Arbuthnot and the door closed. She saw me standing there, and I thought she was going to scream; but the fellow with her in the fur coat—he was the London doctor I heard afterward—took her by the arm.

"Well, she was quiet enough then, but as white as death. She had her bonnet on still, just as she must have put it on to go to church with in the morning, when the young man was taken ill. She beckoned me along, and I went.

"As I was going past the doctor he first shook his head at me, and then whispered as I went on to keep her quiet. I knew there was no hope then for Archie, and I was sorry, very sorry, gentlemen."

The priest shook his own head meditatively once or twice, leaned forward and spat accurately into the heart of the fire.

"Well, it was a big room that I went into, and to tell the truth, I left the door open this time, because I was startled by the screen at the bed and all that.

"The screen stood in the corner by the window to keep off the draught; and the bed to one side of it. I could just catch a glimpse of the lad's face on the pillow and the local doctor close by him. There was a woman or two there as well.

"But the worst was that the lad was talking and moaning out loud, but I didn't attend to him then, and besides, Mrs. Arbuthnot had gone through by another door, and I went after her.

"It was a kind of dressing-room—Archie's perhaps. There was a tall glass and silver things on the table by the window, and a candle or two burning. She turned round there and faced me, and she looked so deadly that I forgot all about the lad for the present. I just looked out to catch her when she fell. I had seen a woman like that once or twice before.

"Well, she said all that I expected—all about the curse and that, and the sins of the fathers; and it was all her fault for taking the beastly place, and how she would swear to clear out—I couldn't get a word in—and at last she said she'd become a Catholic if the boy lived.

"I did get a word in then, and told her not to talk nonsense. The Church didn't want people like that. They must believe first and so on, and all the while I was looking out to catch her.

"Well, she didn't hear a word I said, but she sat down all on a sudden, and I sat down, too, opposite her, and all the while the boy's voice grew louder and louder from the next room.

"Then she started again, but she hadn't been under way a minute before I had given over attending to her. I was listening to the lad."

The priest stopped again abruptly. His pipe had gone out, but he sucked at it hard and seemed not to notice it. His eyes were oddly alert.

"As I listened I looked toward the door into the next room. Both that and the one with the gallery over the hall were open, and I saw the mist coming in like smoke.

"I couldn't catch every word the lad said. He was talking in a high, droning voice, but I caught enough. It was about a face looking at him through smoke.

"'His eyes are like flames,' he said, 'smoky flames—yellow hair—are you a priest? ...What is that red dress?' ...Things like that. Well, it seemed pretty tolerable nonsense, and then I—"

Monsignor Maxwell sat up suddenly.

"Good Lord!" he said.

"Yes," drawled the Canadian, "*Stetit Angelus habens thuribulum aureum.*"

He spoke so placidly that I was almost shocked. It seemed astonishing that a man—Then he went on again.

"Well, I stood up when I heard that, and I faced the old lady.

"'What's the dedication of the chapel?' I said; 'what's the saint? Tell me, woman, tell me!' There! I said it like that.

"Well, she didn't know what I meant, of course, but I got it out of her at last. Of course, it was St. Michael's.

"I sat down then and let her chatter on. I suppose I must have looked a fool, because she took me by the shoulder directly.

"'You aren't listening, Father Jenks,' she said.

"I attended to her then. It seemed as if she wanted me to do something to save him, but I don't think she knew what it was herself, and I'm sure I didn't, not at first, at least.

"Then she began again, and all the while the boy was crying out. She wanted to know if her becoming a Catholic would do any good, and to tell the truth I wasn't so sure then myself as I had been before. Then she said she'd give up the house to Catholics, and then at last she said this:

"'Will you take it off, Father? I know you can. Priests can do anything.'

"Well, I stiffened myself up at that. I was sensible enough not to make a fool of myself, and I said something like this."

He stopped again; sucked vigorously at his cold pipe.

"I said something like this: 'Mind you keep your promise,' I said, 'but as far as I am concerned, I'd let him off.'"

A curious rustle passed round the room, and the priest caught the sound.

"Yes, gentlemen, I said that. I did, indeed, and I guess most of you gentlemen would have done the same in my circumstances.

"And this is what happened.

"First the lad's voice stopped, then there was a whispering, then a footstep in the other room, and the next moment Mrs. Arbuthnot was on her feet, with her mouth opened to scream. I had her down again though in time, and when I turned a woman was at the door, and I could see she had closed the outer door through which the mist came.

"Well, her face told us. The lad had taken the right turn. It was something on the brain, I think, that had dispersed or broken or something—I forget now—but it seemed to come in pat enough, didn't it, gentlemen?"

The Canadian stopped and leaned back. "Was that the end then?"

Father Brent put my question into words: "And what happened?"

"Well," added the other, drawling more than ever, "Mrs. Arbuthnot did not keep her promise. She's there still, for all I know, and attends the Harvest Festivals as regularly as ever. That spoils the story, doesn't it?"

"And the son?" put in the English priest swiftly.

"Well, the son was a bit better. That marriage did not take place. The girl broke it off."

"Well?"

"And Archie's at the English College at this moment studying for the priesthood. I had tea with him at Aragno's yesterday."

Father Martin's Tale

The Father Rector announced to us one day at dinner that a friend of his from England had called upon him a day or two before, and that he had asked him to supper that evening.

"There is a story I heard him tell," he said, "some years ago that I think he would contribute if you cared to ask him, *Monsignor*. It is remarkable; I remember thinking so."

"Tonight?" said *Monsignor*.

"Yes; he is coming tonight."

"That will do very well," said the other; "we have no story for tonight."

Father Martin appeared at supper, a grey-haired old man with a face like a mouse and large brown eyes that were generally cast down. He had a way at table of holding his hands together with his elbows at his side, that bore out the impression of his face.

He looked up deprecatingly and gave a little nervous laugh as *Monsignor* put his request.

"It is a long time since I have told it, *Monsignor*," he said.

"That is the more reason for telling it again," said the other priest with his sharp geniality, "or it may be lost to humanity."

"It has met with incredulity," said the old man.

"It will not meet with it here, then," remarked *Monsignor*. "We have been practising ourselves in the art of believing. Another act of faith will do us no harm."

He explained the circumstances.

Father Martin looked round, and I could see that he was pleased.

"Very well, *Monsignor*," he said; "I will do my best to make it easy."

When we had reached the room upstairs the old priest was put into the armchair in the centre, drawn back a little so that all might see him; he refused tobacco, propped his chin on his two hands, looking more than ever like a venerable mouse, and began his story. I sat at the end of the semicircle, near the fire, and watched him as he talked.

"I regret I have not heard the other tales," he said; "it would encourage me in my own. But perhaps it is better so. I have told this so often that I can only tell it in one way, and you must forgive me, gentlemen, if my way is not yours.

"About twenty years ago I had charge of a mission in Lancashire, some fourteen miles from Blackburn, among the hills. The name of the place is Monkswell; it was a little village then, but I think it is a town now. In those days there was only one street, of perhaps a dozen houses on each side. My little church stood at the head of the street, with the presbytery beside it. The house had a garden at the back, with a path running through it to the gate; and beyond the gate was a path leading on to the moor.

"Nearly all the village was Catholic, and had always been so, and I had perhaps a hundred more of my folk scattered about the moor. Their occupation was weaving; that was before the coal was found at

Monkswell. Now they have a great church there, with a parish of over a thousand.

"Of course, I knew all my people well enough; they are wonderful folk, those Lancashire folk! I could tell you a score of tales of their devotion and faith. There was one woman that I could make nothing of. She lived with her two brothers in a little cottage a couple of miles away from Monkswell; and the three kept themselves by weaving. The two men were fine lads, regular at their religious duties, and at mass every Sunday. But the woman would not come near the church. I went to her again and again, and before any Easter, but it was of no use. She would not even tell me why she would not come; but I knew the reason. The poor creature had been ruined in Blackburn, and could not hold up her head again. Her brothers took her back, and she had lived with them for ten years, and never once during that time, so far as I knew, had set foot outside her little place. She could not bear to be seen, you see."

The little pointed face looked very tender and compassionate now, and the brown, beady eyes ran round the circle deprecatingly.

"Well, it was one Sunday in January that Alfred told me that his sister was unwell. It seemed to be nothing serious, he said, and of course he promised to let me know if she should become worse. But I made up my mind that I would go in any case during that week and see if sickness had softened her at all. Alfred told me, too, that another brother of his, Patrick, on whom, let it be remembered"—and he held up an admonitory hand—"I had never set eyes, was coming up to them on the next day from London for a week's holiday. He promised he would bring him to see me later on in the week.

"There was a fall of snow that afternoon, not very deep, and another next day, and I thought I would put off my walk across the hills until it melted, unless I heard that Sarah was worse.

"It was on the Wednesday evening about six o'clock that I was sent for.

"I was sitting in my study on the ground floor with the curtains drawn when I heard the garden gate open and close, and I ran out into the hall just as the knock came at the back door. I knew that it was unlikely that anyone should come at that hour and in such weather except for a sick call, and I opened the door almost before the knocking had ended.

"The candle was blown out by the draught, but I knew Alfred's voice at once.

"'She is worse, Father,' he said; 'for God's sake come at once. I think she wishes for the sacraments. I am going on for the doctor.'

"I knew by his voice that it was serious, though I could not see his face; I could only see his figure against the snow outside, and before I could say more than that I would come at once he was gone again, and I heard the garden door open and shut. He was gone down to the doctor's house, I knew, a mile further down the valley.

"I shut the hall door without bolting it and went to the kitchen and told my housekeeper to grease my boots well and set them in my room with my cloak and hat and muffler and my lantern. I told her I had had a sick call and did not know when I should be back; she had better put the pot on the fire, and I would help myself when I came home.

"Then I ran into the church through the sacristy to fetch the holy oils and the Blessed Sacrament.

"When I came back I noticed that one of the strings of the purse that held the pyx was frayed, and I set it down on the table to knot it properly. Then again I heard the garden gate open and shut."

The priest lifted his eyes and looked round again; there was something odd in his look.

"Gentlemen, we are getting near the point of the story. I will ask you to listen very carefully and to give me your conclusions afterward. I am relating to you only events as they happened historically. I give you my word as to their truth."

There was a murmur of assent.

"Well, then," he went on, "at first I supposed it was Alfred come back again for some reason. I put down the string and went to the door without a light. As I reached the threshold there came a knocking.

"I turned the handle and a gust of wind burst in as it had done five minutes before. There was a figure standing there, muffled up as the other had been.

"'What is it?' I said. 'I am just coming. Is it you, Alfred?'

"'No, Father,' said a voice—the man was on the steps a yard from me—'I came to say that Sarah is better and does not wish for the sacraments.'

"Of course, I was startled at that.

"'Why, who are you?' I said. 'Are you Patrick?'

"'Yes, Father,' said the man; 'I am Patrick.'

"I cannot describe his voice, but it was not extraordinary in any way; it was a little muffled; I supposed he had a comforter over his mouth. I could not see his face at all. I could not even see if he was stout or thin, the wind blew about his cloak so much.

"As I hesitated the door from the kitchen behind me was flung open, and I heard a very much frightened voice calling:

"'Who's that, Father?' said Hannah.

"I turned round.

"'It is Patrick Oldroyd,' I said; 'he is come from his sister.'

"I could see the woman standing in the light from the kitchen door; she had her hands out before her as if she were frightened at something.

"'Go out of the draught,' I said.

"She went back at that, but she did not close the door, and I knew she was listening to every word.

"'Come in, Patrick,' I said, turning round again.

"I could see he had moved down a step, and was standing on the gravel now.

"He came up again then, and I stood aside to let him go past me into my study. But he stopped at the door. Still I could not see his face; it was dark in the hall, you remember.

"'No, Father,' he said; 'I cannot wait. I must go after Alfred.'

"I put out my hand toward him, but he slipped past me quickly and was out again on the gravel before I could speak.

"'Nonsense!' I said. 'She will be none the worse for a doctor, and if you will wait a minute I will come with you.'

"'You are not wanted,' he said rather offensively, I thought. 'I tell you she is better, Father; she will not see you.'

"I was a little angry at that. I was not accustomed to be spoken to in that way.

"'That is very well,' I said; 'but I shall come for all that, and if you do not wish to walk with me I shall walk alone.'

"He was turning to go, but he faced me again then.

"'Do not come, Father,' he said; 'come tomorrow. I tell you she will not see you. You know what Sarah is.'

"'I know very well,' I said; 'she is out of grace, and I know what will be the end of her if I do not come. I tell you I am coming, Patrick Oldroyd. So, you can do as you please.'

"I shut the door and went back into my room, and as I went the garden gate opened and shut once more.

"My hands trembled a little as I began to knot the string of the pyx;

I supposed then that I had been more angered than I had known"—the old priest looked round again swiftly and dropped his eyes—"but I do not now think that it was only anger. However, you shall hear."

He had moved himself by now to the very edge of his chair, where he sat crouched up with his hands together. The listeners were all very quiet.

"I had hardly begun to knot the string before Hannah came in. She bobbed at the door when she saw what I was holding, and then came forward. I could see that she was very much upset by something.

"'Father,' she said, 'for the love of God do not go with that man.'

"'I am ashamed of you, Hannah,' I told her. 'What do you mean?'

"'Father,' she said, 'I am afraid. I do not like that man. There is something the matter.'

"I rose, laid the pyx down, and went to my boots without saying anything.

"'Father,' she said again, 'for the love of God do not go. I tell you I was frightened when I heard his knock.'

"Still I said nothing, but put on my boots and went to the table where the pyx lay and the case of oils.

"She came right up to me, and I could see that she was as white as death as she stared at me.

"I finished putting on my cloak, wrapped the comforter round my neck, put on my hat and took up the lantern.

"'Father,' she said again.

"I looked her full in the face then as she knelt down.

"'Hannah,' I said, 'I am going. Patrick has gone after his brother.'

"'It is not Patrick,' she cried after me; 'I tell you, Father—'

"Then I shut the door and left her kneeling there.

"It was very dark when I got down the steps, and I hadn't gone a yard along the path before I stepped over my knee into a drift of snow. It had banked up against a gooseberry bush. Well, I saw that I must go carefully, so I stepped back on to the middle of the path, and held my lantern low.

"I could see the marks of the two men plain enough; it was a path that I had made broad on purpose so that I could walk up and down to say my office without thinking much of where I stepped.

"There was one track on this side and one on that.

"Have you ever noticed, gentlemen, that a man in snow will nearly always go back over his own traces in preference to anyone else's? Well, that is so, and it was so in this case.

"When I got to the garden gate I saw that Alfred had turned off to the right on his way to the doctor; his marks were quite plain in the light of the lantern, going down the hill. But I was astonished to see that the other man had not gone after him as he said he would, for there was only one pair of footmarks going down the hill, and the other track was plain enough, coming and going. The man must have gone straight home, I thought.

"Now—"

"One moment, Father Martin," said *Monsignor*, leaning forward; "draw the two lines of tracks here."

He put a pencil and paper into the priest's hands.

Father Martin scribbled for a moment or two and then held up the paper so that we could all see it.

As he explained I understood. He had drawn a square for the house, a line for the garden wall, and through the gap ran four lines, marked with arrows. Two ran to the house and two back as far as the gate; at this point one curved sharply round to the right and one straight across the paper beside that which marked the coming.

"I noticed all this," said the old priest emphatically, "because I determined to follow along the double track so far as Sarah Oldroyd's house, and I kept the light turned on to it. I did not wish to slip into a snowdrift.

"Now, I was very much puzzled. I had been thinking it over, of course, ever since the man had gone, and I could not understand it. I must confess that my housekeeper's words had not made it clearer. I knew she did not know Patrick; he had never been home since she had come to me. I was surprised, too, at his behaviour, for I knew from his brother that he was a good Catholic; and—well, you understand, gentlemen, it was very puzzling. But Hannah was Irish, and I knew they had strange fancies sometimes.

"Then there was something else, which I had better mention before I go any further. Although I had not been frightened when the man came, yet when Hannah had said that she was frightened I knew what she meant. It had seemed to me natural that she should be frightened. I can say no more than that."

He threw out his hands deprecatingly, and then folded them again sedately on his hunched knees.

"Well, I set out across the moor, following carefully in the double track of—of the man who called himself Patrick. I could see Alfred's single track a yard to my right; sometimes the tracks crossed.

"I had no time to look about me much, but I saw now and again the slopes to the north, and once when I turned I saw the lights of the village behind me, perhaps a quarter of a mile away. Then I went on again, and I wondered as I went.

"I will tell you one thing that crossed my mind, gentlemen. I did wonder whether Hannah had not been right, and if this was Patrick after all. I thought it possible—though I must say I thought it very unlikely—that it might be some enemy of Sarah's, someone she had offended, an *infidel*, perhaps, but who wished her to die without the sacraments that she wanted. I thought that, but I never dreamed of—of what I thought afterward and think now."

He looked round again, clasped his hands more tightly and went on.

"It was very rough going, and as I climbed up at last on to the little shoulder of hill that was the horizon from my house, I stopped to get my breath, and turned round again to look behind me.

"I could see my house lights at the end of the village, and the church beside it, and I wondered that I could see the lights so plainly. Then I understood that Hannah must be in my study, and that she had drawn the blind up to watch my lantern going across the snow.

"I am ashamed to tell you, gentlemen, that that cheered me a little; I do not quite know why, but I must confess that I was uncomfortable. I know that I should not have been, carrying what I did, and on such an errand, but I was uneasy. It seemed very lonely out there, and the white sheets of snow made it worse. I do not think that I should have minded the dark so much. There was not much wind and everything was very quiet. I could just hear the stream running down in the valley behind me. The clouds had gone, and there was a clear night of stars overhead."

The old priest stopped; his lips worked a little as I had seen them before two or three times during his story. Then he sighed, looked at us and went on.

"Now, gentlemen, I entreat you to believe me. This is what happened next. You remember that this point at which I stopped to take breath was the horizon from my house. Notice that.

"Well, I turned round and lowered my lantern again to look at the tracks, and a yard in front of me they ceased. They ceased!"

He paused again, and there was not a sound from the circle.

"They ceased, gentlemen; I swear it to you, and I cannot describe what I felt. At first, I thought it was a mistake; that he had leaped a yard or two; that the snow was frozen. It was not so.

"There a yard to the right were Alfred's tracks, perfectly distinct, with the toes pointing the way from which I had come. There was no confusion, no hard or broken ground; there was just the soft surface of the snow, the trampled path of—of the man's footsteps and mine and Alfred's a yard or two away."

The old man did not look like a mouse now; his eyes were large and bright, his mouth severe, and his hands hung in the air in a petrified gesture.

"If he had leaped," he said, "he did not alight again."

He passed his hand over his mouth once or twice.

"Well, gentlemen, I confess that I hesitated. I looked back at the lights and then on again at the slopes in front, and then I was ashamed of myself. I did not hesitate long, for any place was better than that. I went on; I dared not run, for I think I should have gone mad if I had lost self-control; but I walked, and not too fast, either; I put my hand on the pyx as it lay on my breast, but I dared not turn my head to right or left. I just stared at Alfred's tracks in front of me and trod in them.

"Well, gentlemen, I did run the last hundred yards; the door of the Oldroyds' cottage was open, and they were looking out for me, and I gave Sarah the last sacraments, and heard her confession. She died before morning.

"And I have one confession to make myself—I did not go home that night They were very courteous to me when I told them the story, and made out that they did not wish me to leave their sister; so, the doctor and Alfred walked back over the moor together to tell Hannah I should not be back, and that all was well with me.

"There, gentlemen."

"And Patrick?" said a voice.

"Patrick, of course, had not been out that night."

Mr. Bosanquet's Tale

I think that it was on the second Sunday evening that Father Brent brought in his guest. There was a function of some kind at S. Silvestro—I forget the occasion; a Cardinal had given Benediction, and a reception was to follow. At any rate, there were only three of us at home, the German, Father Brent, and myself.

Of course, we talked of our symposium, and the guest, a middle-aged layman, seemed to listen with interest, but he did not say very much. He was a brown-bearded man; he ate slowly and deliberately, and I must confess that I was not particularly impressed with him. Neither did Father Brent try to draw him out. I noticed that he looked at him questioningly once or twice, but he did not actually express his thought till after a little speech from Father Stein.

"But it is a little tiresome to me," said the German, "this talk of footsteps and voices and visions. If that world in which we believe is spiritual, as we know it is, how is it that it presents itself to us under material images? These things are but appearances, but what is the reality?"

Father Brent turned to his friend.

"Well," he said, "what now?"

Mr. Bosanquet smiled and became grave again over his pastry.

"You will repeat it then?" persisted the priest.

The Englishman looked up for an instant, and I met his grave eyes.

"If these gentlemen really wish it," he said briefly.

Father Brent sighed with satisfaction.

"That is excellent," he said.

Then he explained.

Mr. Bosanquet had a story, it seemed, but had entirely refused to relate it to a mixed company. He had had a certain experience once which had changed his life, and it was not an experience to be described at random. There was no ghost in it; it was wholly unsensational, but it had, Father Brent thought, a peculiar interest of its own. He had persuaded his friend to sup with us, knowing that we should be but few, and hoping that the atmosphere might be found favourable. This was the gist of what he was saying, but he was interrupted by the entrance of Beppo with the coffee.

"Shall we have coffee upstairs?" he said.

Then we rose and went upstairs.

It was a few minutes before we settled down, and Mr. Bosanquet seemed in no hurry to begin. But a silence fell presently, and finally the young priest leaned forward.

"Now, Bosanquet," he said.

Mr. Bosanquet set his cup down, crossed his legs, and began. He spoke in a very quiet, unemotional voice.

"My friend has told you that this experience of mine is unsensational. In a manner of speaking he is right. It is unsensational, since it deals with nothing other than that which we must all go through sooner or later; but I think it has a certain interest from the fact that it is an experience of which, except under very peculiar circumstances,

85

none of us will ever be able to give an account. It concerns the act of dying. . . ."

He paused for a moment.

"Yes; the act of dying," he repeated; "for I firmly believe that that is precisely what I did. I passed the point at which death is dogmatically declared by the doctors to have taken place. I underwent, that is, what is called 'legal death,' but I did not, of course, reach that further state called 'somatic death.'"

Father Brent voiced my question.

"Please explain," he said.

"Oh, well, the body, as we know, consists of cells; but there is a certain unity, usually identified with the vital principle, which merges these into one entity, so that if one member suffer, all the members suffer with it. Legal death is when this vital principle leaves the body. The lungs cease to act; the heart is motionless. But when this has taken place there yet remains a further stage. The cells, for a certain period, have a kind of life of their own. There is no vital union between them; the nerve system is suspended; and somatic death, marked by the *rigor mortis*, the stiffening of the cells, indicates the moment when the cells, too, even individually, cease to live. But the man is dead, doctors tell us, sometimes many hours before *rigor mortis* sets in. In fact, in the case of some of the saints, *rigor mortis* appears never to have set in at all; their limbs, we are told, retain softness and elasticity. There is no corruption, at least in the ordinary 'sense.'"

Father Brent grunted and nodded.

"In my case," pursued the Englishman, "I was declared dead, and, as I learned afterward, remained in that state about half an hour. It was after my body had been washed and the face bound up that I returned to life." I sat up in my chair at that. At least he was explicit enough. He glanced at me.

"I can show you my death certificate if you care to come to my hotel tomorrow," he said. "I obtained it from the doctor—cancelled, however, you understand.

"Well, this is what took place.

"The cause of death was exhaustion, following upon angina pectoris, with other complications. I will spare you the details and begin at once at the point at which I was declared to be dying. Up to that point I had suffered extraordinary agony, tempered by morphia. I did not know that such pain was possible. . . . At the moments of the spasms, before each injection took effect, it seemed to me that I did not suffer pain so much as became pain. There was no room for anything else but pain. Then there came the beginning of the dullness of it; it retired and stood off from me. I was still conscious of it, as of a storm passing away, till all sank into a kind of peace. Then, after a long while as it seemed, the dullness lifted, and I came up again to the surface, becoming aware of the world, though of course this bore a certain aspect of unreality, owing to the effects of the drug. . . .

"Well, I said I would leave all that out. . . .

"The last time I came up I knew I was dying. It was all quite different. Things no longer bore that close relation to me that they had had before. I opened my eyes just enough to let me see my hands lying out on the counterpane, and the hillock of my feet, and even the lower part of the brass supports at the end of my bed; but I could not raise my eyelids higher, and almost immediately I closed them again.

"The sense of touch, too, was changed. . . . Once or twice when I have been falling asleep in my chair I have noticed the same phenomenon. I could not tell by feeling, unless I moved them, whether my fingers rested on the counterpane or not. I did move them, with that curious clawing motion that dying people use, simply in order to realise my relations with material surroundings. That, of course, as I know now, is the reason of those motions. It is not an involuntary contraction of the muscles; it is the will trying to get back into touch with the world.

"But the sense of hearing, oddly enough, was almost preternaturally acute. Others undergoing anaesthetics have told me the same. It is the last sense to leave them and the first to return. I could hear a continual minute series of sounds, not at all painfully loud, but absolutely distinct. There was my sister's breathing, irregular and uneven, beside me. I knew by it that she was trying not to break down. I could hear four timepieces ticking—her watch and the doctor's and that of the traveling-clock over the fire and the Dutch clock in the hall below. Then there were the country sounds in the distance and the breeze in the creepers outside my window.

"With regard to taste and smell, they were there, a kind of sour sweetness, if I may say so; but they did not interest me; they were below my level, if I may express it like that. . . .

"Well, I said just now that I knew I was dying. It was as if through all my being there was a steady, smooth retirement from the world. I was perfectly able to reflect—in fact, I reflected as I have never been able to before or since. Do you know the sensation of coming down from town and sitting out in the darkness after dinner in the garden? The silence, after the clatter and glare of London, makes it possible, seems to let the mind free. One is both alert and reflective—both at once. It was rather like that, only far more pronounced. And in that freedom from the pressure of matter I realised perfectly what was happening.

"Now, I must tell you at once that I was not at all frightened. My religion seemed to stand off from me with the rest of the world. I had been up to that time what may be called a 'conventional believer.' I had never doubted exactly, for I always realised that it was absurd for me to criticise what was so obviously the highest standard of morality and faith—I mean Christianity. But neither was I particularly interested. I had lived like other people. I attended church, I repeated my prayers, and I had conventional views of heaven, with which was mixed up a good deal of agnosticism. In a word, I think I may say that I had hope, but not faith, that is, as you Catholics seem to have it."

This was the first hint I had had that Mr. Bosanquet was not a Catholic, and I glanced up at Father Brent. He, too, glanced at me in a half-warning, half-suggestive look. I understood.

"I was not frightened, then," continued the other tranquilly. "My religion, as I see now, was altogether bound up with the world. Even my thoughts went no further than images. I conceived of heaven as in a picture, of Our Lord as a superhuman Man, of death as of a swift passage through the air.... We are all bound, of course, by our limitations to do that; but I had not realised the inadequacy of such images. I conceived of eternity and spiritual existence in terms of time and space, and I had not really even as much faith as that of the agnostic who recognizes that these are inadequate, and therefore foolishly believes that the reality is unknowable—as in one sense indeed it is."

Once more the German priest murmured, and I saw now why this man had been encouraged to tell his story.

"Well, then," he continued, "when the world retired from me with the approach of death, my religion retired naturally with it (that seems to me so obvious now I), and I was left, moving swiftly *inward*, if I may express it so, toward a state of which I was completely ignorant. I was dying as I suppose animals die. I never lost self-consciousness for a moment. As a rule, of course, one realises self-consciousness, as philosophers tell us, by self-differentiation from what is not self. The baby learns it gradually by touching and looking. The dying lose it by ceasing to touch and see, or, rather, they lose that mode of realising, and enter into themselves instead. . . .

"I had then a vague kind of animosity, but I was perfectly peaceful. I had no particular remembrance of sins, no faith or love or hope; nothing but a sense of extreme *naturalness*, if I may express it so. It seemed as if I had known all this all along, as a stone thrown into the air would, if it had consciousness, realise the inevitability of its curve as it neared the earth. I was to die; well, that was the corollary of having lived!

"Well, this inevitable movement inward went on, as it seemed to me, very swiftly. Each instant that I applied my consciousness it seemed to me as if I had gone a great way since the previous instant; the only thing that astonished me was the distance there was to travel. It was a sensation—how shall I express it?—a sensation of sinking swiftly into an inner depth of which I had not guessed the extent. I wondered in a complacent, half-curious kind of way as to what exactly would be the end, how things would be visualized when I passed finally from the body, and such things as I pictured, I pictured, of course, in terms of time and space. I—I thought my essential self, whatever that was, would at a certain moment pass a certain line and emerge on the other side; and the things would be rather as they had been on earth, thinner . . . spiritual. I should see faces, perhaps; forms, places, . . . all in a kind of delicate light. . . . What really happened was a complete surprise."

Mr. Bosanquet paused, and in a meditative kind of way winked several times at the fire. He showed no emotion. He seemed to me merely to be recalling the best phrases to use.

"Well," he said, "I have told this story before, and each time before telling it I have thought that I had got the point and could really describe what happened, and each time I have been disappointed. . . . Of course, it must be so. There are simply no words or illustrations. I must do the best I can.

"Well, this process went on, and after a while I perceived plainly that my senses were fading. I believe I opened my eyes; so, I was told afterwards—opened them wide; but, at any rate, I saw nothing this time except blurred lines and colours, rather like the reverse side of a carpet. They were rather bewildering; but they soon went, leaving nothing but a streaked greyness that darkened rapidly.

"I could no longer move my hands, or, in fact, recall to myself by feeling any material thing at all. I seemed to have lost relations with my body. Neither could I move my lips or tongue; taste had gone. I don't think I had ever understood before how taste depends on the will and the movement of the tongue—much more so than any of the other senses, which are, more or less, passive.

"And then quite suddenly I perceived that hearing had ceased also. There had been no drumming in my ears, as I had half expected; I think there had been at some time previously a clear singing of one high note, which had rather bothered me; and I suppose that it was then that hearing had gone, but I did not notice it till I thought about it.

"And then there was one more thing more strange than all. ... I began to perceive that my will was not myself.

"Most of us are accustomed to think that it is. It is so closely united with that which is the very self that we usually identify them. Sometimes we are even more foolish, and identify our emotions with ourselves, and think that our moods are our character. The fact is, of course, that the intellect is the most superficial of our faculties; there are simply scores of things that we cannot understand in the least, but of which for all that we are as certain as of our own existence. Next to that comes the emotion: it is certainly nearer to us than intellect, though not much; and thirdly comes the will.

"Now the will is quite close to us; it is that through which we consciously act after having heard the reasons for or against action alleged by the other faculties. But the will is, after all, a faculty of self—not self itself.

"I began to see this from the way it was labouring, like an exhausted engine; it was throbbed and moved; it turned this way and that, directing the all but dead faculties outside to move in this or that direction—to think or to perceive. But I began to see clearly now that the real self was something altogether apart, existing simply in another mode. There, that is the point—*in another mode.* . . .

"Now, in this matter I feel hopeless. I simply cannot express what I knew, and know, to be the central fact of our existence. I can say no more than that. Self, that which lies far behind everything else, exists in as different a mode from all else, as—as the inner meaning of a phrase of music is apart from the existence of a dog walking up the street. There is simply no common term which can be applied to them both.

"Well, I perceived my will to be labouring, very slowly and clumsily, and I perceived that it would not be able to move much longer. (You must understand that this 'perceiving' as I call it was not the act of my intellect; it was simply a deep intuitive knowledge dwelling in that which I call Self.)

"Then I suddenly became aware that it was important for my will to fall in the right direction; I understood that this would make—well, the whole difference to me. ... I knew that this would be my last conscious act. . . .

"You ask me how I knew what was the right direction. Well, I must go slowly here. . . ."

He paused for a moment, then he went on very slowly, picking his words.

"I began, I think I may say, to be clearly and vividly conscious of two *centres*; there was Self, and there was Another. This Other was at present completely hidden from me; I was only aware of it as one may be aware of the presence of a huge personality behind an impenetrable curtain. But I perceived that this Other was the only important thing. . . .

"Well, my will was reeling; there was no discomfort, no fear, or pain, or anxiety, and I—whatever that is—watched it as a man may watch a top in its last swift twistings on its side. I had still some control over it; I knew that it was my will; it still was linked to me in a way. . . . Then I put out my energy (remember, there was no conscious perception of anything; nothing but a perfectly blind instinct) and tried to wrench that rolling thing round to a position of rest—ah! how shall I put it?—a position of rest pointing toward this other centre.

"And as I made that effort I lost touch with it. I have no idea whether I succeeded, and at the same instant, if I may call it so, something happened."

Mr. Bosanquet leaned back and sighed.

"Every word is wrong," he said; "you understand that, do you not?"

I nodded two or three times. I kept my eyes on his face. He glanced round at the other two. Then he went on, shifting his attitude a little.

"Well, this something—I suppose I could give half a dozen illustrations, but none of them would be adequate. Let me give you two or three.

"When a man falls in love suddenly his whole centre changes. Up to that point he has probably referred everything to himself—considered things from his own point. When he falls in love the whole thing is shifted; he becomes a part of the circumference—perhaps even the whole circumference; someone else becomes the centre. For example, things he hears and sees are referred in future instantly to this other person; he ceases to be acquisitive; his entire life, if it is really love, is pulled sideways; he does not desire to get, but to give. That is why it is the noblest thing in the world.

"Secondly, imagine that you had lived all your life in a certain house, and had got to know every detail of it perfectly; you had walked about in the garden, too, and looked through the railings, and thought you knew pretty fairly what the country was like. Then one morning, after you had got up and dressed, you went to your bedroom door, opened it, and went out, and that very instant found yourself not in the passage, but on the top of a high mountain with a strange country visible for miles all round, and no house or human being near you.

"Thirdly (and this perhaps is the best illustration after all) , imagine that you were looking at a picture, and had become absorbed in it, and then without any warning at all the picture suddenly became a chord of music which you heard, and which you recognized to be identical with the picture—not merely analogous to it, but the actual picture translated, transubstantiated, and transaccidentated into sound.

"Now, those are the three illustrations I generally use in telling this story; there are others, but I think these are the best.

"Well, it was like that; but you must please to remember that these are only like charcoal sketches of something which is colour rather than shape. But briefly, those are the nearest similitudes I can think of.

"First, although I remained the same, I became aware that I simply was not the centre of what I experienced. It was not I who primarily existed at all. There was Something—I call it Something, because the word Person simply bears no resemblance to the Personality of this Other Existence; at least, no more than a resemblance, because this Other Personality was as different from and as far above our own as the personality of a philosopher is different from the corresponding thing in a people. I became aware—at least, this was what I told myself afterwards—I became aware of real Existence for the first time in my experience. I myself then became merely a speck in a circumference, yet—and this is why I spoke of love—I also became aware that while I had not lost my individuality, yet this Other Being was the only thing that mattered at all, and, further—well, I may as well say it outright, that in the very depth of this Existence was Human Nature; yes, Human Nature. I knew it instantly. I never before had had the faintest idea of what the Incarnation really meant.

"Secondly, the whole of everything was different—as startlingly different as the change of my second illustration. I had expected to find a kind of continuation. There was, in one sense, no continuation at all; nothing in the least like what experience had led me to expect. It was completely abrupt.

"Thirdly, in another sense, what I found was not only the consequence of what had preceded, it was not simply the result, but it was identical with what had preceded. It was the picture becoming sound—the essence of my previous life was here in other terms. It simply was. The whole thing was complete. You may call this Judgment; well, that will do; but it was a Judgment in which there was no question of concurrence or protest. It was inevitably true.

"Let me take even one more illustration.

"Once I went with my brother into a glasshouse in autumn. He smelled a certain flower, and then rather excitedly asked me to smell it. I shut my eyes and smelled it. Practically instantly the whole thing became sound and sight. I saw the terrace at home in summer, and heard the bees. I looked up.

"'Well?' he said.

"'The terrace in summer,' I said.

"'Exactly.'

"Well, it was like that. There was no question about it.

"Now, I have taken some time to tell this; but I must make it clear that there was absolutely no time in the experience—no sense of progression. It was not merely that I was absorbed, but that time had no existence. This is how I knew it.

"Simultaneously with all this I heard one noise; and immediately time began—I began to consider. Presently I heard another noise, then another, like a great drum being beaten. Then the noises went, and there was absolute silence of which I was aware; and others came in—a rustling, a footstep, the sound of words. I was entirely absorbed in these. I heard the sound of water, a door opening, the ticking of a clock. I was conscious of no consideration about these things, and no sensation of any kind; it was as if my brain had become one ear which heard. This went on—well, I may say it was ten seconds or ten years. Time meant nothing to me. I only knew even now that it existed because one thing followed another. I did not reflect at all.

"At last, after this had gone on, it was as if a new note had struck; another sense began to move, the sense of sight. I first became aware of darkness, then came a glimmer, with a sensation of flickering. Then touch. I became aware of a constraint somewhere in the universe; it was a long time before I knew that I myself was feeling it. I did not perceive sensation; I was it.

"Well, these waxed and waxed; then my will stirred; and I became aware that I could choose, that I could acquiesce or resent. Then emotion, and I found myself disliking certain sensations. Then I began to wonder and question again, and ask myself why and what—"

Mr. Bosanquet broke off abruptly.

"Well, I needn't go on. To put it in a word, I was coming back to ordinary life. Half an hour after the doctor had said that I was dead, and about three minutes after the nurse had finished with me—just as she was looking at me, in fact, before going out of the room;—I made a sound with my lips. The rest happened as you would expect; there was nothing interesting in that.

"But this is the point I want to make clear. Those noises I heard like a drum followed by the silence were without doubt the sounds my own body made in dying.

"It was at that point that I died; and the next sounds that I began to hear were the noises the nurse made in washing me and laying me out. There is no question about that. I asked about all the details minutely.

"But the thing that seemed to me so strange at first was the fact that I had died 'before' that, as we say. That complete change of the mode of existence undoubtedly marked death, and the particular instant of death must have been that at which I became aware of the change, and of the severance of my will from myself.

"But I understood it presently. The explanation, I think, must be this.

"There is always a certain space of time between an incident happening and our perception of it—infinitesimally small if we are observing it, but yet it is there. Well, when I made that final effort of will I died, but dying had begun before that. I had only regarded dying from the purely internal side; it took in my soul the form of severance from my will. At that same instant, since we must speak in terms of time, I was in the spiritual mode of existence, where there is simply no time but which includes all time and all one's previous experience; and in practically the same 'instant' I was back again, and experiencing the physical phenomena of dying. The drum-note was either my throat or heart, I suppose; the silence that followed was the body's perception of death worked out in terms of time.

"We may say, then, this, impossible as it sounds—that death had taken place at a given moment in time; that that inner real self behind the will which I have spoken of simultaneously experienced severance

94

from the body, and was immediately in its own mode of existence, which, although reckoned as time, was an instant; was, in fact, simply eternity with its inevitable consequences. But after eternity had been experienced—since I suppose again I must say 'after'—it ceased to be experienced; and all this was enacted in time. Then—"

Mr. Bosanquet sat up, smiling suddenly.

"It is useless; I am boring you."

I roused myself to answer with an energy I had not expected.

"No; please—"

"Well, in one sentence: Then I died."

He leaned back with an air of finality.

"But—but one question," I protested, "you spoke of Judgment. Was the result happiness or unhappiness?"

He shook his head, smiling.

Father Macclesfield's Tale

Monsignor Maxwell announced next day at dinner that he had already arranged for the evening's entertainment. A priest whose acquaintance he had made on the Palatine was leaving for England the next morning, and it was our only chance, therefore, of hearing his story. That he had a story had come to the canon's knowledge in the course of a conversation on the previous afternoon.

"He told me the outline of it," he said; "I think it very remarkable. But I had a great deal of difficulty in persuading him to repeat it to the company this evening. However, he promised at last. I trust, gentlemen, you do not think I have presumed in begging him to do so."

★★★★★★

Father Macclesfield arrived at supper.

He was a little, unimposing, dry man, with a hooked nose and grey hair. He was rather silent at supper, but there was no trace of shyness in his manner as he took his seat upstairs, and without glancing round once began in an even and dispassionate voice:

"I once knew a Catholic girl that married an old Protestant three times her own age. I entreated her not to do so, but it was useless. And when the disillusionment came she used to write to me piteous letters, telling me that her husband had in reality no religion at all. He was a convinced *infidel*, and scouted even the idea of the soul's immortality.

"After two years of married life the old man died. He was about sixty years old, but very hale and hearty till the end.

"Well, when he took to his bed the wife sent for me, and I had half

95

a dozen interviews with him, but it was useless. He told me plainly that he wanted to believe—in fact, he said that the thought of annihilation was intolerable to him. If he had had a child he would not have hated death so much; if his flesh and blood in any manner survived him he could have fancied that he had a sort of vicarious life left; but as it was, there was no kith or kin of his alive, and he could not bear that."

Father Macclesfield sniffed cynically and folded his hands.

"I may say that his deathbed was extremely unpleasant. He was a coarse old fellow, with plenty of strength in him, and he used to make remarks about the churchyard and—and, in fact, the worms, that used to send his poor child of a wife half fainting out of the room. He had lived an immoral life, too, I gathered.

"Just at the last it was—well, disgusting. He had no consideration. God knows why she married him! The agony was a very long one; he caught at the curtains round the bed, calling out, and all his words were about death and the dark. It seemed to me that he caught hold of the curtains as if to hold himself into this world. And at the very end he raised himself clean up in bed and stared horribly out of the window that was open just opposite.

"I must tell you that straight away beneath the window lay a long walk between sheets of dead leaves with laurels on either side and the branches meeting overhead, so that it was very dark there even in summer, and at the end of the walk away from the house was the churchyard gate."

Father Macclesfield paused and blew his nose. Then he went on, still without looking at us.

"Well, the old man died, and he was carried along this laurel path and buried.

"His wife was in such a state that I simply dared not go away. She was frightened to death; and, indeed, the whole affair of her husband's dying was horrible. But she would not leave the house. She had a fancy that it would be cruel to him. She used to go down twice a day to pray at the grave; but she never went along the laurel walk. She would go round by the garden and in at a lower gate and come back the same way, or by the upper garden.

"This went on for three or four days. The man had died on a Saturday and was buried on Monday; it was in July, and he had died about eight o'clock.

"I made up my mind to go on the Saturday after the funeral. My curate had managed alone very well for a few days, but I did not like

96

to leave him for a second Sunday.

"Then on the Friday at lunch—her sister had come down, by the way, and was still in the house—on the Friday the widow said something about never daring to sleep in the room where the old man had died. I told her it was nonsense, and so on; but you must remember she was in a dreadful state of nerves, and she persisted. So, I said I would sleep in the room myself. I had no patience with such ideas then.

"Of course, she said all sorts of things, but I had my way and my things were moved in on Friday evening.

"I went to my new room about a quarter before eight to put on my cassock for dinner. The room was very much as it had been—rather dark because of the trees at the end of the walk outside. There was the four-poster, there with the damask curtains, the table and chairs, the cupboard where his clothes were kept, and so on.

"When I went to put my cassock on I went to the window to look out. To the right and left were the gardens, with the sunlight just off them, but still very bright and gay with the geraniums, and exactly opposite was the laurel walk, like a long, green shady tunnel, dividing the upper and lower lawns.

"I could see straight down it to the churchyard gate, which was about a hundred yards away, I suppose. There were limes overhead and laurels, as I said, on each side.

"Well, I saw someone coming up the walk, but it seemed to me at first that he was drunk. He staggered several times as I watched—I suppose he would be fifty yards away—and once I saw him catch hold of one of the trees and cling to it as if he were afraid of falling. Then he left it and came on again slowly, going from side to side, with his hands out. He seemed desperately keen to get to the house.

"I could see his dress, and it astonished me that a man dressed so should be drunk, for he was quite plainly a gentleman. He wore a white top hat and a grey cutaway coat and grey trousers, and I could make out his white spats.

"Then it struck me he might be ill, and I looked harder than ever, wondering whether I ought to go down.

"When he was about twenty yards away he lifted his face, and it struck me as very odd, but it seemed to me he was extraordinarily like the old man we had buried on Monday; but it was darkish where he was, and the next moment he dropped his face, threw up his hands, and fell flat on his back.

"Well, of course I was startled at that, and I leaned out of the window and called out something. He was moving his hands, I could see, as if he were in convulsions, and I could hear the dry leaves rustling.

"Well, then I turned and ran out and downstairs."

Father Macclesfield stopped a moment.

"Gentlemen," he said abruptly, "when I got there, there was not a sign of the old man. I could see that the leaves had been disturbed, but that was all."

There was an odd silence in the room as he paused, but before any of us had time to speak he went on.

"Of course, I did not say a word of what I had seen. We dined as usual. I smoked for an hour or so by myself after prayers and then I went up to bed. I cannot say I was perfectly comfortable, for I was not, but neither was I frightened.

"When I got to my room I lit all my candles and then went to a big cupboard I had noticed and pulled out some of the drawers. In the bottom of the third drawer I found a gray cutaway coat and grey trousers; I found several pairs of white spats in the top drawer and a white hat on the shelf above. That is the first incident."

"Did you sleep there, Father?" said a voice softly.

"I did," said the priest; "there was no reason why I should not. I did not fall asleep for two or three hours, but I was not disturbed in any way and came to breakfast as usual.

"Well, I thought about it all a bit, and finally I sent a wire to my curate telling him I was detained. I did not like to leave the house just then."

Father Macclesfield settled himself again in his chair and went on in the same dry, uninterested voice.

"On Sunday we drove over to the Catholic church, six miles off, and I said mass. Nothing more happened till the Monday evening.

"That evening I went to the window again about a quarter before eight, as I had done both on the Saturday and Sunday. Everything was perfectly quiet till I heard the churchyard gate unlatch and I saw a man come through.

"But I saw almost at once that it was not the same man I had seen before; it looked to me like a keeper, for he had a gun across his arm; then I saw him hold the gate open an instant, and a dog came through and began to trot up the path toward the house with his master following.

"When the dog was about fifty yards away he stopped dead and pointed.

"I saw the keeper throw his gun forward and come up softly, and as he came the dog began to slink backward. I watched very closely, clean forgetting why I was there, and the next instant something—it was too shadowy under the trees to see exactly what it was—but something about the size of a hare burst out of the laurels and made straight up the path, dodging from side to side, but coming like the wind.

"The beast could not have been more than twenty yards from me when the keeper fired, and the creature went over and over in the dry leaves and lay struggling and screaming. It was horrible! But what astonished me was that the dog did not come up. I heard the keeper snap out something, and then I saw the dog making off down the avenue in the direction of the churchyard as hard as he could go.

"The keeper was running now toward me, but the screaming of the hare, or of whatever it was, had stopped, and I was astonished to see the man come right up to where the beast was struggling and kicking and then stop as if he were puzzled.

"I leaned out of the window and called to him.

"'Right in front of you, man,' I said; 'for God's sake kill the brute.'

"He looked up at me and then down again.

"'Where is it, sir?' he said; 'I can't see it anywhere.'

"And there lay the beast clear before him all the while not a yard away, still kicking.

"Well, I went out of the room and downstairs and out to the avenue.

"The man was standing there still, looking terribly puzzled, but the hare was gone. There was not a sign of it. Only the leaves were disturbed, and the wet earth showed beneath.

"The keeper said that it had been a great hare; he could have sworn to it, and that he had orders to kill all hares and rabbits in the garden enclosure. Then he looked rather odd.

"'Did you see it plainly, sir,' he asked.

"I told him not very plainly; but I thought it a hare, too.

"'Yes, sir,' he said; 'it was a hare, sure enough; but do you know, sir, I thought it to be a kind of silver-grey, with white feet. I never saw one like that before!'

"The odd thing was that not a dog would come near. His own dog was gone, but I fetched the yard dog, a retriever, out of his kennel in the kitchen yard, and if ever I saw a frightened dog it was this one. When we dragged him up at last, all whining and pulling back, he began to snap at us so fiercely that we let go, and he went back like the wind to his kennel. It was the same with the terrier.

"Well, the bell had gone, and I had to go in and explain why I was late; but I didn't say anything about the colour of the hare. That was the second incident."

Father Macclesfield stopped again, smiting reminiscently to himself. I was very much impressed by his quiet air and composure. I think it helped his story a good deal.

Again, before we had time to comment or question, he went on.

"The third incident was so slight that I should not have mentioned it, or thought anything of it, if it had not been for the others; but it seemed to me there was a kind of diminishing gradation of energy which explained. Well, now you shall hear.

"On the other nights of that week I was at my window again, but nothing happened till the Friday. I had arranged to go for certain next day; the widow was much better and more reasonable, and even talked of going abroad herself in the following week.

"On that Friday evening I dressed a little earlier and went down to the avenue this time, instead of staying at my window, at about twenty minutes to eight.

"It was rather a heavy, depressing evening, without a breath of wind, and it was darker than it had been for some days.

"I walked slowly down the avenue to the gate and back again; and I suppose it was fancy, but I felt more uncomfortable than I had felt at all up to then. I was rather relieved to see the widow come out of the house and stand looking down the avenue. I came out myself then and went toward her. She started rather when she saw me and then smiled.

"'I thought it was someone else,' she said. 'Father, I have made up my mind to go. I shall go to town tomorrow, and start on Monday. My sister will come with me.'

"I congratulated her, and then we turned and began to walk back to the lime avenue. She stopped at the entrance, and seemed unwilling to come any further.

"'Come down to the end,' I said, 'and back again. There will be time before dinner.'

"She said nothing, but came with me, and we went straight down to the gate and then turned to come back.

"I don't think either of us spoke a word; I was very uncomfortable indeed by now, and yet I had to go on.

"We were half way back, I suppose, when I heard a sound like

100

a gate rattling; and I whisked round in an instant, expecting to see someone at the gate. But there was no one.

"Then there came a rustling overhead in the leaves; it had been dead still before. Then, I don't know why, but I took my friend suddenly by the arm and drew her to one side out of the path, so that we stood on the right hand, not a foot from the laurels.

"She said nothing, and I said nothing; but I think we were both looking this way and that, as if we expected to see something.

"The breeze died, and then sprang up again, but it was only a breath. I could hear the living leaves rustling overhead, and the dead leaves underfoot, and it was blowing gently from the churchyard.

"Then I saw a thing that one often sees; but I could not take my eyes off it, nor could she. It was a little column of leaves, twisting and turning and dropping and picking up again in the wind, coming slowly up the path. It was a capricious sort of draught, for the little scurry of leaves went this way and that, to and fro across the path. It came up to us, and I could feel the breeze on my hands and face. One leaf struck me softly on the cheek, and I can only say that I shuddered as if it had been a toad. Then it passed on.

"You understand, gentlemen, it was pretty dark; but it seemed to me that the breeze died and the column of leaves—it was no more than a little twist of them—sank down at the end of the avenue.

"We stood there perfectly still for a moment or two, and when I turned she was staring straight at me, but neither of us said one word.

"We did not go up the avenue to the house. We pushed our way through the laurels and came back by the upper garden.

"Nothing else happened; and the next morning we all went off by the eleven o'clock train.

"That is all, gentlemen."

Father Stein's Tale

Old Father Stein was a figure that greatly fascinated me during my first weeks in Rome, after I had got over the slight impatience that his personality roused in me. He was slow of speech and thought and movement, and had that distressing grip of the obvious that is characteristic of the German mind. I soon rejoiced to look at his heavy face, generally unshaven, his deep twinkling eyes, and the ponderous body that had such an air of eternal immovability, and to watch his mind, as through a glass case, labouring like an engine over a fact that he had begun to assimilate. He took a kind of paternal interest in me, too, and would thrust his thick hand under my arm as he stood by me, or clap me heavily on the shoulder as we met. But he was excellently educated, had seen much of the world, although always through a haze of the Fatherland that accompanied him everywhere, and had acquired an exceptional knowledge of English during his labours in a London mission. He used his large vocabulary with a good deal of skill.

I was pleased then when *Monsignor* announced on the following evening that Father Stein was prepared to contribute a story. But the German, knowing that he was master of the situation, would utter nothing at first but hoarse ejaculations at the thought of his reminiscences, and it was not until we had been seated for nearly half an hour before the fire that he consented to begin.

★★★★★★

"It is of a dream," he said; "no more than that; and yet dreams, too, are under the hand of the good God, so I hold. Some, I know, are just folly, and tell us nothing but the confusion of our own nature when the controlling will is withdrawn; but some, I hold, are the whispers of God, and tell us of what we are too dull to hear in our waking life. You do not believe me? Very well; then listen.

"I knew a man in Germany, thirty years ago, who had lived many years away from God. He had been a Catholic, and was well educated in religion till he grew to be a lad. Then he fell into sin, and dared not confess it; and he lied, and made bad confessions, and approached the altar so. He once went to a strange priest to tell his sin, and dared not when the time came; and so added sin to sin, and lost his faith. It is ever so. We know it well. The soul dare not go on in that state, believing in God, and so by an inner act of the will renounces Him. It is not true, it is not true, she cries; and at last the voice of faith is silent and her eyes blind."

The priest stopped and looked round him, and the old Rector nodded once or twice and murmured assent.

"For twenty years he had lived so, without God, and he was not unhappy; for the powers of his soul died one by one, and he could no longer feel. Once or twice they struggled, in their death agony, and he stamped on them again. Once, when his mother died, he nearly lived again; and his soul cried once more within him, and stirred herself; but he would not hear her; it is useless, he said to her; there is no hope for you; lie still; there is nothing for you; you are dreaming; there is no life such as you think; and he trampled her again, and she lay still."

We were all very quiet now. I certainly had not suspected such passion in this old priest; he had seemed to me slow and dull and not capable of any sort of delicate thought or phrase, far less of tragedy; but somehow now his great face was lighted up, his eyebrows twitched as he talked, and it seemed as if we were hearing of a murder that this man had seen for himself. *Monsignor* sat perfectly motionless, staring intently into the fire, and Father Brent was watching the German sideways; Father Stein took a deliberate pinch of snuff, snapped his box, and put it away, and went on.

"This man had lived on the sea coast as a child, but was now in business in a town on the Rhine, and had never visited his old home since he left it with his mother on his father's death. He was now about thirty-five years of age, when God was gracious to him. He was living in a cousin's house, with whom he was partner.

"One night he dreamed he was a child, and walking with one whom he knew was his sister who had died before he was born, but he could not see her face. They were on a white, dusty road, and it was the noon of a hot summer day. There was nothing to be seen round him but great slopes of a dusty country with dry grass, and the burning sky overhead, and the sun. He was tired, and his feet ached, and he was crying as he walked, but he dared not cry loud for fear that his sister would turn and look at him, and he knew she was a—a *revenant*, and did not wish to see her eyes. There was no wind and no birds and no clouds; only the grasshoppers sawed in the dry grass, and the blood drummed in his ears until he thought he would go mad with the noise. And so, they walked, the boy behind his sister, up a long hill. It seemed to him that they had been walking so for hours, for a lifetime, and that there would be no end to it. His feet sank to the ankles in dust, the sun beat on to his brain from above, the white road glared from below, and the tears ran down his cheeks.

"Then there was a breath of salt wind in his face, and his sister began to go faster, noiselessly; and he tried, too, to go faster, but could not; his heart beat like a hammer in his throat, and his feet lagged more and more, and little by little his sister was far in front, and he dared not cry out to her not to leave him for fear she should turn and look at him; and at last he was walking alone, and he dared not lie down or rest.

"The road passed up a slope, and when he reached the top of it at last he saw her again, far away, a little figure that turned to him and waved its hand, and behind her was the blue sea, very faint and in a mist of heat, and then he knew that the end of the bitter journey was very near.

"As he passed up the last slope the sea-line rose higher against the sky, but the line was only as the fine mark of a pencil where sea and sky met, and a dazzling white bird or two passed across it and then dropped below the cliff. By the time he came near his sister the dusty road had died away into the grass, and he was walking over the fresh turf that felt cool to his hot feet. He threw himself down on the edge of it by his sister, where she was lying with her head on her hands looking out at the sea where it spread itself out, a thousand feet below; and still he had not seen her face.

"At the foot of the cliff was a little white beach, and the rocks ran down into deep water on every side of it, and threw a purple shadow across the sand; there were birds here, too, floating out from the cliff and turning and returning; and the sea beneath them was a clear blue, like a Cardinal's ring that I saw once, and the breeze blew up from the water and made him happy again."

Father Stein stopped again, with something of a sob in his old heavy voice, and then he turned to us.

"You know such dreams," he said; "I cannot tell it as—as he told me; but he said it was like the bliss of the redeemed to look down on the sea and feel the breeze in his hair, and taste its saltness.

"He did not wish his sister to speak, though he was afraid of her no more; and yet he knew that there was some secret to be told that would explain all—why they were here, and why she had come back to him, and why the sea was here, and the little beach below them, and the wind and the birds. But he was content to wait until it was time for her to tell him, as he knew she would. It was enough to lie here, after the dusty journey, beside her, and to wait for the word that should be spoken.

"Now, at first, he was so out of breath and his heart beat so in his ears that he could hear nothing but that and his own panting; but it grew quieter soon, and he began to hear something else—the noises of the sea beneath him.

It was a still day, but there was movement down below, and the surge heaved itself softly against the cliff and murmured in deep caves below, like the pedal note of the Frankfort organ, solemn and splendid; and the waves leaned over and crashed gently on the sand. It was all so far beneath that he saw the breaking wave before the sound came up to him, and he lay there and watched and listened; and that great sound made him happier even than the light on the water and the coolness and rest; for it was the sea itself that was speaking now.

"Then he saw suddenly that his sister had turned on her elbow and was looking at him; and he looked into her eyes, and knew her, though she had died before he was born. And she, too, was listening, with her lips parted, to the sound of the surge. And now he knew that the secret was to be told; and he watched her eyes, smiling. And she lifted her hand, as if to hold him silent, and waited, and again the sweet murmur and crash rose up from the sea, and she spoke softly.

"'It is the Precious Blood,' she said."

Father Stein was silent, and we all were silent for a while. As far as I was concerned, at least, the story had somehow held me with an extraordinary fascination, I scarcely knew why.

There was a movement among the others, and presently the Frenchman spoke.

"*Et puis?*" he said.

"The man awoke," said Father Stein, "and found tears on his face."

★★★★★★

It was such a short story that there were still a few minutes before the time for night-prayers, and we sat there without speaking again until the clock sounded in the campanile overhead, and the Rector rose and led the way into the west gallery of the church. I saw Father Stein waiting at the door for me to come up, and I knew why he was waiting.

He took my arm in his thick hand and held it a moment as the others passed down the two steps.

"I was that man," he said.

Mr. Percival's Tale

When I came in from mass into the refectory on the morning following Father Stein's story, I found a layman breakfasting there with the Father Rector. We were introduced to each other, and I learned that Mr. Percival was a barrister, who had arrived from England that morning on a holiday, and was to stay at St. Filippo for a fortnight.

I yield to none in my respect for the clergy; at the same time a layman feels occasionally something of a pariah among them. I suppose this is bound to be so, otherwise I was pleased then to find another dog of my breed with whom I might consort, and even howl, if I so desired. I was pleased, too, with his appearance. He had that trim, academic air that is characteristic of the Bar, in spite of his twenty-two hours' journey, and was dressed in an excellently made grey suit.

He was very slightly bald on his forehead, and had those sharp-cut, mask-like features that mark a man as either lawyer, priest or actor; he had, besides, delightful manners and even, white teeth. I do not think I could have suggested any improvements in person, behaviour, or costume.

By the time that my coffee had arrived the Father Rector had run dry of conversation, and I could see that he was relieved when I joined in.

In a few minutes I was telling Mr. Percival about the symposium we had formed for the relating of preternatural adventures, and I presently asked him whether he had ever had any experience of the kind.

He shook his head.

"I have not," he said in his virile voice; "my business takes my time."

"I wish you had been with us earlier," put in the rector. "I think you would have been interested."

"I am sure of it," he said. "I remember once—but you know, Father, frankly I am something of a sceptic."

"You remember?" I suggested.

He smiled very pleasantly with eyes and mouth.

"Yes, Mr. Benson; I was once next door to such a story. A friend of mine saw something; but I was not with him at the moment." "Well, we thought we had finished last night," I said; "but do you think you would be too tired to entertain us this evening?"

"I shall be delighted to tell the story," he said easily. "But indeed, I am a sceptic in this matter; I cannot dress it up."

"We want the naked fact," I said.

I went sight-seeing with him that day, and found him extremely intelligent and at the same time accurate'. The two virtues do not run often together, and I felt confident that whatever he chose to tell us would be salient and true. I felt, too, that he would need few questions to draw him out; he would say what there was to be said unaided.

When we had taken our places that night he began by again apologising for his attitude of mind.

"I do not know, reverend Fathers," he said, "what are your own theories in this matter; but it appears to me that if what seems to be preternatural can possibly be brought within the range of the natural, one is bound scientifically to treat it in that way. Now in this story of mine—for I will give you a few words of explanation first in order to prejudice your minds as much as possible—in this story the whole matter might be accounted for by the imagination. My friend, who saw what he saw, was under rather theatrical circumstances, and he is an Irishman. Besides that, he knew the history of the place in which he was; and he was quite alone. On the other hand, he has never had an experience of the kind before or since; he is perfectly truthful, and he saw what he saw in moderate daylight. I give you these facts first, and I think you would be perfectly justified in thinking they account for everything. As for my own theory, which is not quite that, I have no idea whether you will agree or disagree with it. I do not say that my judgment is the only sensible one, or anything offensive like that. I merely state what I feel I am bound to accept for the present."

There was a murmur of assent. Then he crossed his legs, leaned back and began:

"In my first summer after I was called to the Bar I went down South Wales for a holiday with another man who had been with me at Oxford. His name was Murphy; he is a J.P. now, in Ireland, I think. I cannot think why we went to South Wales; but there it is. We did.

"We took the train to Cardiff, sent on our luggage up the Taff Valley to an inn of which I cannot remember the name, but it was close to where Lord Bute has a vineyard. Then we walked up to Llandaff, saw St. Tylo's tomb, and went on again to this village.

"Next morning, we thought we would look about us before going on, and we went out for a stroll. It was one of the most glorious mornings I ever remember, quite cloudless and very hot, and we went up through woods to get a breeze at the top of the hill.

"We found that the whole place was full of iron mines, disused now, as the iron is richer further up the country; but I can tell you that they enormously improved the interest of the place. We found shaft after shaft, some protected and some not, but mostly overgrown with bushes, so we had to walk carefully. We had passed half a dozen, I should think, before the thought of going down one of them occurred to Murphy.

"Well, we got down at last, though I rather wished for a rope once or twice, and I think it was one of the most extraordinary sights I have ever seen. You know, perhaps, what the cave of a demon-king is like in the first act of a pantomime. Well, it was like that. There was a kind of blue light that poured down the shafts, refracted from surface to surface, so that the sky was invisible. On all sides passages ran into total darkness; huge reddish rocks stood out fantastically everywhere in the pale light; there was a sound of water falling into a pool from a great height, and presently, striking matches as we went, we came upon a couple of lakes of marvellously clear blue water, through which we could see the heads of ladders emerging from other black holes of unknown depth below.

"We found our way out after a while into what appeared to be the central hall of the mine. Here we saw plain daylight again, for there was an immense round opening at the top, from the edges of which curved among the sides of the shaft, forming a huge circular chamber.

"Imagine the Albert Hall roofless; or, better still, imagine Saint Peter's with the top half of the dome removed. Of course, it was far smaller, but it gave an impression of great size, and it could not have been less than two hundred feet from the edge, over which we saw the trees against the sky, to the tumbled, dusty, rocky floor where we stood.

"I can only describe it as being like a great burnt-out hell in the *Inferno*. Red dust lay everywhere; escape seemed impossible; and vast crags and galleries, with the mouths of passages showing high up, marked by iron bars and chains, jutted out here and there.

"We amused ourselves here for some time by climbing up the sides, calling to one another, for the whole place was full of echoes, rolling down stones from some of the upper edges; but I nearly ended my days there.

"I was standing on a path, about seventy feet up, leaning against the wall. It was a path along which feet must have gone a thousand times when the mine was in working order, and I was watching Murphy, who was just emerging onto a platform opposite me, on the other side of the gulf.

"I put my hand behind me to steady myself, and the next instant very nearly fell forward over the edges at the violent shock to my nerves given by a wood-pigeon who burst out of a hole, brushing my hand as he passed. I gripped on, however, and watched the bird soar out across space, and then up and out at the opening; and then I became aware that my knees were beginning to shake. So, I stumbled along, and threw myself down on the little platform onto which the passage led.

"I suppose I had been more startled than I knew, for I tripped as I went forward, and knocked my knee rather sharply on a stone. I felt for an instant quite sick with the pain on the top of jangling nerves, and lay there saying what I am afraid I ought not to have said.

"Then Murphy came up when I called, and we made our way together through one of the sloping shafts, and came out onto the hillside among the trees."

Mr. Percival paused; his lips twitched a moment with amusement.

"I am afraid I must recall my promise," he said. "I told you all this because I was anxious to give a reason for the feeling I had about the mine, and which I am bound to mention. I felt I never wanted to see the place again—yet in spite of what followed I do not necessarily attribute my feelings to anything but the shock and the pain that I had had. You understand that?"

His bright eyes ran round our faces.

"Yes, yes," said *Monsignor* sharply; "go on, please, Mr. Percival."

"Well, then!"

The lawyer uncrossed his legs and placed them the other way.

"During lunch we told the landlady where we had been, and she begged us not to go there again. I told her that she might rest easy; my knee was beginning to swell. It was a wretched beginning to a walking tour.

"It was not that, she said; but there had been a bad accident there. Four men had been killed there twenty years before by a fall of rock. That had been the last straw on the top of ill-success, and the mine had been abandoned.

"We inquired as to details, and it seemed that the accident had taken place in the central chamber, locally called 'The Cathedral,' and after a few more questions I understood.

"'That was where you were, my friend,' I said to Murphy; 'it was where you were when the bird flew out.'

"He agreed with me, and presently when the woman was gone announced that he was going to the mine again to see the place. Well, I had no business to keep him dangling about. I couldn't walk anywhere myself, so I advised him not to go on to that platform again, and presently he took a couple of candles from the sticks and went off. He promised to be back by four o'clock, and I settled down rather drearily to a pipe and some old magazines.

"Naturally, I fell sound asleep. It was a hot, drowsy afternoon and the magazines were dull. I awoke once or twice, and then slept again deeply.

"I was awakened by the woman coming in to ask whether I would have tea; it was already five o'clock. I told her Yes. I was not in the least anxious about Murphy; he was a good climber, and therefore neither a coward nor a fool.

"As tea came in I looked out of the window again and saw him walking up the path, covered with iron dust, and a moment later I heard his step in the passage, and he came in.

"Mrs. What's-her-name had gone out.

"'Have you had a good time?' I asked.

"He looked at me very oddly and paused before he answered.

"'Oh, yes,' he said; and put his cap and stick in a corner.

"I knew Murphy.

"'Well, why not?' I asked him, beginning to pour out tea.

"He looked round at the door, then he sat down without noticing the cup I pushed across to him.

"'My dear fellow,' he said, 'I think I am going mad.'

"Well, I forget what I said, but I understood that he was very much upset about something, and I suppose I said the proper kind of thing about his not being a damned fool.

"Then he told me his story."

Mr. Percival looked round at us again, still with that slight twitching of the lips that seemed to signify amusement.

"Please remember—" he began, and then broke off. No; I won't—"

"Well.

"He had gone down the same shaft that we went down in the morning, and had spent a couple of hours exploring the passages. He had found an engine-room with tanks and rotten beams in it and rusty chains. He had found some more lakes, too, full of that extraordinary electric-blue water; he had disturbed a quantity of bats somewhere else. Then he had come out again into the central hall, and on looking at his watch had found it after four o'clock, so he thought he would climb up by the way we had come in the morning and go straight home.

"It was as he climbed that his odd sensations began. As he went up, clinging with his hands, he became perfectly certain that he was being watched. He couldn't turn round very well, but he looked up as he went to the opening overhead, but there was nothing there but the dead-blue sky, and the trees very green against it, and the red rocks awning away on every side. It was extraordinarily quiet, he said; the pigeons had not come home from feeding, and he was out of hearing of the dripping water that I told you of.

"Then he reached the platform and the opening of the path where I had my fright in the morning, and turned round to look.

"At first he saw nothing peculiar. The rocks up which he had come fell away at his feet down to the floor of the 'Cathedral' and to the nettles with which he had stung his hands a minute or two before. He looked around at the galleries overhead and opposite, but there was nothing there.

"Then he looked across at the platform where he had been in the morning and where the accident had taken place.

"Let me tell you what this was like. It was about twenty yards in breadth and ten deep, but lay irregular and filled with tumbled rocks. It was a little below the level of his eyes, right across the gulf, and in a straight line would be about fifty or sixty yards away, It lay under the roof, rather retired, so that no light from the sky fell directly on to it; it would have been in complete twilight if it hadn't been for a shaft smaller above it, which shot down a funnel of bluish light, exactly like a stage effect. You see, reverend Fathers, it was very theatrical altogether. That might account, no doubt—"

Mr. Percival broke off again, smiling.

"I am always forgetting," he said. "Well, we must go back to Murphy. At first, he saw nothing but the rocks and the thick, red dust and the broken wall behind it. He was very honest, and told me that as he looked at it he remembered distinctly what the landlady had told us at lunch. It was on that little stage that the tragedy had happened.

"Then he became aware that something was moving among the rocks, and he became perfectly certain that people were looking at him; but it was too dusky to see very clearly at first. Whatever it was, was in the shadows at the back. He fixed his eyes on what was moving. Then this happened."

The lawyer stopped again.

"I will tell you the rest," he said, "in his own words so far as I remember them.

"'I was looking at this moving thing,' he said, 'which seemed exactly of the red colour of the rocks, when it suddenly came out under the funnel of light, and I saw it was a man. He was in a rough suit all iron stained, with a rusty cap, and he had some kind of a pick in his hand. He stopped first in the centre of the light, with his back turned to me, and stood there looking. I cannot say that I was consciously frightened; I honestly do not know what I thought he was. I think that my whole mind was taken up in watching him.

"'Then he turned round slowly and I saw his face. Then I became aware that if he looked at me I should go into hysterics or something of the sort, and I crouched down as low as I could. But he didn't look at me; he was attending to something else, and I could see his face quite clearly. He had a beard and moustache, rather ragged and rusty; he was rather pale, but not particularly. I judged him to be about thirty-five.' Of course," went on the lawyer, "Murphy didn't tell it me quite as I am telling it to you. He stopped a good deal; he drank a sip of tea once or twice and changed his feet about.

"Well, he had seen this man's face very clearly, and described it very clearly.

"It was the expression that struck him most.

"'It was a rather amused expression,' he said; 'rather pathetic and rather tender, and he was looking interestedly about at everything—at the rocks above and beneath; he carried his pick easily in the crook of his arm. He looked exactly like a man whom I once saw visiting his home where he had lived as a child.' (Murphy was very particular about that, though I don't believe he was right.) 'He was smiling a little in his beard and his eyes were half shut. It was so pathetic that I nearly went into hysterics then and there,' said Murphy. 'I wanted to stand up and explain that it was all right, but I knew he knew more than I did. I watched him, I should think, for nearly five minutes; he went to and fro softly in the thick dust, looking here and there, sometimes in the shadow and sometimes out of it. I could not have moved for ten thousand pounds and I could not take my eyes off him.

"'Then just before the end I did look away from him. I wanted to know if it was all real, and I looked at the rocks behind and the openings. Then I saw that there were other people there; at least, there were things moving of the colour of the rocks.

"'I suppose I made some sound then; I was horribly frightened. At any rate, the man in the middle turned right round and faced me, and at that I sank down with the sweat dripping from me, flat on my face, with my hands over my eyes.

"'I thought of a hundred thousand things—of the inn and you and the walk we had had—and I prayed—well, I suppose I prayed. I wanted God to take me right out of this place. I wanted the rocks to open and let me through.'"

Mr. Percival stopped. His voice shook with a tiny tremor. He cleared his throat.

"Well, reverend Fathers, Murphy got up at last and looked about him, and of course there was nothing there but just the rocks and the dust and the sky overhead. Then he came away home the shortest way."

It was a very abrupt ending, and a little sigh ran round the circle.

Monsignor struck a match noisily and kindled his pipe again.

112

"Thank you very much, sir," he said briskly.

Mr. Percival cleared his throat again, but before he could speak Father Brent broke in.

"Now, that is just an instance of what I was saying, *Monsignor*, the night we began. May I ask if you really believe that those were the souls of the miners? Where's the justice of it? What's the point?"

Monsignor glanced at the lawyer.

"Have you any theory, sir?" he asked.

Mr. Percival answered without lifting his eyes.

"I think so," he said shortly; "but I don't feel in the least dogmatic."

Father Brent looked at him almost indignantly.

"I should like to hear it," he said. "If you can square that—"

"I do not square it," said the lawyer. "Personally, I do not believe they were spirits at all."

"Oh?"

"No, I do not, though I do not wish to be dogmatic. To my mind it seems far more likely that this is an instance of Mr. Hudson's theory—the American, you know. His idea is that all apparitions are no more than the result of violent emotions experienced during life. That about the pathetic expression is all nonsense, I believe."

"I don't understand," said Father Brent.

"Well, these men, killed by the fall of the roof, probably went through a violent emotion. This would be heightened in some degree by their loneliness and isolation from the world. This kind of emotion, Mr. Hudson suggests, has a power of saturating material surroundings, which under certain circumstances would once more, like a photograph, give off an image of the agent. In this instance, too, the absence of other human visitors would give this materialized emotion a chance, so to speak, of surviving; there would be very few cross-currents to confuse it. And finally, Murphy was alone; his receptive faculties would be stimulated by that fact, and all that he saw, in my belief, was the psychical wave left by these men in dying."

"Oh! Did you tell him so?"

"I did not. Murphy is a violent man."

I looked up at *Monsignor*, and saw him nodding emphatically to himself.

My Own Tale

I must confess that I was a little taken aback on my last evening before leaving for England when Monsignor Maxwell turned on me suddenly at supper and exclaimed aloud that I had not yet contributed a story.

I protested that I had none; that I was prosaic person; that there was some packing to be done; that my business was to write down the stories of other people; that I had my living to make and could not be liberal with my slender store; that it was a layman's function to sit at holy and learned priests' feet, not to presume to inform them on any subject under the sun.

But it was impossible to resist; it was pointed out to me that I had listened on false pretences if I had not intended to do my share, that telling a story did not hinder my printing it. And, as a final argument, it was declared that unless I occupied the chair that night all present withdrew the leave that had already been given to me to print their stories on my return to England.

There was nothing, therefore, to be done; and as I had already considered the possibility of the request, I did not occupy an unduly long time in pretending to remember what I had to say.

When I was seated upstairs and the fire had been poked according to the ritual and the matches had gone round, and buckled shoes protruded side by side with elastic-ankled boots, I began.

"This is a very unsatisfactory story," I said, "because it has no explanation of any kind. It is quite unlike Mr. Percival's. You will see that even theorising is useless when I have come to the end. It is simply a series of facts that I have to relate; facts that have no significance except one that is supernatural, but it is utterly out of the question even to guess at that significance.

"It is unsatisfactory, too, for a second reason, and that is, that it is on such very hackneyed lines. It is simply one more instance of that very dreamy class of phenomena, named 'haunted houses,' except that there is no ghost in it. Its only claim to interest is, as I have said, the complete futility of any attempt to explain it."

This was rather a pompous exordium, I felt, but thought it best not to raise expectations too high, and I was therefore deliberately dull.

"Sixteen years ago, from last summer I was in France. I had left school, where I had laboured two hours a week at French for four years, and gone away in order to learn it in six weeks. This I accomplished very tolerably, in company with five other boys and an English tutor. Our general adventures are not relevant, but toward the end of our stay we went over one Sunday from Portrieux in order to see a French *château* about three miles away.

"It was a really glorious June day, hot and fresh and exhilarating, and we lunched delightfully in the woods with a funny, fat little French count and his wife, who came with us from the hotel. It is impossible to imagine less uncanny circumstances or companions.

"After lunch we all went cheerfully to the house, whose chimneys we had seen among the trees.

"I know nothing about the dates of houses, but the sort of impression I got of this house was that it was about three hundred years old; but it may equally have been four, or two. I did not know then and do not know now anything about it except its name, which I will not tell you; and its owner's name, which I will not tell you either, and—and something else that I will tell you. We will call the owner, if you please, Comte Jean Marie the First. The house is built in two courts, the right-hand court, through which we entered, was then used as a farmyard; and I should think it probable that it is still so used. This court was exceedingly untidy. There was a large manure heap in the centre, and the servants' quarters to our right looked miserably cared for. There was a cart or two with shafts turned up, near the sheds that were built against the wall opposite the gate; and there was a sleepy old dog with bleared eyes that looked at us intensely from his kennel door.

"Our French friend went across to the servants' cottages with his moustache sticking out on either side of his face; and presently came back with two girls and the keys. There was no objection, he exclaimed dramatically, to our seeing the house!

"The girls went before us, and unlocked the iron gate that led to the second court; and we went through after them.

"Now we had heard at the hotel that the family lived in Paris; but we were not prepared for the dreadful desolation of that inner court. The living part of the house was on our left; and what had once been a lawn to our right; but the house was discoloured and weather-stained; the green paint of the closed shutters and door was cracked and blistered; and the lawn resembled a wilderness; the grass was long and rank; there were rose-trees trailing along the edge and across the path; and a sun-dial on the lawn reminded me strangely of a drunken man petrified in the middle of a stagger. All this, of course, was what was to be expected in an adventure of this kind. It would do for a Christmas number.

"But it was not our business to criticise; and after a moment or two, we followed the girls who had unlocked the front door and were waiting for us to enter.

115

"One of them had gone before to open the shutters.

"It was not a large house, in spite of its name, and we had soon looked through the lower rooms of it. They, too, were what you would expect; the floors were bees-waxed; there were tables and chairs of a tolerable antiquity; a little damask on the walls and so on. But what astonished us was the fact that none of the furniture was covered up, or even moved aside; and the dust lay, I should say, half an inch thick on every horizontal surface. I heard the Frenchman crying on his God in an undertone—as is the custom of Gauls—" (I bowed a little to Father Meuron)—"and finally he burst out with a question as to why the rooms were in this state.

"The girl looked at him stolidly. She was a stout, red-faced girl.

"'It is by the count's orders,' she said.

"'And does the count not come here?' he asked.

"'No, sir.'

"Then we all went upstairs. One of the girls had preceded us again and was sitting with her hand on a door to usher us in.

"'See here is the room the most splendid!' she said; and threw the door open.

"It was certainly the room the most splendid. It was a great bed-chamber hung with tapestry; there were some excellent chairs with carved legs; a splendid gold-framed mirror tilted forward over the carved mantlepiece; and, above all, and standing out from the wall opposite the window was a great four-posted bed, with an elaborately carved head to it, and heavy curtains hanging from the canopy.

"But what surprised us more than anything that we had yet seen, was the sight of the bed. Except for the dust that lay on it, it might have been slept in the night before. There were actually damask sheets upon it, thrown back, and two pillows. All grey with dust. These were not arranged but tumbled about, as a bed is in the morning before it is made.

"As I was looking at this, I heard a boy cry out from the washing-stand.

"'Why, it has had water in it,' he said.

"This did not sound exceptional for a basin, but we all crowded round to look; and it was perfectly true; there was a grey film round the interior of it; and when he had disturbed it as a boy would with his finger we could see the flowered china beneath. The line came two-thirds of the way up the sides of the basin. It must have been partly filled with water a long while ago, which gradually evaporated, leaving its mark in the dust that must have collected there week after week.

"The Frenchman lost his patience at that.

"'My sacred something!' he said, 'why is the room like this?'

"The same girl who had answered him before, answered him again in the same words. She was standing by the mantlepiece watching us.

"'It is the count's orders,' she said stolidly.

"'It is by the count's orders that the bed is not made?' snapped the man.

"'Yes, sir,' said the girl simply.

"Well, that did not content the Frenchman. He exhibited a couple of *francs* and began to question.

"This is the story that he got out of her. She told it quite simply.

"The last time that Count Jean Marie had come to the place, it had been for his honeymoon. He had come down from Paris with his bride. They had dined together downstairs, very happily and gaily; and had slept in the room in which we were at this moment. A message had been sent out for the carriage early next morning; and the couple had driven away with their trunks leaving their servants behind. They had not returned, but a message had come down from Paris that the house was to be closed. It appeared that the servants who had been left behind had had orders that nothing was to be tidied; even the bed was not to be made; the rooms were to be locked up, and left as they were.

"The Frenchman had hardly been able to restrain himself as he heard this unconvincing story; though his wife shook him by the shoulders at each violent gesture that he made, and at the end he had put a torrent of questions.

"'Were they frightened then?'

"'I do not know, sir.'

"'I mean the bride and bridegroom, fool!'

"'I do not know, sir.'

"'Sacred name!—and—and—why do you not know?'

"'I have never seen any of them, sir.'

"'Not seen them! Why you said just now.'

"'Yes, sir; but I was not born then. It was thirty years ago.'

"I do not think I have ever seen people so bewildered as we all were. This was entirely unexpected. The Frenchman's jaw dropped; he licked his lips once or twice; and turned away. We all stood perfectly still a moment, and then we went out."

I indulged myself with a pause just here. I was enjoying myself more than I thought I should. I had not told the story for some while;

and had forgotten what a good one it was. Besides, it had the advantage of being perfectly true. Then I went on again with a pleased consciousness of faces turned to me and black-ended cigarettes.

"I must tell you this," I said. "I was relieved to get out of the room. It is sixteen years ago now; and, I may have embroidered on my sensations; but my impression is that I had been just a little uncomfortable even before the girl's story. I don't think that I felt that there was any presence there, or anything of that kind. It was rather the opposite; it was the feeling of an extraordinary emptiness."

"Like a Catholic Cathedral in Protestant hands," put in a voice.

I nodded at the zealous, convert-making Father Brent.

"It was very like that," I said, "and had, too, the same kind of pathos and terror that one feels in the presence of a child's dead body. It is unnaturally empty, and yet significant; and one does not quite know what it signifies."

I paused again.

"Well, reverend Fathers, that is the first Act. We went back to Portrieux; we made enquiries and got no answer. All shrugged their shoulders, and said that they did not know. There were no tales of the bride's hair turning white in the night, or of any curse or ghost or noises or lights. It was just as I have told you. Then we went back to England; and the curtain came down.

"Now generally such curtains have no resurrection. I suppose we have all had fifty experiences of First Acts; and we do not know to this day whether the whole play is a comedy or a tragedy; or even whether the play has been written at all."

"Do not be modern and allusive, Mr. Benson," said *Monsignor*.

"I beg your pardon, *Monsignor*, I will not. I forgot myself. Well, here is the Second Act. There are only two, and this is a much shorter one.

"Nine years later I was in Paris, staying in the Rue Picot with some Americans. A French friend of theirs was to be married to a man; and I went to the wedding at the Madeleine. It was—well, it was like all other weddings at the Madeleine. No description can be adequate to the appearance of the officiating clergyman and the altar and the bridesmaids and the French gentlemen with polished boots and butterfly ties, and the conversation, and the gaiety, and the general impression of a confectioner's shop and a milliner's and a *salon* and a holy church. I observed the bride and bridegroom and forgot their names for the twentieth time, and exchanged some remarks in the sacristy; with a leader of society who looked like a dissipated priest;

118

with my eyes starting out of my head in my anxiety not to commit a *solécisme* or a *barbarisme*. And then we went home again.

"On the way home we discussed the honeymoon. The pair were going down to a country house in Brittany. I enquired the name of it; and, of course, it was the *château* I had visited nine years before. It had been lent them by Count Jean Marie the Second. The gentleman resided in England, I heard, in order to escape the conscription; he was a connection of the bride's; and was about thirty years of age.

"Well, of course, I was interested; and made enquiries and related my adventure. The Americans were mildly interested, too, but not excited. Thirty-nine years is ancient history to that energetic nation." (I bowed to Father Jenks, before I remembered that he was a Canadian; and then pretended that I had not and went on quickly, and missed a dramatic opportunity.) "But two days afterward they were excited. One of the girls came into *déjeuner*, and said that she had met the bride and bridegroom dining together in the *bois*. They had seemed perfectly well; and had saluted her politely. It seemed that they had come back to Paris after one night at the *château*, exactly as another bride and bridegroom had done thirty-nine years before.

"Before I finish let me sum up the situation.

"In neither case was there apparently any shocking incident, and yet something had been experienced that broke up plans and sent away immediately from a charming house and country two pairs of persons who had deliberately formed the intention of living there for a while. In both cases the persons in question had come back to Paris.

"I need hardly say that I managed to call with my friends upon the bride and bridegroom, and, at the risk of being impertinent, asked the bride point-blank why they had changed their plans and come back to town.

She looked at me without a trace of horror in her eyes, and smiled a little.

"'It was *triste*,' she said; 'a little *triste*. We thought we would come away; we desired crowds.'

I paused again.

"'We desired crowds,' I repeated. "You remember, reverend Fathers, that I had experienced a sense of loneliness, even with my friends, during five minutes spent in that upstairs room. I can only suppose that if I had remained longer I should have experienced such a further degree of that sensation that I should have felt exactly as those two pairs of brides and bridegrooms felt and have come away immediately.

I might even, if I had been in authority, have given orders that nothing was to be touched except my own luggage."

"I do not understand that," said Father Brent, looking puzzled.

"Nor do I altogether," I answered; "but I think I perceive it to be a fact for all that. One might feel that one was an intruder, that one had meddled with something that desired to be left alone, and that one had better not meddle further in any kind of way."

"I suppose you went down there again," observed Monsignor Maxwell.

"I did; a fortnight afterwards. There was only one girl left; the other was married and gone away. She did not remember me; it was nine years ago, and she was a little redder in the face and a little more stolid.

"The lawn had been clipped and mown, but was beginning to grow rank again. Then I went upstairs with her. The room was comparatively clean; there was water in the basin; and clean sheets on the bed; but there was just a little film of dust lying on everything. I pretended I knew nothing and asked questions; and I was told exactly the same story as I had heard nine years before; only this time the date was only a fortnight ago.

"When she had finished she added:

"'It happened so once before, sir; before I was born.'

"'Do you understand it?' I said.

"'No, sir; the house is a little *triste* perhaps. Do you think so, sir?'

"I said that perhaps it was. Then I gave her two *francs* and came away.

"That is all, reverend Fathers."

There was silence for a minute. Then Padre Bianchi made what I consider a tactless remark.

"Bah! that does not terrify me," he said.

"'Terrify' is certainly not the word," remarked Monsignor Maxwell.

"I am not quite sure about that," ended Father Brent.

The bell rang for night-prayers.

"Sum up, Father Rector," said *Monsignor* without moving. "You have heard all the stories and Mr. Benson is going tomorrow."

The old priest smiled as he stood up; and was silent for a moment, looking at us all.

"I can only sum up like this, with the sentiments with which *Monsignor* began," he said: "The longer I live and the more I hear and see, the greater I feel my ignorance to be. I heard a man say the other day that Catholics were the only genuine agnostics alive; and that he respected them for it. They knew some things that others did not; but they did not pretend to affirm or to deny that of which they had no possibility of judging. Is that what you meant me to say, *Monsignor*."

Monsignor nodded meditatively.

"I think that is a sound conclusion," he said. "It is understood then, Mr. Benson, that if you print these stories, you will add that not one of us commits himself to belief in any of them—except, I suppose, each in his own."

"I will mention it," I said.

"Perhaps you might say that we do not even commit ourselves to our own. You can say what you like about yours, of course."

"I will mention that, too," I said, "and I will class myself with the rest. The agnostic position is certainly the soundest in all matters outside the deposit of faith. We all stand, then, exactly where we did at the beginning?"

"Certainly, I do," said Padre Bianchi.

"We all do," said a number of voices.

Then we went to night-prayers together for the last time.

The Necromancers

Chapter 1

"I am very much distressed about it all," murmured Mrs. Baxter.

She was a small, delicate-looking old lady, very true to type indeed, with the silvery hair of the devout widow crowned with an exquisite lace cap, in a filmy black dress, with a complexion of precious china, kind short-sighted blue eyes, and white blue-veined hands busy now upon needlework. She bore about with her always an atmosphere of piety, humble, tender, and sincere, but as persistent as the gentle sandal wood aroma which breathed from her dress. Her theory of the universe, as the girl who watched her now was beginning to find out, was impregnable and unapproachable. Events which conflicted with it were either not events, or they were so exceptional as to be negligible. If she were hard pressed she emitted a pathetic peevishness that rendered further argument impossible.

The room in which she sat reflected perfectly her personality. In spite of the early Victorian date of the furniture, there was in its arrangement and selection a taste so exquisite as to deprive it of even a suspicion of Philistinism. Somehow the rosewood table on which the September morning sun fell with serene beauty did not conflict as it ought to have done with the Tudor panelling of the room. A tapestry screen veiled the door into the hall, and soft curtains of velvety gold hung on either side of the tall, modern windows leading to the garden. For the rest, the furniture was charming and suitable—low chairs, a tapestry couch, a multitude of little leather-covered books on every table, and two low carved bookshelves on either side of the door filled with poetry and devotion.

The girl who sat upright with her hands on her lap was of another type altogether—of that type of which it is impossible to predicate anything except that it makes itself felt in every company. Any respectable astrologer would have had no difficulty in assigning her birth to the sign of the Scorpion. In outward appearance she was not remarkable, though extremely pleasing, and it was a pleasingness that grew upon acquaintance. Her beauty, such as it was, was based upon a good foundation: upon regular features, a slightly cleft rounded chin, a quantity of dark coiled hair, and large, steady, serene brown eyes. Her hands were not small, but beautifully shaped; her figure slender, well made, and always at its ease in any attitude. In fact, she had an air of repose, strength, and all round competence; and, contrasted with this other, she resembled a well-bred sheep-dog eyeing an Angora cat.

They were talking now about Laurie Baxter.

"Dear Laurie is so impetuous and sensitive," murmured his mother, drawing her needle softly through the silk, and then patting her material, "and it is all terribly sad."

This was undeniable, and Maggie said nothing, though her lips opened as if for speech. Then she closed them again, and sat watching the twinkling fire of logs upon the hearth. Then once more Mrs. Baxter took up the tale.

"When I first heard of the poor girl's death," she said, "it seemed to me so providential. It would have been too dreadful if he had married her. He was away from home, you know, on Thursday, when it happened; but he was back here on Friday, and has been like—like a madman ever since. I have done what I could, but—"

"Was she quite impossible?" asked the girl in her slow voice. "I never saw her, you know."

Mrs. Baxter laid down her embroidery.

"My dear, she was. Well, I have not a word against her character, of course. She was all that was good, I believe. But, you know, her home, her father—well, what can you expect from a grocer—and a Baptist," she added, with a touch of vindictiveness.

"What was she like?" asked the girl, still with that meditative air.

"My dear, she was like—like a picture on a chocolate-box. I can say no more than that. She was little and fair-haired, with a very pretty complexion, and a ribbon in her hair always. Laurie brought her up here to see me, you know—in the garden; I felt I could not bear to have her in the house just yet, though, of course, it would have had to have come. She spoke very carefully, but there was an unmistakable accent. Once she left out an aitch, and then she said the word over again quite right."

Maggie nodded gently, with a certain air of pity, and Mrs. Baxter went on encouraged.

"She had a little stammer that—that Laurie thought very pretty, and she had a restless little way of playing with her fingers as if on a piano. Oh, my dear, it would have been too dreadful; and now, my poor boy—"

The old lady's eyes filled with compassionate tears, and she laid her sewing down to fetch out a little lace-fringed pocket-handkerchief.

Maggie leaned back with one easy movement in her low chair, clasping her hands behind her head; but she still said nothing. Mrs. Baxter finished the little ceremony of wiping her eyes, and, still winking a little, bending over her needlework, continued the commentary.

"Do try to help him, my dear. That was why I asked you to come back yesterday. I wanted you to be in the house for the funeral. You see, Laurie's becoming a Catholic at Oxford has brought you two together. It's no good my talking to him about the religious side of it all; he thinks I know nothing at all about the next world, though I'm sure—"

"Tell me," said the girl suddenly, still in the same attitude, "has he been practising his religion? You see, I haven't seen much of him this year, and—"

"I'm afraid not very well," said the old lady tolerantly. "He thought he was going to be a priest at first, you remember, and I'm sure I should have made no objection; and then in the spring he seemed to be getting rather tired of it all. I don't think he gets on with Father Mahon very well. I don't think Father Mahon understands him quite. It was he, you know, who told him not to be a priest, and I think that discouraged poor Laurie."

"I see," said the girl shortly. And Mrs. Baxter applied herself again to her sewing.

It was indeed a rather trying time for the old lady. She was a tranquil and serene soul; and it seemed as if she were doomed to live over a perpetual volcano. It was as pathetic as an amiable cat trying to go to sleep on a rifle-range; she was developing the jumps. The first serious explosion had taken place two years before, when her son, then in his third year at Oxford, had come back with the announcement that Rome was the only home worthy to shelter his aspiring soul, and that he must be received into the Church in six weeks' time. She had produced little books for his edification, as in duty bound, she had summoned Anglican divines to the rescue; but all had been useless, and Laurie had gone back to Oxford as an avowed proselyte.

She had soon become accustomed to the idea, and indeed, when the first shock was over had not greatly disliked it, since her own adopted daughter, of half French parentage, Margaret Marie Deronnais, had been educated in the same faith, and was an eminently satisfactory person. The next shock was Laurie's announcement of his intention to enter the priesthood, and perhaps the Religious Life as well; but this too had been tempered by the reflection that in that case Maggie would inherit this house and carry on its traditions in a suitable manner. Maggie had come to her, upon leaving her convent school three years before, with a pleasant little income of her own—had come to her by an arrangement made previously to her mother's death—and her manner of life, her reasonableness, her adaptability, her presentableness had reassured the old lady considerably as to the tolerableness of the Roman Catholic religion.

Indeed, once she had hoped that Laurie and Maggie might come to an understanding that would prevent all possible difficulty as to the future of his house and estate; but the fourth volcanic storm had once more sent the world flying in pieces about Mrs. Baxter's delicate ears; and, during the last three months she had had to face the prospect of Laurie's bringing home as a bride the rather underbred, pretty, stammering, pink and white daughter of a Baptist grocer of the village.

This had been a terrible affair altogether; Laurie, as is the custom of a certain kind of young male, had met, spoken to, and ultimately kissed this Amy Nugent, on a certain summer evening as the stars came out; but, with a chivalry not so common in such cases, had also sincerely and simply fallen in love with her, with a romance usually reserved for better-matched affections. It seemed, from Laurie's conversation, that Amy was possessed of every grace of body, mind, and soul required in one who was to be mistress of the great house; it was not, so Laurie explained, at all a milkmaid kind of affair; he was not the man, he said, to make a fool of himself over a pretty face. No, Amy was a rare soul, a flower growing on stony soil—sandy perhaps would be the better word—and it was his deliberate intention to make her his wife.

Then had followed every argument known to mothers, for it was not likely that even Mrs. Baxter would accept without a struggle a daughter-in-law who, five years before, had bobbed to her, wearing a pinafore, and carrying in a pair of rather large hands a basket of eggs to her back door. Then she had consented to see the girl, and the interview in the garden had left her more distressed than ever. (It was there that the aitch incident had taken place.) And so the struggle had gone on; Laurie had protested, stormed, sulked, taken refuge in rhetoric and dignity alternately; and his mother had with gentle persistence objected, held her peace, argued, and resisted, conflicting step by step against the inevitable, seeking to reconcile her son by pathos and her God by petition; and then in an instant, only four days ago, it seemed that the latter had prevailed; and today Laurie, in a black suit, rent by sorrow, at this very hour at which the two ladies sat and talked in the drawing-room, was standing by an open grave in the village church-yard, seeing the last of his love, under a pile of blossoms as pink and white as her own complexion, within four elm-boards with a brass plate upon the cover.

Now, therefore, there was a new situation to face, and Mrs. Baxter was regarding it with apprehension.

It is true that mothers know sometimes more of their sons than their sons know of themselves, but there are certain elements of character that sometimes neither mothers nor sons appreciate. It was one or two of those elements that Maggie Deronnais with her hands behind her head, was now considering. It seemed to her very odd that neither the boy himself nor Mrs Baxter in the least seemed to realise the astonishing selfishness of this very boy's actions.

She had known him now for three years, though owing to her own absence in France a part of the time, and his absence in London for the rest, she had seen nothing of this last affair. At first, she had liked him exceedingly; he had seemed to her ardent, natural, and generous. She had liked his affection for his mother and his demonstrativeness in showing it; she had liked his well-bred swagger, his manner with servants, his impulsive courtesy to herself. It was a real pleasure to her to see him, morning by morning, in his knickerbockers and Norfolk jacket, or his tweed suit; and evening by evening in his swallow-tail coat and white shirt, and the knee-breeches and buckled shoes that he wore by reason of the touch of picturesque and defiant romanticism that was so obvious a part of his nature. Then she had begun, little by little, to perceive the egotism that was even more apparent; his self-will, his moodiness, and his persistence.

Though, naturally, she had approved of his conversion to Catholicism, yet she was not sure that his motives were pure. She had hoped indeed that the Church, with its astonishing peremptoriness, might do something towards a moral conversion, as well as an artistic and intellectual change of view. But this, it seemed, had not happened; and this final mad episode of Amy Nugent had fanned her criticism to indignation. She did not disapprove of romance—in fact she largely lived by it—but there were things even more important, and she was as angry as she could be, with decency, at this last manifestation of selfishness.

For the worst of it was that, as she knew perfectly well, Laurie was rather an exceptional person. He was not at all the Young Fool of Fiction. There was a remarkable virility about him, he was tender-hearted to a degree, he had more than his share of brains. It was intolerable that such a person should be so silly.

She wondered what sorrow would do for him. She had come down from Scotland the night before, and down here to Hertfordshire this morning; she had not then yet seen him; and he was now at the funeral. . . .

Well, sorrow would be his test. How would he take it?"

Mrs. Baxter broke in on her meditations.

"Maggy, darling . . . do you think you can do anything? You know I once hoped—"

The girl looked up suddenly, with so vivid an air that it was an interruption. The old lady broke off.

"Well, well," she said. "But is it quite impossible that—"

"Please, don't. I—I can't talk about that. It's impossible—utterly impossible."

The old lady sighed; then she said suddenly, looking at the clock above the oak mantelshelf, "It is half-past. I expect—"

She broke off as the front door was heard to open and close beyond the hall, and waited, paling a little, as steps sounded on the flags; but the steps went up the stairs outside, and there was silence again.

"He has come back," she said. "Oh! my dear."

"How shall you treat him?" asked the girl curiously.

The old lady bent again over her embroidery.

"I think I shall just say nothing. I hope he will ride this afternoon. Will you go with him?"

"I think not. He won't want anyone. I know Laurie."

The other looked up at her sideways in a questioning way, and Maggie went on with a kind of slow decisiveness.

"He will be queer at lunch. Then he will probably ride alone and be late for tea. Then tomorrow—"

"Oh! my dear, Mrs. Stapleton is coming to lunch tomorrow. Do you think he'll mind?"

"Who is Mrs. Stapleton?"

The old lady hesitated.

"She's—she's the wife of Colonel Stapleton. She goes in for what I think is called New Thought; at least, so somebody told me last month. I'm afraid she's not a very steady person. She was a vegetarian last year; now I believe she's given that up again."

Maggie smiled slowly, showing a row of very white, strong teeth.

"I know, auntie," she said. "No; I shouldn't think Laurie'll mind much. Perhaps he'll go back to town in the morning, too."

"No, my dear, he's staying till Thursday."

There fell again one of those pleasant silences that are possible in the country. Outside the garden, with the meadows beyond the village road, lay in that sweet September hush of sunlight and mellow colour that seemed to embalm the house in peace. From the farm beyond the stable-yard came the crowing of a cock, followed by the liquid chuckle of a pigeon perched somewhere overhead among the twisted chimneys. And within this room all was equally at peace. The sunshine lay on table and polished floor, barred by the mullions of the windows, and stained here and there by the little Flemish emblems and coats that hung across the glass; while those two figures, so perfectly in place in their serenity and leisure, sat before the open fire-place and contemplated the very unpeaceful element that had just walked upstairs incarnate in a pale, drawn-eyed young man in black.

The house, in fact, was one of those that have a personality as marked and as mysterious as of a human character. It affected people in quite an extraordinary way. It took charge of the casual guest, entertained and soothed and sometimes silenced him; and it cast upon all who lived in it an enchantment at once inexplicable and delightful. Externally it was nothing remarkable.

It was a large, square-built house, close indeed to the road, but separated from it by a high wrought iron gate in an oak paling, and a short, straight garden-path; originally even ante-Tudor, but matured through centuries, with a Queen Anne front of mellow red brick, and back premises of tile, oak, and modern rough-cast, with old brew-houses that almost enclosed a gravelled court behind. Behind this again lay a great kitchen garden with box-lined paths dividing it all into a dozen rectangles, separated from the orchard and yew walk by a broad double hedge down the centre of which ran a sheltered path. Round the south of the house and in the narrow strip westwards lay broad lawns surrounded by high trees completely shading it from all view of the houses that formed the tiny hamlet fifty yards away.

Within, the house had been modernised almost to a commonplace level. A little hall gave entrance to the drawing-room on the right where these two women now sat, a large, stately room, panelled from floor to ceiling, and to the dining-room on the left; and, again, through to the back, where a smoking-room, an inner hall, and the big kitchens and back premises concluded the ground floor. The two more stories above consisted, on the first floor, of a row of large rooms, airy, high, and dignified, and in the attics of a series of low-pitched chambers, whitewashed, oak-floored, and dormer-windowed, where one or two of the servants slept in splendid isolation. A little flight of irregular steps leading out of the big room on to the first floor, where the housekeeper lived in state, gave access to the further rooms near the kitchen and sculleries.

Maggie had fallen in love with the place from the instant that she had entered it. She had been warned in her French convent of the giddy gaieties of the world and its temptations; and yet it seemed to her after a week in her new home that the world was very much maligned. There was here a sense of peace and sheltered security that she had hardly known even at school; and little by little she had settled down here, with the mother and the son, until it had begun to seem to her that days spent in London or in other friends' houses were no better than interruptions and failures compared with the leisurely, tender life of this place, where it was so easy to read and pray and possess her soul in peace. This affair of Laurie's was almost the first reminder of what she had known by hearsay, that Love and Death and Pain were the bones on which life was modelled.

With a sudden movement she leaned forward, took up the bellows, and began to blow the smouldering logs into flame.

Meanwhile, upstairs on a long couch beside the fire in his big bed-sitting-room lay a young man on his face motionless.

A week ago, he had been one of those men who in almost any company appear easy and satisfactory, and, above all, are satisfactory to themselves. His life was a very pleasant one indeed.

He had come down from Oxford just a year ago, and had determined to take things as they came, to foster acquaintanceships, to travel a little with a congenial friend, to stay about in other people's houses, and, in fact, to enjoy himself entirely before settling down to read law. He had done this most successfully, and had crowned all, as has been related, by falling in love on a July evening with one who, he was quite certain, was the mate designed for him for Time and Eternity. His life, in fact, up to three days ago had developed along exactly those lines along which his temperament travelled with the greatest ease. He was the only son of a widow, he had an excellent income, he made friends wherever he went, and he had just secured the most charming rooms close to the Temple. He had plenty of brains, an exceedingly warm heart, and had lately embraced a religion that satisfied every instinct of his nature. It was the best of all possible worlds, and fitted him like his own well-cut clothes. It consisted of privileges without responsibilities.

And now the crash had come, and all was over.

As the gong sounded for luncheon he turned over and lay on his back, staring at the ceiling.

It should have been a very attractive face under other circumstances. Beneath his brown curls, just touched with gold, there looked out a pair of grey eyes, bright a week ago, now dimmed with tears, and patched beneath with lines of sorrow. His clean-cut, rather passionate lips were set now, with downturned corners, in a line of angry self-control piteous to see; and his clear skin seemed stained and dull. He had never dreamt of such misery in all his days.

As he lay now, with lax hands at his side, tightening at times in an agony of remembrance, he was seeing vision after vision, turning now and again to the contemplation of a dark future without life or love or hope. Again, he saw Amy, as he had first seen her under the luminous July evening, jewelled overhead with peeping stars, amber to the westwards, where the sun had gone down in glory. She was in her sun-bonnet and print dress, stepping towards him across the fresh-scented meadow grass lately shorn of its flowers and growth, looking at him with that curious awed admiration that delighted him with its flattery. Her face was to the west, the reflected glory lay on it as delicate as the light on a flower, and her blue eyes regarded him beneath a halo of golden hair.

He saw her again as she had been one moonlight evening as the two stood together by the sluice of the stream, among the stillness of the woods below the village, with all fairyland about them and in their hearts. She had thrown a wrap about her head and stolen down there by devious ways, according to the appointment, meeting him, as was arranged, as he came out from dinner with all the glamour of the Great House about him, in his evening dress, buckled shoes, and knee-breeches all complete. How marvellous she had been then—a sweet nymph of flesh and blood, glorified by the moon to an ethereal delicacy, with the living pallor of sun-kissed skin, her eyes looking at him like stars beneath her shawl. They had said very little; they had stood there at the sluice gate, with his arm about her, and herself willingly nestling against him, trembling now and again; looking out at the sheeny surface of the slow-flowing stream from which, in the imperceptible night breeze, stole away wraith after wraith of water mist to float and lose themselves in the sleeping woods.

Or, once more, clearer than all else he remembered how he had watched her, himself unseen, delaying the delight of revealing himself, one August morning, scarcely three weeks ago, as she had come down the road that ran past the house, again in her sun-bonnet and print dress, with the dew shining about her on grass and hedge, and the haze of a summer morning veiling the intensity of the blue sky above. He had called her then gently by name, and she had turned her face to him, alight with love and fear and sudden wonder. . . . He remembered even now with a reflection of memory that was nearly an illusion the smell of yew and garden flowers.

This, then, had been the dream; and today the awakening and the end.

That end was even more terrible than he had conceived possible on that horrible Friday morning last week, when he had opened the telegram from her father.

He had never before understood the sordidness of her surroundings, as when, an hour ago, he had stood at the graveside, his eyes wandering from that long elm box with the silver plate and the wreath of flowers, to the mourners on the other side—her father in his broadcloth, his heavy, smooth face pulled in lines of grotesque sorrow; her mother, with her crimson, tear-stained cheeks, her elaborate black, her intolerable crape, and her jet-hung mantle. Even these people had been seen by him up to then through a haze of love; he had thought them simple honest folk, creatures of the soil, yet wholesome, natural, and sturdy. And now that the jewel was lost the setting was worse than empty.

There in the elm-box lay the remnants of the shattered gem. . . . He had seen her in her bed on the Sunday, her fallen face, her sunken eyes, all framed in the detestable whiteness of linen and waxen flowers, yet as pathetic and as appealing as ever, and as necessary to his life. It was then that the supreme fact had first penetrated to his consciousness, that he had lost her—the fact which, driven home by the funeral scene this morning, the rustling crowd come to see the young squire, the elm-box, the heap of flowers—had now flung him down on this couch, crushed, broken, and hopeless, like young ivy after a thunderstorm.

His moods alternated with the rapidity of flying clouds. At one instant he was furious with pain, at the next broken and lax from the same cause. At one moment he cursed God and desired to die, defiant and raging; at the next he sank down into himself as weak as a tortured child, while tears ran down his cheeks and little moans as of an animal murmured in his throat. God was a hated adversary, a merciless Judge ... a Blind Fate ... there was no God ... He was a Fiend ... there was nothing anywhere in the whole universe but Pain and Vanity ...

Yet, through it all, like a throbbing pedal note, ran his need of this girl. He would do anything, suffer anything, make any sacrifice, momentary or lifelong, if he could but see her again, hold her hand for one instant, look into her eyes mysterious with the secret of death. He had but three or four words to say to her, just to secure himself that she lived and was still his, and then ... then he would say goodbye to her, content and happy to wait till death should reunite them. Ah! he asked so little, and God would not give it him.

All, then, was a mockery. It was only this past summer that he had begun to fancy himself in love with Maggie Deronnais. It had been an emotion of very quiet growth, developing gently, week by week, feeding on her wholesomeness, her serenity, her quiet power, her cool, capable hands, and the look in her direct eyes; it resembled respect rather than passion, and need rather than desire; it was a hunger rather than a thirst. Then had risen up this other, blinding and bewildering; and, he told himself, he now knew the difference. His lips curled into bitter and resentful lines as he contemplated the contrast. And all was gone, shattered and vanished; and even Maggie was now impossible.

Again, he writhed over, sick with pain and longing; and so lay.

It was ten minutes before he moved again, and then he only roused himself as he heard a foot on the stairs. Perhaps it was his mother.

He slipped off the couch and stood up, his face lined and creased with the pressure with which he had lain just now, and smoothed his tumbled clothes. Yes, he must go down.

He stepped to the door and opened it.

"I am coming immediately," he said to the servant.

He bore himself at lunch with a respectable self-control, though he said little or nothing. His mother's attitude he found hard to bear, as he caught her eyes once or twice looking at him with sympathy; and he allowed himself internally to turn to Maggie with relief in spite of his meditations just now. She at least respected his sorrow, he told himself. She bore herself very naturally, though with long silences, and never once met his eyes with her own. He made his excuses as soon as he could and slipped across to the stable-yard. At least he would be alone this afternoon. Only, as he rode away half an hour later, he caught a sight of the slender little figure of his mother waiting to have one word with him if she could, beyond the hall-door. But he set his lips and would not see her.

It was one of those perfect September days that fall sometimes as a gift from heaven after the bargain of summer has been more or less concluded. As he rode all that afternoon through lanes and across uplands, his view barred always to the north by the great downs above Royston, grey-blue against the radiant sky, there was scarcely a hint in earth or heaven of any emotion except prevailing peace. Yet the very serenity tortured him the more by its mockery. The birds babbled in the deep woods, the cheerful noise of children reached him now and again from a cottage garden, the mellow light smiled unending benediction, and yet his subconsciousness let go for never an instant of the long elm box six feet below ground, and of its contents lying there in the stifling dark, in the long-grassed churchyard on the hill above his home.

He wondered now and again as to the fate of the spirit that had informed the body and made it what it was; but his imagination refused to work. After all, he asked himself, what were all the teachings of theology but words gabbled to break the appalling silence? Heaven ... Purgatory.... Hell. What was known of these things? The very soul itself—what was that? What was the inconceivable environment, after all, for so inconceivable a thing? ...

He did not need these things, he said—certainly not now—nor those labels and signposts to a doubtful, unimaginable land. He needed Amy herself, or, at least, some hint or sound or glimpse to show him that she indeed was as she had always been; whether in earth or heaven, he did not care; that there was somewhere something that was herself, some definite personal being of a continuous consciousness with that which he had known, characterised still by those graces which he thought he had recognised and certainly loved. Ah! he did not ask much. It would be so easy to God! Here out in this lonely lane where he rode beneath the branches, his reins loose on his horse's neck, his eyes, unseeing, roving over copse and meadow across to the eternal hills—a face, seen for an instant, smiling and gone again; a whisper in his ear, with that dear stammer of shyness; a touch on his knee of those rippling fingers that he had watched in the moonlight playing gently on the sluice-gate above the moonlit stream. . . . He would tell no one if God wished it to be a secret; he would keep it wholly to himself. He did not ask now to possess her; only to be certain that she lived, and that death was not what it seemed to be.

"Is Father Mahon at home?" he asked, as he halted a mile from his own house in the village, where stood the little tin church, not a hundred yards from its elder alienated sister, to which he and Maggie went on Sundays.

The housekeeper turned from her vegetable-gathering beyond the fence, and told him yes. He dismounted, hitched the reins round the gatepost, and went in.

Ah! what an antipathetic little room this was in which he waited while the priest was being fetched from upstairs!

Over the mantelpiece hung a large oleograph of Leo XIII, in cope and tiara, blessing with upraised hand and that eternal, wide-lipped smile; a couple of jars stood beneath filled with dyed grasses; a briar pipe, redolent and foul, lay between them. The rest of the room was in the same key: a bright Brussels carpet, pale and worn by the door, covered the floor; cheap lace curtains were pinned across the windows; and over the littered table a painted deal bookshelf held a dozen volumes, devotional, moral, and dogmatic theology; and by the side of that an illuminated address framed in gilt, and so on.

Laurie looked at it all in dumb dismay. He had seen it before, again and again, but had never realised its horror as he realised it now from the depths of his own misery. Was it really true that his religion could emit such results?

There was a step on the stairs—a very heavy one—and Father Mahon came in, a large, crimson-faced man, who seemed to fill the room with a completely unethereal presence, and held out his hand with a certain gravity. Laurie took it and dropped it.

"Sit down, my dear boy," said the priest, and he impelled him gently to a horsehair-covered armchair.

Laurie stiffened.

"Thank you, father; but I mustn't stay."

He fumbled in his pocket, and fetched out a little paper-covered packet.

"Will you say Mass for my intention, please?" And he laid the packet on the mantelshelf.

The priest took up the coins and slipped them into his waistcoat pocket.

135

"Certainly," he said. "I think I know—"

Laurie turned away with a little jerk.

"I must be going," he said. "I only looked in—"

"Mr. Baxter," said the other, "I hope you will allow me to say how much—"

Laurie drew his breath swiftly, with a hiss as of pain, and glanced at the priest.

"You understand, then, what my intention is?"

"Why, surely. It is for her soul, is it not?"

"I suppose so," said the boy, and went out.

Chapter 2

I have told him," said Mrs. Baxter, as the two women walked beneath the yews that morning after breakfast. "He said he didn't mind."

Maggie did not speak. She had come out just as she was, hatless, but had caught up a spud that stood in the hall, and at that instant had stopped to destroy a youthful plantain that had established himself with infinite pains on the slope of the path. She attacked for a few seconds, extricated what was possible of the root with her strong fingers, tossed the corpse among the ivy, and then moved on.

"I don't know whether to say anything to Mrs. Stapleton or not," pursued the old lady.

"I think I shouldn't, auntie," said the girl slowly.

They spoke of it for a minute or two as they passed up and down, but Maggie only attended with one superficies of her mind.

She had gone up as usual to Mass that morning, and had been astonished to find Laurie already in church; they had walked back together, and, to her surprise, he had told her that the Mass had been for his own intention.

She had answered as well as she could; but a sentence or two of his as they came near home had vaguely troubled her.

It was not that he had said anything he ought not, as a Catholic, to have said; yet her instinct told her that something was wrong. It was his manner, his air, that troubled her. What strange people these converts were! There was so much ardour at one time, so much chilliness at another; there was so little of that steady workaday acceptance of religious facts that marked the born Catholic.

"Mrs. Stapleton is a New Thought kind of person," she said presently.

"So, I understand," said the old lady, with a touch of peevishness.

"A vegetarian last year. And I believe she was a sort of Buddhist five or six years ago. And then she nearly became a Christian Scientist a little while ago."

Maggie smiled.

"I wonder what she'll talk about," she said.

"I hope she won't be very advanced," went on the old lady. "And you think I'd better not tell her about Laurie?"

"I'm sure it's best not," said the girl, "or she'll tell him about Deep Breathing, or saying Om, or something. No; I should let Laurie alone."

It was a little before one o'clock that the motor arrived, and that there descended from it at the iron gate a tall, slender woman, hooded and veiled, who walked up the little path, observed by Maggie from her bedroom, with a kind of whisking step. The motor moved on, wheeled in through the gates at the left, and sank into silence in the stable-yard.

"It's too charming of you, dear Mrs. Baxter," Maggie heard as she came into the drawing-room a minute or two later, "to let me come over like this. I've heard so much about this house. Lady Laura was telling me how very psychical it all was."

"My adopted daughter, Miss Deronnais," observed the old lady.

Maggie saw a rather pretty, *passé* face, triangular in shape, with small red lips, looking at her, as she made her greetings.

"Ah! how perfect all this is," went on the guest presently, looking about her, "how suggestive, how full of meaning!"

She threw back her cloak presently, and Maggie observed that she was busy with various very beautiful little emblems—a scarab, a snake swallowing its tail, and so forth—all exquisitely made, and hung upon a slender chain of some green enamel-like material. Certainly, she was true to type. As the full light fell upon her it became plain that this other-worldly soul did not disdain to use certain toilet requisites upon her face; and a curious Eastern odour exhaled from her dress.

Fortunately, Maggie had a very deep sense of humour, and she hardly resented all this at all, nor even the tactful hints dropped from time to time, after the conventional part of the conversation was over, to the effect that Christianity was, of course, played out, and that a Higher Light had dawned. Mrs. Stapleton did not quite say this outright, but it amounted to as much. Even before Laurie came downstairs it appeared that the lady did not go to church, yet that, such was her broad-mindedness, she did not at all object to do so. It was all one, it seemed, in the Deeper Unity. Nothing particular was true; but all was very suggestive and significant and symbolical of something else to which Mrs. Stapleton and a few friends had the key.

Mrs. Baxter made more than one attempt to get back to more mundane subjects, but it was useless. When even the weather serves as a symbol, the plain man is done for.

Then Laurie came in.

He looked very self-contained and rather pinched this morning, and shook hands with the lady without a word. Then they moved across presently to the green-hung dining-room across the hall, and the exquisite symbol of luncheon made its appearance.

Lady Laura, it appeared, was one of those who had felt the charm of Stantons; only for her it was psychical rather than physical, and all this was passed on by her friend. It seemed that the psychical atmosphere of most modern houses was of a yellow tint, but that this one emanated a brown-gold radiance which was very peculiar and exceptional. Indeed, it was this singularity that had caused Mrs. Stapleton to apply for an invitation to the house. More than once during lunch, in a pause of the conversation, Maggie saw her throw back her head slightly as if to appreciate some odour or colour not experienced by coarser-nerved persons. Once, indeed, she actually put this into words.

"Dear Laura was quite right," cried the lady; "there is something very unique about this place. How fortunate you are, dear Mrs. Baxter!"

"My dear husband's grandfather bought the place," observed the mistress plaintively. "We have always found it very soothing and pleasant."

"How right you are! And—and have you had any experiences here?" Mrs. Baxter eyed her in alarm. Maggie had an irrepressible burst of internal laughter, which, however, gave no hint of its presence in her steady features. She glanced at Laurie, who was eating mutton with a depressed air.

"I was talking to Mr. Vincent, the great spiritualist," went on the other vivaciously, "only last week. You have heard of him, Mrs. Baxter? I was suggesting to him that any place where great emotions have been felt are coloured and stained by them as objectively as old walls are weather-beaten. I had such an interesting conversation, too, with Cardinal Newman on the subject"—she smiled brilliantly at Maggie, as if to reassure her of her own orthodoxy—"scarcely six weeks ago."

There was a pregnant silence. Mrs. Baxter's fork sank to her plate.

"I don't understand," she said faintly. "Cardinal Newman—surely—"

"Why yes," said the other gently. "I know it sounds very startling to orthodox ears; but to us of the Higher Thought all these things are quite familiar. Of course, I need hardly say that Cardinal Newman is no longer—but perhaps I had better not go on."

She glanced archly at Maggie.

"Oh, please go on," said Maggie genially. "You were saying that Cardinal Newman—"

"Dear Miss Deronnais, are you sure you will not be offended?"

"I am always glad to receive new light," said Maggie solemnly.

The other looked at her doubtfully; but there was no hint of irony in the girl's face.

"Well," she began, "of course on the Other Side they see things very differently. I don't mean at all that any religion is exactly untrue. Oh no; they tell us that if we cannot welcome the New Light, that the old lights will do very well for the present. Indeed, when there are Catholics present Cardinal Newman does not scruple to give them a Latin blessing—"

"Is it true that he speaks with an American accent?" asked Maggie gravely. The other laughed with a somewhat shrill geniality.

"That is too bad, Miss Deronnais. Well, of course, the personality of the medium affects the vehicle through which the communications come. That is no difficulty at all when once you understand the principle—"

Mrs. Baxter interrupted. She could bear it no longer.

"Mrs. Stapleton. Do you mean that Cardinal Newman really speaks to you?"

"Why yes," said the other, with a patient indulgence. "That is a very usual experience, but Mr. Vincent does much more than that. It is quite a common experience not only to hear him, but to see him. I have shaken hands with him more than once . . . and I have seen a Catholic kiss his ring."

Mrs. Baxter looked helplessly at the girl; and Maggie came to the rescue once more. "This sounds rather advanced to us," she said. "Won't you explain the principles first?"

Mrs. Stapleton laid her knife and fork down, leaned back, and began to discourse. When a little later her plate was removed, she refused sweets with a gesture, and continued.

Altogether she spoke for about ten minutes, uninterrupted, enjoying herself enormously. The others ate food or refused it in attentive silence. Then at last she ended.

". . . I know all this must sound quite mad and fanatical to those who have not experienced it; and yet to us who have been disciples it is as natural to meet our friends who have crossed over as to meet those who have not. . . . Dear Mrs. Baxter, think how all this enlarges life. There is no longer any death to those who understand. All those limitations are removed; it is no more than going into another room. All are together in the Hands of the All-Father"—Maggie recognised the jetsam of Christian Science. "'O death!' as Paul says, 'where is thy sting? O grave, where is thy victory?'"

Mrs. Stapleton flashed a radiant look of helpfulness round the faces, lingering for an instant on Laurie's, and leaned back.

There followed a silence.

"Shall we go into the drawing-room?" suggested Mrs. Baxter, feebly rising. The guest rose too, again with a brilliant patient smile, and swept out. Maggie crossed herself and looked at Laurie. The boy had an expression, half of disgust, half of interest, and his eyelids sank a little and rose again. Then Maggie went out after the others.

★★★★★★

"A dreadful woman," observed Mrs. Baxter half an hour later, as the two strolled back up the garden path, after seeing Mrs. Stapleton wave a delicately gloved hand encouragingly to them over the back of the throbbing motor.

"I suppose she thinks she believes it all," said Maggie.

"My dear, that woman would believe anything. I hope poor Laurie was not too much distressed."

"Oh! I think Laurie took it all right."

"It was most unfortunate, all that about death and the rest. . . . Why, here comes Laurie; I thought he would be gone out by now."

The boy strolled towards them round the corner of the house, tossing away the fragment of his cigarette. He was still in his dark suit, bare-headed, with no signs of riding about him.

"So, you've not gone out yet, dear boy?" remarked his mother.

"Not yet," he said, and hesitated as they went on.

Mrs. Baxter noticed it.

"I'll go and get ready," she said. "The carriage will be round at three, Maggie."

When she was gone the two moved out together on to the lawn.

"What did you think of that woman?" demanded Laurie with a detached air.

Maggie glanced at him. His tone was a little too much detached.

"I thought her quite dreadful," she said frankly. "Didn't you?" she added.

"Oh yes, I suppose so," said Laurie. He drew out a cigarette and lighted it. "You know a lot of people think there's something in it," he said.

"In what?"

"Spiritualism."

"I daresay," said Maggie.

She perceived out of the corner of her eye that Laurie looked at her suddenly and sharply. For herself, she loathed what little she knew of the subject, so cordially and completely, that she could hardly have put it into words. Nine-tenths of it she believed to be fraud—a matter of wigs and Indian muslin and cross-lights—and the other tenth, by the most generous estimate, an affair of the dingiest and foulest of all the backstairs of life. The prophetic outpourings of Mrs. Stapleton had not altered her opinion.

"Oh! if you feel like that," went on Laurie.

She turned on him.

"Laurie," she said, "I think it perfectly detestable. I acknowledge I don't know much about it; but what little I do know is enough, thank you."

Laurie smiled in a faintly patronising way.

"Well," he said indulgently, if you think that, it's not much use discussing it."

"Indeed, it's not," said Maggie, with her nose in the air.

There was not much more to be said; and the sounds of stamping and whoaing in the stable-yard presently sent the girl indoors in a hurry.

Mrs. Baxter was still mildly querulous during the drive. It appeared to her, Maggie perceived, a kind of veiled insult that things should be talked about in her house which did not seem to fit in with her own scheme of the universe. Mrs. Baxter knew perfectly well that every soul when it left this world went either to what she called Paradise, or in extremely exceptional cases, to a place she did not name; and that these places, each in its own way, entirely absorbed the attention of its inhabitants. Further, it was established in her view that all the members of the spiritual world, apart from the unhappy ones, were a kind of Anglicans, with their minds no doubt enlarged considerably, but on the original lines.

Tales like this of Cardinal Newman therefore were extremely tiresome and upsetting.

And Maggie had her theology also; to her also it appeared quite impossible that Cardinal Newman should frequent the drawing-room of Mr. Vincent in order to exchange impressions with Mrs. Stapleton; but she was more elementary in her answer. For her the thing was simply untrue; and that was the end of it. She found it difficult therefore to follow her companion's train of thought.

"What was it she said?" demanded Mrs. Baxter presently. "I didn't understand her ideas about materialism."

"I think she called it materialisation," explained Maggie patiently. "She said that when things were very favourable, and the medium a very good one, the soul that wanted to communicate could make a kind of body for itself out of what she called the astral matter of the medium or the sitters."

"But surely our bodies aren't like that?"

"No; I can't say that I think they are. But that's what she said."

"My dear, please explain. I want to understand the woman."

Maggie frowned a little.

"Well, the first thing she said was that those souls want to communicate; and that they begin generally by things like table-rapping, or making blue lights. Then when you know they're there, they can go further. Sometimes they gain control of the medium who is in a trance, and speak through him, or write with his hand. Then, if things are favourable, they begin to draw out this matter, and make it into a kind of body for themselves, very thin and ethereal, so that you can pass your hand through it. Then, as things get better and better, they go further still, and can make this body so solid that you can touch it; only this is sometimes rather dangerous, as it is still, in a sort of way, connected with the medium. I think that's the idea."

"But what's the good of it all?"

"Well, you see, Mrs. Stapleton thinks that they really are souls from the other world, and that they can tell us all kinds of things about it all, and what's true, and so on."

"But you don't believe that?"

Maggie turned her large eyes on the old lady; and a spark of humour rose and glimmered in them.

"Of course, I don't," she said.

"Then how do you explain it?"

"I think it's probably all a fraud. But I really don't know. It doesn't

142

seem to me to matter much—"

"But if it should be true?"

Maggie raised her eyebrows, smiling.

"Dear auntie, do put it out of your head. How can it possibly be true?"

Mrs. Baxter set her lips in as much severity as she could.

"I shall ask the vicar," she said. "We might stop at the vicarage on the way back."

Mrs. Baxter did not often stop at the vicarage; as she did not altogether approve of the vicar's wife. There was a good deal of pride in the old lady, and it seemed to her occasionally as if Mrs. Rymer did not understand the difference between the Hall and the parsonage. She envied sometimes, secretly, the Romanist idea of celibacy: it was so much easier to get on with your spiritual adviser if you did not have to consider his wife. But here was a matter which a clergyman must settle for her once and for all; so, she put on a slight air of dignity which became her very well, and a little after four o'clock the victoria turned up the steep little drive that led to the vicarage.

✶✶✶✶✶✶

The dusk was already fallen before Laurie, strolling vaguely in the garden, heard the carriage wheels draw up at the gate outside.

He had ridden again alone, and his mind had run, to a certain extent, as might be expected, upon the recent guest and her very startling conversation. He was an intelligent young man, and he had not been in the least taken in by her pseudo-mystical remarks. Yet there had been something in her extreme assurance that had affected him, as a man may smile sourly at a good story in bad taste. His attitude, in fact, was that of most Christians under the circumstances. He did not, for an instant, believe that such things really and literally happened, and yet it was difficult to advance any absolutely conclusive argument against them. Merely, they had not come his way; they appeared to conflict with experience, and they usually found as their advocates such persons as Mrs. Stapleton.

Two things, however, prevailed to keep the matter before his mind. The first was his own sense of loss, his own experience, sore and hot within him, of the unapproachable emptiness of death; the second, Maggie's attitude. When a plainly sensible and controlled young woman takes up a position of superiority, she is apt, unless the young man in her company happens to be in love with her—and sometimes even when he is—to provoke and irritate him into a camp of opposition. She is still more apt to do so if her relations to him have once been in the line of even greater tenderness.

Laurie then was not in the most favourable of moods to receive the *dicta* of the vicar.

They were announced to him immediately after Mrs. Baxter had received from Maggie's hands her first cup of tea.

"Mr. Rymer tells me it's all nonsense," she said.

Laurie looked up.

"What?" he said.

"Mr. Rymer tells me Spiritualism is all nonsense. He told me about someone called Eglingham, who kept a beard in his portmanteau."

"Eglinton, I think, auntie," put in Maggie.

"I daresay, my dear. Anyhow, it's all the same. I felt sure it must be so." Laurie took a bun, with a thoughtful air.

"Does Mr. Rymer know very much about it, do you think, mother?"

"Dear boy, I think he knows all that anyone need know. Besides, if you come to think of it, how could Cardinal Newman possibly appear in a drawing-room? Particularly when Mrs. Stapleton says he isn't a Christian any longer."

This had a possible and rather pleasing double interpretation; but Laurie decided it was not worthwhile to be humorous.

"What about the Witch of Endor?" he asked innocently, instead.

"That was in the Old Testament," answered his mother rapidly. "Mr. Rymer said something about that too."

"Oh! wasn't it really Samuel who appeared?"

"Mr. Rymer thinks that things were permitted then that are not permitted now."

Laurie drank up his cup of tea. It is a humiliating fact that extreme grief often renders the mourner rather cross. There was a distinct air of crossness about Laurie at this moment. His nerves were very near the top.

"Well, that's very convenient," he said. "Maggie, do you know if there's any book on Spiritualism in the house?"

The girl glanced uneasily near the fireplace.

"I don't know," she said. "Yes; I think there's something up there. I believe I saw it the other day."

Laurie rose and stood opposite the shelves.

"What colour is it? (No, no more tea, thanks.)—"

"Er . . . black and red, I think," said the girl. "I forget."

144

She looked up at him, faintly uneasy, as he very deliberately drew down a book from the shelf and turned the pages.

"Yes . . . this is it," he said. "Thanks very much. . . . No, really no more tea, thanks, mother."

Then he went to the door, with his easy, rather long steps, and disappeared. They heard his steps in the inner hall. Then a door closed overhead.

Mrs. Baxter contentedly poured herself out another cup of tea.

"Poor boy," she said. "He's thinking of that girl still. I'm glad he's got something to occupy his mind."

The end room, on the first floor, was Laurie's possession. It was a big place, with two windows, and a large open fire, and he had skilfully masked the fact that it was a bedroom by disposing his furniture, with the help of a screen, in such a manner as completely to hide the bed and the washing arrangements.

The rest of the room he had furnished in a pleasing male kind of fashion, with a big couch drawn across the fire, a writing-table and chairs, a deep easy chair near the door, and a long, high bookcase covering the wall between the door and the windows. His college oar, too, hung here, and there were pleasant groups and pictures scattered on the other walls.

Maggie did not often come in here, except by invitation, but about seven o'clock on this evening, half an hour before she had to go and dress, she thought she would look in on him for a few minutes. She was still a little uncomfortable; she did not quite know why: it was too ridiculous, she told herself, that a sensible boy like Laurie could be seriously affected by what she considered the wicked nonsense of Spiritualism.

Yet she went, telling herself that Laurie's grief was an excuse for showing him a little marked friendliness. Besides, she would like to ask him whether he was really going back to town on Thursday.

She tapped twice before an answer came; and then it seemed a rather breathless voice which spoke.

The boy was sitting bolt upright on the edge of the sofa, with a couple of candles at his side, and the book in his hands. There was a strained and intensely interested look in his eyes.

"May I come in for a few minutes? It's nearly dressing time," she said.

"Oh—er—certainly."

He got up, rather stiffly, still keeping his place in the book with

145

one finger, while she sat down. Then he too sat again, and there was silence for a moment.

"Why, you're not smoking," she said.

"I forgot. I will now, if you don't mind."

She saw his fingers tremble a little as he put out his hand to a box of cigarettes at his side. But he put the book down, after looking at the page.

She could keep her question in no longer.

"What do you think of that," she said, nodding at the book.

He filled his lungs with smoke and exhaled again slowly.

"I think it's extraordinary," he said shortly.

"In what way?"

Again, he paused before answering. Then he answered deliberately.

"If human evidence is worth anything, those things happen," he said.

"What things?"

"The dead return."

Maggie looked at him, aware of his deliberate attempt at dramatic brevity. He was watching the end of his cigarette with elaborate attention, and his face had that white, rather determined look that she had seen on it once or twice before, in the presence of a domestic crisis.

"Do you really mean you believe that?" she said, with a touch of careful bitterness in her voice.

"I do," he said, "or else—"

"Well?"

"Or else human evidence is worth nothing at all."

Maggie understood him perfectly; but she realised that this was not an occasion to force issues. She still put the tone of faint irony into her voice.

"You really believe that Cardinal Newman comes to Mr. Vincent's drawing-room and raps on tables?"

"I really believe that it is possible to get into touch with those whom we call dead. Each instance, of course, depends on its own evidence."

"And Cardinal Newman?"

"I have not studied the evidence for Cardinal Newman," remarked Laurie in a head-voice.

"Let's have a look at that book," said Maggie impulsively.

He handed it to her; and she began to turn the pages, pausing now and again to read a particular paragraph, and once for nearly a minute while she examined an illustration. Certainly, the book seemed interestingly written, and she read an argument or two that appeared reasonably presented. Yet she was extraordinarily repelled even by the dead paper and ink she had in her hands. It was as if it was something obscene. Finally, she tossed it back on to the couch.

Laurie waited; but she said nothing.

"Well?" he asked at last, still refraining from looking at her.

"I think it's horrible," she said.

Laurie delicately adjusted a little tobacco protruding from his cigarette.

"Isn't that a little unreasonable?" he asked. "You've hardly looked at it yet."

Maggie knew this mood of his only too well. He reserved it for occasions when he was determined to fight. Argument was a useless weapon against it.

"My dear boy," she said with an effort, "I'm sorry. I daresay it is unreasonable. But that kind of thing does seem to me so disgusting. That's all. . . . I didn't come to talk about that. . . . Tell me—"

"Didn't you?" said Laurie.

Maggie was silent.

"Didn't you?"

"Well—yes I did. But I don't want to anymore."

Laurie smiled so that it might be seen.

"Well, what else did you want to say?" (He glanced purposely at the book. Maggie ignored his glance.)

"I just came to see how you were getting on."

"How do you mean? With the book?"

"No; in every way."

He looked up at her swiftly and suddenly, and she saw that his agony of sorrow was acute beneath all his attempts at superiority, his courteous fractiousness, and his set face. She was filled suddenly with an enormous pity.

"Oh! Laurie, I'm so sorry," she cried out. "Can't I do anything?"

"Nothing, thanks; nothing at all," he said quietly.

Again, pity and misery surged up within her, and she cast all prudence to the winds. She had not realised how fond she was of this boy till she saw once more that look in his eyes.

"Oh! Laurie, you know I didn't like it; but—but I don't know what to do, I'm so sorry. But don't spoil it all," she said wildly, hardly knowing what she feared.

"I beg your pardon?"

"You know what I mean. Don't spoil it, by—by fancying things."

"Maggie," said the boy quietly, "you must let me alone. You can't help."

"Can't I?"

"You can't help," he repeated. "I must go my own way. Please don't say any more. I can't stand it."

There followed a dead silence. Then Maggie recovered and stood up. He rose with her.

"Forgive me, Laurie, won't you? I must say this. You'll remember I'll always do anything I can, won't you?"

Then she was gone.

★★★★★★

The ladies went to bed early at Stantons. At ten o'clock precisely a clinking of bedroom candlesticks was heard in the hall, followed by the sound of locking doors. This was the signal. Mrs. Baxter laid aside her embroidery with the punctuality of a religious at the sound of a bell, and said two words—"My dears."

There were occasionally exclamatory expostulations from the two at the picquet-table, but in nine cases out of ten the game had been designed with an eye upon the clock, and hardly any delay followed. Mrs. Baxter kissed her son, and passed her arm through Maggie's. Laurie followed; gave them candles, and generally took one himself.

But this evening there was no picquet. Laurie had stayed later than usual in the dining-room, and had wandered rather restlessly about when he had joined the others. He looked at a London evening paper for a little, paced about, vanished again, and only returned as the ladies were making ready to depart. Then he gave them their candlesticks, and himself came back to the drawing-room.

He was, in fact, in a far more perturbed and excited mood than even Maggie had had any idea of. She had interrupted him half-way through the book, but he had read again steadily until five minutes before dinner, and had, indeed, gone back again to finish it afterwards. He had now finished it; and he wanted to think.

It had had a surprising effect on him, coming as it did upon a state of mind intensely stirred to its depths by his sorrow. Crossness, as I have said, had been the natural psychological result of his emotions; but his emotions were none the less real. The froth of whipped cream is real cream, after all.

Now Laurie had seen perfectly well the extreme unconvincingness

148

of Mrs. Stapleton, and had been genuine enough in his little shrug of disapproval in answer to Maggie's, after lunch; yet that lady's remarks had been sufficient just to ignite the train of thought. This train had smouldered in the afternoon, had been fanned ever so slightly by two breezes—the sense of Maggie's superiority and the faint rebellious reaction which had come upon him with regard to his personal religion. Certainly, he had had Mass said for Amy this morning; but it had been by almost a superstitious rather than a religious instinct. He was, in fact, in that state of religious unreality which occasionally comes upon converts within a year or two of the change of their faith. The impetus of old association is absent, and the force of novelty has died.

Underneath all this then, it must be remembered that the one thing that was intensely real to him was his sense of loss of the one soul in whom his own had been wrapped up. Even this afternoon as yesterday, even this morning as he lay awake, he had been conscious of an irresistible impulse to demand some sign, to catch some glimpse of that which was now denied to him.

It was in this mood that he had read the book; and it is not to be wondered at that he had been excited by it.

For it opened up to him, beneath all its sham mysticism, its intolerable affectations, its grotesque parody of spirituality—of all of which he was largely aware—a glimmering avenue of a faintly possible hope of which he had never dreamed—a hope, at least, of that half self-deception which is so tempting to certain characters.

Here, in this book, written by a living man, whose name and address were given, were stories so startling, and theories so apparently consonant with themselves and with other partly known facts—stories and theories, too, which met so precisely his own overmastering desire, that it is little wonder that he was affected by them.

Naturally, even during his reading, a thousand answers and adverse comments had sprung to his mind—suggestions of fraud, of lying, of hallucination—but yet, here the possibility remained. Here were living men and women who, with the usual complement of senses and reason, declared categorically and in detail, that on this and that date, in this place and the other, after having taken all possible precautions against fraud, they had received messages from the dead—messages of which the purport was understood by none but themselves—that they had seen with their eyes, in sufficient light, the actual features of the dead whom they loved, that they had even clasped their hands, and held for an instant the bodies of those whom they had seen die with their own eyes, and buried.

When the ladies' footsteps had ceased to sound overhead, Laurie went to the French window, opened it, and passed on to the lawn.

He was astonished at the warmth of the September night. The little wind that had been chilly this afternoon had dropped with the coming of the dark, and high overhead he could see the great masses of the leaves motionless against the sky.

He passed round the house, and beneath the yews, and sat down on the garden bench.

It was darker here than outside on the lawn. Beneath his feet were the soft needles from the trees, and above him, as he looked out, still sunk in his thought, he could see the glimmer of a star or two between the branches.

It was a fragrant, kindly night. From the hamlet of half a dozen houses beyond the garden came no sound; and the house, too, was still behind him. An illuminated window somewhere on the first floor went out as he looked at it, like a soul leaving a body; once a sleepy bird somewhere in the shrubbery chirped to its mate and was silent again.

Then as he still laboured in argument, putting this against that, and weighing that against the other, his emotion rose up in an irresistible torrent, and all consideration ceased. One thing remained: he must have Amy, or he must die.

It was five or six minutes before he moved again from that attitude of clenched hands and tensely strung muscles into which his sudden passion had cast him.

During those minutes he had willed with his whole power that she should come to him now and here, down in this warm and fragrant darkness, hidden from all eyes—in this sweet silence, round which sleep kept its guard. Such things had happened before; such things must have happened, for the will and the love of man are the mightiest forces in creation. Surely again and again it had happened; there must be somewhere in the world man after man who had so called back the dead—a husband sobbing silently in the dark, a child wailing for his mother; surely that force had before, in the world's history, willed back again from the mysterious dark of space the dear personality that was all that even heaven could give, had even compelled into a semblance of life some sort of body to clothe it in. These things must have happened—only secrets had been well kept.

So, this boy had willed it; yet the dark had remained empty; and no shadow, no faintly outlined face, had even for an instant blotted out the star on which he stared; no touch on his shoulder, no whisper in his ear. It had seemed as he strove there, in the silence, that it must be done; that there was no limit to power concentrated and intense. Yet it had not happened. . . .

Once he had shuddered a little; and the very shudder of fear had had in it a touch of delicious, trembling expectation. Yet it had not happened.

Laurie relaxed his muscles therefore, let his breath exhale in a long sigh, and once more remembered the book he had read and Mrs. Stapleton's feverish, self-conscious thought.

Half an hour later his mother, listening in her bed, heard his footsteps pass her room.

Chapter 3

Lady Laura Bethell, spinster, had just returned to her house in Queen's Gate, with her dearest friend, Mrs. Stapleton, for a few days of psychical orgy. It was in her house, as much as in any in London, that the modern prophets were to be met with—severe-looking women in shapeless dresses, little men and big, with long hair and cloaks; and it was in her drawing-room that tea and queen cakes were dispensed to inquirers, and papers read and discussed when the revels were over.

Lady Laura herself was not yet completely emancipated from what her friends sometimes called the grave-clothes of so-called Revelation. To her it seemed a profound truth that things could be true and untrue simultaneously—that what might be facts on This Side, as she would have expressed it, might be falsehoods on the Other. She was accustomed, therefore, to attend All Saints', Carlton Gardens, in the morning, and psychical drawing-rooms or halls in the evening, and to declare to her friends how beautifully the one aspect illuminated and interpreted the other.

For the rest, she was a small, fair-haired woman, with pencilled dark eyebrows, a small aquiline nose, gold *pince-nez*, and an exquisite taste in dress.

The two were seated this Tuesday evening, a week after Mrs. Stapleton's visit to the Stantons, in the drawing-room of the Queen's Gate house, over the remnants of what corresponded to five o'clock tea. I say "corresponded," since both of them were sufficiently advanced to have renounced actual tea altogether. Mrs. Stapleton partook of a little hot water out of a copper-jacketed jug; her hostess of boiled milk. They shared their Plasmon biscuits together. These things were considered important for those who would successfully find the Higher Light.

At this instant they were discussing Mr. Vincent.

"Dearest, he seems to me so different from the others," mewed Lady Laura. "He is such a man, you know. So often those others are not quite like men at all; they wear such funny clothes, and their hair always is so queer, somehow."

"Darling, I know what you mean. Yes, there's a great deal of that about James Vincent. Even dear Tom was almost polite to him: he couldn't bear the others: he said that he always thought they were going to paw him."

"And then his powers," continued Lady Laura—"his powers always seem to me so much greater. The magnetism is so much more evident."

Mrs. Stapleton finished her hot water.

"We are going on Sunday?" she said questioningly.

"Yes; just a small party. And he comes here tomorrow, you remember, just for a talk. I have asked a clergyman I know in to meet him. It seems to me such a pity that our religious teachers should know so little of what is going on."

"Who is he?"

"Oh, Mr. Jamieson ... just a young clergyman I met in the summer. I promised to let him know the next time Mr. Vincent came to me."

Mrs. Stapleton murmured her gratification.

These two had really a great deal in common besides their faith. It is true that Mrs. Stapleton was forty, and her friend but thirty-one; but the former did all that was possible to compensate for this by adroit *toilette* tactics. Both, too, were accustomed to dress in soft materials, with long chains bearing various emblems; they did their hair in the same way; they cultivated the same kinds of tones in their voices—a purring, mewing manner—suggestive of intuitive kittens. Both alike had a passion for proselytism. But after that the differences began. There was a deal more in Mrs. Stapleton besides the kittenish qualities. She was perfectly capable of delivering a speech in public; she had written some really well-expressed articles in various Higher periodicals; and she had a will-power beyond the ordinary. At the point where Lady Laura began to deprecate and soothe, Mrs. Stapleton began to clear decks for action, so to speak, to be incisive, to be fervent, even to be rather eloquent. She kept "dear Tom," the Colonel, not crushed or beaten, for that was beyond the power of man to do, but at least silently acquiescent in her programme: he allowed her even to entertain her prophetical friends at his expense, now and then; and, even when among men, refrained from too bitter speech. It was said by the Colonel's friends that Mrs. Colonel had a tongue of her own. Certainly, she ruled her house well and did her duty; and it was only because of her husband's absence in Scotland that during this time she was permitting herself the refreshment of a week or two among the Illuminated.

At about six o'clock Lady Laura announced her intention of retiring for her evening meditation. Opening out of her bedroom was a small dressing-room that she had fitted up for this purpose with all the broad suggestiveness that marks the Higher Thought: decked with ornaments emblematical of at least three religions, and provided with a faldstool and an exceedingly easy chair. It was here that she was accustomed to spend an hour before dinner, with closed eyes, emancipating herself from the fetters of sense; and rising to a due appreciation of that Nothingness that was All, from which All came and to which it retired.

"I must go, dearest; it is time."

A ring at the bell below made her pause.

"Do you think that can be Mr. Vincent?" she said, pleasantly apprehensive. "It's not the right day, but one never knows."

A footman's figure entered.

"Mr. Baxter, my lady. . . . . Is your ladyship at home?"

"Mr. Baxter—"

Mrs. Stapleton rose.

"Let me see him instead, dearest. . . . You remember . . . from Stantons."

"I wonder what he wants?" murmured the hostess.

"Yes, do see him, Maud; you can always fetch me if it's anything."

Then she was gone. Mrs. Stapleton sank into a chair again; and in a minute Laurie was shaking hands with her.

Mrs. Stapleton was accustomed to deal with young men, and through long habit had learned how to flatter them without appearing to do so. Laurie's type, however, was less familiar to her. She preferred the kind that grow their hair rather long and wear turn-down collars, and have just found out the hopeless banality of all orthodoxy whatever. She even bore with them when they called themselves unmoral. But she remembered Laurie, the silent boy at lunch last week, she had even mentioned him to Lady Laura, and received information about the village girl, more or less correct. She was also aware that he was a Catholic.

She gave him her hand without rising.

"Lady Laura asked me to excuse her absence to you, Mr. Baxter. To be quite truthful, she is at home, but had just gone upstairs for her meditation."

"Indeed!"

"Yes, you know; we think that so important, just as you do. Do sit down, Mr. Baxter. You have had tea?"

"Yes, thanks."

"I hope she will be down before you go. I don't think she'll be very long this evening. Can I give her any message, Mr. Baxter, in case you don't see her?"

Laurie put his hat and stick down carefully, and crossed his legs.

"No; I don't think so, thanks," he said. "The fact is, I came partly to find out your address, if I might."

Mrs. Stapleton rustled and rearranged herself.

"Oh! but that's charming of you," she said. "Is there anything particular?"

"Yes," said Laurie slowly; "at least it seems rather particular to me. It's what you were talking about the other day."

"Now how nice of you to say that! Do you know, I was wondering as we talked. Now do tell me exactly what is in your mind, Mr. Baxter."

Mrs. Stapleton was conscious of a considerable sense of pleasure. Usually she found this kind of man very imperceptive and gross. Laurie seemed perfectly at his ease, dressed quite in the proper way, and had an air of presentableness that usually only went with Philistinism. She determined to do her best.

"May I speak quite freely, please?" he asked, looking straight at her.

"Please, please," she said, with that touch of childish intensity that her friends thought so innocent and beautiful.

"Well, it's like this," said Laurie. "I've always rather disliked all that kind of thing, more than I can say. It did seem to me so—well—so feeble, don't you know; and then I'm a Catholic, you see, and so—"

"Yes; yes?"

"Well, I've been reading Mr. Stainton Moses, and one or two other books; and I must say that an awful lot of it seems to me still great rubbish; and then there are any amount of frauds, aren't there, Mrs. Stapleton, in that line?"

"Alas! Ah, yes!"

"But then I don't know what to make of some of the evidence that remains. It seems to me that if evidence is worth anything at all, there must be something real at the back of it all. And then, if that is so, if it really is true that it is possible to get into actual touch with people who are dead—I mean really and truly, so that there's no kind of doubt about it—well, that does seem to me about the most important thing in the world. Do you see?"

She kept her eyes on his face for an instant or two. Plainly he was really moved; his face had gone a little white in the lamplight and his hands were clasped tightly enough over his knee to whiten the knuckles. She remembered Lady Laura's remarks about the village girl, and understood. But she perceived that she must not attempt intimacy just yet with this young man: he would resent it. Besides, she was shrewd enough to see by his manner that he did not altogether like her.

She nodded pensively once or twice. Then she turned to him with a bright smile. "I understand entirely," she said. "(May I too speak quite freely? Yes?) Well, I am so glad you have spoken out. Of course, we are quite accustomed to being distrusted and feared. After all, it is the privilege of all truth-seekers to suffer, is it not? Well, I will say what is in my heart.

"First, you are quite right about some of our workers being dishonest sometimes. They are, Mr. Baxter. I have seen more than one, myself, exposed. But that is natural, is it not? Why, there have been bad Catholics, too, have there not? And, after all, we are only human; and there is a great temptation sometimes not to send people away disappointed. You have heard those stories, I expect, Mr. Baxter?"

"I have heard of Mr. Eglinton."

"Ah! Poor Willie. , . . Yes. But he had great powers, for all that. . . . Well, but the point you want to get at is this, is it not? Is it really true, underneath it all? Is that it?"

Laurie nodded, looking at her steadily. She leaned forward.

"Mr. Baxter, by all that I hold most sacred, I assure you that it is, that I myself have seen and touched ... *touched* ... my own father, who crossed over twenty years ago. I have received messages from his own lips ... and communications in other ways too, concerning matters only known to him and to myself. Is that sufficient? No"; (she held up a delicate silencing hand) ".... no, I will not ask you to take my word. I will ask you to test it for yourself."

Laurie too leaned forward now in his low chair, his hands clasped between his knees.

"You will—you will let me test it?" he said in a low voice.

She sat back easily, pushing her draperies straight. She was in some fine silk that fell straight from her high slender waist to her copper-coloured shoes.

"Listen, Mr. Baxter. Tomorrow there is coming to this house certainly the greatest medium in London, if not in Europe. (Of course, we cannot compete with the East. We are only children beside them.) Well, this man, Mr. Vincent—I think I spoke of him to you last week—he is coming here just for a talk to one or two friends. There shall be no difficulty if you wish it. I will speak to Lady Laura before you go."

Laurie looked at her without moving.

"I shall be very much obliged," he said. "You will remember that I am not yet in the least convinced? I only want to know."

"That is exactly the right attitude. That is all we have any right to ask. We do not ask for blind faith, Mr. Baxter—only for believing after having seen."

Laurie nodded slowly.

"That seems to me reasonable," he said.

There was silence for a moment. Then she determined on a bold stroke.

"There is someone in particular—Mr. Baxter—forgive me for asking—someone who has passed over—?"

She sank her voice to what she had been informed was a sympathetic tone, and was scarcely prepared for the sudden tightening of that face.

"That is my affair, Mrs. Stapleton."

Ah well, she had been premature. She would fetch Lady Laura, she said; she thought she might venture for such a purpose. No, she would not be away three minutes. Then she rustled out.

Laurie went to the fire to wait, and stood there, mechanically warming his hands and staring down at that sleeping core of red coal.

He had taken his courage in both hands in coming at all. In spite of his brave words to Maggie, he had been conscious of a curious repulsion with regard to the whole matter—a repulsion not only of contempt towards the elaborate affectations of the woman he had determined to consult. Yet he had come.

What he had said just now had been perfectly true. He was not yet in the least convinced, but he was anxious, intensely and passionately anxious, goaded too by desire.

Ah! surely it was absurd and fantastic—here in London, in this century. He turned and faced the lamp-lit room, letting his eyes wander round the picture-hung walls, the blue stamped paper, the Empire furniture, the general appearance of beautiful comfort and sane modern life. It was absurd and fantastic; he would be disappointed again, as he had been disappointed in everything else. These things did not happen—the dead did not return. Step by step those things that for centuries had been deemed evidence of the supernatural, one by one had been explained and discounted. Hypnotism, water-divining, witchcraft, and the rest. All these had once been believed to be indisputable proofs of a life beyond the grave, of strange supernormal personalities, and these, one by one, had been either accounted for or discredited. It was mad of him to be alarmed or excited. No, he would go through with it, expecting nothing, hoping nothing. But he would just go through with it to satisfy himself. . . .

The door opened, and the two ladies came in.

"I am delighted that you called, Mr. Baxter; and on such an errand!"

Lady Laura put out a hand, tremulous with pleasure at welcoming a possible disciple.

"Mrs. Stapleton has explained—" began Laurie.

"I understand everything. You come as a sceptic—no, not as a sceptic, but as an inquirer, that is all that we wish. . . . Then tomorrow, at about half-past four."

Chapter 4

It was a mellow October afternoon, glowing towards sunset, as Laurie came across the south end of the park to his appointment next day; and the effect of it upon his mind was singularly unsuggestive of supernatural mystery. Instead, rather, the warm sky, the lights beginning to peep here and there, though an hour before sunset, turned him rather in the direction of the natural and the domestic.

He wondered what his mother and Maggie would say if they knew his errand, for he had sufficient self-control not to have told them of his intentions. As regards his mother he did not care very much. Of course, she would deprecate it and feebly dissuade; but he recognised that there was no particular principle behind, beyond a sense of discomfort at the unknown. But it was necessary for him to argue with himself about Maggie. The angry kind of contempt that he knew she would feel needed an answer; and he gave it by reminding himself that she had been brought up in a convent-school, that she knew nothing of the world, and that, lastly, he himself did not take the matter seriously. He was aware, too, that the instinctive repulsion that she felt so keenly found a certain echo in his own feelings; but he explained this by the novelty of the thing.

In fact, the attitude of mind in which he more or less succeeded in arraying himself was that of one who goes to see a serious conjurer. It would be rather fun, he thought, to see a table dancing. But there was not wholly wanting that inexplicable tendency of some natures deliberately to deceive themselves on what lies nearest to their hearts.

Mr. Vincent had not yet arrived when he was shown upstairs, even though Laurie himself was late. (This was partly deliberate. He thought it best to show a little nonchalance.) There was only a young clergyman in the room with the ladies; and the two were introduced.

"Mr. Baxter—Mr. Jamieson."

He seemed a harmless young man, thought Laurie, and plainly a little nervous at the situation in which he found himself, as might a greyhound carry himself in a kennel of well-bred foxhounds. He was very correctly dressed, with Roman collar and stock, and obviously had not long left a theological college. He had an engaging kind of courtesy, ecclesiastically cut features, and curly black hair. He sat balancing a delicate cup adroitly on his knee.

"Mr. Jamieson is so anxious to know all that is going on," explained Lady Laura, with a voluble frankness. "He thinks it so necessary to be abreast of the times, as he said to me the other day."

Laurie assented, grimly pitying the young man for his indiscreet confidences. The clergyman looked priggish in his efforts not to do so.

"He has a class of young men on Sundays," continued the hostess—"(Another biscuit, Maud darling?)—whom he tries to interest in all modern movements. He thinks it so important."

Mr. Jamieson cleared his throat in a virile manner.

"Just so," he said; "exactly so."

"And so, I told him he must really come and meet Mr. Vincent. . . . I can't think why he is so late; but he has so many calls upon his time, that I am sure I wonder—"

"Mr. Vincent," announced the footman.

A rather fine figure of a man came forward into the room, dressed in much better taste than Laurie somehow had expected, and not at all like the type of an insane dissenting minister in broadcloth which he had feared. Instead, it was a big man that he saw, stooping a little, inclined to stoutness, with a full curly beard tinged with grey, rather overhung brows, and a high forehead, from which the same kind of curly greyish hair was beginning to retreat. He was in a well-cut frock-coat and dark trousers, with the collar of the period and a dark tie.

Lady Laura was in a flutter of welcome, pouring out little sentences, leading him to a seat, introducing him, and finally pressing refreshments into his hands.

"It is too good of you," she said; "too good of you, with all your engagements. . . .These gentlemen are most anxious. . . . Mrs. Stapleton of course you know. . . . And you will just sit and talk to us . . . like friends . . . won't you. . . . No, no! no formal speech at all . . . just a few words . . . and you will allow us to ask you questions. . . ."

And so on.

Meanwhile Laurie observed the high-priest carefully and narrowly, and was quite unable to see any of the unpleasant qualities he had expected. He sat easily, without self-consciousness or arrogance or unpleasant humility. He had a pair of pleasant, shrewd, and rather kind eyes; and his voice, when he said a word or two in answer to Lady Laura's volubility, was of that resonant softness that is always a delight to hear. In fact, his whole bearing and personality was that of a rather exceptional average man—a publisher, it might be, or a retired lawyer—a family man with a sober round of life and ordinary duties, who brought to their fulfilment a wholesome, kindly, but distinctly strong character of his own. Laurie hardly knew whether he was pleased or disappointed. He would almost have preferred a wild creature with rolling eyes, in a cloak; yet he would have been secretly amused and contemptuous at such a man.

"The sitting is off for Sunday, by the way, Lady Laura," said the newcomer.

"Indeed! How is that?"

"Oh! there was some mistake about the rooms; it's the secretary's fault; you mustn't blame me."

Lady Laura cried out her dismay and disappointment, and Mrs. Stapleton played chorus. It was *too* tiresome, they said, too provoking, particularly just now, when "Annie" was so complacent. (Mrs. Stapleton explained kindly to the two young gentlemen that "Annie" was a spirit who had lately made various very interesting revelations.) What was to be done? Were there no other rooms?

Mr. Vincent shook his head. It was too late, he said, to make arrangements now.

While the ladies continued to buzz, and Mr. Jamieson to listen from the extreme edge of his chair, Laurie continued to make mental comments. He felt distinctly puzzled by the marked difference between the prophet and his disciples. These were so shallow; this so impressive by the most ordinary of all methods, and the most difficult of imitation, that is, by sheer human personality. He could not grasp the least common multiple of the two sides. Yet this man tolerated these women, and, indeed, seemed very kind and friendly towards them. He seemed to possess that sort of competence which rises from the fact of having well-arranged ideas and complete certitude about them.

And at last a pause came. Mr. Vincent set down his cup for the second time, refused buttered bun, and waited.

"Yes, do smoke, Mr. Vincent."

The man drew out his cigarette-case, smiling, offering it to the two men. Laurie took one; the clergyman refused.

"And now, Mr. Vincent."

Again, he smiled, in a half-embarrassed way.

"But no speeches, I think you said," he remarked.

"Oh! well, you know what I mean; just like friends, you know. Treat us all like that."

(Mrs. Stapleton rose, came nearer the circle, rustled down again, and sank into an elaborate silence.)

"Well, what is it these gentlemen wish to hear?"

"Everything—everything," cried Lady Laura. "They claim to know nothing at all."

Laurie thought it time to explain himself a little. He felt he would not like to take this man at an unfair advantage.

"I should just like to say this," he said. "I have told Mrs. Stapleton already. It is this. I must confess that so far as I am concerned I am not a believer. But neither am I a sceptic. I am just a real agnostic in this matter. I have read several books; and I have been impressed. But there's a great deal in them that seems to me nonsense; perhaps I had better say which I don't understand. This materialising business, for instance. . . . I can understand that the minds of the dead can affect ours; but I don't see how they can affect matter—in table-rapping, for instance, and still more in appearing, and our being able to touch and see them. . . . I think that's my position," he ended rather lamely.

The fact was that he was a little disconcerted by the other's eyes. They were, as I have said, kind and shrewd eyes, but they had a good deal of power as well. Mr. Vincent sat motionless during this little

160

speech, just looking at him, not at all offensively, yet with the effect of making the young man feel rather like a defiant and naughty little boy who is trying to explain.

Laurie sat back and drew on his cigarette rather hard.

"I understand perfectly," said the steady voice. "You are in a very reasonable position. I wish all were as open-minded. May I say a word or two?"

"Please."

"Well, it is materialisation that puzzles you, is it?"

"Exactly," said Laurie. "Our theologians tell us. By the way, I am a Catholic." (The other bowed a little.) "Our theologians, I believe, tell us that such a thing cannot be, except under peculiar circumstances, as in the lives of the saints, and so on."

"Are you bound to believe all that your theologians say?" asked the other quietly.

"Well, it would be very rash indeed" began Laurie.

"Exactly, I see. But what if you approach it from the other side, and try to find out instead whether these things actually do happen. I do not wish to be rude, Mr. Baxter; but you remember that your theologians—I am not so foolish as to say the Church, for I know that that was not so—but your theologians, you know, made a mistake about Galileo."

Laurie winced a little. Mr. Jamieson cleared his throat in gentle approval.

"Now I don't ask you to accept anything contrary to your faith," went on the other gently; "but if you really wish to look into this matter, you must set aside for the present all other presuppositions. You must not begin by assuming that the theologians are always right, nor even in asking how or why these things should happen. The one point is, *do they happen?*"

His last words had a curious little effect as of a sudden flame. He had spoken smoothly and quietly; then he had suddenly put an unexpected emphasis into the little sentence at the end. Laurie jumped, internally. Yes, that was the point, he assented internally.

"Now," went on the other, again in that slow, reassuring voice, flicking off the ash of his cigarette, "is it possible for you to doubt that these things happen? May I ask you what books you have read?"

Laurie named three or four.

"And they have not convinced you?"

"Not altogether."

"Yet you accept human evidence for a great many much more remarkable things than these—as a Catholic."

"That is Divine Revelation," said Laurie, sure of his ground.

"Pardon me," said the other. "I do not in the least say it is not Divine Revelation—that is another question—but you receive the statement that it is so, on the word of man. Is that not true?"

Laurie was silent. He did not quite know what to say; and he almost feared the next words. But he was astonished that the other did not press home the point.

"Think over that, Mr. Baxter. That is all I ask. And now for the real thing. You sincerely wish to be convinced?"

"I am ready to be convinced."

The medium paused an instant, looking intently at the fire. Then he tossed the stump of his cigarette away and lighted another. The two ladies sat motionless.

"You seem fond of a *priori* arguments, Mr. Baxter," he began, with a kindly smile. "Let us have one or two, then.

"Consider first the relation of your soul to your body. That is infinitely mysterious, is it not? An emotion rises in your soul, and a flush of blood marks it. That is the subconscious mechanism of your body. But to say that, does not explain it. It is only a label. You follow me? Yes? Or still more mysterious is your conscious power. You will to raise your hand, and it obeys. Muscular action? Oh yes; but that is but another label." (He turned his eyes, suddenly sombre, upon the staring, listening young man, and his voice rose a little.) "Go right behind all that, Mr. Baxter, down to the mysteries. What is that link between soul and body? You do not know! Nor does the wisest scientist in the world. Nor ever will. Yet there the link is!"

Again, he paused.

Laurie was aware of a rising half-excited interest far beyond the power of the words he heard. Yet the manner of these too was striking. It was not the sham mysticism he had expected. There was a certain reverence in them, an admitting of mysteries, that seemed hard to reconcile with the ideas he had formed of the dogmatism of these folk.

"Now begin again," continued the quiet, virile voice. "You believe, as a Christian, in the immortality of the soul, in the survival of personality after death. Thank God for that! All do not, in these days. Then I need not labour at that.

"Now, Mr. Baxter, imagine to yourself some soul that you have loved passionately, who has crossed over to the other side." (Laurie drew a long, noiseless breath, steadying himself with clenched hands.) "She has come to the unimaginable glories, according to her measure; she is at an end of doubts and fears and suspicions. She knows because she sees. . . . But do you think that she is absorbed in these things? You know nothing of human love, Mr. Baxter" (the voice trembled with genuine emotion) . . . if you can think that! . . . . If you can think that her thought turns only to herself and her joys. Why, her life has been lived in your love by our hypothesis—you were at her bedside when she died, perhaps; and she clung to you as to God Himself, when the shadow deepened.

"Do you think that her first thought, or at least her second, will not be of you? . . . . In all that she sees, she will desire you to see it also. She will strive, crave, hunger for you—not that she may possess you, but that you may be one with her in her own possession; she will send out vibration after vibration of sympathy and longing; and you, on this side, will be tuned to her as none other can be—you, on this side, will be empty for her love, for the sight and sound of her. . . . Is death then so strong?—stronger than love? Can a Christian believe that?"

The change in the man was extraordinary. His heavy beard and brows hid half his face, but his whole being glowed passionately in his voice, even in his little trembling gestures, and Laurie sat astonished. Every word uttered seemed to fit his own case, to express by an almost perfect vehicle the vague thoughts that had struggled in his own heart during this last week. It was Amy of whom the man spoke, Amy with her eyes and hair, peering from the glorious gloom to catch some glimpse of her lover in his meaningless light of earthly day.

Mr. Vincent cleared his throat a little, and at the sound the two motionless women stirred and rustled a little. The sound of a hansom, the spanking trot and wintry jingle of bells swelled out of the distance, passed, and went into silence before he spoke again. Then it was in his usual slow voice that he continued.

"Conceive such a soul as that, Mr. Baxter. She desires to communicate with one she loves on earth, with you or me, and it is a human and innocent desire. Yet she has lost that connection, that machinery of which we have spoken—that connection of which we know nothing, between matter and spirit, except that it exists. What is she to do? Well, at least she will do this, she will bend every power that she possesses upon that medium—I mean matter—through which alone the communication can be made; as a man on an island, beyond the power of a human voice, will use any instrument, however grotesque, to signal to a passing ship. Would any decent man, Mr. Baxter, mock at the pathos and effort of that, even if it were some grotesque thing, like a flannel shirt on the end of an oar? Yet men mock at the tapping of a table! . . .

"Well, then, this longing soul uses every means at her disposal, concentrates every power she possesses. Is it so very unreasonable, so very unchristian, so very dishonouring to the love of God, to think that she sometimes succeeds? . . . that she is able, under comparatively exceptional circumstances, to re-establish that connection with material things, that was perfectly normal and natural to her during her earthly life. . . . Tell me, Mr. Baxter."

Laurie shifted a little in his chair.

"I cannot say that it does," he said, in a voice that seemed strange in his own ears. The medium smiled a little.

"So much for a *priori* reasoning," he said. "There remains only the fact whether such things do happen or not. There I must leave you to yourself, Mr. Baxter."

Laurie sat forward suddenly.

"But that is exactly where I need your help, sir," he said.

A murmur broke from the ladies' lips simultaneously, resembling applause. Mr. Jamieson sat back and swallowed perceptibly in his throat.

"You have said so much, sir," went on Laurie deliberately, "that you have, so to speak, put yourself in my debt. I must ask you to take me further."

Mr. Vincent smiled full at him.

"You must take your place with others," he said. "These ladies—"

"Mr. Vincent, Mr. Vincent," cried Lady Laura. "He is quite right, you must help him. You must help us all."

"Well, Sunday week," he began deprecatingly.

Mrs. Stapleton broke in.

"No, no; now, Mr. Vincent, now. Do something now. Surely the circumstances are favourable."

"I must be gone again at six-thirty," said the man hesitatingly.

Laurie broke in. He felt desperate.

"If you can show me anything of this, sir, you can surely show it now. If you do not show it now—"

"Well, Mr. Baxter?" put in the voice, sharp and incisive, as if expecting an insult and challenging it.

Laurie broke down.

"I can only say," he cried, "that I beg and entreat of you to do what

164

you can—now and here."

There was a silence.

"And you, Mr. Jamieson?"

The young clergyman started, as if from a daze. Then he rose abruptly.

"I—I must be going, Lady Laura," he said. "I had no idea it was so late. I—I have a confirmation class."

An instant later he was gone.

"That is as well," observed the medium. "And you are sure, Mr. Baxter, that you wish me to try? You must remember that I promise nothing."

"I wish you to try."

"And if nothing happens?"

"If nothing happens, I will promise to—to continue my search. I shall know then that—that it is at least sincere."

Mr. Vincent rose to his feet.

"A little table just here, Lady Laura, if you please, and a pencil and paper. . . . Will you kindly take your seats? . . . Yes, Mr. Baxter, draw up your chair . . . here. Now, please, we must have complete silence, and, so far as possible, silence of thought."

★★★★★★

The table, a small, round rosewood one, stood, bare of any cloth, upon the hearthrug. The two ladies sat, motionless statues once more, upon the side furthest from the fire, with their hands resting lightly upon the surface. Laurie sat on one side and the medium on the other. Mr. Vincent had received his paper and pencil almost immediately, and now sat resting his right hand with the pencil upon the paper as if to write, his left hand upon his knee as he sat, turned away slightly from the centre.

Laurie looked at him closely. , . .

And now he began to be aware of a certain quite indefinable change in the face at which he looked. The eyes were open—no, it was not in them that the change lay, nor in the lines about the mouth, so far as he could see them, nor any detail, anywhere. Neither was it the face of a dreamer or a sleepwalker, or of the dead, when the lines disappear and life retires. It was a living, conscious face, yet it was changed. The lips were slightly parted, and the breath came evenly between them. It was more like the face of one lost in deep, absorbed, introspective thought. Laurie decided that this was the explanation.

He looked at the hand on the paper—well shaped, brownish, capable—perfectly motionless, the pencil held lightly between the finger and thumb.

Then he glanced up at the two ladies.

They too were perfectly motionless, but there was no change in them. The eyes of both were downcast, fixed steadily upon the paper. And as he looked he saw Lady Laura begin to lift her lids slowly as if to glance at him. He looked himself upon the paper and the motionless fingers.

He was astonished at the speed with which the situation had developed. Five minutes ago, he had been listening to talk, and joining in it. The clergyman had been here; he himself had been sitting a yard further back. Now they sat here as if they had sat for an hour. It seemed that the progress of events had stopped. . . .

Then he began to listen for the sounds of the world outside, for within here it seemed as if a silence of a very strange quality had suddenly descended and enveloped them. It was as if a section—that place in which he sat—had been cut out of time and space. It was apart here, it was different altogether. . . .

He began to be intensely and minutely conscious of the world outside—so entirely conscious that he lost all perception of that at which he stared; whether it was the paper, or the strong, motionless hand, or the introspective face, he was afterwards unaware. But he heard all the quiet roar of the London evening, and was able to distinguish even the note of each instrument that helped to make up that untiring, inconclusive orchestra. Far away to the northwards sounded a great thoroughfare, the rolling of wheels, a myriad hoofs, the pulse of motor vehicles, and the cries of street boys; upon all these his attention dwelt as they came up through the outward windows into that dead silent, lamp-lit room of which he had lost consciousness. Again a hansom came up the street, with the rap of hoofs, the swish of a whip, the wintry jingle of bells. . . .

He began gently to consider these things, to perceive, rather than to form, little inward pictures of what they signified; he saw the lighted omnibus, the little swirl of faces round a news-board.

Then he began to consider what had brought him here; it seemed that he saw himself, coming in his dark suit across the park, turning into the thoroughfare and across it. He began to consider Amy; and it seemed to him that in this intense and living silence he was conscious of her for the first time without sorrow since ten days ago. He began to consider.

166

Something brought him back in an instant to the room and his perception of it, but he had not an idea what this was, whether a movement or a sound. But on considering it afterwards he remembered that it was as that sound is that wakes a man at the very instant of his falling asleep, a sharp momentary tick, as of a clock. Yet he had not been in the least sleepy.

On the contrary, he perceived now with an extreme and alert attention the hand on the paper; he even turned his head slightly to see if the pencil had moved. It was as motionless as at the beginning.

He glanced up, with a touch of surprise, at his hostess's face, and caught her in the very act of turning her eyes from his. There was no impatience in her movement: rather her face was of one absorbed, listening intently, not like the bearded face opposite, introspective and intuitive, but eagerly, though motionlessly, observant of the objective world. He looked at Mrs. Stapleton. She too bore the same expression of intent regarding thought on her usually rather tiresome face.

Then once again the silence began to come down, like a long, noiseless hush.

This time, however, his progress was swifter and more sure. He passed with the speed of thought through those processes that had been measurable before, faintly conscious of the words spoken before the sitting began—

". . . If possible, the silence of thought."

He thought he understood now what this signified, and that he was experiencing it. No longer did he dwell upon, or consider, with any voluntary activity, the images that passed before him. Rather they moved past him while he simply regarded them without understanding. His perception ran swiftly outwards, as through concentric circles, yet he was not sure whether it were outwards or inwards that he went. The roar of London, with its flight of ocular visions, sank behind him, and without any further sense of mental travel, he found himself perceiving his own home, whether in memory, imagination, or fact he did not know. But he perceived his mother, in the familiar lamp-lit room, over her needlework, and Maggie—Maggie looking at him with a strange, almost terrified expression in her great eyes. Then these too were gone; and he was out in some warm silence, filled with a single presence—that which he desired; and there he stopped.

He was not in the least aware of how long this lasted. But he found himself at a certain moment in time, looking steadily at the white paper on the table, from which the hand had gone, again conscious of the sudden passing of some clear sound that left no echo—as sharp as the crack of a whip. Oh! the paper—that was the important point! He bent a little closer, and was aware of a sharp disappointment as he saw it was stainless of writing. Then he was astonished that the hand and pencil had gone from it, and looked up quickly.

Mr. Vincent was looking at him with a strange expression.

At first, he thought he might have interrupted, and wondered with dismay whether this were so. But there was no sign of anger in those eyes—nothing but a curious and kindly interest.

"Nothing happened?" he exclaimed hastily. "You have written nothing?"

He looked at the ladies.

Lady Laura too was looking at him with the same strange interest as the medium. Mrs. Stapleton, he noticed, was just folding up, in an unobtrusive manner, several sheets of paper that he had not noticed before.

He felt a little stiff, and moved as if to stand up; but, to his astonishment, the big man was up in an instant, laying his hands on his shoulders.

"Just sit still quietly for a few minutes," said the kindly voice. "Just sit still."

"Why—why—" began Laurie, bewildered.

"Yes, just sit still quietly," went on the voice; "you feel a little tired."

"Just a little," said Laurie. "But—"

"Yes, yes; just sit still. No; don't speak."

Then a silence fell again.

Laurie began to wonder what this was all about. Certainly, he felt tired, yet strangely elated. But he felt no inclination to move; and sat back, passive, looking at his own hands on his knees. But he was disappointed that nothing had happened.

Then the thought of time came into his mind. He supposed that it would be about ten minutes past six. The sitting had begun a little before six. He glanced up at the clock on the mantelpiece; but it was one of those bulgy-faced Empire gilt affairs that display everything except the hour. He still waited a moment, feeling all this to be very unusual and unconventional. Why should he sit here like an invalid, and why should these three sit here and watch him so closely?

He shifted a little in his chair, feeling that an effort was due from him. The question of the time of day struck him as a suitably conventional remark with which to break the embarrassing silence.

"What is the time?" he said. "I am afraid I ought to be—"

"There is plenty of time," said the grave voice across the table.

With a sudden movement Laurie was on his feet, peering at the clock, knowing that something was wrong somewhere. Then he turned to the company bewildered and suspicious.

"Why, it is nearly eight," he cried.

Mr. Vincent smiled reassuringly.

"It is about that," he said. "Please sit down again, Mr. Baxter."

"But—but—" began Laurie.

"Please sit down again, Mr. Baxter," repeated the voice, with a touch of imperiousness that there was no resisting.

Laurie sat down again; but he was alert, suspicious, and intensely puzzled.

"Will you kindly tell me what has happened?" he asked sharply.

"You feel tired?"

"No; I am all right. Kindly tell me what has happened."

He saw Lady Laura whisper something in an undertone he could not hear. Mr. Vincent stood up with a nod and leaned himself against the mantelpiece, looking down at the rather indignant young man.

"Certainly," he said. "You are sure you are not exhausted, Mr. Baxter?"

"Not in the least," said Laurie.

"Well, then, you passed into trance about five minutes—"

"*What?*"

"You passed into trance about five minutes past six; you came out of it five minutes ago."

"Trance?" gasped Laurie.

"Certainly. A very deep and satisfactory trance. There is nothing to be frightened of, Mr. Baxter. It is an unusual gift, that is all. I have seldom seen a more satisfactory instance. May I ask you a question or two, sir?"

Laurie nodded vaguely. He was still trying hopelessly to take in what had been said.

"You nearly passed into trance a little earlier. May I ask whether you heard or saw anything that recalled you?"

Laurie shut his eyes tight in an effort to think. He felt dimly rather proud of himself.

"It was quite short. Then you came back and looked at Lady Laura. Try to remember."

169

"I remember thinking I had heard a sound."

The medium nodded.

"Just so," he said.

"That would be the third," said Lady Laura, nodding sagely.

"Third what?" said Laurie rather rudely.

No one paid any attention to him.

"Now can you give any account of the last hour and a half?" continued the medium tranquilly.

Laurie considered again. He was still a little confused.

"I remember thinking about the streets," he said, "and then of my own home, and then—"

He stopped.

"Yes; and then?"

"Then of a certain private matter."

"Ah! We must not pry then. But can you answer one question more? Was it connected with any person who has crossed over?"

"It was," said Laurie shortly.

"Just so," said the medium.

Laurie felt suspicious.

"Why do you ask that?" he said.

Mr. Vincent looked at him steadily.

"I think I had better tell you, Mr. Baxter; it is more straightforward, though you will not like it. You will be surprised to hear that you talked very considerably during this hour and a half; and from all that you said I should suppose you were controlled by a spirit recently crossed over—a young girl who on being questioned gave the name of Amy Nugent—"

Laurie sprang to his feet, furious.

"You have been spying, sir. How dare you—"

"Sit down, Mr. Baxter, or you shall not hear a word more," rang out the imperious, unruffled voice. "Sit down this instant."

Laurie shot a look at the two ladies. Then he remembered himself. He sat down.

"I am not at all angry, Mr. Baxter," came the voice, suave and kindly again. "Your thought was very natural. But I think I can prove to you that you are mistaken."

Mr. Vincent glanced at Mrs. Stapleton with an almost imperceptible frown, then back at Laurie.

"Let me see, Mr. Baxter. . . . Is there anyone on earth besides yourself who knew that you had sat out, about ten days ago or so, under some yew trees in your garden at home, and thought of this young girl —that you—"

Laurie looked at him in dumb dismay; some little sound broke from his mouth.

"Well, is that enough, Mr. Baxter?"

Lady Laura slid in a sentence here.

"Dear Mr. Baxter, you need not be in the least alarmed. All that has passed here is, of course, as sacred as in the confessional. We should not dream, without your leave—"

"One moment," gasped the boy.

He drove his face into his hands and sat overwhelmed.

Presently he looked up.

"But *I* knew it," he said. "*I* knew it. It was just my own self which spoke."

The medium smiled.

"Yes," he said, "of course that is the first answer." He placed one hand on the table, leaning forward, and began to play his fingers as if on a piano. Laurie watched the movement, which seemed vaguely familiar.

"Can you account for that, Mr. Baxter? You did that several times. It seemed uncharacteristic of you, somehow."

Laurie looked at him, mute. He remembered now. He half raised a hand in protest.

"And . . . and do you ever stammer?" went on the man.

Still Laurie was silent. It was beyond belief or imagination.

"Now if those things were characteristic—"

"Stop, sir," cried the boy; and then, "But those too might be unconscious imitation."

"They might," said the other. "But then we had the advantage of watching you. And there were other things."

"I beg your pardon?"

"There was the loud continuous rapping, at the beginning and the end. You were awakened twice by these."

Laurie remained perfectly motionless without a word. He was still striving to marshal this flood of mad ideas. It was incredible, amazing.

Then he stood up.

"I must go away," he said. "I—I don't know what to think."

"You had better stay a little longer and rest," said the medium kindly.

The boy shook his head.

"I must go at once," he said. "I cannot trust myself."

He went out without a word, followed by the medium. The two ladies sat eyeing one another.

"It has been astonishing . . . astonishing," sighed Mrs. Stapleton. "What a find!"

There was no more said. Lady Laura sat as one in trance herself.

Then Mr. Vincent returned.

"You must not lose sight of that young man," he said abruptly. "It is an extraordinary case."

"I have all the notes here," remarked Mrs. Stapleton.

"Yes; you had better keep them. He must not see them at present."

Chapter 5

As the weeks went by Maggie's faint uneasiness disappeared. She was one of those fortunate persons who, possessing what are known as nerves, are aware of the possession, and discount their effects accordingly.

That uneasiness had culminated a few days after Laurie's departure one evening as she sat with the old lady after tea—in a sudden touch of terror at she knew not what.

"What is the matter, my dear?" the old lady had said without warning.

Maggie was reading, but it appeared that Mrs. Baxter had noticed her lower her book suddenly, with an odd expression.

Maggie had blinked a moment.

"Nothing," she said. "I was just thinking of Laurie; I don't know why."

But since then she had been able to reassure herself. Her fancies were but fancies, she told herself; and they had ceased to trouble her. The boy's letters to his mother were ordinary and natural: he was reading fairly hard; his coach was as pleasant a person as he had seemed; he hoped to run down to Stantons for a few days at Christmas. There was nothing whatever to alarm anyone; plainly his ridiculous attitude about Spiritualism had been laid by; and, better still, he was beginning to recover himself after his sorrow in September.

It was an extraordinarily peaceful and uneventful life that the two led together—the kind of life that strengthens previous proclivities and adds no new ones; that brings out the framework of character and motive as dropping water clears the buried roots of a tree. This was all very well for Mrs. Baxter, whose character was already fully formed, it may be hoped; but not so utterly satisfactory for the girl, though the process was pleasant enough.

After Mass and breakfast, she spent the morning as she wished, overseeing little extra details of the house—gardening plans, the poultry, and so forth—and reading what she cared to. The afternoon was devoted to the old lady's airing; the evening till dinner to anything she wished; and after dinner again to gentle conversation. Very little happened. The vicar and his wife dined there occasionally, and still more occasionally Father Mahon. Now and then there were vague entertainments to be patronised in the village schoolroom, in an atmosphere of ink and hair-oil; and a mild amount of rather dreary and stately gaiety connected with the big houses round. Mrs. Baxter occasionally put in appearances, a dignified and aristocratic old figure with her gentle eyes and black lace veil; and Maggie went with her.

The pleasure of this life grew steadily upon Maggie. She was one of that fraction of the world that finds entertainment to lie, like the kingdom of God, within. She did not in the least wish to be "amused" or stimulated and distracted. She was perfectly and serenely content with the fowls, the garden, her small selected tasks, her religion, and herself.

The result was, as it always is in such cases, she began to revolve about three or four main lines of thought, and to make a very fair progress in the knowledge of herself. She knew her faults quite well; and she was not unaware of her virtues. She knew perfectly that she was apt to give way to internal irritation, of a strong though invisible kind, when interruptions happened; that she now and then gave way to an unduly fierce contempt of tiresome people, and said little bitter things that she afterwards regretted. She also knew that she was quite courageous, that she had magnificent physical health, and that she could be perfectly content with a life that a good many other people would find narrow and stifling.

Her own character then was one thing that she had studied—not in the least in a morbid way—during her life at Stantons. And another thing she was beginning to study, rather to her own surprise, was the character of Laurie. She began to become a little astonished at the frequency with which, during a silent drive, or some mild mechanical labour in the gardens, the image of that young man would rise before her.

Indeed, as has been said, she had new material to work on. She had not realised till the *affaire* Amy that boy's astonishing selfishness; and it became for her a rather pleasant psychological exercise to build up his characteristics into a consistent whole. It had not struck her, till this specimen came before her notice, how generosity and egotism, for example, so far from being mutually exclusive, can very easily be complements, each of the other.

So then she passed her days—exteriorly a capable and occupied person, interested in half a dozen simple things; interiorly rather introspective, rather scrupulous, and intensely interested in the watching of two characters—her own and her adopted brother's. Mrs. Baxter's character needed no dissection; it was a consistent whole, clear as crystal and as rigid.

It was still some five weeks before Christmas that Maggie became aware of what, as a British maiden, she ought, of course, to have known long before—namely, that she was thinking just a little too much about a young man who, so far as was apparent, thought nothing at all about her. It was true that once he had passed through a period of sentimentality in her regard; but the extreme discouragement it had met with had been enough.

Her discovery happened in this way.

Mrs. Baxter opened a letter one morning, smiling contentedly to herself.

"From Laurie," she said. Maggie ceased eating toast for a second, to listen.

Then the old lady uttered a small cry of dismay.

"He thinks he can't come, after all," she said.

Maggie had a moment of very acute annoyance.

"What does he say? Why not?" she asked.

There was a pause. She watched Mrs. Baxter's lips moving slowly, her glasses in place; saw the page turned, and turned again. She took another piece of toast. There are few things more irritating than to have fragments of a letter doled out piecemeal.

"He doesn't say. He just says he's very busy indeed, and has a great deal of way to make up." The old lady continued reading tranquilly, and laid the letter down.

"Nothing more?" asked Maggie, consumed with annoyance.

"He's been to the theatre once or twice. . . . Dear Laurie! I'm glad he's recovering his spirits."

Maggie was very angry indeed. She thought it abominable of the boy to treat his mother like that. And then there was the shooting—not much, indeed, beyond the rabbits, which the man who acted as occasional keeper told her wanted thinning, and a dozen or two of wild pheasants—yet this shooting had always been done, she understood, at Christmas, ever since Master Laurie had been old enough to hold a gun.

She determined to write him a letter.

When breakfast was over, with a resolved face she went to her room. She would really tell this boy a home-truth or two. It was a—a sister's place to do so. The mother, she knew well enough, would do no more than send a little wail, and would end by telling the dear boy that, of course, he knew best, and that she was very happy to think that he was taking such pains about his studies. Someone must point out to the boy his overwhelming selfishness, and it seemed that no one was at hand but herself. Therefore, she would do it.

She did it, therefore, politely enough but unmistakably; and as it was a fine morning, she thought that she would like to step up to the village and post it. She did not want to relent; and once the letter was in the post-box, the thing would be done.

It was, indeed, a delicious morning. As she passed out through the iron gate the trees overhead, still with a few brown belated leaves, soared up in filigree of exquisite workmanship into a sky of clear November blue, as fresh as a hedge-sparrow's egg. The genial sound of cock-crowing rose, silver and exultant, from the farm beyond the road, and the tiny street of the hamlet looked as clean as a Dutch picture.

She noticed on the right, just before she turned up to the village on the left, the grocer's shop, with the name "Nugent" in capitals as bright and flamboyant as on the depot of a merchant king. Mr. Nugent could be faintly descried within, in white shirt-sleeves and an apron, busied at a pile of cheeses. Overhead, three pairs of lace curtains, each decked with a blue bow, denoted the bedrooms. One of them must have been Amy's. She wondered which. . . .

All up the road to the village, some half-mile in length, she pondered Amy. She had never seen her, to her knowledge; but she had a tolerably accurate mental picture of her from Mrs. Baxter's account. . . .Ah! how could Laurie? How could he? . . . Laurie, of all people! It was just one more example. . . .

After dropping her letter into the box at the corner, she hesitated for an instant. Then, with an odd look on her face, she turned sharply aside to where the church tower pricked above the leafless trees.

It was a typical little country church, with that odour of the respectable and rather stuffy sanctity peculiar to the class; she had wrinkled her nose at it more than once in Laurie's company. But she passed by the door of it now, and, stepping among the wet grasses, came down the little slope among the headstones to where a very white marble angel clasped an equally white marble cross. She passed to the front of this, and looked, frowning a little over the intolerable taste of the thing.

The cross, she perceived, was wreathed with a spray of white marble ivory; the angel was a German female, with a very rounded leg emerging behind a kind of button; and there, at the foot of the cross, was the inscription, in startling black—

AMY NUGENT
THE DEAR AND ONLY DAUGHTER
OF
AMOS AND MARIA NUGENT
OF STANTONS
DIED SEPTEMBER 21ST 1901
RESPECTED BY ALL
"I SHALL SEE HER BUT NOT NOW."

Below, as vivid as the inscription, there stood out the maker's name, and of the town where he lived.

So, she lay there, reflected Maggie. It had ended in that. A mound of earth, cracking a little, and sunken. She lay there, her nervous fingers motionless and her stammer silent. And could there be a more eloquent monument of what she was? . . . Then she remembered herself, and signed herself with the cross, while her lips moved an instant for the repose of the poor girlish soul. Then she stepped up again on to the path to go home.

It was as she came near the church gate that she understood herself, that she perceived why she had come, and was conscious for the first time of her real attitude of soul as she had stood there, reading the inscription, and, in a flash, there followed the knowledge of the inevitable meaning of it all.

In a word it was this.

She had come there, she told herself, to triumph, to gloat. Oh! she spared herself nothing, as she stood there, crimson with shame, to gloat over the grave of a rival. Amy was nothing less than that, and she herself—she, Margaret Marie Deronnais—had given way to jealousy of this grocer's daughter, because . . . because . . . she had begun to care, really to care, for the man to whom she had written that letter this morning, and this man had scarcely said one word to her, or given her one glance, beyond such as a brother might give to a sister. There was the naked truth.

Her mind fled back. She understood a hundred things now. She perceived that that sudden anger at breakfast had been personal disappointment—not at all that lofty disinterestedness on behalf of the mother that she had pretended. She understood too, now, the meaning of those long contented meditations as she went up and down the garden walks, alert for plantains, the meaning of the zeal she had shown, only a week ago, on behalf of a certain hazel which the gardener wanted to cut down.

"You had better wait till Mr. Laurence comes home," she had said. "I think he once said he liked the tree to be just there."

She understood now why she had been so intuitive, so condemnatory, so critical of the boy—it was that she was passionately interested in him, that it was a pleasure even to abuse him to herself, to call him selfish and self-centred, that all this lofty disapproval was just the sop that her subconsciousness had used to quiet her uneasiness.

Little scenes rose before her— all passed almost in a flash of time— as she stood with her hand on the medieval-looking latch of the gate, and she saw herself in them all as a proud, unmaidenly, pharisaical prig, in love with a man who was not in love with her.

She made an effort, unlatched the gate, and moved on, a beautiful, composed figure, with great steady eyes and well-cut profile, a model of dignity and grace, interiorly a raging, self-contemptuous, abject wretch.

It must be remembered that she was convent-bred.

******

By the time that Laurie's answer came, poor Maggie had arranged her emotions fairly satisfactorily. She came to the conclusion, arrived at after much heart-searching, that after all she was not yet actually in love with Laurie, but was in danger of being so, and that therefore now that she knew the danger, and could guard against it, she need not actually withdraw from her home, and bury herself in a convent or the foreign mission-field.

She arrived at this astonishing conclusion by the following process of thought. It may be presented in the form of a syllogism.

All girls who are in love regard the beloved as a spotless, reproachless hero.

Maggie Deronnais did not regard Laurie Baxter as a spotless, reproachless hero.

Ergo. Maggie Deronnais was not in love with Laurie Baxter.

Strange as it may appear to non-Catholic readers, Maggie did not confide her complications to the ear of Father Mahon. She mentioned, no doubt, on the following Saturday, that she had given way to thoughts of pride and jealousy, that she had deceived herself with regard to a certain action, done really for selfish motives, into thinking she had done it for altruistic motives, and there she left it. And, no doubt, Father Mahon left it there too, and gave her absolution without hesitation.

Then Laurie's answer arrived, and had to be dealt with, that is, it had to be treated interiorly with a proper restraint of emotions. He wrote:

My dear Maggie,
Why all this fury? What have I done? I said to mother that I didn't know for certain whether I could come or not, as I had a lot to do. I don't think she can have given you the letter to read, or you wouldn't have written all that about my being away from home at the one season of the year, etc. Of course, I'll come, if you or anybody feels like that. Does mother feel upset too? Please tell me if she ever feels that, or is in the least unwell, or anything. I'll come instantly. As it is, shall we say the 20th of December, and I'll stay at least a week. Will that do?"
Yours,

L. B.

This was a little overwhelming, and Maggie wrote off a penitent letter, refraining carefully, however, from any expressions that might have anything of the least warmth, but saying that she was very glad he was coming, and that the shooting should be seen to.

She directed the letter; and then sat for an instant looking at Laurie's—at the neat Oxford-looking hand, the artistic appearance of the paragraphs, and all the rest of it.

She would have liked to keep it—to put it with half a dozen others she had from him; but it seemed better not.

Then as she tore it up into careful strips, her conscience smote her again, shrewdly; and she drew out the top left-hand drawer of the table at which she sat.

There they were, a little pile of them, neat and orderly. She looked at them an instant; then she took them out, turned them quickly to see if all were there, and then, gathering up the strips of the one she had received that morning, went over to the wood fire and dropped them in.

It was better so, she said to herself.

The days went pleasantly enough after that. She would not for an instant allow to herself that any of their smoothness arose from the fact that this boy would be here again in a few weeks. On the contrary, it was because she had detected a weakness in his regard, she told herself, and had resolutely stamped on it, that she was in so serene a peace. She arranged about the shooting—that is to say, she informed the acting keeper that Master Laurie would be home for Christmas as usual—all in an unemotional manner, and went about her various affairs without effort.

She found Mrs. Baxter just a little trying now and then. That lady had come to the conclusion that Laurie was unhappy in his religion—certainly references to it had dropped out of his letters—and that Mr. Rymer must set it right.

"The vicar must dine here at least twice while Laurie is here," she observed at breakfast one morning. "He has a great influence with young men."

Maggie reflected upon a remark or two, extremely unjust, made by Laurie with regard to the clergyman.

"Do you think—do you think he understands Laurie," she said.

"He has known him for fifteen years," remarked Mrs. Baxter.

"Perhaps it's Laurie that doesn't understand him then," said Maggie tranquilly.

"I daresay."

"And—and what do you think Mr. Rymer will be able to do?" asked the girl.

"Just settle the boy. . . . I don't think Laurie's very happy. Not that I would willingly disturb his mind again; I don't mean that, my dear. I quite understand that your religion is just the one for certain temperaments, and Laurie's is one of them; but a few helpful words sometimes—" Mrs. Baxter left it at an aposiopesis, a form of speech she was fond of.

There was a grain of truth, Maggie thought, in the old lady's hints, and she helped herself in silence to marmalade. Laurie's letters, which she usually read, did not refer much to religion, or to the Brompton Oratory, as his custom had been at first. She tried to make up her mind that this was a healthy sign; that it showed that Laurie was settling down from that slight feverishness of zeal that seemed the inevitable atmosphere of most converts. Maggie found converts a little trying now and then; they would talk so much about facts, certainly undisputed, and for that very reason not to be talked about. Laurie had been a marked case, she remembered; he wouldn't let the thing alone, and his contempt of Anglican clergy, whom Maggie herself regarded with respect, was hard to understand. In fact she had remonstrated on the subject of the vicar. . . .

Maggie perceived that she was letting her thoughts run again on disputable lines; and she made a remark about the Balkan crisis so abruptly that Mrs. Baxter looked at her in bewilderment.

"You do jump about so, my dear. We were speaking of Laurie, were we not?"

"Yes," said Maggie.

"It's the twentieth he's coming on, is it not?"

"Yes," said Maggie.

"I wonder what train he'll come by?"

"I don't know," said Maggie.

A few days before Laurie's arrival she went to the greenhouse to see the chrysanthemums. There was an excellent show of them.

"Mrs. Baxter doesn't like them hairy ones," said the gardener.

"Oh! I had forgotten. Well, Ferris, on the nineteenth I shall want a big bunch of them. You'd better take those—those hairy ones. And some maidenhair. Is there plenty?"

"Yes, miss."

"Can you make a wreath, Ferris?"

"Yes, miss."

"Well, will you make a good wreath of them, please, for a grave? The morning of the twentieth will do. There'll be plenty left for the church and house?"

"Oh yes, miss."

"And for Father Mahon?"

"Oh yes, miss."

"Very well, then. Will you remember that? A good wreath, with fern, on the morning of the twentieth. If you'll just leave it here I'll call for it about twelve o'clock. You needn't send it up to the house."

"Very good, miss."

Chapter 6

Laurie was sitting in his room after breakfast, filling his briar pipe thoughtfully, and contemplating his journey to Stantons.

It was more than six weeks now since his experience in Queen's

Gate, and he had gone through a variety of emotions. Bewildered terror was the first, a nervous interest the next, a truculent scepticism the third; and lately, to his astonishment, the nervous interest had begun to revive.

At first, he had been filled with unreasoning fear. He had walked back as far as the gate of the park, hardly knowing where he went, conscious only that he must be in the company of his fellows; upon finding himself on the south side of Hyde Park Corner, where travellers were few, he had crossed over in nervous haste to where he might jostle human beings. Then he had dined in a restaurant, knowing that a band would be playing there, and had drunk a bottle of champagne; he had gone to his rooms, cheered and excited, and had leapt instantly into bed for fear that his courage should evaporate. For he was perfectly aware that fear, and a sickening kind of repulsion, formed a very large element in his emotions.

For nearly two hours, unless three persons had lied consummately, he—his essential being, that sleepless self that underlies all—had been in strange company, had become identified in some horrible manner with the soul of a dead person. It was as if he had been informed some morning that he had slept all night with a corpse under his bed. He woke half a dozen times that night in the pleasant curtained bedroom, and each time with the terror upon him. What if stories were true, and this Thing still haunted the air? It was remarkable, he considered afterwards, how the sign which he had demanded had not had the effect for which he had hoped. He was not at all reassured by it.

Then as the days went by, and he was left in peace, his horror began to pass. He turned the thing over in his mind a dozen times a day, and found it absorbing. But he began to reflect that, after all, he had nothing more than he had had before in the way of evidence. An hypnotic sleep might explain the whole thing. That little revelation he had made in his unconsciousness, of his sitting beneath the yews, might easily be accounted for by the fact that he himself knew it, that it had been a deeper element in his experience than he had known, and that he had told it aloud. It was no proof of anything more.

There remained the rapping and what the medium had called his "appearance" during the sleep; but of all this he had read before in books. Why should he be convinced any more now than he had been previously? Besides, it was surely doubtful, was it not, whether the rapping, if it had really taken place, might not be the normal cracks and sounds of woodwork, intensified in the attention of the listeners? or if it was more than this, was there any proof that it might not be produced in some way by the intense will-power of some living person present? This was surely conceivable—more conceivable, that is, than any other hypothesis. . . . Besides, what had it all got to do with Amy?

Within a week of his original experience, scepticism was dominant. These lines of thought did their work by incessant repetition. The normal life he lived, the large, business-like face of the lawyer whom he faced day by day, a theatre or two, a couple of dinners—even the noise of London streets and the appearance of workaday persons—all these gradually reassured him.

When therefore he received a nervous little note from Lady Laura, reminding him of the seance to be held in Baker Street, and begging his attendance, he wrote a most proper letter back again, thanking her for her kindness, but saying that he had come to the conclusion that this kind of thing was not good for him or his work, and begging her to make his excuses to Mr. Vincent.

A week or two passed, and nothing whatever happened. Then he heard again from Lady Laura, and again he answered by a polite refusal, adding a little more as to his own state of mind; and again, silence fell.

Then at last Mr. Vincent called on him in person one evening after dinner.

Laurie's rooms were in Mitre Court, very convenient to the Temple—two rooms opening into one another, and communicating with the staircase.

He had played a little on his grand piano, that occupied a third of his sitting-room, and had then dropped off to sleep before his fire. He awakened suddenly to see the big man standing almost over him, and sat up confusedly.

"I beg your pardon, Mr. Baxter; the porter's boy told me to come straight up. I found your outer door open."

Laurie hastened to welcome him, to set him down in a deep chair, to offer whisky and to supply tobacco. There was something about this man that commanded deference.

"You know why I have come, I expect," said the medium, smiling.

Laurie smiled back, a little nervously.

"I have come to see whether you will not reconsider your decision."

The boy shook his head.

"I think not," he said.

"You found no ill effects, I hope, from what happened at Lady

Laura's?"

"Not at all, after the first shock."

"Doesn't that reassure you at all, Mr. Baxter?"

Laurie hesitated.

"It's like this," he said; "I'm not really convinced. I don't see any-thing final in what happened."

"Will you explain, please?"

Laurie set the results of his meditations forth at length. There was nothing, he said, that could not be accounted for by a very abnormal state of subjectivity. The fact that this . . . this young person's name was in his mind . . . and so forth. . . .

". . . And I find it rather distracting to my work," he ended. "Please don't think me rude or ungrateful, Mr. Vincent."

(He thought he was being very strong and sensible!)

The medium was silent for a moment.

"Doesn't it strike you as odd that I myself was able to get no results that night?" he said presently.

"How? I don't understand."

"Why, as a rule, I find no difficulty at all in getting some sort of response by automatic handwriting. Are you aware that I could do nothing at all that night?"

Laurie considered it.

"Well," he said at last, "this may sound very foolish to you; but granting that I have got unusual gifts that way—they are your own words, Mr. Vincent—if that is so, I don't see why my own concentra-tion of thought, or hypnotic sleep or trance—or whatever it was—might not have been so intense as to—"

"I quite see," interrupted the other. "That is, of course, conceivable from your point of view. It had occurred to me that you might think that. . . . Then I take it that your theory is that the subconscious self is sufficient to account for it all—that in this hypnotic sleep, if you care to call it so, you simply uttered what was in your heart, and identified yourself with . . . with your memory of that young girl."

"I suppose so," said Laurie shortly.

"And the rapping, loud, continuous, unmistakable?"

"That doesn't seem to me important. I did not actually hear it, you know."

"Then what you need is some unmistakable sign?"

"Yes . . . but I see perfectly that this is impossible. Whatever I said in my sleep, either I can't identify it as true, in which case it is worthless as evidence, or I can identify it, because I already know it, and in that case, it is worthless again."

The medium smiled, half closing his eyes.

"You must think us very childish, Mr. Baxter," he said.

He sat up a little in his chair; then, putting his hand into his breast pocket, drew out a note-book, holding it still closed on his knee.

"May I ask you a rather painful question?" he said gently.

Laurie nodded. He felt so secure.

"Would you kindly tell me—first, whether you have seen the grave of this young girl since you left the country; secondly, whether anyone happens to have mentioned it to you?"

Laurie swallowed in his throat.

"Certainly no one has mentioned it to me. And I have not seen it since I left the country."

"How long ago was that?"

"That was . . . about September the twenty-seventh."

"Thank you! . . ." (He opened the note-book and turned the pages a moment or two.) "And will you listen to this, Mr. Baxter?—'Tell Laurie that the ground has sunk a little above my grave; and that cracks are showing at the sides.'"

"What is that book?" said the boy hoarsely.

The medium closed it and returned it to his pocket.

"That book, Mr. Baxter, contains a few extracts from some of the things you said during your trance. The sentence I have read is one of them, an answer given to a demand made by me that the control should give some unmistakable proof of her identity. She . . . you hesitated some time before giving that answer."

"Who took the notes?"

"Mrs. Stapleton. You can see the originals if you wish. I thought it might distress you to know that such notes had been taken; but I have had to risk that. We must not lose you, Mr. Baxter."

Laurie sat, dumb and bewildered.

"Now all you have to do," continued the medium serenely, "is to find out whether what has been said is correct or not. If it is not correct, there will be an end of the matter, if you choose. But if it is correct—"

"Stop; let me think!" cried Laurie.

He was back again in the confusion from which he thought he had escaped. Here was a definite test, offered at least in good faith—just such a test as had been lacking before; and he had no doubt whatever that it would be borne out by facts. And if it were—was there any conceivable hypothesis that would explain it except the one offered so confidently by this grave, dignified man who sat and looked at him with something of interested compassion in his heavy eyes? Coincidence? It was absurd. Certainly, graves did sink, sometimes—but . . . Thought-transference from someone who noticed the grave? . . . But why that particular thought, so vivid, concise, and pointed? . . .

If it were true? . . .

He looked hopelessly at the man, who sat smoking quietly and waiting.

And then again, another thought, previously ignored, pierced him like a sword. If it were true; if Amy herself, poor pretty Amy, had indeed been there, were indeed near him now, hammering and crying out like a child shut out at night, against his own sceptical heart . . . if it were indeed true that during those two hours she had had her heart's desire, and had been one with his very soul, in a manner to which no earthly union could aspire . . . how had he treated her? Even at this thought a shudder of repulsion ran through him. . . . It was unnatural, detestable . . . yet how sweet! . . . What did the Church say of such things? . . . But what if religion were wrong, and this indeed were the satiety of the higher nature of which marriage was but the material expression? . . .

The thoughts flew swifter than clouds as he sat there, bewildering, torturing, beckoning. He made a violent effort. He must be sane, and face things.

"Mr. Vincent," he cried.

The kindly face turned to him again.

"Mr. Vincent—"

"Hush, I quite understand," said the fatherly voice. "It is a shock, I know; but Truth is a little shocking sometimes. Wait. I perfectly understand that you must have time. You must think it all over, and verify this. You must not commit yourself. But I think you had better have my address. The ladies are a little too emotional, are they not? I expect you would sooner come to see me without them."

He laid his card on the little tea-table and stood up. "Goodnight, Mr. Baxter."

Laurie took his hand, and looked for a moment into the kind eyes. Then the man was gone.

★★★★★★

That was a little while ago, now, and Laurie sitting over breakfast

185

had had time to think it out, and by an act of sustained will to suspend his judgment.

He had come back again to the state I have described—to nervous interest—no more than that. The terror seemed gone, and certainly the scepticism seemed gone too. Now he had to face Maggie and his mother, and to see the grave. . . .

Somehow, he had become more accustomed to the idea that there might be real and solid truth under it all, and familiarity had bred ease. Yet there was nervousness there too at the thought of going home. There were moods in which, sitting or walking alone, he passionately desired it all to be true; other moods in which he was acquiescent; but in both there was a faint discomfort in the thought of meeting Maggie, and a certain instinct of propitiation towards her. Maggie had begun to stand for him as a kind of embodiment of a view of life which was sane, wholesome, and curiously attractive; there was a largeness about her, a strength, a sense of fresh air that was delightful. It was that kind of thing, he thought, that had attracted him to her during this past summer.

The image of Amy, on the other hand, more than ever now since those recent associations, stood for something quite contrary—certainly for attractiveness, but of a feverish and vivid kind, extraordinarily unlike the other. To express it in terms of time, he thought of Maggie in the morning, and of Amy in the evening, particularly after dinner. Maggie was cool and sunny; Amy suited better the evening fever and artificial light.

And now Maggie had to be faced.

First, he reflected that he had not breathed a hint, either to her or his mother, as to what had passed. They both would believe that he had dropped all this. There would then be no arguing, that at least was a comfort. But there was a curious sense of isolation and division between him and the girl.

Yet, after all, he asked himself indignantly, what affair was it of hers? She was not his confessor; she was just a convent-bred girl who couldn't understand. He would be aloof and polite. That was the attitude. And he would manage his own affairs.

He drew a few brisk draughts of smoke from his pipe and stood up. That was settled.

It was in this determined mood then that he stepped out on to the platform at the close of this wintry day, and saw Maggie, radiant in furs, waiting for him, with her back to the orange sunset.

These two did not kiss one another. It was thought better not. But he took her hand with a pleasant sense of welcome and home-coming.

"Auntie's in the brougham," she said. "There's lots of room for the luggage on the top. . . . Oh! Laurie, how jolly this is!"

It was a pleasant two-mile drive that they had.

Laurie sat with his back to the horses. His mother patted his knee once or twice under the fur rug, and looked at him with benevolent pleasure. It seemed at first a very delightful home-coming. Mrs. Baxter asked after Mr. Morton, Laurie's coach, with proper deference.

But places have as strong a power of retaining associations as persons, and even as they turned down into the hamlet Laurie was aware that this was particularly true just now. He carefully did not glance out at Mr. Nugent's shop, but it was of no use. The whole place was as full to him of the memory of Amy—and more than the memory, it seemed—as if she was still alive. They drew up at the very gate where he had whispered her name; the end of the yew walk, where he had sat on a certain night, showed beyond the house; and half a mile behind lay the meadows, darkling now, where he had first met her face to face in the sunset, and the sluice of the stream where they had stood together silent. And all was like a landscape seen through coloured paper by a child, it was of the uniform tint of death and sorrow.

Laurie was rather quiet all that evening. His mother noticed it, and it produced a remark from her that for an instant brought his heart into his mouth.

"You look a little peaked, dearest," she said, as she took her bedroom candlestick from him. "You haven't been thinking any more about that Spiritualism?"

He handed a candlestick to Maggie, avoiding her eyes.

"Oh, for a bit," he said lightly, "but I haven't touched the thing for over two months."

He said it so well that even Maggie was reassured. She had just hesitated for a fraction of a second to hear his answer, and she went to bed well content.

Her contentment was even deeper next morning when Laurie, calling to her through the cheerful frosty air, made her stop at the turning to the village on her way to church.

"I'm coming," he said virtuously; "I haven't been on a weekday for ages."

They talked of this and that for the half-mile before them. At the church door she hesitated again.

"Laurie, I wish you'd come to the Protestant churchyard with me for a moment afterwards, will you?"

He paled so suddenly that she was startled.

"Why?" he said shortly.

"I want you to see something."

He looked at her still for an instant with an incomprehensible expression. Then he nodded with set lips.

When she came out he was waiting for her. She determined to say something of regret.

"Laurie, I'm dreadfully sorry if I shouldn't have said that. ... I was stupid. ... But perhaps—"

"What is it you want me to see?" he said without the faintest expression in his voice.

"Just some flowers," she said. "You don't mind, do you?"

She saw him trembling a little.

"Was that all?"

"Why yes. ... What else could it be?"

They went on a few steps without another word. At the church gate he spoke again.

"It's awfully good of you, Maggie ... I ... I'm rather upset still, you know; that's all."

He hurried, a little in front of her, over the frosty grass beyond the church; and she saw him looking at the grave very earnestly as she came up. He said nothing for a moment.

"I'm afraid the monument's rather ... rather awful. ... Do you like the flowers, Laurie?"

She was noticing that the chrysanthemums were a little blackened by the frost; and hardly attended to the fact that he did not answer.

"Do you like the flowers?" she said again presently.

He started from his prolonged stare downwards.

"Oh yes, yes," he said; "they're ... they're lovely. ... Maggie, the grave's all right, isn't it: the mound, I mean?"

At first, she hardly understood.

"Oh yes ... what do you mean?"

He sighed, whether in relief or not she did not know.

"Only ... only I have heard of mounds sinking sometimes, or cracking at the sides. But this one—"

"Oh yes," interrupted the girl. "But this was very bad yesterday. ... What's the matter, Laurie?"

He had turned his face with some suddenness, and there was in it a look of such terror that she herself was frightened.

"What were you saying, Maggie?"

"It was nothing of any importance," said the girl hurriedly. "It wasn't in the least disfigured, if that—"

"Maggie, will you please tell me exactly in what condition this grave was yesterday? When was it put right?"

"I . . . I noticed it when I brought the chrysanthemums up yesterday morning. The ground was sunk a little, and cracks were showing at the sides. I told the sexton to put it right. He seems to have done it. . . . Laurie, why do you look like that?"

He was staring at her with an expression that might have meant anything. She would not have been surprised if he had burst into a fit of laughter. It was horrible and unnatural.

"Laurie! Laurie! Don't look like that!"

He turned suddenly away and left her. She hurried after him.

On the way to the house he told her the whole story from beginning to end.

★★★★★★

The two were sitting together in the little smoking-room at the back of the house on the last night of Laurie's holidays. He was to go back to town next morning.

Maggie had passed a thoroughly miserable week. She had had to keep her promise not to tell Mrs. Baxter—not that that lady would have been of much service, but the very telling would be a relief—and things really were not serious enough to justify her telling Father Mahon.

To her the misery lay, not in any belief she had that the spiritualistic claim was true, but that the boy could be so horribly excited by it. She had gone over the arguments again and again with him, approving heartily of his suggestions as to the earlier part of the story, and suggesting herself what seemed to her the most sensible explanation of the final detail. Graves did sink, she said, in two cases out of three, and Laurie was as aware of that as herself. Why in the world should not this then be attributed to the same subconscious mind as that which, in the hypnotic sleep—or whatever it was—had given voice to the rest of his imaginations? Laurie had shaken his head. Now they were at it once more. Mrs. Baxter had gone to bed half an hour before.

"It's too wickedly grotesque," she said indignantly. "You can't seriously believe that poor Amy's soul entered into your mind for an hour

189

and a half in Lady Laura's drawing-room. Why, what's purgatory, then, or heaven? It's so utterly and ridiculously impossible that I can't speak of it with patience."

Laurie smiled at her rather wearily and contemptuously.

"The point," he said, "is this: Which is the simplest hypothesis? You and I both believe that the soul is somewhere; and it's natural, isn't it, that she should want—oh! dash it all! Maggie, I think you should remember that she was in love with me—as well as I with her," he added.

Maggie made a tiny mental note.

"I don't deny for an instant that it's a very odd story," she said. "But this kind of explanation is just—oh, I can't speak of it. You allowed yourself that up to this last thing you didn't really believe it; and now because of this coincidence the whole thing's turned upside down. Laurie, I wish you'd be reasonable."

Laurie glanced at her.

She was sitting with her back to the curtained and shuttered window, beyond which lay the yew walk; and the lamplight from the tall stand fell full upon her. She was dressed in some rich darkish material, her breast veiled in filmy white stuff, and her round, strong arms lay, bare to the elbow, along the arms of her chair. She was a very pleasant wholesome sight. But her face was troubled, and her great serene eyes were not so serene as usual. He was astonished at the persistence with which she attacked him. Her whole personality seemed thrown into her eyes and gestures and quick words.

"Maggie," he said, "please listen. I've told you again and again that I'm not actually convinced. What you say is just conceivably possible. But it doesn't seem to me to be the most natural explanation. The most natural seems to me to be what I have said; and you're quite right in saying that it's this last thing that has made the difference. It's exactly like the grain that turns the whole bottle into solid salt. It needed that. . . . But, as I've said, I can't be actually and finally convinced until I've seen more. I'm going to see more. I wrote to Mr. Vincent this morning."

"You did?" cried the girl.

"Don't be silly, please. . . . Yes, I did. I told him I'd be at his service when I came back to London. Not to have done that would have been cowardly and absurd. I owe him that."

"Laurie, I wish you wouldn't," said the girl pleadingly.

He sat up a little, disturbed by this very unusual air of hers.

"But if it's all such nonsense," he said, "what's there to be afraid of?"

"It's—it's morbid," said Maggie, "morbid and horrible. Of course, it's nonsense; but it's—it's wicked nonsense."

Laurie flushed a little.

"You're polite," he said.

"I'm sorry." she said penitently. "But you know, really—"

The boy suddenly blazed up a little.

"You seem to think I've got no heart," he cried. "Suppose it was true—suppose really and truly Amy was here, and—"

A sudden clear sharp sound like the crack of a whip sounded from the corner of the room. Even Maggie started and glanced at the boy. He was dead white on the instant; his lips were trembling.

"What was that?" he whispered sharp and loud.

"Just the woodwork," she said tranquilly; "the thaw has set in to-night."

Laurie looked at her; his lips still moved nervously.

"But—but—" he began.

"Dear boy, don't you see the state of nerves—"

Again, came the little sharp crack, and she stopped. For an instant she was disturbed; certain possibilities opened before her, and she regarded them. Then she crushed them down, impatiently and half timorously. She stood up abruptly.

"I'm going to bed," she said. "This is too ridiculous—"

"No, no; don't leave me. . . . Maggie . . . I don't like it."

She sat down again, wondering at his childishness, and yet conscious that her own nerves, too, were ever so slightly on edge. She would not look at him, for fear that the meeting of eyes might hint at more than she meant. She threw her head back on her chair and remained looking at the ceiling. But to think that the souls of the dead—ah, how repulsive!

Outside the night was very still.

The hard frost had kept the world iron-bound in a sprinkle of snow during the last two or three days, but this afternoon the thaw had begun. Twice during dinner there had come the thud of masses of snow falling from the roof on to the lawn outside, and the clear sparkle of the candles had seemed a little dim and hazy. "It would be a comfort to get at the garden again," she had reflected.

And now that the two sat here in the windless silence the thaw became more apparent every instant. The silence was profound, and the little noises of the night outside, the drip from the eaves slow and deliberate, the rustle of released leaves, and even the gentle thud on the lawn from the yew branches—all these helped to emphasise the stillness. It was not like the murmur of day; it was rather like the gnawing of a mouse in the wainscot of some death-chamber.

It requires almost superhumanly strong nerves to sit at night, after a conversation of this kind, opposite an apparently reasonable person who is white and twitching with terror, even though one resolutely refrains from looking at him, without being slightly affected. One may argue with oneself to any extent, tap one's foot cheerfully on the floor, fill the mind most painstakingly with normal thoughts; yet it is something of a conflict, however victorious one may be.

Even Maggie herself became aware of this.

It was not that now for one single moment she allowed that the two little sudden noises in the room could possibly proceed from any cause whatever except that which she had stated—the relaxation of stiffened wood under the influence of the thaw. Nor had all Laurie's arguments prevailed to shake in the smallest degree her resolute conviction that there was nothing whatever preternatural in his certainly queer story.

Yet, as she sat there in the lamplight, with Laurie speechless before her, and the great curtained window behind, she became conscious of an uneasiness that she could not entirely repel. It was just, physical, she said; it was the result of the change of weather; or, at the most, it was the silence that had now fallen and the proximity of a terrified boy.

She looked across at him again.

He was lying back in the old green armchair, his eyes rather shadowed from the lamp overhead, quite still and quiet, his hands still clasping the lion-bosses of his chair-arms. Beside him, on the little table, lay his still smouldering cigarette-end in the silver tray. . . .

Maggie suddenly sprang to her feet, slipped round the table, and caught him by the arm.

"Laurie, Laurie, wake up. . . . What's the matter?"

A long shudder passed through him. He sat up, with a bewildered look.

"Eh? What is it?" he said. "Was I asleep?"

He rubbed his hands over his eyes and looked round.

"What is it, Maggie? Was I asleep?"

(Was the boy acting? Surely it was good acting!)

Maggie threw herself down on her knees by the chair.

"Laurie! Laurie! I beg you not to go to see Mr. Vincent. It's bad for you. . . . I do wish you wouldn't."

He still blinked at her a moment.

"I don't understand. What do you mean, Maggie?"

She stood up, ashamed of her impulsiveness.

"Only I wish you wouldn't go and see that man. Laurie, please don't."

He stood up too, stretching. Every sign of nervousness seemed gone.

"Not see Mr. Vincent? Nonsense; of course, I shall. You don't understand, Maggie."

Chapter 7

What a relief," sighed Mrs. Stapleton. "I thought we had lost him."

The three were sitting once again in Lady Laura's drawing-room soon after lunch. Mr. Vincent had just looked in with Laurie's note to give the news. It was a heavy fog outside, woolly in texture and orange in colour, and the tall windows seemed opaque in the lamplight; the room, by contrast, appeared a safe and pleasant refuge from the reek and stinging vapour of the street.

Mrs. Stapleton had been lunching with her friend. The Colonel had returned for Christmas, so his wife's duties had recalled her for the present from those spiritual conversations which she had enjoyed in the autumn. It was such a refreshment, she had said with a patient smile, to slip away sometimes into the purer atmosphere.

Mr. Vincent folded the letter and restored it to his pocket.

"We must be careful with him," he said. "He is extraordinarily sensitive. I almost wish he were not so developed. Temperaments like his are apt to be thrown off their balance."

Lady Laura was silent.

For herself she was not perfectly happy. She had lately come across one or two rather deplorable cases. A very promising girl, daughter of a publican in the suburbs, had developed the same kind of powers, and the end of it all had been rather a dreadful scene in Baker Street. She was now in an asylum. A friend of her own, too, had lately taken to lecturing against Christianity in rather painful terms. Lady Laura wondered why people could not be as well balanced as herself.

"I think he had better not come to the public *séances* at present," went on the medium. "That, no doubt, will come later; but I was going to ask a great favour from you, Lady Laura."

She looked up.

"That bother about the rooms is not yet settled, and the Sunday *séances* will have to cease for the present. I wonder if you would let us come here, just a few of us only, for three or' four Sundays, at any rate."

She brightened up.

"Why, it would be the greatest pleasure," she said. "But what about the cabinet?"

"If necessary, I would send one across. Will you allow me to make arrangements?"

Mrs. Stapleton beamed.

"What a privilege!" she said. "Dearest, I quite envy you. I am afraid dear Tom would never consent—"

"There are just one or two things on my mind," went on Mr. Vincent so pleasantly that the interruption seemed almost a compliment, "and the first is this. I want him to see for himself. Of course, for ourselves, his trance is the point; but hardly for him. He is tremendously impressed; I can see that; though he pretends not to be. But I should like him to see something unmistakable as soon as possible. We must prevent his going into trance, if possible. . . . And the next thing is his religion."

"Catholics are supposed not to come," observed Mrs. Stapleton.

"Just so. . . . Mr. Baxter is a convert, isn't he? . . .I thought so."

He mused for a moment or two.

The ladies had never seen him so interested in an amateur. Usually his manner was remarkable for its detachment and severe assurance; but it seemed that this case excited even him. Lady Laura was filled again with sudden compunction.

"Mr. Vincent," she said, "do you really think there is no danger for this boy?"

He glanced up at her.

"There is always danger," he said. "We know that well enough. We can but take precautions. But pioneers always have to risk something."

She was not reassured.

"But I mean special danger. He is extraordinarily sensitive, you know. There was that girl from Surbiton. . . ."

"Oh! she was exceptionally hysterical. Mr. Baxter's not like that. I do not see that he runs any greater risk than we run ourselves."

"You are sure of that?"

He smiled deprecatingly.

"I am sure of nothing," he said. "But if you feel you would sooner not—"

Mrs. Stapleton rustled excitedly, and Lady Laura grabbed at her retreating opportunity.

"No, no," she cried. "I didn't mean that for one moment. Please, please come here. I only wondered whether there was any particular precaution "

"I will think about it," said the medium. "But I am sure we must be careful not to shock him. Of course, we don't all take the same view about religion; but we can leave that for the present. The point is that Mr. Baxter should, if possible, see something unmistakable. The rest can take care of itself. . . . Then, if you consent, Lady Laura, we might have a little sitting here next Sunday night. Would nine o'clock suit you?"

He glanced at the two ladies.

"That will do very well," said the mistress of the house. "And, about preparations—"

"I will look in on Saturday afternoon. Is there anyone particular you think of asking?"

"Mr. Jamieson came to see me again a few days ago," suggested Lady Laura tentatively.

"That will do very well. Then we three and those two. That will be quite enough for the present."

He stood up—a big, dominating figure—a reassuring man to look at, with his kindly face, his bushy, square beard, and his appearance of physical strength. Lady Laura sat vaguely comforted.

"And about my notes," asked Maud Stapleton.

"I think they will not be necessary. . . . Good day. . . . Saturday afternoon."

The two sat on silently for a minute or two after he was gone.

"What is the matter, dearest?"

Lady Laura's little anxious face did not move. She was staring thoughtfully at the fire. Mrs. Stapleton laid a sympathetic hand on the other's knee.

"Dearest" she began.

"No; it is nothing, darling," said Lady Laura.

Meanwhile the medium was picking his way through the foggy streets. Figures loomed up, sudden and enormous, and vanished again. Smoky flares of flame shone like spots of painted fire, bright and unpenetrating, from windows overhead; and sounds came to him through the woolly atmosphere, dulled and sonorous. It would, so to speak, have been a suitably dramatic setting for his thoughts if he had been thinking in character, vaguely suggestive of presences and hints and peeps into the unknown.

But he was a very practical man. His spiritualistic faith was a reality to him, as unexciting as Christianity to the normal Christian; he entertained no manner of doubt as to its truth.

Beyond all the fraud, the self-deception, the amazing feats of the sub-conscious self, there remained certain facts beyond doubting— facts which required, he believed, an objective explanation, which none but the spiritualistic thesis offered. He had far more evidence, he considered sincerely enough, for his spiritualism than most Christians for their Christianity.

He had no very definite theory as to the spiritual world beyond thinking that it was rather like this world. For him it was peopled with individualities of various characters and temperaments, of various grades and achievements; and of these a certain number had the power of communicating under great difficulties with persons on this side who were capable of receiving such communications. That there were dangers connected with this process, he was well aware; he had seen often enough the moral sense vanish and the mental powers decay. But these were to him no more than the honourable wounds to which all who struggle are liable.

The point for him was that here lay the one certain means of getting into touch with reality. Certainly, that reality was sometimes of a disconcerting nature, and seldom of an illuminating one; he hated, as much as anyone, the tambourine business, except so far as it was essential; and he deplored the fact that, as he believed, it was often the most degraded and the least satisfactory of the inhabitants of the other world that most easily got into touch with the inhabitants of this. Yet, for him, the main tenets of spiritualism were as the bones of the universe; it was the only religion which seemed to him in the least worthy of serious attention.

He had not practised as a medium for longer than ten or a dozen years. He had discovered, by chance as he thought, that he possessed mediumistic powers in an unusual degree, and had begun then to take up the life as a profession. He had suffered, so far as he was aware, no ill effects from this life, though he had seen others suffer; and, as his fame grew, his income grew with it.

It is necessary, then, to understand that he was not a conscious charlatan; he loathed mechanical tricks such as he occasionally came across; he was perfectly and serenely convinced that the powers which

196

he possessed were genuine, and that the personages he seemed to come across in his mediumistic efforts were what they professed to be; that they were not hallucinatory, that they were not the products of fraud, that they were not necessarily evil. He regarded this religion as he regarded science; both were progressive, both liable to error, both capable of abuse. Yet as a scientist did not shrink from experiment for fear of risk, neither must the spiritualist.

As he picked his way to his lodgings on the north of the park, he was thinking about Laurie Baxter. That this boy possessed in an unusual degree what he would have called "occult powers" was very evident to him. That these powers involved a certain risk was evident too. He proposed, therefore, to take all reasonable precautions. All the catastrophes he had witnessed in the past were due, he thought, to a too rapid development of those powers, or to inexperience. He determined, therefore, to go slowly.

First, the boy must be convinced; next, he must be attached to the cause; thirdly, his religion must be knocked out of him; fourthly, he must be trained and developed. But for the present he must not be allowed to go into trance if it could be prevented. It was plain, he thought, that Laurie had a very strong "affinity," as he would have said, with the disembodied spirit of a certain "Amy Nugent." His communication with her had been of a very startling nature in its rapidity and perfection. Real progress might be made, then, through this channel.

(Yes; I am aware that this sounds grotesque nonsense.)

★★★★★★

Laurie came back to town in a condition of interior quietness that rather astonished him. He had said to Maggie that he was not convinced; and that was true so far as he knew. Intellectually, the spiritualistic theory was at present only the hypothesis that seemed the most reasonable; yet morally he was as convinced of its truth as of anything in the world. And this showed itself by the quietness in which he found his soul plunged.

Moral conviction—that conviction on which a man acts—does not always coincide with the intellectual process. Occasionally it outruns it; occasionally lags behind; and the first sign of its arrival is the cessation of strain. The intellect may still be busy, arranging, sorting, and classifying; but the thing itself is done, and the soul leans back.

A certain amount of excitement made itself felt when he found Mr. Vincent's letter waiting for his arrival to congratulate him on his decision, and to beg him to be at Queen's Gate not later than half-past eight o'clock on the following Sunday; but it was not more than momentary. He knew the thing to be inevitably true now; the time and place at which it manifested itself was not supremely important.

Yes, he wrote in answer; he would certainly keep the appointment suggested.

He dined out at a restaurant, returned to his rooms, and sat down to arrange his ideas.

These, to be frank, were not very many, nor very profound.

He had already, in the days that had passed since his shock, no lighter because expected, when he had learned from Maggie that the test was fulfilled, and that a fact known to no one present, not even himself, in Queen's Gate, had been communicated through his lips— since that time the idea had become familiar that the veil between this world and the next was a very thin one. After all, a large number of persons in the world believe that, as it is, and they are not, in consequence, in a continuous state of exaltation. Laurie had learned this, he thought, experimentally. Very well, then, that was so; there was no more to be said.

Next, the excitement of the thought of communicating with Amy in particular had to a large extent burned itself out. It was nearly four months since her death; and in his very heart of hearts he was beginning to be aware that she had not been so entirely his twin-soul as he would still have maintained. He had reflected a little, in the meantime, upon the grocer's shop, the dissenting tea-parties, the odour of cheeses. Certainly these things could not destroy an "affinity" if the affinity were robust; but it would need to be. . . .

He was still very tender towards the thought of her; she had gained too, inevitably, by dying, a dignity she had lacked while living, and it might well be that intercourse with her in the manner proposed would be an extraordinarily sweet experience. But he was no longer excited—passionately and overwhelmingly—by the prospect. It would be delightful? Yes. But . . .

Then Laurie began to look at his religion, and at that view he stopped dead. He had no ideas at all on the subject; he had not a notion where he stood. All he knew was that it had become uninteresting. True? Oh, yes, he supposed so. He retained it still as many retain faith in the supernatural—a reserve that could be drawn upon in extremities.

He had not yet missed hearing Mass on Sunday; in fact, he proposed to go even next Sunday. "A man must have a religion," he said to himself; and, intellectually, there was at present no other possible religion for him except the Catholic. Yet as he looked into the future he was doubtful.

He drew himself up in his chair and began to fill his pipe. . . . In three days, he would be seated in a room with three or four persons, he supposed. Of these two—and certainly the two strongest characters—had no religion except that supplied by spiritualism, and he had read enough to know this was, at any rate in the long run, non-Christian. And these three or four persons, moreover, believed with their whole hearts that they were in relations with the invisible world, far more evident and sensible than those claimed by any other believers on the face of the earth. And, after all, Laurie reflected, there seemed to be justice in their claim. He would be seated in that room, he repeated to himself, and it might be that before he left it he would have seen with his own eyes, and possibly handled, living persons who had, in the common phrase, "died" and been buried. Almost certainly, at the very least, he would have received from such intelligences unmistakable messages. . . .

He was astonished that he was not more excited.

He asked himself again whether he really believed it; he compared his belief in it with his belief in the existence of New Zealand. Yes, if that were belief, he had it. . . . But the excitement of doubt was gone, as no doubt it was gone when New Zealand became a geographical expression.

He was astonished at its naturalness—at the extraordinary manner in which, when once the evidence had been seen and the point of view grasped, the whole thing fell into place. It seemed to him as if he must have known it all his life; yet, he knew, six months ago he had hardly known more than that there were upon the face of the earth persons called Spiritualists, who believed, or pretended to believe, what he then was quite sure was fantastic nonsense. And now he was, to all intents, one of them. . . .

He was being drawn forward, it seemed, by a process as inevitable as that of spring or autumn; and, once he had yielded to it, the conflict and the excitement were over. Certainly, this made very few demands. Christianity said that those were blessed who had not seen and yet believed; Spiritualism said that the only reasonable belief was that which followed seeing.

So then Laurie sat and meditated.

Once or twice that evening he looked round him tranquilly without a touch of that terror that had seized him in the smoking-room at home.

If all this were true—and he repeated to himself that he knew it was true—these presences were about him now, why was it that he was no longer frightened?

He looked carefully into the dark corner behind him, beyond the low jutting bookshelf, in the angle between the curtained windows, at his piano, glossy and mysterious in the gloom, at the door half-open into his bedroom. All was quiet here, shut off from the hum of Fleet Street; circumstances were propitious. Why was he not frightened? .. Why, what was there to frighten him? These presences were natural and normal; even as a Catholic he believed in them. And if they manifested themselves, what was there to fear in that?

He looked steadily and serenely; and as he looked, like the kindling of a fire, there rose within him a sense of strange exaltation.

"Amy," he whispered.

But there was no movement or hint.

Laurie smiled a little, wearily. He felt tired; he would sleep a little. He beat out his pipe, crossed his feet before the fire, and closed his eyes.

★★★★★★

There followed that smooth rush into gulfs of sleep that provides perhaps the most exquisite physical sensation known to man, as the veils fall thicker and softer every instant, and the consciousness gathers itself inwards from hands and feet and limbs, like a dog curling himself up for rest; yet retains itself in continuous being, and is able to regard its own comfort. All this he remembered perfectly half an hour later; but there followed in his memory that inevitable gap in which self loses itself before emerging into the phantom land of dreams, or returning to reality.

But that into which he emerged, he remembered afterwards, was a different realm altogether from that which is usual—from that country of grotesque fancy and jumbled thoughts, of thin shadows of truth and echoes from the common world where most of us find ourselves in sleep.

His dream was as follows:—

He was still in his room, he thought, but no longer in his chair. Instead, he stood in the very centre of the floor, or at least poised somewhere above it, for he could see at a glance, without turning, all that the room contained. He directed his attention—for it was this, rather than sight, through which he perceived—to the piano, the chiffonier, the chairs, the two doors, the curtained windows; and finally, with scarcely even a touch of surprise, to himself still sunk in the chair before the fire. He regarded himself with pleased interest, remembering even in that instant that he had never before seen himself with closed eyes. . . .

All in the room was extraordinarily vivid and clear-cut. It was true that the firelight still wavered and sank again in billows of soft colour about the shadowed walls, but the changing light was no more an interruption to the action of that steady medium through which he perceived than the movement of summer clouds across the full sunlight. It was at that moment that he understood that he saw no longer with eyes, but with that faculty of perception to which sight is only analogous—that faculty which underlies and is common to all the senses alike.

His reasoning powers, too, at this moment, seemed to have gone from him like a husk. He did not argue or deduce; simply he understood. And, in a flash, simultaneous with the whole vision, he perceived that he was behind all the slow processes of the world, by which this is added to that, and a conclusion drawn; by which light travels, and sounds resolve themselves and emotions run their course. He had reached, he thought, the ultimate secret. . . . It was This that lay behind everything.

Now it is impossible to set down, except progressively, all this sum of experiences that occupied for him one interminable instant. Neither did he remember afterwards the order in which they presented themselves; for it seemed to him that there was no order; all was simultaneous.

But he understood plainly by intuition that all was open to him. Space no longer existed for him; nothing, to his perception, separated this from that. He was able, he saw, without stirring from his attitude to see in an instant any place or person towards which he chose to exercise his attention. It seemed a marvellously simple point, this—that space was little more than an illusion; that it was, after all, nothing else but a translation into rather coarse terms of what may be called "differences." "Here" and "There" were but relative terms; certainly they corresponded to facts, but they were not those facts themselves. . . . And since he now stood behind them he saw them on their inner side, as a man standing in the interior of a globe may be said to be equally present to every point upon its surface.

The fascination of the thought was enormous; and, like a child who begins to take notice and to learn the laws of extension and distance, so he began to learn their reverse. He saw, he thought (as he had seen once before, only, this time, without the sense of movement), the interior of the lighted drawing-room at home, and his mother nodding in her chair; he directed his attention to Maggie, and perceived her passing across the landing toward the head of the stairs with a candle in her hand. It was this sight that brought him to a further discovery, to the effect that time also was of very nearly no importance either; for he perceived that by bending his attention upon her he could restrain her, so to speak, in her movement. There she stood, one foot outstretched, the candle flame leaning motionless backward; and he knew too that it was not she who was thus restrained, but that it was the intensity and directness of his thought that fixed, so to say, in terms of eternity, that instant of time. . . .

So, it went on; or, rather, so it was with him. He pleased himself by contemplating the London streets outside, the darkness of the garden in some square, the interior of the Oratory where a few figures kneeled—all seen beyond the movements of light and shadow in this clear invisible radiance that was to his perception as common light to common eyes. The world of which he had had experience—for he found himself unable to see that which he had never experienced— lay before his will like a movable map: this or that person or place had but to be desired, and it was present.

And then came the return; and the Horror. . . .

He began in this way.

He understood that he wished to awake, or, rather, to be reunited with the body that lay there in deep sleep before the fire. He observed it for a moment or two, interested and pleased, the face sunk a little on the hand, the feet lightly crossed on the fender. He looked at his own profile, the straight nose, the parted lips through which the breath came evenly. He attempted even to touch the face, wondering with gentle pleasure what would be the result. . . .

Then, suddenly, an impulse came to him to enter the body, and with the impulse the process, it seemed, began.

That process was not unlike that of falling asleep. In an instant perception was gone; the lighted room was gone, and that obedient world which he had contemplated just now. Yet self-consciousness for a while remained; he still had the power of perceiving his own personality, though this dwindled every moment down to that same gulf of nothingness through which he had found his way.

But at the very instant in which consciousness was passing there met him an emotion so fierce and overwhelming that he recoiled in terror back from the body once more and earth-perceptions; and a panic seized him.

It was such a panic as seizes a child who. fearfully courageous, has stolen at night from his room; and turning in half-simulated terror finds the door fast against him, or is aware of a malignant presence come suddenly into being, standing between himself and the safety of his own bed.

On the one side his fear drove him onwards; on the other a Horror faced him. He dared not recoil, for he understood where security lay; he longed, like the child screaming in the dark and beating his hands, to get back to the warmth and safety of bed; yet there stood before him a Presence, or at the least an Emotion of some kind, so hostile, so terrible, that he dared not penetrate it. It was not that an actual restraint lay upon him: he knew, that is, that the door was open; yet it needed an effort of the will of which his paralysis of terror rendered him incapable. . . .

The tension became intolerable.

"O God . . . God . . . God . . . " he cried.

And in an instant the threshold was vacated; the swift rush asserted itself, and the space was passed.

Laurie sat up abruptly in his chair.

★★★★★★

Mr. Vincent was beginning to think about going to bed. He had come in an hour before, had written half a dozen letters, and was smoking peacefully before the fire.

His rooms were not remarkable in any way, except for half a dozen objects standing on the second shelf of his bookcase, and the selection of literature ranged below them. For the rest, all was commonplace enough; a mahogany knee-hold table, a couple of easy chairs, much worn, and a long, extremely comfortable sofa standing by itself against the wall with evident signs, in its tumbled cushions and rubbed fabric, of continual and frequent use. A second door gave entrance to his bedroom.

He beat out his pipe slowly, yawned, and stood up.

It was at this instant that he heard the sudden tingle of the electric bell in the lobby outside, and, wondering at the interruption at this hour, went quickly out and opened the door on to the stairs.

"Mr. Baxter! Come in, come in; I'm delighted to see you."

Laurie came in without a word, went straight up to the fireplace, and faced about.

"I'm not going to apologise," he said, "for coming at this time. You told me to come and see you at any time, and I've taken you at your word."

The young man had an odd embarrassed manner, thought the other; an air of having come in spite of uneasiness; he was almost shame-faced.

The medium impelled him gently into a chair.

"First a cigarette," he said; "next a little whisky; and then I shall be delighted to listen. . . . No; please do as I say."

Laurie permitted himself to be managed; there was a strong, almost paternal air in the other's manner that was difficult to resist. He lit his cigarette, he sipped his whisky; but his movements were nervously quick.

"Well, then . . ." and he interrupted himself. "What are those things, Mr. Vincent?" (He nodded towards the second shelf in the bookcase.)

Mr. Vincent turned on the hearthrug.

"Those? Oh! those are a few rather elementary instruments for my work."

He lifted down a crystal ball on a small black polished wooden stand and handed it over.

"You have heard of crystal-gazing? Well, that is the article."

"Is that crystal?"

"Oh no: common glass. Price three shillings and sixpence."

Laurie turned it over, letting the shining globe run on to his hand. "And this is——" he began.

"And this," said the medium, setting a curious windmill-shaped affair, its sails lined with looking-glass, on the little table by the fire, "this is a French toy. Very elementary."

"What's that?"

"Look."

Mr. Vincent wound a small handle at the back of the windmill to a sound of clockwork, set it down again, and released it. Instantly the sails began to revolve, noiseless and swift, producing the effect of a rapidly flashing circle of light across which span lines, waxing and waning with extraordinary speed.

"What the——"

"It's a little machine for inducing sleep. Oh! I haven't used that for months. But it's useful sometimes. The hypnotic subject just stares at that steadily. . . . Why, you're looking dazed yourself, already, Mr. Baxter," smiled the medium.

He stopped the mechanism and pushed it on one side.

"And what's the other?" asked Laurie, looking again at the shelf.

"Ah!"

The medium, with quite a different air, took down and set before him an object resembling a tiny heart-shaped table on three wheeled legs, perhaps four or five inches across. Through the centre ran a pencil perpendicularly of which the point just touched the table-cloth on which the thing rested. Laurie looked at it, and glanced up.

"Yes, that's Planchette," said the medium.

"For . . . for automatic writing?"

The other nodded.

"Yes," he said. "The experimenter puts his fingers lightly upon that, and there's a sheet of paper beneath. That is all."

Laurie looked at him, half curiously. Then with a sudden movement he stood up.

"Yes," he said. "Thank you. But—"

"Please sit down, Mr. Baxter. . . . I know you haven't come about that kind of thing. Will you kindly tell me what you have come about?"

He, too, sat down, and, without looking at the other, began slowly to fill his pipe again, with his strong capable fingers. Laurie stared at the process, unseeing.

"Just tell me simply," said the medium again, still without looking at him.

Laurie threw himself back.

"Well, I will," he said. "I know it's absurdly childish; but I'm a little frightened. It's about a dream."

"That's not necessarily childish."

"It's a dream I had tonight—in my chair after dinner."

"Well?"

Then Laurie began.

For about ten minutes he talked without ceasing. Mr. Vincent smoked tranquilly, putting what seemed to Laurie quite unimportant questions now and again, and nodding gently from time to time.

"And I'm frightened," ended Laurie; "and I want you to tell me what it all means."

The other drew a long inhalation through his pipe, expelled it, and leaned back.

205

"Oh, it's comparatively common," he said; "common, that is, with people of your temperament, Mr. Baxter—and mine. . . . You tell me that it was prayer that enabled you to get through at the end? That is interesting."

"But—but—was it more than fancy—more, I mean, than an ordinary dream?"

"Oh, yes; it was objective. It was a real experience."

"You mean"

"Mr. Baxter, just listen to me for a minute or two. You can ask any questions you like at the end. First, you are a Catholic, you told me; you believe, that is to say, among other things, that the spiritual world is a real thing, always present more or less. Well, of course, I agree with you; though I do not agree with you altogether as to the geography and—and other details of that world. But you believe, I take it, that this world is continually with us—that this room, so to speak, is a great deal more than that of which our senses tell us; that there are with us, now and always, a multitude of influences, good, bad, and indifferent, really present to our spirits?"

"I suppose so," said Laurie.

"Now begin again. There are two kinds of dreams. (I am just stating my own belief, Mr. Baxter. You can make what comments you like afterwards.) The one kind of dream is entirely unimportant; it is merely a hash, a *réchauffée*, of our own thoughts, in which little things that we have experienced reappear in a hopeless sort of confusion. It is the kind of dream that we forget altogether, generally, five minutes after waking, if not before. But there is another kind of dream that we do not forget. It leaves as vivid an impression upon us as if it were a waking experience—an actual incident. And that is exactly what it is."

"I don't understand."

"Have you ever heard of the subliminal consciousness, Mr. Baxter?"

"No."

The medium smiled.

"That is fortunate," he said. "It's being run to death just now. . . . Well, I'll put it in an untechnical way. There is a part of us, (is there not?) that lies below our ordinary waking thoughts—that part of us in which our dreams reside, our habits take shape, our instincts, intuitions, and all the rest, are generated. Well, in ordinary dreams, when we are asleep, it is this part that is active. The pot boils, so to speak, all by itself, uncontrolled by reason. A madman is a man in whom this

206

part is supreme in his waking life as well. Well, it is through this part of us that we communicate with the spiritual world. There are, let us say, two doors in it—that which leads up to our senses, through which come down our waking experiences to be stored up; and—and the other door...."

"Yes?"

The medium hesitated.

"Well," he said, "in some natures—yours, for instance, Mr. Baxter—this door opens rather easily. It was through that door that you went, I think, in what you call your 'dream.' You yourself said it was quite unlike ordinary dreams."

"Yes."

"And I am the more sure that this is so, since your experience is exactly that of so many others under the same circumstances."

Laurie moved uncomfortably in his chair.

"I don't quite understand," he said sharply. "You mean it was not a dream?"

"Certainly not. At least, not a dream in the ordinary sense. It was an actual experience."

"But—but I was asleep."

"Certainly. That is one of the usual conditions—an almost indispensable condition, in fact. The objective self—I mean the ordinary workaday faculties—was lulled; and your subjective self—call it what you like—but it is your real self, the essential self that survives death—this self, simply went through the inner door, and—and saw what was to be seen."

Laurie looked at him intently. But there was a touch of apprehension in his face, too.

"You mean," he said slowly, "that—that all I saw—the limitations of space, and so forth—that these were facts and not fancies?"

"Certainly. Doesn't your theology hint at something of the kind?"

Laurie was silent. He had no idea of what his theology told him on the point.

"But why should I—I of all people—have such an experience?" he asked suddenly.

The medium smiled.

"Who can tell that?" he said. "Why should one man be an artist, and another not? It is a matter of temperament. You see you've begun to develop that temperament at last; and it's a very marked one to begin with. As for—"

Laurie interrupted him.

"Yes, yes," he said. "But there's another point. What about that fear I had when I tried to—to awaken?"

There passed over the medium's face a shade of gravity. It was no more than a shade, but it was there. He reached out rather quickly for his pipe which he had laid aside, and blew through it carefully before answering.

"That?" he said, with what seemed to the boy an affected carelessness. "That? Oh, that's a common experience. Don't think about that too much, Mr. Baxter. It's never very healthy—"

"I am sorry," said Laurie deliberately. "But I must ask you to tell me what you think. I must know what I'm doing."

The medium filled his pipe again. Twice he began to speak, and checked himself; and in the long silence Laurie felt his fears gather upon him tenfold.

"Please tell me at once, Mr. Vincent," he said. "Unless I know everything that is to be known, I will not go another step along this road. I really mean that."

The medium paused in his pipe-filling.

"And what if I do tell you?" he said in his slow virile voice. "Are you sure you will not be turned back?"

"If it is a well-known danger, and can be avoided with prudence, I certainly shall not turn back."

"Very well, Mr. Baxter, I will take you at your word. . . . Have you ever heard the phrase, 'The Watcher on the Threshold'?"

Laurie shook his head.

"No," he said. "At least I don't think so."

"Well," said the medium quietly, "that is what we call the Fear you spoke of. . . . No; don't interrupt. I'll tell you all we know. It's not very much."

He paused again, stretched his hand for the matches, and took one out. Laurie watched him as if fascinated by the action.

Outside roared Oxford Street in one long rolling sound as of the sea; but within here was that quiet retired silence which the boy had noticed before in the same company. Was that fancy, too, he wondered? . . .

The medium lit his pipe and leaned back.

"I'll tell you all we know," he said again quietly. "It's not very much. Really the phrase I used just now sums it up pretty well. We who have tried to get beyond this world of sense have become aware of certain facts of which the world generally knows nothing at all. One of these facts is that the door between this life and the other is guarded by a certain being of whom we know really nothing at all, except that his presence causes the most appalling fear in those who experience it. He is set there—God only knows why—and his main business seems to be to restrain, if possible, from re-entering the body those who have left it. Just occasionally his presence is perceived by those on this side, but not often. But I have been present at death-beds where he has been seen—"

"Seen?"

"Oh! yes. Seen by the dying person. It is usually only a glimpse; it might be said to be a mistake. For myself I believe that that appalling terror that now and then shows itself, even in people who do not fear death itself, who are perfectly resigned, who have nothing on their conscience—well, personally, I believe the fear comes from a sight of this—this Personage."

Laurie licked his dry lips. He told himself that he did not believe one word of it.

"And . . . and he is evil?" he asked.

The other shrugged his shoulders.

"Isn't that a relative term?" he said. "From one point of view, certainly; but not necessarily from all."

"And . . . and what's the good of it?"

The medium smiled a little.

"That's a question we soon cease to ask. You must remember that we hardly know anything at all yet. But one thing seems more and more certain the more we investigate, and that is that our point of view is not the only one, nor even the principal one. Christianity, I fancy, says the same thing, does it not? The 'glory of God,' whatever that may be, comes before even the 'salvation of souls.'"

Laurie wrenched his attention once more to a focus.

"Then I was in danger?" he said.

"Certainly. We are always in danger—"

"You mean, if I hadn't prayed—"

"Ah! that is another question. . . . But, in short, if you hadn't succeeded in getting past—well, you'd have failed."

Again, there fell a silence.

It seemed to Laurie as if his world were falling about him. Yet he was far from sure whether it were not all an illusion. But the extreme quietness and confidence of this man in enunciating these startling theories had their effect. It was practically impossible for the boy to sit here, still nervous from his experience, and hear, unmoved, this apparently reasonable and connected account of things that were certainly incomprehensible on any other hypothesis. His remembrance of the very startling uniqueness of his dream was still vivid. . . . Surely it all fitted in . . . yet . . .

"But there is one thing," broke in the medium's quiet voice. "Should you ever experience this kind of thing again, I should recommend you not to pray. Just exercise your own individuality; assert yourself; don't lean on another. You are quite strong enough."

"You mean—"

"I mean exactly what I say. What is called Prayer is really an imaginative concession to weakness. Take the short cut, rather. Assert your own—your own individuality."

Laurie changed his attitude. He uncrossed his feet and sat up a little.

"Oh! pray if you want to," said the medium. "But you must remember, Mr. Baxter, that you are quite an exceptional person. I assure you that you have no conception of your own powers. I must say that I hope you will take the strong line." (He paused.) "These *séances*, for instance. Now that you know a little more of the dangers, are you going to turn back?"

His overhung kindly eyes looked out keenly for an instant at the boy's restless face.

"I don't know," said Laurie; "I must think—"

He got up.

"Look here, Mr. Vincent," he said, "it seems to me you're extraordinarily—er—extraordinarily plausible. But I'm even now not quite sure whether I'm not going mad. It's like a perfectly mad dream—all these things one on the top of the other."

He paused, looking sharply at the elder man, and away again.

"Yes?"

Laurie began to finger a pencil that lay on the chimney-shelf.

"You see what I mean, don't you?" he said. "I'm not disputing—er—your point of view, nor your sincerity. But I do wish you would give me another proof or two."

"You haven't had enough?"

"Oh! I suppose I have—if I were reasonable. But, you know, it all seems to me as if you suddenly demonstrated to me that twice two made five."

"But then, surely no proof—"

"Yes; I know. I quite see that. Yet I want one—something quite absolutely ordinary. If you can do all these things—spirits and all the rest—can't you do something ever so much simpler, that's beyond mistake?"

"Oh, I daresay. But wouldn't you ask yet another after that?"

"I don't know."

"Or wouldn't you think you'd been hypnotised?"

Laurie shook his head.

"I'm not a fool," he said.

"Then give me that pencil," said the medium, suddenly extending his hand.

Laurie stared a moment. Then he handed over the pencil.

On the little table by the arm-chair, a couple of feet from Laurie, stood the whisky apparatus and a box of cigarettes. These the medium, without moving from his chair, lifted off and set on the floor beside him, leaving the woven-grass surface of the table entirely bare. He then laid the pencil gently in the centre—all without a word. Laurie watched him carefully.

"Now kindly do not speak one word or make one movement," said the man peremptorily. "Wait! You're perfectly sure you're not hypnotised, or any other nonsense?"

"Certainly not."

"Just go round the room, look out of the window, poke the fire—anything you like."

"I'm satisfied," said the boy.

"Very good. Then kindly watch that pencil."

The medium leaned a little forward in his chair, bending his eyes steadily upon the little wooden cylinder lying, like any other pencil, on the top of the table. Laurie glanced once at him, then back again. There it lay, common and ordinary.

For at least a minute nothing happened at all, except that from the intentness of the elder man there seemed once more to radiate out that curious air of silence that Laurie was beginning to know so well—that silence that seemed impenetrable to the common sounds of the world and to exist altogether independent of them. Once and again he glanced round at the ordinary-looking room, the curtained windows, the dull furniture; and the second time he looked back at the pencil he was almost certain that some movement had just taken place with it. He resolutely fixed his eyes upon it, bending every faculty he possessed into one tense attitude of attention. And a moment later he could not resist a sudden movement and a swift indrawing of breath; for there, before his very eyes, the pencil tilted, very hesitatingly and quiveringly, as if pulled by a spider's thread. He heard, too, the tiny tap of its fall.

He glanced at the medium, who jerked his head impatiently, as if for silence. Then once more the silence came down.

A minute later there was no longer the possibility of a doubt.

There before the boy's eyes, as he stared, white-faced, with parted lips, the pencil rose, hesitated, quivered; but, instead of falling back again, hung so for a moment on its point, forming with itself an acute angle with the plane of the table in an entirely impossible position; then, once more rising higher, swung on its point in a quarter circle, and after one more pause and quiver, rose to its full height, remained poised one instant, then fell with a sudden movement, rolled across the table and dropped on the carpet.

The medium leaned back, drawing a long breath.

"There," he said; and smiled at the bewildered young man.

"But—but—" began the other.

"Yes, I know," said the man. "It's startling, isn't it? and indeed it's not as easy as it looks. I wasn't at all sure—"

"But, good Lord, I saw—"

"Of course, you did; but how do you know you weren't hypnotised?"

(Laurie sat down suddenly, unconscious that he had done so.)

The medium put out his hand for his pipe once more.

"Now, I'm going to be quite honest," he said. "I have quite a quantity of comments to make on that. First, it doesn't prove anything whatever, even if it really happened—"

"Even if it!"

"Certainly. . . . Oh, yes; I saw it too; and there's the pencil on the floor—" (he stooped and picked it up).

"But what if we were both hypnotised—both acted upon by self-suggestion? We can't prove we weren't."

Laurie was dumb.

"Secondly, it doesn't prove anything, in any case, as regards the other matters we were speaking of. It only shows—if it really happened, as I say—that the mind has extraordinary control over matter. It hasn't anything to do with immortality, or—or spiritualism."

"Then why did you do it?" gasped the boy.

"Merely fireworks . . . only to show off. People are convinced by such queer things."

Laurie sat regarding, still with an unusual pallor in his face and brightness in his eyes. He could not in the last degree put into words why it was that the tiny incident of the pencil affected him so profoundly. Vaguely, only, he perceived that it was all connected somehow with the ordinariness of the accessories, and more impressive therefore than all the paraphernalia of planchette, spinning mirrors, or even his own dreams.

He stood up again suddenly.

"It's no good, Mr. Vincent," he said, putting out his hand, "I'm knocked over. I can't imagine why. It's no use talking now. I must think. Goodnight."

"Goodnight, Mr. Baxter," said the medium serenely.

Chapter 8

Her ladyship told me to show you in here, sir," said the footman at half-past eight on Sunday evening.

Laurie put down his hat, slipped off his coat, and went into the dining-room.

The table was still littered with dessert-plates and napkins. Two people had dined there he observed. He went round to the fire, wondering vaguely as to why he had not been shown upstairs, and stood, warming his hands behind him, and looking at the pleasant gloom of the high picture-hung walls.

In spite of himself he felt slightly more excited than he had thought he would be; it was one thing to be philosophical at a prospect of three days' distance; and another when the gates of death actually rise in sight. He wondered in what mood he would see his own rooms again. Then he yawned slightly—and was a little pleased that it was natural to yawn.

There was a rustle outside; the door opened, and Lady Laura slipped in.

"Forgive me, Mr. Baxter," she said. "I wanted to have just a word with you first. Please sit down a moment."

She seemed a little anxious and upset, thought Laurie, as he sat down and looked at her in her evening dress with the emblematic chain more apparent than ever. Her frizzed hair sat as usual on the top of her head, and her *pince-nez* glimmered at him across the hearthrug like the eyes of a cat.

"It is this," she said hurriedly. "I felt I must just speak to you. I wasn't sure whether you quite realised the . . . the dangers of all this. I didn't want you to . . . to run any risks in my house. I should feel responsible, you know."

She laughed nervously.

"Risks? Would you mind explaining?" said Laurie.

"There . . . there are always risks, you know."

"What sort?"

"Oh . . . you know . . . nerves, and so on. I . . . I have seen people very much upset at *séances*, more than once."

Laurie smiled.

"I don't think you need be afraid, Lady Laura. It's awfully kind of you; but, do you know, I'm ashamed to say that, if anything, I'm rather bored."

The *pince-nez* gleamed.

"But—but don't you believe it? I thought Mr. Vincent said—"

"Oh yes, I believe it; but, you know, it seems to me so natural now. Even if nothing happens tonight, I don't think I shall believe it any the less."

She was silent an instant.

"You know there are other risks," she said suddenly.

"What? Are things thrown about?"

"Please don't laugh at it, Mr. Baxter. I am quite serious."

"Well—what kind do you mean?"

Again, she paused.

"It's very awful," she said; "but, you know, people's nerves do break down entirely sometimes, even though they're not in the least afraid. I saw a case once—"

She stopped.

"Yes?"

"It—it was a very awful case. A girl—a sensitive—broke down altogether under the strain. She's in an asylum."

"I don't think that's likely for me," said Laurie, with a touch of humour in his voice. "And, after all, you run these risks, don't you—and Mrs. Stapleton?"

"Yes; but you see we're not sensitives. And even I—"

"Yes?"

"Well, even I feel sometimes rather overcome. . . . Mr. Baxter, do you quite realise what it all means?"

"I think so. To tell the truth—"

He stopped.

"Yes; but the thing itself is really overwhelming. . . . There's—there's an extraordinary power sometimes. You know I was with Maud Stapleton when she saw her father—"

She stopped again.

"Yes?"

"I saw him too, you know. . . . Oh! there was no possibility of fraud. It was with Mr. Vincent. It—it was rather terrible."

"Yes?"

"Maud fainted. . . . Please don't tell her I told you, Mr. Baxter; she wouldn't like you to know that. And then other things happen sometimes which aren't nice. Do you think me a great coward? I—I think I've got a fit of nerves tonight."

Laurie could see that she was trembling.

"I think you're very kind," he said, "to take the trouble to tell me all this. But indeed, I was quite ready to be startled. I quite understand what you mean—but—"

"Mr. Baxter, you can't understand unless you've experienced it. And, you know, the other day here you knew nothing at all: you were not conscious. Now tonight you're to keep awake; Mr. Vincent's going to arrange to do what he can about that. And—and I don't quite like it."

"Why, what on earth can happen?" asked Laurie, bewildered.

"Mr. Baxter, I suppose you realise that it's you that they—whoever they are—are interested in? There's no kind of doubt that you'll be the centre tonight. And I did just want you to understand fully that there are risks. I shouldn't like to think—"

Laurie stood up.

"I understand perfectly," he said. "Certainly, I always knew there were risks. I hold myself responsible, and no one else. Is that quite clear?"

The wire of the front-door bell suddenly twitched in the hall, and a peal came up the stairs.

"He's come," said the other. "Come upstairs, Mr. Baxter. Please don't say a word of what I've said."

She hurried out, and he after her, as the footman came up from the lower regions.

The drawing-room presented an unusual appearance to Laurie as he came in. All the small furniture had been moved away to the side where the windows looked into the street, and formed there what looked like an amateur barricade. In the centre of the room, immediately below the electric light, stood a solid small round table with four chairs set round it as if for Bridge. There was on the side further from the street a kind of ante-room communicating with the main room by a high, wide archway nearly as large as the room to which it gave access; and within this, full in sight, stood a curious erection, not unlike a confessional, seated within for one, roofed, walled, and floored with thin wood. The front of this was open, but screened partly by two curtains that seemed to hang from a rod within. The rest of the little extra room was entirely empty except for the piano that stood closed in the corner.

There were two persons standing rather disconsolately on the vacant hearthrug—Mrs. Stapleton and the clergyman whom Laurie had met on his last visit here. Mr. Jamieson wore an expression usually associated with funerals, and Mrs. Stapleton's face was full of suppressed excitement.

"Dearest, what a time you've been! Was that Mr. Vincent?"

"I think so," said Lady Laura.

The two men nodded to one another, and an instant later the medium came in.

He was in evening clothes; and, more than ever, Laurie thought how average and conventional he looked. His manner was not in the least pontifical, and he shook hands cordially and naturally, but gave one quick glance of approval at Laurie.

"It struck me as extraordinarily cold," he said. "I see you have an excellent fire." And he stooped, rubbing his hands together to warm them.

"We must screen that presently," he said.

Then he stood up again.

"There's no use in wasting time. May I say a word first, Lady Laura?"

She nodded, looking at him almost apprehensively.

"First, I must ask you gentlemen to give me your word on a certain point. I have not an idea how things will go, or whether we shall get any results; but we are going to attempt materialisation. Probably, in any case, this will not go very far; we may not be able to do more than to see some figure or face. But in any case, I want you two gentlemen to give me your word that you will attempt no violence. Anything in the nature of seizing the figure may have very disastrous results indeed to myself. You understand that what you will see, if you see anything, will not be actual flesh or blood; it will be formed of a certain matter of which we understand very little at present, but which is at any rate intimately connected with myself or with someone present. Really, we know no more of it than that. We are all of us inquirers equally. Now will you gentlemen give me your words of honour that you will obey me in this; and that in all other matters you will follow the directions of ... (he glanced at the two ladies)—"of Mrs. Stapleton, and do nothing without her consent?"

He spoke in a brisk, matter-of-fact way, and looked keenly from face to face of the two men as he ended.

"I give you my word," said Laurie.

"Yes; just so," said Mr. Jamieson.

"Now there is one matter more," went on the medium. "Mr. Baxter, you are aware that you are a sensitive of a very high order. Now I do not wish you to pass into trance tonight. Kindly keep your attention fixed upon me steadily. Watch me closely: you will be able to see me quite well enough, as I shall explain presently. Mrs. Stapleton will sit with her back to the fire, Lady Laura opposite, Mr. Jamieson with his back to the cabinet, and you, Mr. Baxter, facing it. (Yes, Mr. Jamieson, you may turn round freely, so long as you keep your hands upon the table.) Now, if you feel anything resembling sleep or unconsciousness coming upon you irresistibly, Mr. Baxter, I wish you just lightly to tap Mrs. Stapleton's hand. She will then, if necessary, break up the circle. Give the signal directly you feel the sensation is really coming on, or if you find it very difficult to keep your attention fixed. You will do this?"

"I will do it," said Laurie.

"Then that is really all."

He moved a step away from the fire. Then he paused.

"By the way, I may as well just tell you our methods. I shall take my place within the cabinet, drawing the curtains partly across at the top so as to shade my face. But you will be able to see the whole of my body, and probably even my face as well. You four will please to sit at the table in the order I have indicated, with your hands resting upon it. You will not speak unless you are spoken to, or until Mrs. Stapleton gives the signal. That is all. You then wait. Now it may be ten minutes, half an hour, an hour—anything up to two hours before anything happens. If there is no result, Mrs. Stapleton will break up the circle at eleven o'clock, and awaken me if necessary."

He broke off.

"Kindly just examine the cabinet and the whole room first, gentlemen. We mediums must protect ourselves."

He smiled genially and nodded to the two.

Laurie went straight across the open floor to the cabinet. It was raised on four feet, about twelve inches from the ground. Heavy green curtains hung from a bar within. Laurie took these, and ran them to and fro; then he went into the cabinet. It was entirely empty except for a single board that formed the seat. As he came out he encountered the awestruck face of the clergyman who had followed him in dead silence, and now went into the cabinet after him. Laurie passed round behind: the little room was empty except for the piano at the back, and two low bookshelves on either side of the fireless hearth. The window looking presumably into the garden was shuttered from top to bottom, and barred, and the curtains were drawn back so that it could be seen. A cat could not have hidden in the place. It was all perfectly satisfactory.

He came back to where the others were standing silent, and the clergyman followed him.

"You are satisfied, gentlemen?" said the medium, smiling.

"Perfectly," said Laurie, and the clergyman bowed.

"Well, then," said the other, "it is close upon nine."

He indicated the chairs, and himself went past towards the cabinet, his heavy step making the room vibrate as he went. As he came near the door, he fumbled with the button, and all the lights but one went out.

The four sat down. Laurie watched Mr. Vincent step up into the cabinet, jerk the curtains this way and that, and at last sit easily back, in such a way that his face could be seen in a kind of twilight, and the rest of his body perfectly visible.

Then silence came down upon the room.

★★★★★★

The cat of the next house decided to go a-walking after an excellent supper of herring-heads. He had an appointment with a friend. So he cleaned himself carefully on the landing outside the pantry, evaded a couple of caresses from the young footman lately come from the country, and finally leapt on the window-sill, and sat there regarding the back garden, the smoky wall beyond seen in the light of the pantry window, and the chimney-pots high and forbidding against the luminous night sky. His tail moved with a soft ominous sinuousness as he looked.

Presently he climbed cautiously out beneath the sash, gathered himself for a spring, and the next instant was seated on the boundary wall between his own house and that of Lady Laura's.

Here again he paused. That which served him for a mind, that mysterious bundle of intuitions and instincts by which he reckoned time, exchanged confidences, and arranged experiences, informed him that the night was yet young, and that his friend would not yet be arrived. He sat there so still and so long, that if it had not been for his resolute head and the blunt spires of his ears, he would have appeared to an onlooker below as no more than a humpy finial on an otherwise regularly built wall. Now and again the last inch of his tail twitched slightly, like an independent member, as he contemplated his thoughts.

Overhead the last glimmer of day was utterly gone, and in the place of it the mysterious glow of night over a city hung high and luminous. He, a town-bred cat, descended from generations of town bred cats, listened passively to the gentle roar of traffic that stood, to him, for the running of brooks and the sighing of forest trees. It was to him the auditory background of adventure, romance, and bitter war.

The energy of life ran strong in his veins and sinews. Once and again as that, which was for him imaginative vision and anticipation, asserted itself, he crisped his strong claws into the crumbling mortar, shooting them, by an unconscious muscular action, from the padded sheaths in which they lay. Once a furious yapping sounded from a lighted window far beneath; but he scorned to do more than turn a slow head in the direction of it: then once more he resumed his watch.

The time came at last, conveyed to him as surely as by a punctual clock, and he rose noiselessly to his feet. Then again, he paused, and stretched first one strong foreleg and then the other to its furthest reach, shooting again his claws, conscious with a faint sense of well-being of those tightly-strung muscles rippling beneath his loose striped skin. They would be in action presently. And, as he did so, there looked over the parapet six feet above him, at the top of the trellis up which presently he would ascend, another resolute little head and blunt-spired ears, and a soft indescribable voice spoke a gentle insult. It was his friend . . . and, he knew well enough, on some high ridge in the background squatted a young female beauty, with flattened ears and waving tail, awaiting the caresses of the victor.

As he saw the head above him, to human eyes a shapeless silhouette, to his eyes a grey-pencilled picture perfect in all its details, he paused in his stretching. Then he sat back, arranged his tail, and lifted his head to answer. The cry that came from him, not yet *fortissimo*, sounded in human ears beneath no more than a soft broken-hearted wail, but to him who sat above it surpassed in insolence even his own carefully modulated offensiveness.

Again, the other answered, this time lifting himself to his full height, sending a message along the nerves of his back that prickled his own skin and passed out along the tail with an exquisite ripple of movement. And once more came the answer from below.

So, the preliminary challenge went on. Already in the voice of each there had begun to show itself that faint note of hysteria that culminates presently in a scream of anger and a torrent of spits, leading again in their turn to an ominous silence and the first fierce clawing blows at eyes and ears. In another instant the watcher above would recoil for a moment as the swift rush was made up the trellis, and then the battle would be joined: but that instant never came. There fell a sudden silence; and he, peering down into the grey gloom, chin on paws, and tail twitching eighteen inches behind, saw an astonishing sight. His adversary had broken off in the midst of a long crescendo cry, and was himself crouched flat upon the narrow wall staring now not upwards, but downwards, diagonally, at a certain curtained window eight feet below.

This was all very unusual and contrary to precedent. A dog, a human hand armed with a missile, a furious minatory face—these things were not present to account for the breach of etiquette. Vaguely he perceived this, conscious only of inexplicability; but he himself also ceased, and watched for developments.

Very slowly they came at first. That crouching body beneath was motionless now; even the tail had ceased to twitch and hung limply behind, dripping over the edge of the narrow wall into the unfathomable pit of the garden; and as the watcher stared, he felt himself some communication of the horror so apparent in the other's attitude. Along his own spine, from neck to flank, ran the paralysing nervous movement; his own tail ceased to move; his own ears drew back instinctively, flattening themselves at the sides of the square strong head. There was a movement nearby, and he turned quick eyes to see the lithe young love of his heart stepping softly into her place beside him.

When he turned again his adversary had vanished.

Yet he still watched. Still there was no sound from the window at which the other had stared just now: no oblong of light shone out into the darkness to explain that sudden withdrawal from the fray.

All was as silent as it had been just now; on all sides windows were closed; now and then came a human voice, just a word or two, spoken and answered from one of those pits beneath, and the steady rumble of traffic went on far away across the roofs; but here, in the immediate neighbourhood, all was at peace. He knew well enough the window in question; he had leapt himself upon the sill once and again and seen the foodless waste of floor and carpet and furniture within.

Yet as he watched and waited his own horror grew. That for which in men we have as yet no term was strong within him, as in every beast that lives by perception rather than reason; and he too by this strange faculty knew well enough that something was abroad, raying out from that silent curtained unseen window—something of an utterly different order from that of dog or flung shoe and furious vituperation—something that affected certain nerves within his body in a new and awful manner. Once or twice in his life he had been conscious of it before, once in an empty room, once in a room tenanted by a mere outline beneath a sheet and closed by a locked door.

His heart too seemed melted within him; his tail too hung limply behind the stucco parapet, and he made no answering movement to the tiny crooning note that sounded once in his ears.

And still the horror grew. . . .

Presently he withdrew one claw from the crumbling edge, raising his head delicately; and then the other. For an instant longer he waited, feeling his back heave uncontrollably. Then, dropping noiselessly on to the lead, he fled beneath the sheltering parapet, a noiseless shadow in the gloom; and his mate fled with him.

Chapter 9

Laurie turned slowly over in bed, drew a long breath, expelled it, and, releasing his arms from the bedclothes, sat up. He switched on the light by his bed, glanced at his watch, switched off the light, and sank down again into the sheets. He need not get up just yet.

Then he remembered.

When an event of an entirely new order comes into experience, it takes a little time to be assimilated. It is as when a large piece of furniture is brought into a room; all the rest of the furniture takes upon itself a different value. A picture that did very well up to then over the fire-place must perhaps be moved. Values, relations, and balance all require readjustment.

Now up to last night Laurie had indeed been convinced, in one sense, of spiritualistic phenomena; but they had not yet for him

221

reached the point of significance when they affected everything else. The new sideboard, so to speak, had been brought into the room, but it had been put temporarily against the wall in a vacant space to be looked at; the owner of the room had not yet realised the necessity of rearranging the whole. But last night something had happened that changed all this. He was now beginning to perceive the need of a complete review of everything.

As he lay there, quiet indeed, but startlingly alert, he first reviewed the single fact.

About an hour or so had passed away before anything particular happened. They had sat there, those four, in complete silence, their hands upon the table, occasionally shifting a little, hearing the sound of one another's breathing or the faint rustle of one of the ladies' dresses, in sufficient light from the screened fire and the single heavily shaded electric burner to recognise faces, and even, after the first few minutes, to distinguish even small objects, or to read large print.

For the most part Laurie had kept his eyes upon the medium in the cabinet. There the man had leaned back, plainly visible for the most part, with even the paleness of his face and the dark blot of his beard clearly discernible in the twilight. Now and then the boy's eyes had wandered to the other faces, to the young clergyman's opposite downcast and motionless, with a sort of apprehensive look and a de-termination not to give way—to the three-quarter profiles of the two women, and the gleam of the *pince-nez* below Lady Laura's frizzed hair.

So, he had sat, the thoughts at first racing through his brain, then, as time went on, moving more and more slowly, with his own brain be-coming ever more passive, until at last he had been compelled to make a little effort against the drowsiness that had begun to envelop him. He had had to do this altogether three or four times, and had even begun to wonder whether he should be able to resist much longer, when a sudden trembling of the table had awakened him, alert and conscious in a moment, and he had sat with every faculty violently attentive to what should follow.

That trembling was a curious sensation beneath his hands. At first it was no more than might be caused by the passing of a heavy van in the street; only there was no van. But it had increased, with spasms and recoils, till it resembled a continuous shudder as of a living rigid body. It began also to tilt slightly this way and that.

Now all this, Laurie knew well, meant nothing at all—or rather, it need not. And when the movement passed again through all the reverse motions, sinking at last into complete stillness, he was conscious of disappointment. A moment later, however, as he glanced up again at the medium in the cabinet, he drew his breath sharply, and Mr. Jamieson, at the sound, wheeled his head swiftly to look.

There, in the cabinet, somewhere overhead behind the curtain, a faint but perfectly distinct radiance was visible. It was no more than a diffused glimmer, but it was unmistakable, and it shone out faintly and clearly upon the medium's face. By its light Laurie could make out every line and every feature, the drooping clipped moustache, the strong jutting nose, the lines from nostril to mouth, and the closed eyes. As he watched the light deepened in intensity, seeming to concentrate itself in the hidden corner at the top. Then, with a smooth, steady motion it emerged into full sight, in appearance like a softly luminous globe of a pale bluish colour, undefined at the edges, floating steadily forward with a motion like that of an air balloon, out into the room. Once outside the cabinet it seemed to hesitate, hanging at about the height of a man's head—then, after an instant, it retired once more, re-entered the cabinet, disappeared in the direction from which it had come, and once more died out.

Well, there it had been; there was no doubt about it. . . . And Laurie was unacquainted with any mechanism that could produce it.

The clergyman too had seemed affected. He had watched, with turned-back head, the phenomenon from beginning to end, and at the close, with a long indrawing of breath, had looked once at Laurie, licked his dry lips with a motion that was audible in that profound silence, and once more dropped his eyes. The ladies had been silent, and all but motionless throughout.

Well, the rest had happened comparatively quickly.

Once more, after the lapse of a few minutes, the radiance had begun to re-form; but this time it had emerged almost immediately, diffused and misty like a nebula; had hung again before the cabinet, and then, with a strange, gently whirling motion, had seemed to arrange itself in lines and curves.

Gradually, as he stared at it, it had begun to take the shape and semblance of a head, swathed in drapery, with that same drapery, hanging, as it appeared in folds, dripping downwards to the ground, where it lost itself in vagueness. Then, as he still stared, conscious of nothing but the amazing fact, features appeared to be forming—first blots and lines as of shadow, finally eyes, nose, mouth, and chin as of a young girl. . . .

A moment later there was no longer a doubt. It was the face of Amy Nugent that was looking at him, grave and steady—as when he had seen it in the moonlight above the sluice—and behind, seen half through the strange drapery, and half apart from it, a couple of feet behind, the face of the sleeping medium.

At that sight he had not moved nor spoken. It was enough that the fact was there. Every power he possessed was concentrated in the one effort of observation. . . .

He heard from somewhere a gasping sigh, and there rose up between him and the face the figure of the clergyman, with his head turned back staring at the apparition, and one hand only on the table, yet with that hand so heavy upon it that the whole table shuddered with his shudder.

There was a movement on the left, and he heard a fierce feminine whisper—

"Sit down, sir; sit down this instant. . . ."

When the clergyman had again sunk down into his seat with that same strong shudder, the luminous face was already incoherent; the features had relapsed again into blots and shadows, the drapery was absorbing itself upwards into the centre from which it came. Once more the nebula trembled, moved backwards, and disappeared. The next instant the radiance went out, as if turned off by a switch. The medium groaned gently and awoke.

Well, that had ended it. Laurie scarcely remembered the talking that followed, the explanations, the apologies, the hardly concealed terror of the young clergyman. The medium had come out presently, dazed and confused. They had talked . . . and so forth. Then Laurie had come home, still trying to assimilate the amazing fact, of which he said that it could make no difference—that he had seen with his own eyes the face of Amy Nugent four months after her death.

Now here he was in bed on the following morning, trying to assimilate it once more.

It seemed to him as if sleep had done its work—that the sub-conscious intelligence had been able to take the fact in—and that henceforth it was an established thing in his experience. He was not excited now, but he was intensely and overwhelmingly interested. There the thing was. Now what difference did it make?

First, he understood that it made an enormous difference to the value of the most ordinary things. It really was true—as true as tables and chairs—that there was a life after this, and that personality survived.

Never again could he doubt that for one instant, even in the gloomiest mood. So long as a man walks by faith, by the acceptance of authority, human or Divine, there is always psychologically possible the assertion of self, the instinct that what one has not personally experienced may just conceivably be untrue. But when one has seen—so long as memory does not disappear—this agnostic instinct is an impossibility. Every single act therefore has a new significance. There is no venture about it anymore; there is, indeed, very little opportunity for heroism. Once it is certain, by the evidence of the senses, that death is just an interlude, this life becomes merely part of a long process. . . .

Now as to the conduct of that life—what of religion? And here, for a moment or two, Laurie was genuinely dismayed. For, as he looked at the Catholic religion, he perceived that the whole thing had changed. It no longer seemed august and dominant. As he contemplated himself as he had been at Mass on the previous morning, he seemed to have been rather absurd. Why all this trouble, all this energy, all these innumerable acts and efforts of faith? It was not that his religion seemed necessarily untrue; it was certainly possible for a man to hold simultaneously Catholic and spiritualistic beliefs; there had not been a hint last night against Christianity, and yet, in the face of this evidence of the senses, Catholicism seemed a very shadowy thing.

It might well be true, as any philosophy may be true, but—did it matter very much? To be enthusiastic about it was the frenzy of an artist, who loves the portrait more than the original—and possibly a very misleading and inadequate portrait. Laurie had seen for himself the original last night; he had seen a disembodied soul in a garb assumed for the purpose of identification. . . . Did he need, then, a "religion?" Was not his experience all-sufficing? . . .

Then suddenly all speculation fled away in the presence of the personal element.

Three days ago, he had contemplated the thought of Amy with comparative indifference. She had been to him lately little more than a "test case" of the spiritual world, clothed about with the memory of sentiment. Now once more she sprang into vivid vital life as a person. She was not lost; his relations with her were not just incidents of the past; they were as much bound up with the present as courtship has a continuity with married life. She existed—her very self—and communication was possible between them. . . .

Laurie rolled over on to his back. The thought was violently overwhelming; there was a furious, absorbing fascination in it. The gulf had been bridged; it could be bridged again. Even if tales were true, it could be bridged far more securely yet. It was possible that the phantom he had seen could be brought yet more forward into the world of sense, that he could touch again with his very hand a tabernacle enclosing her soul. So far spiritualism had not failed him; why should he suspect it of failure in the future? It had been done before; it could, and should, be done again. Besides, there was the pencil incident. . . .

He threw off the clothes and sprang out of bed. It was time to get up; time to begin again this fascinating, absorbingly interesting earthly life, which now had such enormous possibilities.

✶✶✶✶✶✶

The rooms of Mr. James Morton were conveniently situated up four flights of stairs in one of those blocks of buildings, so mysterious to the layman, that lie not a very long way from Charing Cross. There is a silence always here as of college life, and the place is frequented by the same curious selections from the human race as haunt University courts. Here are to be seen cooks, aged and dignified men, errand-boys, and rather shabby old women.

The interior of the rooms, too, is not unlike that of an ordinary rather second-rate college; and Mr. James Morton's taste did not redeem the chambers in which he sat. From roof to floor the particular apartment in which he sat was lined with bookshelves filled with unprepossessing volumes and large black tin boxes. A large table stood in the middle of the room, littered with papers, with bulwarks of the same kind of tin boxes rising at either end.

Mr. Morton himself was a square-built man of some forty years, clean-shaven, and rather pale and stout, with strongly marked features, a good loud voice, and the pleasant, brusque manners that befit a University and public school man who has taken seriously to business.

Laurie and he got on excellently together. The younger man had an admiration for the older, whose reputation as a rather distinguished barrister certainly deserved it, and was sufficiently in awe of him to pay attention to his directions in all matters connected with law. But they did not meet much on other planes. Laurie had asked the other down to Stantons once, and had dined with him three or four times in return. And there their acquaintance found its limitations.

This morning, however, the boy's interested air, with its hints of suppressed excitement and his marked inattention to the books and papers which were his business, at last caused the older man to make a remark. It was in his best manner.

"What's the matter, eh?" he suddenly shot at him, without prelude of any kind.

Laurie's attention came back with a jump, and he flushed a little.

"Oh!—er—nothing particular," he murmured. And he set himself down to his books again in silence, conscious of the watchful roving eye on the other side of the table.

About half-past twelve Mr. Morton shut his own book with a slap, leaned back, and began to fill his pipe.

"Nothing seems very important," he said.

As the last uttered word had been spoken an hour previously, Laurie was bewildered, and looked it.

"It won't do, Baxter," went on the other. "You haven't turned a page an hour this morning."

Laurie smiled doubtfully, and leaned back too. Then he had a spasm of confidence.

"Yes. I'm rather upset this morning," he said. "The fact is, last night ..."

Mr. Morton waited.

"Well?" he said. "Oh! don't tell if me you don't want to."

Laurie looked at him.

"I wonder what you'd say," he said at last.

The other got up with an abrupt movement, pushed his books together, selected a hat, and put it on.

"I'm going to lunch," he said. "Got to be in the Courts at two; and ..."

"Oh! wait a minute," said Laurie. "I think I want to tell you."

"Well, make haste." He stood, in attitude to go.

"What do you think of spiritualism?"

"Blasted rot," said Mr. Morton. "Anything more I can do for you?"

"Do you know anything about it?"

"No. Don't want to. Is that all?"

"Well, look here," said Laurie. . . . "Oh! sit down for two minutes."

Then he began. He described carefully his experiences of the night before, explaining so much as was necessary of antecedent events. The other during the course of it tilted his hat back, and half leaned, half sat against a side-table, watching the boy at first with a genial contempt, and finally with the same curious interest that one gives to a man with a new disease.

"Now, what d'you make of that?" ended Laurie, flushed and superb.

"D'you want to know?" came after a short silence.

227

Laurie nodded.

"What I said at the beginning, then."

"What?"

"Blasted rot," said Mr. Morton again.

Laurie frowned sharply, and affected to put his books together.

"Of course, if you take it like that," he said. "But I don't know what respect you can possibly have for any evidence, if . . ."

"My dear chap, that isn't evidence. No evidence in the world could make me believe that the earth was upside down. These things don't happen."

"Then how do you explain . . .?"

"I don't explain," said Mr. Morton. "The thing's simply not worth looking into. If you really saw that, you're either mad or else there was a trick. . . . Now come along to lunch."

"But I'm not the only one," cried Laurie hotly.

"No, indeed you're not. . . . Look here, Baxter, that sort of thing plays the devil with nerves. Just drop it once and for all. I knew a chap once who went in for all that. Well, the end was what everybody knew would happen. . . ."

"Yes?" said Laurie.

"Went off his chump," said the other briefly. "Nasty mess all over the floor. Now come to lunch."

"Wait a second. You can't argue from particulars to universals. Was he the only one you ever knew?"

The other paused a moment.

"No," he said. "As it happens, he wasn't. I knew another chap—he's a solicitor. . . . Oh! by the way, he's one of your people—a Catholic, I mean."

"Well, what about him?"

"Oh! he's all right," admitted Mr. Morton, with a grudging air. "But he gave it up and took to religion instead."

"Yes? What's his name?"

"Cathcart."

He glanced up at the clock.

"Good Lord," he said, "ten to one."

Then he was gone.

Laurie was far too exalted to be much depressed by this counsel's opinion; and had, indeed, several minutes of delightful meditation on the crass complacency of a clever man when taken off his ground. It was deplorable, he said to himself, that men should be so content with their limitations. But it was always the way, he reflected. To be a specialist in one point involved the pruning of all growth on every other. Here was Morton, almost in the front rank of his particular subject, and, besides, very far from being a bookworm; yet, when taken an inch out of his rut, he could do nothing but flounder. He wondered what Morton would make of these things if he saw them himself.

In the course of the afternoon Morton himself turned up again. The case had ended unexpectedly soon. Laurie waited till the closing of the shutters offered an opportunity for a break in the work, and once more returned to the charge.

"Morton," he said, "I wish you'd come with me one day."

The other looked up.

"Eh?"

"To see for yourself what I told you."

Mr. Morton snorted abruptly.

"Lord!" he said, "I thought we'd done with that. No, thank you: Egyptian Hall's all I need."

Laurie sighed elaborately.

"Oh! of course, if you won't face facts, one can't expect . . ."

"Look here, Baxter," said the other almost kindly, "I advise you to give this up. It plays the very devil with nerves, as I told you. Why, you're as jumpy as a cat yourself. And it isn't worth it. If there was anything in it, why it would be another thing; but . . ."

"I . . . I wouldn't give it up for all the world," stammered Laurie in his zeal. "You simply don't know what you're talking about. Why . . . why, I'm not a fool . . . I know that. And do you think I'm ass enough to be taken in by a trick? And as if a trick could be played like that in a drawing-room! I tell you I examined every inch. . . ."

"Look here," said Morton, looking curiously at the boy—for there was something rather impressive about Laurie's manner—"look here; you'd better see old Cathcart. Know him? . . . Well, I'll introduce you any time. He'll tell you another tale. Of course, I don't believe all the rot he talks; but, at any rate, he's sensible enough to have given it all up. Says he wouldn't touch it with a pole. And he was rather a big bug at it in his time, I believe."

Laurie sneered audibly.

"Got frightened, I suppose," he said. "Of course, I know well enough that it's rather startling—"

"My dear man, he was in the thick of it for ten years. I'll acknowledge his stories are hair-raising, if one believed them; but then, you

229

see—"

"What's his address?"

Morton jerked his head towards the directories in the bookshelf.

"Find him there," he said. "I'll give you an introduction if you want it. Though, mind you, I think he talks as much rot as anyone—"

"What does he say?"

"Lord!—I don't know. Some theory or other. But, at any rate, he's given it up."

Laurie pursed his lips.

"I daresay I'll ask you some time," he said. "Meanwhile—"

"Meanwhile, for the Lord's sake, get on with that business you've got there."

Mr. Morton was indeed, as Laurie had reflected, extraordinarily uninterested in things outside his beat; and his beat was not a very extended one. He was a quite admirable barrister, competent, alert, merciless and kindly at the proper times, and, while at his business, thought of hardly anything else at all. And when he was not at his business, he threw himself with equal zest into two or three other occupations—golf, dining out, and the collection of a particular kind of chairs. Beyond these things there was for him really nothing of value.

But, owing to circumstances, his beat had been further extended to include Laurie Baxter, whom he was beginning to like extremely. There was an air of romance about Laurie, a pleasant enthusiasm, excellent manners, and a rather delightful faculty of hero-worship. Mr. Morton himself, too, while possessing nothing even resembling a religion, was, like many other people, not altogether unattracted towards those who had, though he thought religiousness to be a sign of a slightly incompetent character; and he rather liked Laurie's Catholicism, such as it was. It must be rather pleasant, he considered (when he considered it at all), to believe "all that," as he would have said.

So, this new phase of Laurie's interested him far more than he would have allowed, so soon as he became aware that it was not merely superficial; and, indeed, Laurie's constant return to the subject, as well as his air of enthusiastic conviction, soon convinced him that this was so.

Further, after a week or two, he became aware that the young man's work was suffering; and he heard from his lips the expression of certain views that seemed to the elder man extremely unhealthy.

For example, on a Friday evening, not much afterwards, as Laurie was putting his books together, Mr. Morton asked him where he was going to spend the weekend.

"Stopping in town," said the boy briefly.

"Oh! I'm going to my brother's cottage. Care to come? Afraid there's no Catholic church near."

Laurie smiled.

"That wouldn't deter me," he said. "I've made up my mind—"

"Yes?"

"Oh, it doesn't matter," said Laurie. "No—thanks awfully, but I've got to stop in town."

"Lady Laura's again?"

"Yes."

"Same old game?"

Laurie sat down.

"Look here," he said, "I know you don't mean anything; but I wish you'd understand."

"Well?"

The boy's face flushed with sudden nervous enthusiasm.

"Do you understand," he said, "that this is just everything to me? Do you know it's beginning to seem to me just the only thing that matters? I'm quite aware that you think it all the most utter bunkum; but, you see, I know it's true. And the whole thing is just like heaven opening. . . . Look here ... I didn't tell you half the other day. The fact is, that I was just as much in love with this girl as—as a man could be. She died; and now—"

"Look here, what were you up to last Sunday?"

Laurie quieted a little.

"You wouldn't understand," he said.

"Have you done any more of that business?"

"What business?"

"Well—thinking you saw her All right, seeing her, if you like."

The boy shook his head.

"No. Vincent's away in Ireland. We've been going on other lines."

"Tell me; I swear I won't laugh."

"All right; I don't care if you do. . . . Well, automatic handwriting."

"What's that?"

Laurie hesitated.

"Well, I go into trance, you see, and—"

"Good Lord, what next?"

"And then this girl writes through my hand," said Laurie deliberately, "when I'm unconscious. See?"

"I see you're a damned young fool," said Morton seriously.

"But if it's all rot, as you think?"

"Of course, it's all rot! Do you think I believe for one instant "He broke off. "And so's a nervous breakdown all rot, isn't it, and D.T.? They aren't real snakes, you know."

Laurie smiled in a superior manner.

"And you're getting yourself absorbed in all this—"

Laurie looked at him with a sudden flash of fanaticism.

"I tell you," he said, "that it's all the world to me. And so, would it be to you, if—"

"Oh, Lord! don't become Salvation Army.... Seen Cathcart yet?"

"No. I haven't the least wish to see Cathcart."

Morton rose, put his pens in the drawer, locked it; slid half a dozen papers into a black tin box, locked that too, and went towards his coat and hat, all in silence.

As he went out he turned on the threshold.

"When's that man coming back from Ireland?" he said.

"Who? Vincent? Oh! another month yet. We're going to have another try when he comes."

"Try? What at?"

"Materialisation," said Laurie. "That's to say—"

"I don't want to know what the foul thing means."

He still paused, looking hard at the boy. Then he sniffed.

"A young fool," he said. "I repeat it.... Lock up when you come. ... Goodnight."

Chapter 10

Mrs. Baxter possessed one of the two secrets of serenity. The other need not be specified; but hers arose from the most pleasant and most human form of narrow-mindedness. As has been said before, when things did not fit with her own scheme, either they were not things, but only fancies of somebody inconsiderable, or else she resolutely disregarded them. She had an opportunity of testing her serenity on one day early in February.

She rose as usual at a fixed hour—eight o'clock—and when she was ready knelt down at her *prie-Dieu*. This was quite an elaborate structure, far more elaborate than the devotions offered there. It was a very beautiful inlaid Florentine affair, and had a little shelf above it filled with a number of the little leather-bound books in which her soul delighted. She did not use these books very much; but she liked to see them there. It would not be decent to enter the sanctuary of Mrs. Baxter's prayers; it is enough to say that they were not very long. Then she rose from her knees, left her large comfortable bedroom, redolent with soap and hot water, and came downstairs, a beautiful slender little figure in black lace veil and rich dress, through the sunlight of the staircase, into the dining-room.

There she took up her letters and packets. They were not exciting. There was an unimportant note from a friend, a couple of bills, and a *Bon Marché* catalogue; and she scrutinised these through her spectacles, sitting by the fire. When she had done she noticed a letter lying by Maggie's place, directed in a masculine hand. An instant later Maggie came in herself, in her hat and furs, a charming picture, fresh from the winter sunlight and air, and kissed her.

While Mrs. Baxter poured out tea she addressed a remark or two to the girl, but only got back those vague inattentive murmurs that are the sign of a distracted mind; and, looking up presently with a sense of injury, noticed that Maggie was reading her letter with extraordinary diligence.

"My dear, I am speaking to you," said Mrs. Baxter, with an air of slightly humorous dignity.

"Er—I am sorry," murmured Maggie, and continued reading.

Mrs. Baxter put out her hand for the *Bon Marché* catalogue in order to drive home her sense of injury, and met Maggie's eyes, suddenly raised to meet her own, with a curious strained look in them.

"Darling, what is the matter?"

Maggie still stared at her a moment, as if questioning both herself and the other, and finally handed the letter across with an abrupt movement.

"Read it," she said.

It was rather a business to read it. It involved spectacles, a pushing aside of a plate, and a slight turning to catch the light. Mrs. Baxter read it, and handed it back, making three or four times the sound written as "Tut."

"The tiresome boy!" she said querulously, but without alarm.

"What are we to do? You see, Mr. Morton thinks we ought to do something. He mentions a Mr. Cathcart."

Mrs. Baxter reached out for the toast-rack.

"My dear, there's nothing to be done. You know what Laurie is. It'll only make him worse."

Maggie looked at her uneasily.

"I wish we could do something," she said.

"My dear, he'd have written to me—Mr. Morton, I mean—if Laurie had been really unwell. You see he only says he doesn't attend to his work as he ought."

Maggie took up the letter, put it carefully back into the envelope, and went on with breakfast. There was nothing more to be said just then.

But she was uneasy, and after breakfast went out into the garden, spud in hand, to think it all over, with the letter in her pocket.

Certainly, the letter was not alarming *per se*, but *per accidens*—that is to say, taking into account who it was that had written, she was not so sure. She had met Mr. Morton but once, and had formed of him the kind of impression that a girl would form of such a man in the hours of a weekend—a brusque, ordinary kind of barrister without much imagination and a good deal of shrewd force. It was surely rather an extreme step for a man like this to write to a girl in such a condition of things, asking her to use her influence to dissuade Laurie from his present course of life. Plainly the man meant what he said; he had not written to Mrs. Baxter, as he explained in the letter, for fear of alarming her unduly, and, as he expressly said, there was nothing to be alarmed about. Yet he had written.

Maggie stopped at the lower end of the orchard path, took out the letter, and read the last three or four sentences again:

"Please forgive me if you think it was unnecessary to write. Of course, I have no doubt whatever that the whole thing is nothing but nonsense; but even nonsense can have a bad effect, and Mr. Baxter seems to me to be far too much wrapt up in it. I enclose the address of a friend of mine in case you would care to write to him on the subject. He was once a Spiritualist, and is now a devout Catholic. He takes a view of it that I do not take; but at any rate his advice could do no harm. You can trust him to be absolutely discreet.

"Believe me,

"Yours sincerely,

"James Morton."

It really was very odd and unconventional; and Mr. Morton had not seemed at all an odd or unconventional person. He mentioned, too, a particular date, February 25, as the date by which the medium would have returned, and some sort of further effort was going to be made; but he did not attempt to explain this, nor did Maggie understand it. It only seemed to her rather sinister and unpleasant.

She turned over the page, and there was the address he had mentioned—a Mr. Cathcart. Surely he did not expect her to write to this stranger. . . .

She walked up and down with her spud for another half-hour before she could come to any conclusion. Certainly, she agreed with Mr. James Morton that the whole thing was nonsense; yet, further, that this nonsense was capable of doing a good deal of harm to an excitable person. Besides, Laurie obviously had a bad conscience about it, or he would have mentioned it.

She caught sight of Mrs. Baxter presently through the thick hedge, walking with her dainty, dignified step along the paths of the kitchen garden; and a certain impatience seized her at the sight. This boy's mother was so annoyingly serene. Surely it was her business, rather than Maggie's own, to look after Laurie; yet the girl knew perfectly well that if Laurie was left to his mother nothing at all would be done. Mrs. Baxter would deplore it all, of course, gently and tranquilly, in Laurie's absence, and would, perhaps, if she were hard pressed, utter a feeble protest even in his presence; and that was absolutely all. . . .

"Maggie! Maggie!" came the gentle old voice, calling presently; and then to some unseen person, "Have you seen Miss Deronnais anywhere?"

Maggie put the letter in her pocket and hurried through from the orchard.

"Yes?" she said, with a half hope.

"Come in, my dear, and tell me what you think of those new tea-cups in the *Bon Marché* catalogue," said the old lady. "There seem some beautiful new designs, and we want another set."

Maggie bowed to the inevitable. But as they passed up the garden her resolution was precipitated.

"Can you let me go by twelve," she said. "I rather want to see Father Mahon about something."

"My dear, I shall not keep you three minutes," protested the old lady.

And they went in to talk for an hour and threequarters.

★★★★★★

Father Mahon was a conscientious priest. He said his mass at eight o'clock; he breakfasted at nine; he performed certain devotions till half-past ten; read the paper till eleven, and theology till twelve. Then he considered himself at liberty to do what he liked till his dinner at one. (The rest of his day does not concern us just now.)

He, too, was looking round his garden this morning—a fine, solid figure of a man, in rather baggy trousers, short coat, and expansive waistcoat, with every button doing its duty. He too, like Mr. James Morton, had his beat, an even narrower one than the barrister's, and even better trodden, for he never strayed off it at all, except for four short weeks in the summer, when he hurried across to Ireland and got up late, and went on picnics with other ecclesiastics in straw hats, and joined in cheerful songs in the evening.

He was a priest, with perfectly defined duties, and of admirable punctuality and conscientiousness in doing them. He disliked the English quite extraordinarily; but his sense of duty was such that they never suspected it; and his flock of Saxons adored him as people only can adore a brisk, business-like man with a large heart and peremptory ways, who is their guide and father, and is perfectly aware of it. His sermons consisted of cold-cut blocks of dogma taken perseveringly from sermon outlines and served up Sunday by Sunday with a sauce of a slight and delightful brogue. He could never have kindled the Thames, nor indeed any river at all, but he could bridge them with solid stones; and this is, perhaps, even more desirable.

Maggie had begun by disliking him. She had thought him rather coarse and stupid; but she had changed her mind. He was not what may be called subtle; he had no patience at all with such things as scruples, *nuances*, and shades of tone and meaning; but if you put a plain question to him plainly, he gave you a plain answer, if he knew it; if not, he looked it up then and there; and that is always a relief in this intricate world. Maggie therefore did not bother him much; she went to him only on plain issues; and he respected and liked her accordingly.

"Good morning, my child," he said in his loud, breezy voice, as he came in to find her in his hideous little sitting-room. "I hope you don't mind the smell of tobacco-smoke."

The room indeed reeked; he had started a cigar, according to rule, as the clock struck twelve, and had left it just now upon a stump outside when his housekeeper had come to announce a visitor.

"Not in the least, thanks, Father. . . . May I sit down? It's rather a long business, I'm afraid."

The priest pulled out an armchair covered with horsehair and an anti-macassar.

"Sit down, my child."

Then he sat down himself, opposite her, in his trousers at once tight and baggy, with his rather large boots cocked one over the other, and his genial red face smiling at her.

"Now then," he said.

"It's not about myself, Father," she began rather hurriedly. "It's about Laurie Baxter. May I begin at the beginning?"

He nodded. He was not sorry to hear something about this boy, whom he didn't like at all, but for whom he knew himself at least partly responsible. The English were bad enough, but English converts were indescribably trying; and Laurie had been on his mind lately, he scarcely knew why.

Then Maggie began at the beginning, and told the whole thing, from Amy's death down to Mr. Morton's letter. He put a question or two to her during her story, looking at her with pressed lips, and finally put out his hand for the letter itself.

"Mrs. Baxter doesn't know what I've come about," said the girl. "You won't give her a hint, will you, Father?"

He nodded reassuringly to her, absorbed in the letter, and presently handed it back, with a large smile.

"He seems a sensible fellow," he said.

"Ah! that's what I wanted to ask you, Father. I don't know anything at all about spiritualism. Is it—is it really all nonsense? Is there nothing in it at all?"

He laughed loud.

"I don't think you need be afraid," he said. "Of course we know that souls don't come back like that. They're somewhere else." "Then it's all fraud?"

"It's practically all fraud," he said, "but it's very superstitious, and is forbidden by the Church."

This was straight enough. It was at least a clear issue to begin to attack Laurie upon.

"Then—then that's the evil of it?" she said. "There's no real power underneath? That's what Mr. Rymer said to Mrs. Baxter; and it's what I've always thought myself."

The priest's face became theological.

"Let's see what Sabetti says," he said. "I fancy—"

He turned in his chair and fetched out a volume behind him.

"Here we are. . . ."

He ran his finger down the heavy paragraphs, turned a page or two, and began a running comment and translation: "'*Necromantia ex*' . . . 'Necromancy arising from invocation of the dead.' . . . Let's see . . . yes,

237

'Spiritism, or the consulting of spirits in order to know hidden things, especially that pertain to the future life, certainly is divination properly so called, and is . . . is full of even more impiety than is magnetism, or the use of turning tables. The reason is, as the Baltimore fathers testify, that such knowledge must necessarily be ascribed to Satanic intervention, since in no other manner can it be explained.'"

"Then—" began Maggie.

"One moment, my child . . . Yes . . . just so. 'Express divination.' . . . . No, no. Ah! here we are, 'Tacit divination, . . . even if it is openly protested that no commerce with the Demon is intended, is *per se* grave sin; but it can sometimes be excused from mortal sin, on account of simplicity or ignorance or a lack of certain faith.' You see, my child"—(he set the book back in its place)—"so far as it's not fraud it's diabolical. And that's an end of it."

"But do you think it's not all fraud, then?" asked the girl, paling a little.

He laughed again, with a resonance that warmed her heart.

"I should pay just no attention to it all. Tell him, if you like, what I've said, and that it's grave sin for him to play with it; but don't get thinking that the devil's in everything."

Maggie was puzzled.

"Then it's not the devil?" she asked—"at least not in this case, you think?"

He smiled again reassuringly.

"I should suspect it was a clever trick," he said. I don't think Master Laurie's likely to get mixed up with the devil in that way. There's plenty of easier ways than that."

"Do you think I should write to Mr. Cathcart?"

"Just as you like. He's a convert, isn't he? I believe I've heard his name."

"I think so."

"Well, it wouldn't do any harm; though I should suspect not much good."

Maggie was silent.

"Just tell Master Laurie not to play tricks," said the priest. "He's got a good, sensible friend in Mr. Morton. I can see that. And don't trouble your head too much about it, my child."

When Maggie was gone, he went out to finish his cigar, and found to his pleasure that it was still alight, and after a puff or two it went very well.

He thought about his interview for a few minutes as he walked up and down, taking the bright winter air. It explained a good deal. He had begun to be a little anxious about this boy. It was not that Laurie had actually neglected his religion while at Stantons; he was always in his place at mass on Sundays, and even, very occasionally, on weekdays as well. And he had had a mass said for Amy Nugent. But even as far back as the beginning of the previous year, there had been an air about him not altogether reassuring.

Well, this at any rate was a small commentary on the present situation. . . .

(The priest stopped to look at some bulbs that were coming up in the bed beside him, and stooped, breathing heavily, to smooth the earth round one of them with a large finger.)

. . . And as for this Spiritualistic nonsense—of course the whole thing was a trick. Things did not happen like that. Of course, the devil could do extraordinary things: or at any rate had been able to do them in the past; but as for Master Laurie Baxter—whose home was down there in the hamlet, and who had been at Oxford and was now reading law—as for the thought that this rather superior Saxon young man was in direct communication with Satan at the present time—well, that needed no comment but loud laughter.

Yet it was very unwholesome and unhealthy. That was the worst of these converts; they could not be content with the sober workaday facts of the Catholic creed. They must be always running after some novelty or other. . . . And it was mortal sin anyhow, if the sinner had the faintest idea

A large dinner-bell pealed from the back door; and the priest went in to roast beef with Yorkshire pudding, apple dumplings, and a single glass of port wine to end up with.

✶✶✶✶✶✶

It was strange how Maggie felt steadied and encouraged in the presence of something at least resembling danger. So long as Laurie was merely tiresome and foolish, she distrusted herself, she made little rules and resolutions, and deliberately kept herself interiorly detached from him. But now that there was something definite to look to, her sensitiveness vanished.

As to what that something was, she did not trust herself to decide. Father Mahon had given her a point to work at—the fact that the thing, as a serious pursuit, was forbidden; as to what the reality behind was, whether indeed there were any reality at all, she did not allow herself to consider. Laurie was in a state of nerves sufficiently trouble-some to bring a letter from his friend and guide; and he was in that state through playing tricks on forbidden ground; that was enough.

Her interview with Father Mahon precipitated her half-formed resolution; and after tea she went upstairs to write to Mr. Cathcart.

It was an unconventional thing to do, but she was sufficiently per-turbed to disregard that drawback, and she wrote a very sensible letter, explaining first who she was; then, without any names being men-tioned, she described her adopted brother's position, and indicated his experiences: she occupied the last page in asking two or three ques-tions, and begging for general advice.

Mrs. Baxter displayed some symptoms after dinner which the girl recognised well enough. They comprised a resolute avoidance of Lau-rie's name, a funny stiff little air of dignity, and a touch of patronage. And the interpretation of these things was that the old lady did not wish the subject to be mentioned again, and that, interiorly, she was doing her best to ignore and forget it. Maggie felt, again, vaguely comforted; it left her a freer hand.

She lay awake a long time that night.

Her room was a little square one on the top of the stairs, above the smoking-room where she had that odd scene with Laurie a month or so before, and looking out upon the yew walk that led to the orchard. It was a cheerful little place enough, papered in brown, hung all over with water colours, with her bed in one corner; and it looked a reas-suring familiar kind of place in the firelight, as she lay open-eyed and thinking.

It was not that she was at all frightened; it was no more than a little natural anxiety; and half a dozen times in the hour or two that she lay thinking, she turned resolutely over in bed, dismissed the little pictures that her mind formed in spite of herself, and began to think of pleasant, sane subjects.

But the images recurred. They were no more than little vignettes—Laurie talking to a severe-looking tall man with a sardonic smile; Lau-rie having tea with Mrs. Stapleton; Laurie in an empty room, looking at a closed door. . . .

It was this last picture that recurred three or four times at the very instant that the girl was drowsing off into sleep; and it had therefore that particular vividness that characterises the thoughts when the con-scious attention is dormant. It had too a strangely perturbing effect upon her; and she could not imagine why.

After the third return of it her sense of humour came to the rescue: it was too ridiculous, she said, to be alarmed at an empty room and Laurie's back. Once more she turned on her side, away from the fire-light, and resolved, if it recurred again, to examine the details closely.

Again, the moments passed: thought followed thought, in those quiet waves that lull the mind towards sleep; finally, once more the picture was there, clear and distinct.

Yes; she would look at it this time.

It was a bare room, wainscoted round the walls a few inches up, papered beyond in some common palish pattern. Laurie stood in the centre of the uncarpeted boards, with his back turned to her, looking, it seemed, with an intense expectation at the very dull door in the wall opposite him. He was in his evening dress, she saw, knee-breeches and buckles all complete; and his hands were clenched, as they hung, held out a little from his sides, as he himself, crouching a little, stared at the door.

She, too, looked at the door, at its conventional panels and its brass handle; and it appeared to her as if both he and she were expectant of some visitor. The door would open presently, she perceived; and the reason why Laurie was so intent upon the entrance, was that he, no more than she, had any idea as to the character of the person who was to come in. She became quite interested as she watched—it was a method she followed sometimes when wooing sleep—and she began, in her fancy, to go past Laurie as if to open the door. But as she passed him she was aware that he put out a hand to check her, as if to hold her back from some danger; and she stopped, hesitating, still looking, not at Laurie, but at the door.

She began then, with the irresponsibility of deepening sleep, to imagine instead what lay beyond the door—to perceive by intuitive vision the character of the house. She got so far as understanding that it was all as unfurnished as this room, that the house stood solitary among trees, and that even these, and the tangled garden that she de-termined must surround the house, were as listening and as expectant as herself and the waiting figure of the boy. Once more, as if to verify her semi-passive imaginative excursion, she moved to the door. . . .

Ah! what nonsense it was. Here she was, wide awake again, in her own familiar room, with the firelight on the walls.

. . . Well, well; sleep was a curious thing; and so was imagination . . .

. . . At any rate she had written to Mr. Cathcart.

Chapter 11

The "Cock Inn" is situated in Fleet Street, not twenty yards from Mitre Court and scarcely fifty from the passage that leads down to the court where Mr. James Morton still has his chambers.

It was a convenient place, therefore, for Laurie to lunch in, and he generally made his appearance there a few minutes before one o'clock to partake of a small rump steak and a pewter mug of beer. Sometimes he came alone, sometimes in company; and by a carefully thought out system of tips he usually managed to have reserved for him at least until one o'clock a particular seat in a particular partition in that row of stable-like shelters that run the length of the room opposite the door on the first floor.

On the twenty-third of February, however—it was a Friday, by the way, and boiled plaice would have to be eaten instead of rump steak—he was a little annoyed to find his seat already occupied by a small, brisk-looking man with a grey beard and spectacles, who, with a newspaper propped in front of him, was also engaged in the consumption of boiled plaice.

The little man looked up at him sharply, like a bird disturbed in a meal, and then down again upon the paper. Laurie noticed that his hat and stick were laid upon the adjoining chair as if to retain it.

He hesitated an instant; then he slid in on the other side, opposite the stranger, tapped his glass with his knife, and sat down.

When the waiter came, a familiarly deferential man with whiskers, Laurie, with a slight look of peevishness, gave his order, and glanced reproachfully at the occupied seat. The waiter gave the ghost of a shrug with his shoulders, significant of apologetic helplessness, and went away.

A minute later Mr. Morton entered, glanced this way and that, nodding imperceptibly to Laurie, and was just moving off to a less occupied table when the stranger looked up.

"Mr. Morton," he cried, "Mr. Morton!" in an odd voice that seemed on the point of cracking into *falsetto*. (Certainly, he was very like a portly bird, thought Laurie.)

The other turned round, nodded with short geniality, and slid into the chair from which the old man moved his hat and stick with zealous haste.

"And what are you doing here?" said Mr. Morton.

"Just taking a bite like yourself," said the other. "Friday—worse luck."

Laurie was conscious of a touch of interest. This man was a Catholic, then, he supposed.

"Oh, by the way," said Mr. Morton, "have you—er" and he indicated Laurie. "No? . . . Baxter, let me introduce Mr. Cathcart."

For a moment the name meant nothing to Laurie; then he remembered; but his rising suspicions were quelled instantly by his friend's next remark.

"By the way, Cathcart, we were talking of you a week or two ago."

"Indeed! I am flattered," said the old man perkily. (Yes, "perky" was the word, thought Laurie.)

"Mr. Baxter here is interested in Spiritualism—(rump steak, waiter, and pint of bitter)—and I told him you were the man for him."

Laurie interiorly drew in his horns.

"A—er—an experimenter?" asked the old man, with courteous interest, his eyes giving a quick gleam beneath his glasses.

"A little."

"Yes. Most dangerous—most dangerous. . . . And any success, Mr. Baxter?"

Laurie felt his annoyance deepen.

"Very considerable success," he said shortly.

"Ah, yes—you must forgive me, sir; but I have had a good deal of experience, and I must say—— You are a Catholic, I see," he said, interrupting himself. "Or a High Churchman."

"I am a Catholic," said Laurie.

"So'm I. But I gave up spiritualism as soon as I became one. Very interesting experiences, too; but—well, I value my soul too much, Mr. Baxter."

Mr. Morton put a large piece of potato into his mouth with a detached air.

It was really rather trying, thought Laurie, to be catechised in this way; so, he determined to show superiority.

"And you think it all superstition and nonsense?" he asked.

"Indeed, no," said the old man shortly.

Laurie pushed his plate on one side, and drew the cheese towards him. This was a little more interesting, he thought, but he was still far from feeling communicative.

"What then?" he asked.

"Oh, very real indeed," said the old man. "That is just the danger."

"The danger?"

"Yes, Mr. Baxter. Of course, there's plenty of fraud and trickery; we all know that. But it's the part that's not fraud that's—— May I ask what medium you go to?"

"I know Mr. Vincent. And I've been to some public *séances*, too."

The old man looked at him with sudden interest, but said nothing.

"You think he's not honest?" said Laurie, with cool offensiveness.

"Oh, yes; he's perfectly honest," said the other deliberately. "I'll trouble you for the sugar, Mr. Morton."

Laurie was determined not to begin the subject again. He felt that he was being patronised and lectured, and did not like it. And once again the suspicion crossed his mind that this was an arranged meeting. It was so very neat—two days before the *séance*—the entry of Morton—his own seat occupied. Yet he did not feel quite courageous enough to challenge either of them. He ate his cheese deliberately and waited, listening to the talk between the two on quite irrelevant subjects, and presently determined on a bit of bravado.

"May I look at the *Daily Mirror*, Mr. Cathcart?" he asked.

"There is no doubt of his guilt," the old man said, as he handed the paper across (the two were deep in a law case now). "I said so to Markham a dozen times" and so on.

But there was no more word of spiritualism. Laurie propped the paper before him as he finished his cheese, and waited for coffee, and read with unseeing eyes. He was resenting as hard as he could the abruptness of the opening and closing of the subject, and the complete disregard now shown to him. He drank his coffee, still leisurely, and lit a cigarette; and still the two talked.

He stood up at last and reached down his hat and stick. The old man looked up.

"You are going, Mr. Baxter? . . . Good day. . . . Well then; and as I was waiting in court—"

Laurie passed out indignantly, and went down the stairs.

So that was Mr. Cathcart. . . . Well, he was thankful he hadn't written to him, after all. He was not his kind in the least.

★★★★★★

The moment he passed out of the door the old man stopped his fluent talking and waited, looking after the boy. Then he turned again to his friend.

"I'm a blundering idiot," he said.

Mr. Morton sniffed.

"I've put him against me now—Lord knows how; but I've done it;

and he won't listen to me."

"Gad!" said Mr. Morton; "what funny people you all are! And you really meant what you said?"

"Every word," said the old man cheerfully. . . . "Well; our little plot's over."

"Why don't you ask him to come and see you?"

"First," said the old man, with the same unruffled cheerfulness, "he wouldn't have come. We've muddled it. We'd much better have been straightforward. Secondly, he thinks me an old fool—as you do, only more so. No; we must set to work some other way now. . . . Tell me about Miss Deronnais: I showed you her letter?"

The other nodded, helping himself to cheese.

"I told her that I was at her service, of course; and I haven't heard again. Sensible girl?"

"Very sensible, I should say."

"Sort of girl that wouldn't scream or faint in a crisis?"

"Exactly the opposite, I should say. But I've hardly seen her, you know."

"Well, well. . . . And the mother?"

"No good at all," said Mr. Morton.

"Then the girl's the sheet anchor. . . . In love with him, do you know?"

"Lord! How d'you expect me to know that?"

The old man pondered in silence, seeming to assimilate the situation.

"He's in a devil of a mess," he said, with abrupt cheerfulness. "That man Vincent—"

"Well?"

"He's the most dangerous of the lot. Just because he's honest."

"Good God!" broke in the other again suddenly. "Do all Catholics believe this rubbish?"

"My dear friend, of course they don't. Not one in a thousand. I wish they did. That's what's the matter. But they laugh at it—laugh at it!" . . . (His voice cracked into shrill *falsetto*.) . . . "Laugh at hell-fire. . . Is Sunday the day, did you say?"

"He told me the twenty-fifth."

"And at that woman's in Queen's Gate, I suppose?"

"Expect so. He didn't say. Or I forget."

"I heard they were at their games there again," said Mr. Cathcart with meditative geniality. "I'd like to blow up the stinking hole."

Mr. Morton chuckled audibly.

"You're the youngest man of your years I've ever come across," he said. "No wonder you believe all that stuff. When are you going to grow up, Cathcart?"

The old man paid no attention at all.

"Well—that plot's over," he said again. "Now for Miss Deronnais. But we can't stop this Sunday affair; that's certain. Did he tell you anything about it? Materialisation? Automatic——"

"Lord, I don't know all that jargon. . . ."

"My dear Morton, for a lawyer, you're the worst witness I've ever Well, I'm off. No more to be done today."

The other sat on a few minutes over his pipe.

It seemed to him quite amazing that a sensible man like Cathcart could take such rubbish seriously. In every other department of life, the solicitor was an eminently shrewd and sane man, with, moreover, a youthful kind of brisk humour that is perhaps the surest symptom of sanity that it is possible to have.

He had seen him in court for years past under every sort of circumstance, and if it had been required of him to select a character with which superstition and morbid humbug could have had nothing in common, he would have laid his hand upon the senior partner of Cathcart and Cathcart. Yet here was this sane man, taking this fantastic nonsense as if there were really something in it. He had first heard him speak of the subject at a small bachelor dinner party of four in the rooms of a mutual friend; and, as he had listened, he had had the same sensation as one would have upon hearing a Cabinet Minister, let us say, discussing stump-cricket with enthusiasm. Cathcart had said all kinds of things when once he was started—all with that air of business-like briskness that was so characteristic of him and so disconcerting in such a connection.

If he had apologised for it as an amiable weakness, if he had been in the least shamefaced or deprecatory, it would have been another matter; one would have forgiven it as one forgives any little exceptional eccentricity. But to hear him speak of materialisation as of a process as normal (though unusual) as the production of radium, and of planchette as of wireless telegraphy—as established, indubitable facts, though out of the range of common experience—this had amazed this very practical man. Cathcart had hinted too of other things— things which he would not amplify—of a still more disconcertingly impossible nature—matters which Morton had scarcely thought had been credible even to the darkest medievalists; and all this with that same sharp, sane humour that lent an air of reality to all that he said.

For romantic young asses like Laurie Baxter such things were not so hopelessly incongruous, though obviously they were bad for him; they were all part of the wild credulousness of a religious youth; but for Cathcart, aged sixty-two, a solicitor in good practice, with a wife and two grown-up daughters, and a reputation for exceptionally sound shrewdness—! But it must be remembered he was a Catholic!

So Mr. James Morton sat in the "Cock" and pondered. He was not sorry he had tried to take steps to choke off this young fool, and he was just a little sorry that so far, they had failed. He had written to Miss Deronnais in an impulse, after an unusually feverish outburst from the boy; and she, he had learnt later, had written to Mr. Cathcart. The rest had been of the other's devising.

Well, it had failed so far. Perhaps next week things would be better.

He paid his bill, left two pence for the waiter, and went out. He had a case that afternoon.

******

Laurie left chambers as it was growing dark that afternoon, and went back to his rooms for tea. He had passed, as was usual now, an extremely distracted couple of hours, sitting over his books with spasmodic efforts only to attend to them. He was beginning, in fact, to be not quite sure whether Law after all was his vocation. . . .

His kettle was singing pleasantly on the hob, and a tray glimmered in the firelight on the little table, as the woman had left it; and it was not until he had poured himself out a cup of tea that he saw on the white cloth an envelope, directed to him, inscribed "By hand," in the usual handwriting of persons engaged in business. Even then he did not open it at once; it was probably only some note connected with his chief's affairs.

For half an hour more he sat on, smoking after tea, pondering that which was always in his mind now, and dwelling with a vague pleasant expectancy on what Sunday night should bring forth. Mr. Vincent, he knew, was returning to town that afternoon. Perhaps, even, he might look in for a few minutes, if there were any last instructions to be given.

The effect of the medium on the young man's mind had increased enormously during these past weeks. That air of virile masterfulness, all the more impressive because of its extreme quiet assurance, had proved even more deep than had at first appeared.

It is very hard to analyse the elements of a boy's adoration for a solid middle-aged gentleman with a "personality"; yet the thing is an enormously potent fact, and plays at least as big a part in the subcurrents that run about the world as any more normal human emotions. Psychologists of the materialistic school would probably say that it was a survival of the tribe-and-war instinct. At any rate, there it is.

Added to all this was the peculiar relation in which the medium stood to the boy; it was he who had first opened the door towards that strange other world that so persistently haunts the imaginations of certain temperaments; it was through him that Laurie had had brought before the evidence of his senses, as he thought, the actuality of the things of which he had dreamed'—an actuality which his religion had somehow succeeded in evading. It was not that Laurie had been insincere in his religion; there had been moments, and there still were, occasionally, when the world that the Catholic religion preached by word and symbol and sacrament, became apparent; but the whole thing was upon a different plane. Religion bade him approach in one way, spiritualism in the other. The senses had nothing to do with one; they were the only ultimate channels of the other. And it is extraordinarily easy for human beings to regard as more fundamentally real the evidence of the senses than the evidence of faith. . . .

Here then were the two choices—a world of spirit, to be taken largely on trust, to be discerned only in shadow and outline upon rare and unusual occasions of exaltation, of a particular quality which had almost lost its appeal; and a world of spirit that took shape and form and practical intelligibility, in ordinary rooms and under very nearly ordinary circumstances—a world, in short, not of a transcendent God and the spirits of just men made perfect, of vast dogmas and theories, but of a familiar atmosphere, impregnated with experience, inhabited by known souls who in this method or that made themselves apparent to those senses which, Laurie believed, could not lie. . . . And the point of contact was Amy Nugent herself. . . .

As regards his exact attitude to this girl it is more difficult to write. On the one side the human element—those associations directly connected with the senses—her actual face and hands, physical atmosphere and surroundings—those had disappeared; they were dispersed, or they lay underground; and it had been with a certain shock of surprise, in spite of the explanations given to him, that he had seen what he believed to be her face in the drawing-room in Queen's Gate. But he had tried to arrange all this in his imagination, and it had fallen into shape and proportion again. In short, he thought he understood now that it is character which gives unity to the transient qualities of a person on earth, and that, when those qualities disappear, it is as unimportant as the wasting of tissue: when, according to the spiritualists' gospel that character manifests itself from the other side, it naturally reconstitutes the form by which it had been recognised on earth.

Yet, in spite of this sense of familiarity with what he had seen, there had fallen between Amy and himself that august shadow that is called Death. . . . And in spite of the assurances he had received, even at the hands of his own senses, that this was indeed the same girl that he had known on earth, there was a strange awe mingled with his old rather shallow passion. There were moments, as he sat alone in his rooms at night, when it rose almost to terror; just as there were other moments when awe vanished for a while, and his whole being was flooded with an extraordinary ecstatic semi-earthly happiness at the thought that he and she could yet speak with one another. . . . Imagine, if you please, a child who on returning home finds that his mother has become queen, and meets her in the glory of ermine and diadem. . . .

But the real deciding point—which, somehow, he knew must come—the moment at which these conflicting notes should become a chord, was fixed for Sunday evening next. Up to now he had had evidence of her presence, he had received intelligible messages, though fragmentary and half stammered through the mysterious veil, he had for an instant or two looked upon her face; but the real point, he hoped, would come in two days. The public seances had not impressed him. He had been to three or four of these in a certain road off Baker Street, and had been astonished and disappointed.

The kind of people that he had met there—sentimental *bourgeois* with less power of sifting evidence than the average child, with a credulity that was almost supernatural—the medium, a stout woman who rolled her eyes and had damp fat fingers; the hymn-singing, the wheezy harmonium, the amazing pseudo-mystical oracular messages that revealed nothing which a religiose fool could not invent—in fact the whole affair, from the sham stained-glass lamp-shade to the ghostly tambourines overhead, the puerility of the tricks played on the inquirers, and all the rest of it—this seemed as little connected with what he had experienced with Mr. Vincent as a *dervish* dance with High Mass. He had reflected with almost ludicrous horror upon the impression it would make on Maggie, and the remarks it would elicit.

But this other engagement was a very different matter.

They were going to attempt a further advance. It had, indeed, been explained to him that these attempts were but tentative and experimental; it was impossible to dictate exactly what should fall; but the object on Sunday night was to go a step further, and to bring about, if possible, the materialisation process to such a point that the figure could be handled, and could speak. And it seemed to Laurie as if this would be final indeed. . . .

So, he sat this evening, within forty-eight hours of the crisis, thinking steadily. Half a dozen times, perhaps, the thought of Maggie recurred to him; but he was learning how to get rid of that.

Then he took up the note and opened it. It was filled with four pages of writing. He turned to the end and read the signature. Then he turned back and read the whole letter.

It was very quiet as he sat there thinking over what he had read. The noise of Fleet Street came up here only as the soothing murmur of the sea upon a beach; and he himself sat motionless, the firelight falling upwards upon his young face, his eyes, and his curly hair. About him stood his familiar furniture, the grand piano a pool of glimmering dark wood in the background, the tall curtained windows suggestive of shelter and warmth and protection.

Yet, if he had but known it, he was making an enormous choice. The letter was from the man he had met at midday, and he was deciding how to answer it. He was soothed and quieted by his loneliness, and his irritation had disappeared: he regarded the letter from a youthfully philosophical standpoint, pleased with his moderation, as the work of a fanatic; he was considering only whether he would yield, for politeness' sake, to the importunity, or answer shortly and decisively. It seemed to him remarkable that a mature and experienced man could write such a letter.

At last he got up, went to his writing-table, and sat down. Still he hesitated for a minute; then he dipped his pen and wrote.

When he had finished and directed it, he went back to the fire. He had an hour yet in which to think and think before he need dress. He had promised to dine with Mrs. Stapleton at half-past seven. He had a touch of headache, and perhaps might sleep it off.

Chapter 12

Lady Laura crossed the road by Knightsbridge Barracks and turned again homewards through the park.

It was one of those days that occasionally fall in late February which almost cheer the beholder into a belief that spring has really begun. Overhead the sky was a clear pale blue, flecked with summer-looking clouds, gauzy and white; beneath, the whole earth was waking drowsily from a frost so slight as only to emphasise the essential softness of the day that followed: the crocuses were alight in the grass, and an indescribable tint lay over all that had life, like the flush in the face of an awakening child. But these days are too good to last, and Lady Laura, who had looked at the forecast of a Sunday paper, had determined to take her exercise immediately after church.

She had come out not long before from All Saints'; she had listened to an excellent though unexciting sermon and some extremely beautiful singing; and even now, saturated with that atmosphere and with the soothing physical air in which she walked, her anxieties seemed less acute. There were enough of her acquaintances, too, in groups here and there—she had to bow and smile sufficiently often—to prevent these anxieties from reasserting themselves too forcibly. And it may be supposed that not a creature who observed her, in her exceedingly graceful hat and mantle, with her fair head a little on one side, and her gold-rimmed *pince-nez* delicately gleaming in the sunlight, had the very faintest suspicion that she had any anxieties at all.

Yet she felt strangely unwilling even to go home.

The men were to set about clearing the drawing-room while she was at church; and somehow the thought that it would be done when she got home, that the temple would, so to speak, be cleared for sacrifice, was a distasteful one.

She did not quite know when the change had begun; in fact, she was scarcely yet aware that there was a change at all. Upon one point only her attention fixed itself, and that was the increasing desire she felt that Laurie Baxter should go no further in his researches under her auspices.

Up to within a few weeks ago she had been all ardour. It had seemed to her, as has been said, that the apparent results of spiritualism were all to the good, that they were in no point contrary to the religion she happened to believe—in fact, that they made real, as does an actual tree in the foreground of a panorama, the rather misty sky and hills of Christianity. She had even called them very "teaching."

It was about eighteen months since she had first taken this up under the onslaught of Mrs. Stapleton's enthusiasm; but things had not been as satisfactory as she wished, until Mr. Vincent had appeared. Then indeed matters had moved forward; she had seen extraordinary things, and the effect of them had been doubled by the medium's obvious honesty and his strong personality. He was to her as a resolute priest to a timid penitent; he had led her forward, supported by his own conviction and his extremely steady will, until she had begun to feel at home in this amazing new world, and eager to make proselytes.

Then Laurie had appeared, and almost immediately a dread had seized her that she could neither explain nor understand. She had attempted a little tentative conversation on the point with dearest Maud, but dearest Maud had appeared so entirely incapable of understanding her scruples that she had said no more. But her inexplicable anxiety had already reached such a point that she had determined to say a word to Laurie on the subject. This had been done, without avail; and now a new step forward was to be made.

As to of what this step consisted she was perfectly aware.

The "controls," she believed—the spirits that desired to communicate—had a series of graduated steps by which the communications could be made, from mere incoherent noises (as a man may rap a message from one room to another), through appearances, also incoherent and intangible, right up to the final point of assuming visible tangible form, and of speaking in an audible voice. This process, she believed, consisted first in a mere connection between spirit and matter, and finally passed into an actual assumption of matter, moulded into the form of the body once worn by the spirit on earth.

For nearly all of this process she had had the evidence of her own senses; she had received messages, inexplicable to her except on the hypothesis put forward, from departed relations of her own; she had seen lights, and faces, and even figures formed before her eyes, in her own drawing-room; but she had not as yet, though dearest Maud had been more fortunate, been able to handle and grasp such figures, to satisfy the sense of touch, as well as of sight, in proof of the reality of the phenomenon. Yes; she was satisfied even with what she had seen; she had no manner of doubt as to the theories put before her by Mr. Vincent; yet she shrank (and she scarcely knew why) from that final consummation which it was proposed to carry out if possible that evening. But the shrinking centred round some half-discerned danger to Laurie Baxter rather than to herself.

It was these kinds of thoughts that beset her as she walked up beneath the trees on her way homewards—checked and soothed now somewhat by the pleasant air and the radiant sunlight, yet perceptible beneath everything. And it was not only of Laurie Baxter that she thought; she spared a little attention for herself.

For she had begun to be aware, for the first time since her initiation, of a very faint distaste—as slight and yet as suggestive as that caused by a half-perceived consciousness of a delicately disagreeable smell. There comes such a moment in the life of cut flowers in water, when the impetus of growing energy ceases, and a new tone makes itself felt in their scent, of which the end is certain. It is not sufficient to cause the flowers to be thrown away; they still possess volumes of fragrance; yet these decrease, and the new scent increases, until it has the victory.

So, it was now to the perceptions of this lady. Oh! yes; spiritualism was very "teaching" and beautiful; it was perfectly compatible with orthodox religion; it was undeniably true. She would not dream of giving it up. Only it would be better if Laurie Baxter did not meddle with it: he was too sensitive. . . . However, he was coming that evening again. . . . There was the fact.

As she turned southwards at last, crossing the road again towards her own street, it seemed to her that the day even now was beginning to cloud over. Over the roofs of Kensington, a haze was beginning to make itself visible, as impalpable as a skein of smoke; yet there it was. She felt a little languid, too. Perhaps she had walked too far. She would rest a little after lunch, if dearest Maud did not mind; for dearest Maud was to lunch with her, as was usual on Sundays when the Colonel was away.

As she came, slower than ever, down the broad opulent pavement of Queen's Gate, through the silence and emptiness of Sunday—for the church bells were long ago silent—she noticed coming towards her, with a sauntering step, an old gentleman in frock coat and silk hat of a slightly antique appearance, spatted and gloved, carrying his hands behind his back, as if he were waiting to be joined by some friend from one of the houses. She noticed that he looked at her through his glasses, but thought no more of it till she turned up the steps of her own house. Then she was startled by the sound of quick footsteps and a voice.

"I beg your pardon, madam . . ."

She turned, with her key in the door, and there he stood, hat in hand.

"Have I the pleasure of speaking to Lady Laura Bethell?"

There was a pleasant brisk ring about his voice that inclined her rather favourably towards him.

"Is there anything . . . Did you want to speak to me? . . . Yes, I am Lady Laura Bethell."

"I was told you were at church, madam, and that you were not at home to visitors on Sunday."

"That is quite right. . . . May I ask . . .?"

"Only a few minutes, Lady Laura, I promise you. Will you forgive my persistence?"

(Yes; the man was a gentleman; there was no doubt of that.)

"Would not tomorrow do? I am rather engaged today."

He had his card-case ready, and without answering her at once, he came up the steps and handed it to her.

The name meant nothing at all to her.

"Will not tomorrow . . .?" she began again.

"Tomorrow will be too late," said the old gentleman. "I beg of you, Lady Laura. It is on an extremely important matter."

She still hesitated an instant; then she pushed the door open and went in.

"Please come in," she said.

She was so taken aback by the sudden situation that she forgot completely that the drawing-room would be upside down, and led the way straight upstairs; and it was not till she was actually within the door, with the old gentleman close on her heels, that she saw that, with the exception of three or four chairs about the fire and the table set out near the hearthrug, the room was empty of furniture.

"I forgot," she said; "but will you mind coming in here. . . . We . . . we have a meeting here this evening."

She led the way to the fire, and at first did not notice that he was not following her. When she turned round she saw the old gentleman, with his air of antique politeness completely vanished, standing and looking about him with a very peculiar expression. She also noticed, to her annoyance, that the cabinet was already in place in the little ante-room and that his eyes almost immediately rested upon it. Yet there was no look of wonder in his face; rather it was such a look as a man might have on visiting the scene of a well-known crime—interest, knowledge, and loathing.

"So, it is here—" he said in quite a low voice.

Then he came across the room towards her.

******

For an instant his bearded face looked so strangely at her that she half moved towards the bell. Then he smiled, with a little reassuring gesture.

"No, no," he said. "May I sit down a moment?"

She began hastily to cover her confusion.

"It is a meeting," she said, "for this evening. I am sorry—"

"Just so," he said. "It is about that that I have come."

"I beg your pardon . . .?"

"Please sit down, Lady Laura. . . . May I say in a sentence what I have come to say?"

(This seemed a very odd old man.)

"Why, yes—" she said.

"I have come to beg you not to allow Mr. Baxter to enter the house. . . . No, I have no authority from anyone, least of all from Mr. Baxter. He has no idea that I have come. He would think it an unwarrantable piece of impertinence."

"Mr. Cathcart . . . I—I cannot—"

"Allow me," he said, with a little compelling gesture that silenced her. "I have been asked to interfere by a couple of people very much interested in Mr. Baxter; one of them, if not both, completely disbelieves in spiritualism."

"Then you know—"

He waved his hand towards the cabinet.

"Of course, I know," he said. "Why, I was a spiritualist for ten years myself. No, not a medium; not a professional, that is to say. I know all about Mr. Vincent; all about Mrs. Stapleton and yourself, Lady Laura. I still follow the news closely; I know perfectly well—"

"And you have given it up?"

"I have given it up for a long while," he said quietly. "And I have come to ask you to forbid Mr. Baxter to be present this evening, for—for the same reason for which I have given it up myself."

"Yes? And that—"

"I don't think we need go into that," he said. "It is enough, is it not, for me to say that Mr. Baxter's work, and, in fact, his whole nervous system, is suffering considerably from the excitement; that one of the persons who have asked me to do what I can is Mr. Baxter's own law-coach: and that even if he had not asked me, Mr. Baxter's own appearance—"

"You know him?"

"Practically, no. I lunched at the same table with him on Friday; the symptoms are quite unmistakable."

"I don't understand. Symptoms?"

"Well, we will say symptoms of nervous excitement. You are aware, no doubt, that he is exceptionally sensitive. Probably you have seen for yourself—"

"Wait a moment," said Lady Laura, her own heart beating furiously. "Why do you not go to Mr. Baxter himself?"

"I have done so. I arranged to meet him at lunch, and somehow, I took a wrong turn with him: I have no tact whatever, as you perceive. But I wrote to him on Friday night, offering to call upon him, and just giving him a hint. Well, it was useless. He refused to see me."

"I don't see what I—"

"Oh yes," chirped the old gentleman almost gaily. "It would be quite unusual and unconventional. I just ask you to send him a line—I will take it myself, if you wish it—telling him that you think it would be better for him not to come, and saying that you are making other arrangements for tonight."

He looked at her with that odd little air of birdlike briskness that she had noticed in the street; and it pleasantly affected her even in the midst of the uneasiness that now surged upon her again tenfold more than before. She could see that there was something else behind his manner; it had just looked out in the glance he had given round the room on entering; but she could not trouble at this moment to analyse what it was. She was completely bewildered by the strangeness of the encounter, and the extraordinary coincidence of this man's judgment with her own. Yet there were a hundred reasons against her taking his advice. What would the others say? What of all the arrangements . . . the expectation? . . .

"I don't see how it's possible now," she began. "I think I know what you mean. But—"

"Indeed, I trust you have no idea," cried the old gentleman, with a queer little *falsetto* note coming into his voice—"no idea at all. I come to you merely on the plea of nervous excitement; it is injuring his health, Lady Laura."

She looked at him curiously.

"But—" she began.

"Oh, I will go further," he said. "Have you never heard of—of insanity in connection with all this? We will call it insanity, if you wish."

For a moment her heart stood still. The word had a sinister sound, in view of an incident she had once witnessed; but it seemed to her that some meaning behind, unknown to her, was still more sinister. Why had he said that it might be "called insanity" only? . . .

"Yes. . . . I—I have once seen a case," she stammered.

"Well," said the old gentleman, "is it not enough when I tell you that I—I who was a spiritualist for ten years—have never seen a more dangerous subject than Mr. Baxter? Is the risk worth it? . . . Lady Laura, do you quite understand what you are doing?"

He leaned forward a little; and again, she felt anxiety, sickening and horrible, surge within her. Yet, on the other hand . . . .

The door opened suddenly, and Mr. Vincent came in.

******

There was silence for a moment; then the old gentleman turned round, and in an instant was on his feet, quiet, but with an air of bristling about his thrust-out chin and his tense attitude.

Mr. Vincent paused, looking from one to the other.

"I beg your pardon, Lady Laura," he said courteously. "Your man told me to wait here; I think he did not know you had come in."

"Well—er—this gentleman . . ." began Lady Laura. "Why, do you know Mr. Vincent?" she asked suddenly, startled by the expression in the old gentleman's face.

"I used to know Mr. Vincent," he said shortly.

"You have the advantage of me," smiled the medium, coming forward to the fire.

"My name is Cathcart, sir."

The other started, almost imperceptibly.

"Ah! yes," he said quietly. "We did meet a few times, I remember."

Lady Laura was conscious of distinct relief at the interruption: it seemed to her a providential escape from a troublesome decision.

"I think there is nothing more to be said, Mr. Cathcart. . . . No, don't go, Mr. Vincent. We had finished our talk."

"Lady Laura," said the old gentleman with a rather determined air, "I beg of you to give me ten minutes more private conversation."

She hesitated, clearly foreseeing trouble either way. Then she decided.

"There is no necessity today," she said. "If you care to make an appointment for one day next week, Mr. Cathcart—"

"I am to understand that you refuse me a few minutes now?"

"There is no necessity that I can see—"

"Then I must say what I have to say before Mr. Vincent—"

"One moment, sir," put in the medium, with that sudden slight air of imperiousness that Lady Laura knew very well by now. "If Lady Laura consents to hear you, I must take it on myself to see that nothing offensive is said." He glanced as if for leave towards the woman.

She made an effort.

"If you will say it quickly," she began. "Otherwise—"

The old gentleman drew a breath as if to steady himself. It was plain that he was very strongly moved beneath his self-command: his air of cheerful geniality was gone.

"I will say it in one sentence," he said. "It is this: You are ruining that boy between you, body and soul; and you are responsible before his Maker and yours. And if—"

"Lady Laura," said the medium, "do you wish to hear any more?"

She made a doubtful little gesture of assent.

"And if you wish to know my reasons for saying this," went on Mr. Cathcart, "you have only to ask for them from Mr. Vincent. He knows well enough why I left spiritualism—if he dares to tell you."

Lady Laura glanced at the medium. He was perfectly still and quiet—looking, watching the old man curiously and half humorously under his heavy eyebrows.

"And I understand," went on the other, "that tonight you are to make an attempt at complete materialisation. Very good; then after to-night it may be too late. I have tried to appeal to the boy: he will not hear me. And you too have refused to hear me out. I could give you evidence, if you wished. Ask this gentleman how many cases he has known in the last five years, where complete ruin, body and soul—"

The medium turned a little to the fire, sighing as if for weariness: and at the sound the old man stopped, trembling. It was more obvious than ever that he only held himself in restraint by a very violent effort: it was as if the presence of the medium affected him in an extraordinary degree.

Lady Laura glanced again from one to the other.

"That is all, then?" she said.

His lips worked. Then he burst out—

"I am sick of talking," he cried—"sick of it! I have warned you. That is enough. I cannot do more."

He wheeled on his heel and went out. A minute later the two heard the front door bang.

She looked at Mr. Vincent. He was twirling softly in his strong fingers a little bronze candlestick that stood on the mantelpiece: his manner was completely unconcerned; he even seemed to be smiling a little.

For herself she felt helpless. She had taken her choice, impelled to it, though she scarcely recognised the fact, by the entrance of this strong personality; and now she needed reassurance once again. But before she had a word to say, he spoke—still in his serene manner.

"Yes, yes," he said. "I remember now. I used to know Mr. Cathcart once. A very violent old gentleman."

"What did he mean?"

"His reasons for leaving us? Indeed, I scarcely remember. I suppose it was because he became a Catholic."

"Was there nothing more?"

He looked at her pleasantly.

"Why, I daresay there was. I really can't remember, Lady Laura. I suppose he had his nerves shaken. You can see for yourself what a fanatic he is."

But in spite of his presence, once more a gust of anxiety shook her.

"Mr. Vincent, are you sure it's safe—for Mr. Baxter, I mean?"

"Safe? Why, he's as safe as any of us can be. We all have nervous systems, of course."

"But he's particularly sensitive, isn't he?"

"Indeed, yes. That is why even this evening he must not go into trance. That must come later, after a good training."

She stood up, and came herself to stand by the mantelpiece.

"Then really there's no danger?"

He turned straight to her, looking at her with kind, smiling eyes.

"Lady Laura," he said, "have I ever yet told you that there was no danger? I think not. There is always danger, for every one of us, as there is for the scientist in the laboratory, and the engineer in his machinery. But what we can do is to reduce that danger to a minimum, so that, humanly speaking, we are reasonably and sufficiently safe. No doubt you remember the case of that girl? Well, that was an accident: and accidents will happen; but do me the justice to remember that it was the first time that I had seen her. It was absolutely impossible to foresee. She was on the very edge of a nervous breakdown before she entered the room. But with regard to Mr. Baxter, I have seen him again and again; and I tell you that I consider him to be running a certain risk—but a perfectly justifiable one, and one that is reduced to a minimum. If I did not think that we were taking every precaution, I would not have him in the room for all the world. . . . Are you satisfied, Lady Laura?"

Every word he said helped her back to assurance. It was all so reasonable and well weighed. If he had said there was no danger, she would have feared the more; but his very recognition of it gave her security. And above all, his tranquillity and his strength were enormous assets on his side.

She drew a breath, and decided to go forward.

"And Mr. Cathcart?" she asked.

He smiled again.

"You can see what he is," he said. "I should advise you not to see him again. It's of no sort of use."

Chapter 13

The weather forecasts had been in the right; and the few that struggled homewards that night from church fought against a south-west wind that tore, laden with driving rain, up the streets and across the open spaces, till the very lights were dimmed in the tall street lamps and shone only through streaming panes that seemed half opaque with mist and vapour. In Queen's Gate hardly one lighted window showed that the houses were inhabited. So fierce was the clamour and storm of the broad street that men made haste to shut out every glimpse of the night, and the fanlights above the doors, or here and there a line of brightness where some draught had tossed the curtains apart, were the only signs of human life.

Outside the broad pavements stared like surfaces of some canal, black and mirror-like, empty of passengers, catching every spark or hint of light from house and lamp, transforming it to a tall streak of glimmering wetness. The housekeeper's room in this house on the right was the more delightful from the contrast. It was here that the august assembly was held every evening after supper, set about with rigid etiquette and ancient rite. Its windows looked on to the little square garden at the back, but were now tight shuttered and curtained; and the room was a very model of comfort and warmth. Before the fire a square table was drawn up, set out with pudding and fruit, for it was here that the upper servants withdrew after the cold meat and beer of the servants' hall, to be waited upon by the butler's boy: and it was round this that the four sat in state—housekeeper, butler, lady's maid, and cook.

It was already after ten o'clock; and Mr. Parker was permitted to smoke a small cigar. They had discussed the weather, the sermon that Miss Baker had heard in the morning, and the prospects of a Dissolution; and they had once more returned to the mysteries that were being enacted upstairs. They were getting accustomed to them now, and there was not a great deal to say, unless they repeated themselves, which they had no objection to do. Their attitude was one of tolerant scepticism, tempered by an agreeable tendency on the part of Miss Baker to become agitated after a certain point. Mr. Vincent, it was generally conceded, was a respectable sort of man, with an air about him that could hardly be put into words, and it was thought to be a pity that he lent himself to such superstition. Mrs. Stapleton had been long ago dismissed as a silly sort of woman, though with a will of her own; and her ladyship, of course, must have her way; it could not last long, it was thought.

But young Mr. Baxter was another matter, and there was a deal to say about him. He was a gentleman—that was certain; and he seemed to have sense; but it was a pity that he was so often here now on this business. He had not said one word to Mr. Parker this evening as he took off his coat; Mr. Parker had not thought that he looked very well.

"He was too quiet-like," said the butler.

As to the details of the affair upstairs—these were considered in a purely humorous light. It was understood that tables danced a hornpipe, and that tambourines were beaten by invisible hands; and it was not necessary to go further into principles, particularly since all these things were done by machinery at the Egyptian Hall. Faces also, it was believed, were seen looking out of the cabinet which Mr. Parker had once more helped to erect this morning; but these, it was explained, were "done" by luminous paint. Finally, if people insisted on looking into causes, Electricity was a sufficient answer for all the rest. No one actually suggested water-power.

As for human motives, these were not called in question at all. It appeared to amuse some people to do this kind of thing, as others might collect old china or practise the *cotillon*. There it was, a fact, and there was no more to be said about it. Old Lady Carraden, where Mr. Parker had once been under-butler, had gone in for pouter pigeons; and Miss Baker had heard tell of a nobleman who had a carpenter's shop of his own.

These things were so, then; and meantime here was a cigar to be smoked by Mr. Parker, and a little weak tea to be taken by the three ladies.

It was about a quarter-past ten when a reversion was made to the weather. Within here all was supremely comfortable. A black stuff mat, with a red fringed border, lay before the blazing fire, convenient to the feet; the heavy red curtains shut out the darkness, and where the glass cases of china permitted it, large photographs of wedding groups and the houses of the nobility hung upon the walls. A King Charles' spaniel, in another glass case, looked upon the company with an eternal snarl belied by the mildness of his brown eyes; and, corresponding to him on the other side of the fire, a numerous family of humming-birds, a little dusty and dim, poised perpetually above the flowers of a lichened tree, with a flaming sunset to show them up.

But, without, the wind tore unceasingly, laden with rain, through the gusty darkness of the little garden, and, in the pauses, the swift dripping from the roof splashed and splashed upon the paved walk. It was a very wild night, as Mr. Parker observed four times: he only hoped that no one would require a hansom cab. He had been foolish enough to take the responsibility tonight of letting the guests out himself, and of allowing William to go to bed when he wished. And these were late affairs, seldom over before eleven, and often not till nearly midnight.

Mrs. Martin, in her blouse, moved a little nearer the fire, and said she must be off soon to bed; Mrs. Mayle, in her black silk, added that there was no telling when her ladyship would get to bed, what with Mrs. Stapleton and all, and commiserated Miss Baker; Miss Baker moaned a little in self-pity; and Mr. Parker remarked for the fifth time that it was a wild night. It was an astonishingly serene and domestic atmosphere: no effort of imagination or wit was required from anybody; it was enough to make observations when they occurred to the brain, and they would meet with a tranquil response.

As half-past ten tingled out from the little yellow marble clock on the mantelpiece—it had been won by Mrs. Mayle's deceased husband in a horticultural exhibition—Mrs. Martin said that she must go and have a look at the scullery to see that all was as it should be; there was no knowing with these girls nowadays what they might not leave undone; and Mrs. Mayle preened herself gently with the thought that her responsibilities were on a higher plane. Mr. Parker made a courteous movement as if to rise, and remained seated, as the cook rustled out. Miss Baker sighed again as she contemplated the long conversation that might take place between the two ladies upstairs before she could get her mistress to bed.

Once more the tranquil atmosphere settled down on the warm room; the brass lamp burned brightly with a faint and reassuring smell of paraffin; the fire presented a radiant cavern of red coals fringed by dancing flames; and Mr. Parker leaned forwards to shake off the ash of his cigar.

Then, on a sudden, he paused, for from the passage outside came the passionless tingle of an electric bell—then another, and another, and another, as if some person overhead strove by reiteration on that single note to cry out some overwhelming need.

★★★★★★

Overhead in the great empty drawing-room the noise of the wind and rain, the almost continuous spatter on the glass, and the long hooting of the gusts, had been far more noticeable than in the base-ment beneath. Below stairs the company had been natural and nor-mal, talking of this and that, in a brightly lighted room, dwelling only on matters that fell beneath the range of their senses, lulled by warmth and food and cigar-smoke into a kind of rapt self-contemplation. But up here, in the gloom, lighted only on this occasion by a single shaded candle, in a complete interior silence, three persons had sat round a table for more than an hour, striving by passivity and a kind of inde-scribable concentration to ignore all that was presented by the senses, and to await some movement from that which lies beyond them.

Lady Laura had sat down that night in a state of mind which she could not analyse. It was not that her anxieties had been lulled so much as counterbalanced; they were still there, at once poignant and heavy, but on the other side there had been the assured air of the me-dium, his reasonableness and his personality, as well as the enthusiasm of her friend, and her astonished remonstrances. She had decided to acquiesce, not because she was satisfied, but because on the whole anxiety was outweighed by confidence. She could not have taken ac-tion under such circumstances, but she could at least refrain from it.

Laurie, as Mr. Parker had noticed, had been "quiet-like"; he had said very little indeed, but a nervous strain was evident in the bright-ness of his eyes; but in answer to a conventional inquiry he had de-clared himself extremely well. Mr. Vincent had looked at him for just an instant longer than usual as he shook hands, but he said nothing. Mrs. Stapleton had made an ecstatic remark or two on the envy with which she regarded the boy's sensitive faculties.

At the beginning of the seance the medium had repeated his warnings as to Laurie's avoiding of trance, and had added one or two other precautions. Then he had gone into the cabinet; the fire had been pressed down under ashes, and a single candle lighted and placed behind the angle of the little adjoining room in such a position that its shaded light fell upon the cabinet only and the figure of the medium within.

When the silence became fixed, Lady Laura for the first time perceived the rage of wind and rain outside. The very intensity of the interior stillness and the rapture of attention emphasised to an extraordinary degree the windy roar without. Yet the silence seemed to her, now as always, to have a peculiar faculty of detaching the psychical from the physical atmosphere. In spite of the batter of rain not ten feet away, the sighing between the shutters, and even the lift now and again of the heavy curtains in the draught, she seemed to herself as remote from it as a man crouching in the dark under some ruin feels himself at an almost infinite distance from the pick and the hammer of the rescuers. These were in one world, she in another.

For over an hour no movement was made. She herself sat facing the fire, Laurie on her left looking towards the cabinet with his back to the windows, Mrs. Stapleton opposite to her.

An endless procession of thoughts defiled before her as she sat, yet these too were somewhat remote—far up, so to speak, on the superficies of consciousness: they did not approach that realm of the will poised now and attentive on another range of existence. Once and again she glanced up without moving her head at the three-quarter profile on her left, at the somewhat Zulu-like outline opposite to her; then down again at the polished little round table and the six hands laid upon it. And meanwhile her brain revolved images rather than thoughts, memories rather than reflections—vignettes, so to speak,— old Mr. Cathcart in his spats and frock-coat, the look on the medium's face, there and gone again in an instant as he had heard the stranger's name; the carved oak stalls of the chancel towards which she had faced this morning, the look of the park, the bloom upon the still leafless trees, the radiance of the blue spring sky. . . .

It must have been, she thought, after a little over an hour that the first expected movement made itself felt— a long trembling shudder through the wood beneath her hands, followed by a strange sensation of lightness, as if the whole table rose a little from the floor. Then, almost before the movement subsided, a torrent of little taps poured itself out, as delicate and as swift and, it seemed, as perfectly calculated, as the rapping of some minute electric hammer. This was new to her, yet not so unlike other experiences as to seem strange or perturbing in any way. . . . Again, she bent her attention to the table as the vibration ceased. There followed a long silence.

It must have been about ten minutes later that she became aware of the next phenomenon; and her attention had been called to it by a sudden noiseless uplifting of the profile on her left. She turned her face to the cabinet and looked; and there, perfectly discernible, was some movement going on between the curtains. For the moment she could see the medium clearly, his arms folded, indicated by the white lines of his cuffs across his breast, his head sunk forward in deep sleep; and at the next instant the curtains flapped two or three times, as if jerked from within, and finally rested completely closed.

She glanced quickly at the boy on her left, and in the diffused light from the other room could see him distinctly, his eyes open and watching, his lips compressed as if in some tense effort of self-control.

When she looked at the cabinet again she could see that some movement had begun again behind the curtains, for these swayed and jerked convulsively, as if some person with but little room was moving there. And she could hear now, as the gusts outside lulled for a moment, the steady rather stertorous breathing of the medium. Then once again the wind gathered strength outside; the rain tore at the glass like a streaming handful of tiny pebbles, and the great curtains at her side lifted and sighed in the draught through the shutters.

When it quieted again the breathing had become a measured moaning, as that which a dreaming dog emits at the end of each expiration; and she herself drew a long trembling breath, overwhelmed by the sense of some struggle in the room such as she had not experienced before.

It was impossible for her to express this even to herself; yet the perception was clear—as clear as some presentment of the senses. She knew during those moments, as she watched the swaying curtains of the cabinet in the shaded light that fell upon them, and heard now and again that low moan from behind them, that some kind of stress lay upon something that was new to her in this connection. For the time she forgot her undertone of anxiety as to this boy at her side, and a curious terrified excitement took its place. Once, even then, she glanced at him again, and saw the motionless profile watching, always watching. . . .

Then in an instant the climax came, and this is what she saw.

The commotion of the curtains ceased suddenly, and they hung in straight folds from roof to floor of the little cabinet. Then they gently parted—she saw the long fingers that laid hold of them—and the form of a person came out, descended the single step, and stood on the floor before her eyes, in the plain candle-light, not four steps away.

It was the figure of a young girl, perfectly formed in all its parts, swathed in some light stuff resembling muslin that fell almost to the feet and shrouded the upper part of the head. Her hands were clasped across her breast, her bare feet were visible against the dark floor, and her features were unmistakably clear. There was a certain beauty in the face—in the young lips, the open eyes, and the dark lines of the brows over them; and the complexion was waxen, clear as of a blonde.

But, as the observer had noticed before on the three or four occasions on which she had seen these phenomena, there was a strange mask-like set of the features, as if the life that lay behind them had not perfectly saturated that which expressed it. It was something utterly different from the face of a dead person, yet also not completely alive, though the eyes turned a little in their sockets, and the young down-curved lips smiled. Behind her, plain between the tossed-back curtains, was the figure of the medium sunk in sleep.

And so, for a few seconds the apparition remained.

It seemed to the watcher that during those seconds the whole world was still. Whether in truth the wind had dropped, or whether the absorbed attention perceived nothing but the marvel before it, yet so it seemed. Even the breathing of the medium had stopped; Lady Laura heard only the ticking of the watch upon her own wrist.

Then, as once more a gust tore up from the southwest, the figure moved forward a step nearer the table, coming with a motion as of a living person, causing, it even appeared, that faint vibration on the floor as of a living body.

She stood so near now, though with her back to the diffused light of the ante-room, that her features were more plain than before—the stained lips, the open eyes, the shadow beneath the nostrils and chin, even the white fingers clasped across the breast. There was none of that vague mistiness that had been seen once before in that room; every line was as clear-cut as in the face of a living person; even the swell of the breast beneath the hands, the slender sloping shoulders, the long curved line from hip to ankle, all were real and discernible. And once again the staring eyes of the watcher took in, and her mind perceived, that slight mask-like look on the pretty appealing face.

Once again, the figure came forward, straight on to the table; and then, so swift that not a motion or a word could check it, the catastrophe fell.

There was a violent movement on Lady Laura's left hand, a chair shot back and fell, and with a horrible tearing cry from the throat, the boy dashed himself face forwards across the table, snatched at and for an instant seized something real and concrete that stood there; and as the two women sprang up, losing sight for an instant of the figure that had been there a moment ago, the boy sank forward, moaning and sobbing, and a crash as of a heavy body falling sounded from the cabinet.

For a space of reckonable time there was complete silence. Then once more a blast of wind tore up from the south-west, rain shattered against the window, and the house vibrated to the shock.

Chapter 14

As the date approached Maggie felt her anxieties settle down, like a fire, from turbulence to steady flame. On the Sunday she had with real difficulty kept it to herself, and the fringe of the storm of wind and rain that broke over Hertfordshire in the evening had not been reassuring. Yet on one thing her will kept steady hold, and that was that Mrs. Baxter must not be consulted. No conceivable good could result, and there might even be harm: either the old lady would be too much or not enough concerned: she might insist on Laurie's return to Stantons, or might write him a cheering letter encouraging him to amuse himself in any direction that he pleased. So, Maggie passed the evening in fits of alternate silence and small conversation, and succeeded in making Mrs. Baxter recommend a good long night.

Monday morning, however, broke with a cloudless sky, an air like wine, and the chatter of birds; and by the time that Maggie went to look at the crocuses immediately before breakfast, she was all but at her ease again. Enough, however, of anxiety remained to make her hurry out to the stable-yard when she heard the postman on his way to the back door.

There was one letter for her, in Mr. Cathcart's handwriting; and she opened it rather hastily as she turned in again to the garden.

It was reassuring. It stated that the writer had approached—(that was the word)—Mr. Baxter, though unfortunately with ill-success, and that he proposed on the following day—(the letter was dated on Saturday evening)—also to approach Lady Laura Bethell. He felt fairly confident, he said, that his efforts would succeed in postponing, at any rate, Mr. Baxter's visit to Lady Laura; and in that case he would write further as to what was best to be done. In the meanwhile, Miss Deronnais was not to be in the least anxious. Whatever happened, it was extremely improbable that one visit more or less to a *séance* would carry any great harm: it was the habit, rather than the act, that was usually harmful to the nervous system. And the writer begged to remain her obedient servant.

Maggie's spirits rose with a bound. How extraordinarily foolish she had been, she told herself, to have been filled with such forebodings last night! It was more than likely that the *séance* had taken place without Laurie; and, even at the worst, as Mr. Cathcart said, he was probably only a little more excited than usual this morning.

So, she began to think about future arrangements; and by the time that Mrs. Baxter looked benignantly out at her from beneath the Queen Anne doorway to tell her that breakfast was waiting, she was conceiving of the possibility of going up herself to London in a week or two on some shopping excuse, and of making one more genial attempt to persuade Laurie to be a sensible boy again.

During her visit to the fowl-yard after breakfast she began to elaborate these plans.

She was clear now, once again, that the whole thing was a fantastic delusion, and that its sole harm was that it was superstitious and nerve-shaking. (She threw a large handful of maize, with a meditative eye.) It was on that ground and that only that she would approach Laurie. Perhaps even it would be better for her not to go and see him; it might appear that she was making too much of it: a good sensible letter might do the work equally well.... Well, she would wait at least to hear from Mr. Cathcart once more. The second post would probably bring a letter from him. (She emptied her bowl.)

She was out again in the spring sunshine, walking up and down before the house with a book by the time that the second post was due. But this time, through the iron gate, she saw the postman go past the house without stopping. Once more her spirits rose, this time, one might say, to par; and she went indoors.

Her window looked out on to the front; and she moved her writing-table to it to catch as much as possible of the radiant air and light of the spring day. She proposed to begin to sketch out what she would say to Laurie, and suggest, if he wished it, to come up and see him in a week or two. She would apologise for her fussiness, and say that the reason why she was writing was that she did not want his mother to be made anxious.

"My dear Laurie . . ."

She bit her pen gently, and looked out of the window to catch inspiration for the particular frame of words with which she should begin. And as she looked an old gentleman suddenly appeared beyond the iron gate, shook it gently, glanced up in vain for a name on the stone posts, and stood irresolute. It was an old trap, that of the front gate; there was no bell, and it was necessary for visitors to come straight in to the front door.

Then, so swiftly that she could not formulate it, an anxiety leapt at her, and she laid her pen down, staring. Who was this?

She went quickly to the bell and rang it; standing there waiting, with beating heart and face suddenly gone white....

"Susan," she said, "there is an old gentleman at the gate. Go out and see who it is.... Stop: if it is anyone for me ... if—if he gives the name of Mr. Cathcart, ask him to be so kind as to go round the turn to the village and wait for me.... Susan, don't say anything to Mrs. Baxter; it may just possibly be bad news."

From behind the curtain she watched the maid go down the path, saw a few words pass between her and the stranger, and then the maid come back. She waited breathless.

"Yes, miss. It is a Mr. Cathcart. He said he would wait for you."

Maggie nodded.

"I will go," she said. "Remember, please do not say a word to anyone. It may be bad news, as I said."

As she walked through the hamlet three minutes later, she began to recognise that the news must be really serious; and that beneath all her serenity she had been aware of its possibility. So intense now was that anxiety—though perfectly formless in its details—that all other faculties seemed absorbed into it. She could not frame any imagination as to what it meant; she could form no plan, alternative or absolute, as to what must be done. She was only aware that something had happened, and that she would know the facts in a few seconds.

About fifty yards up the turning she saw the old gentleman waiting. He was in his London clothes, silk-hatted and spatted, and made a curiously incongruous picture there in the deep-banked lane that led upwards to the village. On either side towered the trees, still leafless, yet bursting with life; and overhead chattered the birds against the tender midday sky of spring.

He lifted his hat as she came to him; but they spoke no word of greeting.

"Tell me quickly," she said. "I am Maggie Deronnais."

He turned to walk by her side, saying nothing for a moment.

"The facts or the interpretation?" he asked in his brisk manner. "I will just say first that I have seen him this morning."

"Oh! the facts," she said. "Quickly, please."

"Well, he is going to Mr. Morton's chambers this afternoon; he says . . ."

"What?"

"One moment, please. . . . Oh! he is not seriously ill, as the world counts illness. He thought he was just very tired this morning. I went round to call on him. He was in bed at half-past ten when I left him. Then I came straight down here."

For a moment she thought the old man mad. The relief was so intense that she flushed scarlet, and stopped dead in the middle of the road.

"You came down here," she repeated. "Why, I thought—"

He looked at her gravely, in spite of the incessant twinkle in his eyes. She perceived that this old man's eyes would twinkle at a death-bed. He stroked his grey beard smoothly down.

"Yes; you thought that he was dead, perhaps? Oh, no. But for all that, Miss Deronnais, it is just as serious as it can be."

She did not know what to think. Was the man a madman himself?

"Listen, please. I am telling you simply the facts. I was anxious, and I went round this morning first to Lady Laura Bethell. To my astonishment she saw me. I will not tell you all that she said, just now. She was in a terrible state, though she did not know one-tenth of the harm Well, after what she told me I went round straight to Mitre Court. The porter was inclined not to let me in. Well, I went in, and straight into Mr. Baxter's bedroom; and I found there—"

He stopped.

"Yes?"

"I found exactly what I had feared, and expected."

"Oh! tell me quickly," she cried, wheeling on him in anger.

He looked at her as if critically for a moment. Then he went on abruptly.

"I found Mr. Baxter in bed. I made no apology at all. I said simply that I had come to see how he was after the *séance*."

"It took place, then—"

"Oh! yes. . . . I forgot to mention that Lady Laura would pay no attention to me yesterday. . . . Yes, it took place . . . Well, Mr. Baxter did not seem surprised to see me. He told me he felt tired. He said that the *séance* had been a success. And while he talked I watched him. . . . Then I came away and caught the ten-fifty."

"I don't understand in the least," said Maggie.

"So, I suppose," said the other drily. "I imagine you do not believe in spiritualism at all—I mean that you think that the whole thing is fraud or hysteria?"

"Yes, I do," said Maggie bravely.

He nodded once or twice.

"So do most sensible people. . . . Well, Miss Deronnais, I have come to warn you. I did not write, because it was impossible to know what to say until I had seen you and heard your answer to that question. At the same time, I wanted to lose no time. Anything may happen now at any moment. . . . I wanted to tell you this: that I am at your service now altogether. When—" he stopped; then he began again, "If you hear no further news for the present, may I ask when you expect to see Mr. Baxter again?"

"In Easter week."

"That is a fortnight off. . . . Do you think you could persuade him to come down here next week instead? I should like you to see him for yourself: or even sooner."

She was still hopelessly confused with these apparent alternations. She still wondered whether Mr. Cathcart were as mad as he seemed. They turned, as the village came in sight ahead, up the hill.

"Next week? I could try," she said mechanically. "But I don't understand—"

He held up a gloved hand.

"Wait till you have seen him," he said. "For myself, I shall make a point of seeing Mr. Morton every day to hear the news. . . . Miss Deronnais, I tell you plainly that you alone will have to bear the weight of all this, unless Mrs. Baxter—"

"Oh, do explain," she said almost irritably.

He looked at her with those irresistibly twinkling eyes, but she perceived a very steady will behind them.

"I will explain nothing at all," he said, "now that I have seen you, and heard what you think, except this single point. What you have to be prepared for is the news that Mr. Baxter has suddenly gone out of his mind."

It was said in exactly the same tone as his previous sentences, and for a moment she did not catch the full weight of its meaning. She stopped and looked at him, paling gradually.

"Yes, you took that very well," he said, still meeting her eyes steadily. "Stop . . . Keep a strong hold on yourself. That is the worst you have to hear, for the present. Now tell me immediately whether you think

Mrs. Baxter should be informed or not."

Her leaping heart slowed down into three or four gulping blows at the base of her throat. She swallowed with difficulty.

"How do you know—"

"Kindly answer my question," he said. "Do you think Mrs. Baxter—"

"Oh, God! Oh, God!" sobbed Maggie.

"Steady, steady," said the old man. "Take my arm, Miss Deronnais."

She shook her head, keeping her eyes fixed on his.

He smiled in his grey beard.

"Very good," he said, "very good. And do you think—"

She shook her head again.

"No: not one word. She is his mother. Besides—she is not the kind—she would be of no use."

"Yes: it is as I thought. Very well, Miss Deronnais; you will have to be responsible. You can wire for me at any moment. You have my address?"

She nodded.

"Then I have one or two things to add. Whatever happens, do not lose heart for one moment. I have seen these cases again and again. . . . Whatever happens, too, do not put yourself into a doctor's hands until I have seen Mr. Baxter for myself. The thing may come suddenly or gradually. And the very instant you are convinced it is coming, telegraph to me. I will be here two hours after. . . . Do you understand?"

They halted twenty yards from the turning into the hamlet. He looked at her again with his kindly humorous eyes.

She nodded slowly and deliberately, repeating in her own mind his instructions; and beneath, like a whirl of waters, questions surged to and fro, clamouring for answer. But her self-control was coming back each instant.

"You understand, Miss Deronnais?" he said again.

"I understand. Will you write to me?"

"I will write this evening. . . . Once more, then. Get him down next week. Watch him carefully when he comes. Consult no doctor until you have telegraphed to me, and I have seen him."

She drew a long breath, nodding almost mechanically.

"Goodbye, Miss Deronnais. Let me tell you that you are taking it magnificently. Fear nothing; pray much."

He took her hand for a moment. Then he raised his hat and left her standing there.

★★★★★★

Mrs. Baxter was exceedingly absorbed just now in a new pious book of meditations written by a clergyman. A nicely bound copy of it, which she had ordered specially, had arrived by the parcels post that morning; and she had been sitting in the drawing-room ever since looking through it, and marking it with a small silver pencil. Religion was to this lady what horticulture was to Maggie, except of course that it was really important, while horticulture was not. She often wondered that Maggie did not seem to understand: of course, she went to mass every morning, dear girl; but religion surely was much more than that; one should be able to sit for two or three hours over a book in the drawing-room, before the fire, with a silver pencil.

So, at lunch she prattled of the book almost continuously, and at the end of it thought Maggie more unsubtle than ever: she looked rather tired and strained, thought the old lady, and she hardly said a word from beginning to end.

The drive in the afternoon was equally unsatisfactory. Mrs. Baxter took the book with her, and the pencil, in order to read aloud a few extracts here and there; and she again seemed to find Maggie rather vacuous and silent.

"Dearest child, you are not very well, I think," she said at last.

Maggie roused herself suddenly.

"What, Auntie?"

"You are not very well, I think. Did you sleep well?"

"Oh! I slept all right," said Maggie vaguely.

But after tea Mrs. Baxter did not feel very well herself. She said she thought she must have taken a little chill. Maggie looked at her with unperceptive eyes.

"I am sorry," she said mechanically.

"Dearest, you don't seem very overwhelmed. I think perhaps I shall have dinner in bed. Give me my book, child. . . . Yes, and the pencil-case."

Mrs. Baxter's room was so comfortable, and the book so fascinatingly spiritual, that she determined to keep her resolution and go to bed. She felt feverish, just to the extent of being very sleepy and at her ease. She rang her bell and issued her commands.

"A little of the *volaille*," she said, "with a spoonful of soup before it. . . . No, no meat; but a custard or so, and a little fruit. Oh! yes, Charlotte, and tell Miss Maggie not to come and see me after dinner."

It seemed that the message had roused the dear girl at last, for Maggie appeared ten minutes later in quite a different mood. There was really some animation in her face.

"Dear Auntie, I am so very sorry. . . . Yes; do go to bed, and breakfast there in the morning too. I'm just writing to Laurie, by the way."

Mrs. Baxter nodded sleepily from her deep chair.

"He's coming down in Easter week, isn't he?"

"So, he says, my dear."

"Why shouldn't he come next week instead, Auntie, and be with us for Easter? You'd like that, wouldn't you?"

"Very nice indeed, dear child; but don't bother the boy."

"And you don't think it's influenza?" put in Maggie swiftly, laying a cool hand on the old lady's.

She maintained it was not. It was just a little chill, such as she had had this time last year: and it became necessary to rouse herself a little to enumerate the symptoms. By the time she had done, Maggie's attention had begun to wander again: the old lady had never known her so unsympathetic before, and said so with gentle peevishness.

Maggie kissed her quickly.

"I'm sorry, Auntie," she said. "I was just thinking of something. Sleep well; and don't get up in the morning."

Then she left her to a spoonful of soup, a little *volaille*, a custard, some fruit, her spiritual book and contentment.

Downstairs she dined alone in the green-hung dining-room; and she revolved for the twentieth time the thoughts that had been continuously with her since midday, moving before her like a kaleidoscope, incessantly changing their relations, their shapes, and their suggestions. These tended to form themselves into two main alternative classes. Either Mr. Cathcart was a harmless fanatic, or he was unusually sharp. But these again had almost endless subdivisions, for at present she had no idea of what was really in his mind—as to what his hints meant.

Either this curious old gentleman with shrewd, humorous eyes was entirely wrong, and Laurie was just suffering from a nervous strain, not severe enough to hinder him from reading law in Mr. Morton's chambers; and this was all the substratum of Mr. Cathcart's mysteries: or else Mr. Cathcart was right, and Laurie was in the presence of some danger called insanity which Mr. Cathcart interpreted in some strange fashion she could not understand. And beneath all this again moved the further questions as to what spiritualism really was—what it professed to be, or mere superstitious nonsense, or something else.

She was amazed that she had not demanded greater explicitness this morning; but the thing had been so startling, so suggestive at first, so insignificant in its substance, that her ordinary common sense had deserted her. The old gentleman had come and gone like a wraith, had uttered a few inconclusive sentences, and promised to write, had been disappointed with her at one moment and enthusiastic the next. Obviously, their planes ran neither parallel nor opposing; they cut at unexpected points; and Maggie had no notion as to the direction in which his lay. All she saw plainly was that there was some point of view other than hers.

So, then, she revolved theories, questioned, argued, doubted with herself. One thing only emerged—the old lady's feverish cold afforded her exactly the opportunity she wished; she could write to Laurie with perfect truthfulness that his mother had taken to her bed, and that she hoped he would come down next week instead of the week after.

After dinner she sat down and wrote it, pausing many times to consider a phrase.

Then she read a little, and soon after ten went upstairs to bed.

★★★★★★

It was a little before sunset on that day that Mr. James Morton turned down on to the embankment to walk up to the Westminster underground to take him home. He was a great man on physical exercise, and it was a matter of principle with him to live far from his work. As he came down the little passage he found his friend waiting for him, and together they turned up towards where in the distance the Westminster towers rose high and blue against the evening sky.

"Well?" said the old man.

Mr. Morton looked at him with a humorous eye.

"You are a hopeless case," he said.

"Kindly tell me what you noticed."

"My dear man," he said, "there's absolutely nothing to say. I did exactly what you said: I hardly spoke to him at all: I watched him very carefully indeed. I really can't go on doing that day after day. I've got my own work to do. It's the most utter bunkum I ever—"

"Tell me anything odd that you saw."

"There was nothing odd at all, except that the boy looked tired, as you saw for yourself this morning."

"Did he behave exactly as usual?"

"Exactly, except that he was quieter. He fidgeted a little with his

275

fingers."

"Yes?"

"And he seemed very hard at work. I caught him looking at me once or twice."

"Yes? How did he look?"

"He just looked at me—that was all. Good Lord! what do you want—"

"And there was nothing else—absolutely nothing else?"

"Absolutely nothing else."

"He didn't complain of . . . of anything?"

"Lord! . . . Oh, yes; he did say something about a headache."

"Ah!" (The old man leaned forward.) "A headache? What kind?"

"Back of his head."

The old man sat back with pursed lips.

"Did he talk about last night?" he went on again suddenly.

"Not a word."

"Ah!"

Mr. Morton burst into a rude uproarious laugh.

"Upon my word!" he said. "I think, Cathcart, you're the most amazingly—"

The other held up a gloved hand in deprecation; but he did not seem at all ruffled.

"Yes, yes; we can take all that as said. . . . I'm accustomed to it, my dear fellow. Well, I saw Miss Deronnais, as I told you I should in my note. . . . You're quite right about her."

"Pleased to hear it, I'm sure," said Mr. Morton solemnly.

"She's one in a thousand. I told her right out, you know, that I feared insanity."

"Oh! you did! That's tactful! How did she—"

"She took it admirably."

"And did you tell her your delightful theories?"

"I did not. She will see all that for herself, I expect. Meantime—"

"Oh, you didn't tell me about your interview with Lady Laura."

The old face grew a little grim.

"Ah! that's not finished yet," he said. "I'm on my way to her now. I don't think she'll play with the thing again just yet."

"And the others—the medium, and so on?"

"They will have to take their chance. It's absolutely useless going to them."

"They're as bad as I am, I expect."

276

The old man turned a sharp face to him.

"Oh! you know nothing whatever about it," he said. "You don't count. But they do know quite enough."

In the underground the two talked no more; but Mr. Morton, affecting to read his paper, glanced up once or twice at the old shrewd face opposite that stared so steadily out of the window into the roaring darkness. And once more he reflected how astonishing it was that anyone in these days—anyone, at least, possessing common sense—and common sense was written all over that old bearded face—could believe such fantastic rubbish as that which had been lately discussed. It was not only the particular points that regarded Laurie Baxter—all these absurd, though disquieting hints about insanity and suicide and the rest of it—but the principles that old Cathcart declared to be beneath—those principles which he had, apparently, not confided to Miss Deronnais. Here was the twentieth century; here was an electric railway, padded seats, and the *Pall Mall!* . . .Was further comment required?

The train began to slow up at Gloucester Road; and old Cathcart gathered up his umbrella and gloves.

"Then tomorrow," he said, "at the same time?"

Mr. Morton made a resigned gesture.

"But why don't you go and have it out with him yourself?" he asked.

"He would not listen to me—less than ever now. Goodnight."

The train slid on again into the darkness; and the lawyer sat for a moment with pursed lips. Yes, of course the boy was overwrought: anyone could see that: he had stammered a little—a sure sign. But why make all this fuss? A week in the country would set him right.

Then he opened the *Pall Mall* again resolutely.

Chapter 15

Mr. and Mrs. Nugent were enjoying their holiday exceedingly. On Good Friday they had driven laboriously in a waggonette to Royston, where they had visited the hermit's cave in company with other grandees of their village, and held a stately picnic on the downs. They had returned, the gentlemen of the party slightly flushed with brandy and water from the various hostelries on the home journey, and the ladies severe, with watercress on their laps. Accordingly, on the Saturday, Mrs. Nugent had thought it better to stay indoors and despatch her husband to the scene of the first cricket match of the season, a couple of miles away.

At about five o'clock she made herself a cup of tea, and did not wake up from the sleep which followed until the evening was closing in. She awoke with a start, remembering that she had intended to give a good look between the spare bedroom that had been her daughter's, and possibly make a change or two of the furniture. There was a mahogany wardrobe . . . and so forth.

She had not entered this room very often since the death. It had come to resemble to her mind a sort of melancholy sanctuary, symbolical of glories that might have been; for she and her husband were full of the glorious day that had begun to dawn when Laurie, very constrained though very ardent, had called upon them in state to disclose his intentions. Well, it had been a false dawn; but at least it could be, and was, still talked about in sad and suggestive whispers.

It seemed full then of a mysterious splendour when she entered it this evening, candle in hand, and stood regarding it from the threshold. To the outward eye it was nothing very startling. A shrouded bed protruded from the wall opposite with the words "The Lord preserve thee from all evil "illuminated in pink and gold by the girl's own hand. An oleograph of Queen Victoria in coronation robes hung on one side and the painted photograph of a Nonconformist divine, Bible in hand, whiskered and cravatted, upon the other. There was a small cloth-covered table at the foot of the bed, adorned with an almost continuous line of brass-headed nails as a kind of beading round the edge, in the centre of which rested the plaster image of a young person clasping a cross. A hymn-book and a Bible stood before this, and a small jar of wilted flowers. Against the opposite wall, flanked by dejected-looking wedding -groups, and another text or two, stood the great mahogany wardrobe, whose removal was vaguely in contemplation.

Mrs. Nugent regarded the whole with a tender kind of severity, shaking her head slowly from side to side, with the tin candlestick slightly tilted. (She was a full-bodied lady, in clothes rather too tight for her, and panted a little after the ascent of the stairs.) It seemed to her once more a strangely and inexplicably perverse act of Providence, to whom she had always paid deference, by which so incalculable a rise in the social scale had been denied to her.

Then she advanced a step, her eyes straying from the shrouded bed to the wardrobe and back again. Then she set the candlestick upon the table and turned round.

It must now be premised that Mrs. Nugent was utterly without a trace of what is known as superstition; for the whole evidential value of what follows, such as it is, depends upon that fact. She would not, by preference, sleep in a room immediately after a death had taken place in it, but solely for the reason of certain ill-defined physical theories which she would have summed up under the expression that "it was but right that the air should be changed." Her views on human nature and its component parts were undoubtedly practical and common-sense. To put it brutally, Amy's body was in the churchyard and Amy's soul, crowned and robed, in heaven; so, there was no more to account for. She knew nothing of modern theories, nothing of the revival of ancient beliefs; she would have regarded with kindly compassion, and met with practical comments, that unwilling shrinking from scenes of death occasionally manifested by certain kind of temperaments.

She turned, then, and looked at the wardrobe, still full of Amy's belongings, with her back to the bed in which Amy had died, without even the faintest premonitory symptom of the unreasoning terror that presently seized upon her.

It came about in this way.

She kneeled down, after a careful scrutiny of the polished surface of the mahogany, pulled out a drawer filled to brimming over with linen of various kinds and uses, and began to dive among these with careful housewifely hands to discover their tale. Simultaneously, as she remembered afterwards, there came from the hill leading down from the direction of the station, the sound of a trotting horse.

She paused to listen, her mind full of that faint gossipy surmise that surges so quickly up in the thoughts of village dwellers, her hands for an instant motionless among the linen. It might be the doctor, or Mr. Paton, or Mr. Grove. Those names flashed upon her; but an instant later were drowned again in a kind of fear of which she could give afterwards no account.

It seemed to her, she said, that there was something coming to-wards her that set her a-tremble; and when, a moment later, the trotting hoofs rang out sharp and near, she positively relapsed into a kind of sitting position on the floor, helpless and paralysed by a furious up-rush of terror.

For it appeared, so far as Mrs. Nugent could afterwards make it out, as if a sort of double process went on. It was not merely that Fear, full-armed, rushed upon with the approaching wheels, outside and therefore harmless; but that the room itself in which she crouched, itself filled with some atmosphere, swift as water in a rising lock, that held her there motionless, blind and dumb with horror, unable to move, even to lift her hands or turn her head. As one approached, the other rose.

Again, sounded the hoofs and wheels, near now and imminent. Again, they hushed as the corner was approached. Then once more, as they broke out, clear and distinct, not twenty yards away at the turning into the village, Mrs. Nugent, no longer able even to keep that rigid position of fear, sank gently backwards and relapsed in a huddle on the floor.

******

Mr. Nugent was astonished and even a little peevish when, on arriving home after dark, he found the parlour lamp a-smoke and his wife absent.

He inquired for her; the mistress had slipped upstairs scarcely ten minutes ago. He shouted at the bottom of the stairs, but there was no response. And after he had taken his boots off, and his desire for supper had become poignant, he himself stepped upstairs to see into the matter. . . .

It was several minutes, even after the conveyal of an apparently inanimate body downstairs, that his wife first made clear signs of intelligence; and even these were little more than grotesque expressions of fear—rolling eyes and exclamations. It was another quarter of an hour before any kind of connected story could be got out of her. One conclusion only was evident, that Mrs. Nugent did not propose to fetch the forgotten candle still burning on the cloth-covered, brass-nailed table, but that it must be fetched instantly; the door locked on the outside, and the key laid before her on that tablecloth. These were the terms that must be conceded before any further details were gone into.

Plainly there was but one person to carry out these instructions, for the little servant-maid was already all eyes and mouth at the few pregnant sentences that had fallen from her mistress's lips. So Mr. Nugent himself, cloth cap and all, stepped upstairs once more.

He paused at the door and looked in.

All was entirely as usual. In spite of the unpleasant expectancy roused, in spite of himself and his godliness, by the words of his wife and her awful head-nodding, the room gave back to him no echo or lingering scent of horror. The little bed stood there, white and innocent in the candlelight, the drawer still gaped, showing its pathetic contents; the furniture, pictures, texts, and all the rest remained in their places, harmless and undefiled as when Amy herself had set them there.

He looked carefully round before entering; then, stepping forward, he took the candle, closed the drawer, not without difficulty, glanced round once more, and went out, locking the door behind him.

"A pack of nonsense!" he said, as he tossed the key on to the table before his wife.

The theological discussion waxed late that night, and by ten o'clock Mrs. Nugent, under the influence of an excellent supper and a touch of stimulant, had begun to condemn her own terrors, or rather to cease to protest when her husband condemned them for her. A number of solutions had been proposed for the startling little incident, to none of which did she give an unqualified denial. It was the stooping that had done it; there had been a rush of blood to the head that had emptied the heart and caused the sinking feeling. It was the watercress eaten in such abundance on the previous afternoon.

It was the fact that she had passed an unoccupied morning, owing to the closing of the shop. It was one of those things, or all of them, or some other like one of them. Even the little maid was reassured, when she came to take away the supper things, by the cheerful conversation of the couple, though she registered a private vow that for no consideration under heaven would she enter the bedroom on the right at the top of the stairs.

About half-past ten Mrs. Nugent said that she would step up to bed; and in that direction she went, accompanied by her husband, whose programme it was presently to step round to the "Wheatsheaf "for an hour with the landlord after the bar was shut up.

At the door on the right hand he hesitated, but his wife passed on sternly; and as she passed into their own bedroom a piece of news came to his mind.

"That was Mr. Laurie you heard, Mary," said he. "Jim told me he saw him go past just after dark. . . . Well; I'll take the house-key with me."

Chapter 16

When is he coming?" asked Mrs. Baxter with a touch of peevishness, as she sat propped up in her tall chair before the bedroom fire.

"He will be here about six," said Maggie. "Are you sure you have finished?"

The old lady turned away her head from the rice pudding in a kind of gesture of repulsion. She was in the fractious period of influenza, and Maggie had had a hard time with her.

Nothing particular had happened for the last ten days. Mrs. Baxter's feverish cold had developed, and she was but now emerging from the nightdress and flannel-jacket stage to that of the petticoat and dressing-gown. It was all very ordinary and untragic, and Maggie had had but little time to consider the events on which her sub-conscious attention still dwelt. Mr. Cathcart had had no particular news to give her. Laurie, it seemed, was working silently with his coach, talking little. Yet the old man did not for one instant withdraw one word that he had said. Only, in answer to a series of positive inquiries from the girl two days before, he had told her to wait and see him for herself, warning her at the same time to show no signs of perturbation to the boy.

And now the day was come—Easter Eve, as it happened— and she would see him before night. He had sent no answer to her first letter; then, finally, a telegram had come that morning announcing his train.

She was wondering with all her might that afternoon as to what she would see. In a way she was terrified; in another way she was contemptuous. The evidence was so extraordinarily confused. If he were in danger of insanity, how was it that Mr. Cathcart advised her to get him down to a house with only two women and a few maids? Who was there besides this old gentleman who ever dreamed that such a danger was possible? How, if it was so obvious that she would see the change for herself, was it that others—Mr. Morton, for example—had not seen it too? More than ever the theory gained force in her mind that the whole thing was grossly exaggerated by this old man, and that all that was the matter with Laurie was a certain nervous strain.

Yet, for all that, as the afternoon closed in, she felt her nerves tightening. She walked a little in the garden while the old lady took her nap; she came in to read to her again from the vellum-bound little book as the afternoon light began to fade. Then, after tea, she went under orders to see for herself whether Laurie's room was as it should be.

It struck her with an odd sense of strangeness as she went in; she scarcely knew why; she told herself it was because of what she had heard of him lately. But all was as it should be. There were spring flowers on the table and mantelshelf, and a pleasant fire on the hearth. It was even reassuring after she had been there a minute or two.

Then she went to look at the smoking-room where she had sat with him and heard the curious noise of the cracking wood on the night of the thaw, when the boy had behaved so foolishly. Here, too, was a fire, a tall porter's chair drawn on one side with its back to the door, and a deep leather couch set opposite. There was a box of Laurie's cigarettes set ready on the table—candles, matches, flowers, the illustrated papers—yes, everything.

But she stood looking on it all for a few moments with an odd emotion. It was familiar, homely, domestic—yet it was strange. There was an air of expectation about it all. . . . Then on a sudden the emotions precipitated themselves in tenderness. . . . Ah! poor Laurie. . . .

"It is all perfectly right," she said to the old lady.

"Are the cigarettes there?"

"Yes: I noticed them particularly."

"And flowers?"

"Yes, flowers too."

"What time is it, my dear? I can't see."

Maggie peered at the clock.

"It's just after six, Auntie. Will you have the candles?"

The old lady shook her head.

"No, my dear: my eyes can't stand the light. Why hasn't the boy come?"

"Why, it's hardly time yet. Shall I bring him up at once?"

"Just for two minutes," sighed the old lady. "My head's bad again."

"Poor dear," said Maggie.

"Sit down, my dearest, for a few minutes. You'll hear the wheels from here. . . . No, don't talk or read."

There, then, the two women sat waiting.

Outside the twilight was falling, layer on layer, over the spring garden, in a great stillness. The chilly wind of the afternoon had dropped, and there was scarcely a sound to be heard from the living things about the house that once more were renewing their strength. Yet over all, to the Catholic's mind at least, there lay a shadow of death, from associations with that strange anniversary that was passing, hour by hour. . . .

As to what Maggie thought during those minutes of waiting, she could have given afterwards no coherent description. Matters were too complicated to think clearly; she knew so little; there were so many hypotheses. Yet one emotion dominated the rest—expectancy with a tinge of fear. Here she sat, in this peaceful room, with all the homely paraphernalia of convalescence about her—the fire, the bed laid invitingly open with a couple of books, and a reading-lamp on the little table at the side, the faint smell of sandal-wood; and before the fire dozed a peaceful old lady full too of gentle expectation of her son, yet knowing nothing whatever of the vague perils that were about him, that had, indeed, whatever they were, already closed in on him. . . . And that son was approaching nearer every instant through the country lanes. . . .

She rose at last and went on tiptoe to the window.

The curtains had not yet been drawn, and she could see in the fading light the elaborate ironwork of the tall gate in the fence, and the common road outside it, gleaming here and there in puddles that caught the green colour from the dying western sky. In front, on the lawn on this side, burned tiny patches of white where the crocuses sprouted.

As she stood there, there came a sound of wheels, and a carriage came in sight. It drew up at the gate, and the door opened.

★★★★★★

"He is come," said the girl softly, as she saw the tall ulstered figure appear from the carriage. There was no answer, and as she went on tiptoe to the fire, she saw that the old lady was asleep. She went noiselessly out of the room, and stood for an instant, every pulse racing with horrible excitement, listening to the footsteps and voices in the hall. Then she drew a long trembling breath, steadied herself with a huge effort of the will, and went downstairs.

"Mr. Laurie's gone into the smoking-room, miss," said the servant, looking at her oddly.

He was standing by the table as she went in; so much she could see: but the candles were unlighted, and no more was visible of him than his outline against the darkening window.

"Well, Laurie?" she said.

"Well, Maggie," said his voice in answer. And their hands met.

Then in an instant she knew that something was wrong. Yet at the moment she had not an idea as to what it was that told her that. It was Laurie's voice surely!

"You're all in the dark," she said.

There was no movement or word in answer. She passed her hand along the mantelpiece for the matches she had seen there just before; but her hand shook so much that some little metal ornament fell with a crash as she fumbled there, and she drew a long almost vocal breath of sudden nervous alarm. And still there was no movement in answer. Only the tall figure stood watching her it seemed—a pale luminous patch showing her his face.

Then she found the matches and struck one; and, keeping her face downcast, lighted, with fingers that shook violently, the two candles on the little table by the fire. She must just be natural and ordinary, she kept on telling herself. Then with another fierce effort of will she began to speak, lifting her eyes to his face as she did so.

"Auntie's just fallen . . ." (her voice died suddenly for an instant, as she saw him looking at her)—Then she finished—"just fallen asleep. Will . . . you come up presently . . . Laurie?"

Every word was an effort, as she looked steadily into the eyes that looked so steadily into hers.

(It was Laurie—yes—but, good God! . . .)

"You must just kiss her and come away," she said, driving out the words with effort after effort.

"She has a bad headache this evening . . . Laurie—a bad headache."

With a sudden twitch she turned away from those eyes.

"Come, Laurie," she said. And she heard his steps following her.

They passed so through the inner hall and upstairs: and, without turning again, holding herself steady only by the consciousness that some appalling catastrophe was imminent if she did not, she opened the door of the old lady's room.

"Here he is," she said. "Now, Laurie, just kiss her and come away."

"My dearest," came the old voice from the gloom, and two hands were lifted.

Maggie watched, as the tall figure came obediently forward, in an indescribable terror. It was as when one watches a man in a tiger's den. . . . But the figure bent obediently, and kissed.

Maggie instantly stepped forward.

"Not a word," she said. "Auntie's got a headache. Yes, Auntie, he's very well; you'll see him in the morning. Go out at once, please, Laurie."

Without a word he passed out, and, as she closed the door after him, heard him stop irresolute on the landing.

"My dearest child," came the peevish old voice, "you might have allowed my own son—"

"No, no, Auntie, you really mustn't. I know how bad your head is. . . . Yes, yes; he's very well. You'll see him in the morning."

(And all the while she was conscious of the figure that must be faced again presently, waiting on the landing.)

"Shall I go and see that everything's all right in his room?" she said. "Perhaps they've forgotten—"

"Yes, my dearest, go and see. And send Charlotte to me."

The old voice was growing drowsy again.

Maggie went out swiftly without a word. There again stood the figure waiting. The landing lamp had been forgotten. She led the way to his room.

"Come, Laurie," she said. "I'll just see that everything's all right."

She found the matches again, lighted the candles, and set them on his table, still without a look at that face that turned always as she went.

"We shall have to dine alone," she said, striving to make her voice natural, as she reached the door.

Then once more she raised her eyes to his, and looked him bravely in the face as he stood by the fire.

"Do just as you like about dressing," she said. "I expect you're tired."

She could bear it no more. She went out without another word, passed steadily across the length of the landing to her own room, locked the door, and threw herself on her knees.

★★★★★★

She was roused by a tap on the door—how much later she did not know. But the agony was passed for the present—the repulsion and the horror of what she had seen. Perhaps it was that she did not yet understand the whole truth. But at least her will was dominant; she was as a man who has fought with fear alone, and walks, white and trembling, yet perfectly himself, to the operating table.

She opened the door; and Susan stood there with a candle in one hand and a scrap of white in the other.

"For you, miss," said the maid.

Maggie took it without a word, and read the name and the pencilled message twice.

"Just light the lamp out here," she said. "Oh . . . and, by the way, send Charlotte to Mrs. Baxter at once."

"Yes, miss. . . ."

The maid still paused, eyeing her, as if with an unspoken question. There was terror too in her eyes.

"Mr. Laurie is not very well," said Maggie steadily. "Please take no notice of anything. And . . . and, Susan, I think I shall dine alone this evening. Just a tray up here will do. If Mr. Laurie says anything, just explain that I am looking after Mrs. Baxter. And . . . Susan—"

"Yes, miss."

"Please see that Mrs. Baxter is not told that I am not dining downstairs."

"Yes, miss."

Maggie still stood an instant, hesitating. Then a thought recurred again.

"One moment," she said.

She stepped across the room to her writing-table, beckoning the maid to come inside and shut the door; then she wrote rapidly for a minute or so, enclosed her note, directed it, and gave it to the girl.

"Just send up someone at once, will you, with this to Father Mahon—on a bicycle."

When the maid was gone, she waited still for an instant looking across the dark landing, expectant of some sound or movement. But all was still. A line of light showed only under the door where the boy who was called Laurie Baxter stood or sat. At least he was not moving about. There in the darkness Maggie tested her power of resisting panic. Panic was the one fatal thing: so much she understood. Even if that silent door had opened, she knew she could stand there still.

She went back, took a wrap from the chair where she had tossed it down on coming in from the garden that afternoon, threw it over her head and shoulders, passed down the stairs and out through the garden once more in the darkness of the spring evening.

All was quiet in the tiny hamlet as she went along the road. A blaze of light shone from the tap-room window where the fathers of families were talking together, and within Mr. Nugent's shuttered shop she could see through the doorway the grocer himself in his shirt-sleeves, shifting something on the counter. So great was the tension to which she had strung herself that she did not even envy the ordinariness of these people: they appeared to be in some other world, not attainable by herself. These were busied with domestic affairs, with beer or cheese or gossip. Her task was of another kind: so much she knew; and as to what that task was, she was about to learn.

As she turned the corner, the figure she expected was waiting there; and she could see in the deep twilight that he lifted his hat to her. She went straight up to him.

"Yes," she said, "I have seen for myself. You are right so far. Now tell me what to do."

It was no time for conventionality. She did not ask why the solicitor was there. It was enough that he had come.

"Walk this way then with me," he said. "Now tell me what you have seen."

"I have seen a change I cannot describe at all. It's just someone else—not Laurie at all. I don't understand it in the least. But I just want to know what to do. I have written to Father Mahon to come."

He was silent for a step or two.

"I cannot tell you what to do. I must leave that to yourself. I can only tell you what not to do."

"Very well."

"Miss Deronnais, you are magnificent! . . . There, it is said. Now then. You must not get excited or frightened whatever happens. I do not believe that you are in any clanger— not of the ordinary kind, I mean. But if you want me, I shall be at the inn. I have taken rooms there for a night or so. And you must not yield to him interiorly. I wonder if you understand."

"I think I shall understand soon. At present I understand nothing. I have said I cannot dine with him."

"But—"

"I cannot . . . before the servants. One of them at least suspects something. But I will sit with him afterwards, if that is right."

"Very good. You must be with him as much as you can. Remember, it is not the worst yet. It is to prevent that worst happening that you must use all the power you've got."

"Am I to speak to him straight out? And what shall I tell Father Mahon?"

"You must use your judgment. Your object is to fight on his side, remember, against this thing that is obsessing him. Miss Deronnais, I must give you another warning."

She bowed. She did not wish to use more words than were necessary. The strain was frightful.

"It is this: whatever you may see—little tricks of speech or movement—you must not for one instant yield to the thought that the creature that is obsessing him is what he thinks it is. Remember the thing is wholly evil, wholly evil; but it may, perhaps, do its utmost to hide that, and to keep up the illusion. It is intelligent, but not brilliant; it has the intelligence only of some venomous brute in the slime. Or it may try to frighten you. You must not be frightened."

(She understood hints here and there of what the old man said— enough, at any rate, to act.)

"And you must keep up to the utmost pitch your sympathy with *him* himself. You must remember that he is somewhere there, underneath, in chains; and that, probably, he is struggling too, and needs you. It is not Possession yet: he is still partly conscious . . . Did he know you?"

"Yes; he just knew me. He was puzzled, I think."

"Has he seen anyone else he knows?"

288

"His mother . . . yes. He just knew her too. He did not speak to her. I would not let him."

"Miss Deronnais, you have acted admirably. . . . What is he doing now?"

"I don't know. I left him in his room. He was quite quiet."

"You must go back directly. . . . Shall we turn? I don't think there's much more to say just now."

Then she noticed that he had said nothing about the priest.

"And what about Father Mahon?" she said.

The old man was silent a moment.

"Well?" she said again.

"Miss Deronnais, I wouldn't rely on Father Mahon. I've hardly ever met a priest who takes these things seriously. In theory—yes, of course; but not in concrete instances. However, Father Mahon may be an exception. And the worst of it is that the priesthood has enormous power, if they only knew it."

The tingle of a bicycle bell sounded down the road behind them. Maggie wheeled on the instant, and caught the profile she was expecting.

"Is that you?" she said, as the rider passed.

The man jumped off, touched his hat, and handed her a note. She tore it open, and glanced through it in the light of the bicycle lamp. Then she crumpled it up and threw it into the ditch with a quick, impatient movement.

"All right," she said. "Goodnight."

The gardener mounted his bicycle again and moved off.

"Well?" said the old man.

"Father Mahon's called away suddenly. It's from his housekeeper. He'll only be back in time for the first mass tomorrow."

The other nodded, three or four times, as if in assent.

"Why do you do that?" asked the girl suddenly.

"It is what I should have expected to happen."

"What! Father Mahon?—Do you mean it . . . it is arranged?"

"I know nothing. It may be coincidence. Speak no more of it. You have the facts to think of."

About them as they walked back in silence lay the quiet spring night. From the direction of the hamlet came the banging of a door, then voices wishing goodnight, and the sound of footsteps. The steps passed the end of the lane and died away again. Over the trees to the right were visible the high twisted chimney of the old house where the terror dwelt.

"Two points then to remember," said the voice in the darkness— "Courage and Love. Can you remember?"

Maggie bowed her head again in answer.

"I will call and ask to see you as soon as the household is up. If you can't see me, I shall understand that things are going well—or you can send out a note to me. As for Mrs. Baxter—"

"I shall not say one word to her until it becomes absolutely necessary. And if—"

"If it becomes necessary I will wire for a doctor from town. I will undertake all the preliminary arrangements, if you will allow me."

Ten steps before the corner they stopped. "God bless you, Miss Deronnais. Remember, I am at the inn if you need me."

★★★★★★

Mrs. Baxter dined placidly in bed at about half-past seven; but she was more sleepy than ever when she had done. She was rash enough to drink a little claret and water.

"It always goes straight to my head, Charlotte," she explained. "Well, set the book—no, not that one—the one bound in white parchment. . . . Yes, just so, down here; and turn the reading lamp so that I can read if I want to. . . . Oh! ask Miss Maggie to tap at my door very softly when she comes out from dinner. Has she gone down yet?"

"I think I heard her step just now, ma'am."

"Very well; then you can just tell Susan to let her know. How was Mr. Laurie looking, Charlotte?"

"I haven't seen him, ma'am."

"Very well. Then that is all, Charlotte. You can just look in here after Miss Maggie and settle me for the night."

Then the door closed, and Mrs. Baxter instantly began to doze off.

She was one of those persons whose moments between sleeping and waking, especially during a little attack of feverishness, are occupied in contemplating a number of little vivid pictures of all kinds that present themselves to the mental vision; and she saw as usual a quantity of these, made up of tiny details of the day that was gone, and of other details markedly unconnected with it. She saw for example little scenes in which Maggie and Charlotte and medicine bottles and Chinese faces and printed pages of a book all moved together in a sort of convincing incoherence; and she was just beginning to lose herself in the depths of sleep, and to forget her firm resolution of reading another page or so of the book by her side, when a little sound came, and she opened, as she thought, her eyes.

Her reading lamp cast a funnel of light across her bed, and the rest of the room was lit only by the fire dancing in the chimney. Yet this was bright enough, she thought at the time, to show her perfectly distinctly, though with shadows fleeting across it, her son's face peering in at the door. She thought she said something; but she was not sure afterwards. At any rate, the face did not move; and it seemed to her that it bore an expression of such extraordinary malignity that she would hardly have known it for her son's. In a sudden panic she raised herself in bed, staring; and as the shadows came and went, as she stared, the face was gone again. Mrs. Baxter drew a quick breath or two as she looked; but there was nothing. Yet again she could have sworn that she heard the faint jar of the closing door.

She reached out and put her hand on the bell-string that hung clown over her bed. Then she hesitated. It was too ridiculous, she told herself. Besides, Charlotte would have gone to her room.

But the fear did not go immediately; though she told herself again and again that it was just one of those little waking visions that she knew so well.

She lay back on the pillow, thinking. . . . Why, they would have reached the fish by now. No; she would tell Maggie when she came up. How Laurie would laugh tomorrow! Then, little by little, she dozed off once more.

The next thing of which she was aware was Maggie bending over her.

"Asleep, Auntie dear?" said the girl softly.

The old lady murmured something. Then she sat up, suddenly.

"No, my dear. Have you finished dinner?"

"Yes, Auntie."

"Where's Laurie? I should like to see him for a minute."

"Not tonight, Auntie; you're too tired. Besides, I think he's gone to the smoking-room."

She acquiesced placidly.

"Very well, dearest. . . . Oh! Maggie, such a queer thing happened just now—when you were at dinner."

"Yes?"

"I thought I saw Laurie look in, just for an instant. But he looked awful, somehow. It was just one of my little waking visions I've told you of, I suppose."

The girl was silent; but the old lady saw her suddenly straighten herself.

"Just ask him whether he did look in, after all. It may just have been the shadow on his face."

"What time was it?"

"About ten past eight, I suppose, dearest. You'll ask him, won't you?"

"Yes, Auntie. . . . I think I'd better lock your door when I go out. You won't fancy such things then, will you ?"

"Very well, dearest. As you think best."

The old voice was becoming sleepy again: and Maggie stood watching a moment or two longer.

"Send Charlotte to me, dearest . . . Goodnight, my pet . . . I'm too sleepy again. My love to Laurie."

"Yes, Auntie."

The old lady felt the girl's warm lips on her forehead. They seemed to linger a little. Then Mrs. Baxter lost herself once more.

The public bar of the Wheatsheaf Inn was the scene this evening of a lively discussion. Some thought the old gentleman, arrived that day from London, to be a new kind of commercial traveller, with designs upon the gardens of the gentry; others that he was a sort of scientific collector; others, again, that he was a private detective; and since there was no evidence at all, good or bad, in support of any one of these suggestions, a very pretty debate became possible.

A silence fell when his step was heard to pass down the stairs and out into the street, and another half an hour later when he returned. Then once more the discussion began.

At ten o'clock the majority of the men moved out into the moonlight to disperse homewards, as the landlord began to put away the glasses and glance at the clock. Overhead the lighted blind showed where the mysterious stranger still kept vigil; and over the way, beyond the still leafless trees, towered up the twisted chimneys of Mrs. Baxter's house. No word had been spoken connecting the two, yet one or two of the men glanced across the way in vague surmise.

Nearly a couple of hours later the landlord himself came to the door to give the great Mr. Nugent himself, with whom he had been sitting in the inner parlour, a last goodnight, and he too noticed that the bedroom window was still lighted up. He jerked his finger in the direction of it.

"A late old party" he said in an undertone.

Mr. Nugent nodded. He was still a little flushed with whisky and with his previous recountings of what would have happened if his poor daughter had lived to marry the young squire, of his (Mr. Nugent's) swift social advancement and its outward evidences, and of the hobnobbing with the gentry that would have taken place. He looked reflectively across at the silhouette of the big house, all grey and silver in the full moon. The landlord followed the direction of his eyes; and for some reason unknown to them both, the two stood there silent for a full half-minute. Yet there was nothing exceptional to be seen.

Immediately before them, across the road, rose the high oak paling that enclosed the lawn on this side, and the immense limes that towered, untrimmed and undipped, in delicate soaring filigree against the peacock sky of night. Behind them showed the chimneys, above the dusky front of red-brick and the parapet. The moon was not yet full upon the house, and the windows glimmered only here and there, in lines and sudden patches where they caught the reflected light.

Yet the two looked at it in silence. They had seen such a sight fifty times before, for the landlord and the other at least twice a week spent such an evening together, and usually parted at the door. But they stood here on this evening and looked.

All was as still as a spring night can be. Unseen and unheard the life of the earth streamed upwards in twig and blade and leaf, pushing on to the miracle of the prophet Jonas, to be revealed in wealth of colour and scent and sound a fortnight later. The wind had fallen; the last doors were shut, and the two figures standing here were as still as all else. To neither of them occurred even the thinnest shadow of a suspicion as to the cause that held them here—two plain men—in silence, staring at an old house—not a thought of any hidden life beyond that of matter, that life by which most men reckon existence. For them this was but one more night such as they had known for half a century. There was a moon. It was fine. That was Mrs. Baxter's house. This was the village street:—that was the sum of the situation. . . .

Mr. Nugent moved off presently with a brisk air, bidding his friend goodnight, and the landlord, after another look, went in. There came the sound of bolts and bars, the light in the window of the parlour beside the bar suddenly went out, footsteps creaked upstairs; a door shut, and all was silence.

Half an hour later a shadow moved across the blind upstairs: an arm appeared to elongate itself; then, up went the blind, the window followed it, and a bearded face looked out into the moonlight. Behind was the table littered with papers, for Mr. Cathcart, laborious even in the midst of anxiety, had brought down with him for the Sunday a quantity of business that could not easily wait; and had sat there patiently docketing, correcting, and writing ever since his interview in the lane nearly five hours before.

Even now his face seemed serene enough; it jerked softly this way and that, up the street and down again; then once more settled down to stare across the road at the grey and silver pile beyond the trees. Yet even he saw nothing there beyond what the landlord had seen. It stood there, uncrossed by lights or footsteps or sounds, keeping its secret well, even from him who knew what it contained.

Yet to the watcher the place was as sinister as a prison. Behind the solemn walls and the superficial flash of the windows, beneath the silence and the serenity, lay a life more terrible than death, engaged now in some drama of which he could not guess the issue. A conflict was proceeding there, more silent than the silence itself. Two souls fought for one against a foe of unknown strength and unguessed possibilities. The servants slept apart, and the old mistress apart, yet in one of those rooms (and he did not know which) a battle was locked of which the issue was more stupendous than that of any struggle with disease. Yet he could do nothing to help, except what he already did, with his fingers twisting and gripping a string of beads beneath the window-sill. Such a battle as this must be fought by picked champions; and since the priesthood in this instance could not help, a girl's courage and love must take its place.

From the village above the hill came the stroke of a single bell; a bird in the garden-walk beyond the paling chirped softly to his mate; then once more silence came down upon the moonlit street, the striped shadows, the tall house and trees, and the bearded face watching at the window.

Chapter 17

The little inner hall looked very quiet and familiar as Maggie Deronnais stood on the landing, passing through her last struggle with herself before the shock of battle. The stairs went straight down, with the old carpet, up and down which she had gone a thousand times, with every faint patch and line where it was a little worn at the edges, visible in the lamplight from overhead; and she stared at these, standing there silent in her white dress, bare-armed and bare-necked, with her hair in great coils on her head, as upright as a lance. Beneath lay the little hall, with the tiger-skin, the red-papered walls, and a few miscellaneous things—an old cloak of hers she used on rainy days in the garden, a straw hat of Laurie's, and a cap or two, hanging on the pegs opposite.

In front was the door to the outer hall, to the left, that of the smoking-room. The house was perfectly quiet. Dinner had been cleared away already through the hatch into the kitchen passage, and the servants' quarters were on the other side of the house. No sound of any kind came from the smoking-room; not even the faint whiff of tobacco-smoke that had a way of stealing out when Laurie was smoking really seriously within.

She did not know why, she had stopped there, half-way down the stairs.

She had dined from a tray in her own room, as she had said; and had been there alone ever since, for the most part at her *prie-Dieu*, in dead silence, conscious of nothing connected, listening to the occasional tread of a maid in the hall beneath, passing to and from the dining-room. There she had tried to face the ordeal that was coming— the ordeal, at the nature of which even now she only half guessed, and she had realised nothing, formed no plan, considered no eventuality. Things were so wholly out of her experience that she had no process whereby to deal with them. Just two words came over and over again before her consciousness—Courage and Love.

She looked again at the door.

Laurie was there, she said. Then she questioned herself. Was it Laurie? . . .

"He is there, underneath," she whispered to herself softly; "he is waiting for me to help him." She remembered that she must make that act of faith. Yet was it Laurie who had looked in at his mother's door? . . . Well, the door was locked now. But that secretive visit seemed to her terrible.

What, then, did she believe?

She had put that question to herself fifty times, and found no answer. The old man's solution was clear enough now: he believed no less than that out of that infinitely mysterious void that lies beyond the veils of sense there had come a Personality, strong, malignant, degraded, and seeking to degrade, seizing upon this lad's soul, in the disguise of a dead girl, and desiring to possess it. How fantastic that sounded! Did she believe it? She did not know. Then there was the solution of a nervous strain, rising to a climax of insanity. This was the answer of the average doctor. Did she believe that? Was that enough to account for the look in the boy's eyes? She did not know.

She understood perfectly that the fact of herself living under conditions of matter made the second solution the more natural; yet that did not content her. For her religion informed her emphatically that discarnate Personalities existed which desired the ruin of human souls, and, indeed, forbade the practices of spiritualism for this very reason. Yet there was hardly a Catholic she knew who regarded the possibility in these days as more than a theoretical one. So she hesitated, holding her judgment in suspense. One thing only she saw clearly, and that was that she must act as if she believed the former solution: she must treat the boy as one obsessed, whether indeed he were so or not. There was no other manner in which she could concentrate her force upon the heart of the struggle. If there were no evil Personality in the affair, it was necessary to assume one.

And still she waited.

There came back to her an old childish memory.

Once, as a child of ten, she had had to undergo a small operation. One of the nuns had taken her to the doctor's house. When she had understood that she must come into the next room and have it done, she had stopped dead. The nun had encouraged her.

"Leave me quite alone, please, Mother, just for one minute. Please don't speak. I'll come in a minute."

After a minute's waiting, while they looked at her, she had gone forward, sat down in the chair and behaved quite perfectly. Yes; she understood that now. It was necessary first to collect forces, to concentrate energies, to subdue the imagination: after that almost anything could be borne.

So, she stood here now, without even the thought of flight, not arguing, not reassuring herself, not analysing anything; but just gathering strength, screwing the will tight, facing things.

And there was yet another psychological fact that astonished her, though she was only conscious of it in a parenthetical kind of way, and that was the strength of her feeling for Laurie himself. It seemed to her curious, when she considered it, how the horror of that which lay over the boy seemed, like death itself, to throw out as on a clear background the best of himself. His figure appeared to her memory as wholly good and sweet; the shadows on his character seemed absorbed in the darkness that lay over him; and towards this figure she experienced a sense of protective love and energy that astonished her. She desired with all her power to seize and rescue him.

Then she drew a long steady breath, thrust out her strong white hand to see if the fingers trembled; went down the stairs, and, without knocking, opened the smoking-room door and went straight in, closing it behind her. There was a screen to be passed round.

She passed round it.

And he sat there on the couch looking at her.

★★★★★★

For the first instant she remained there standing motionless; it was like a declaration of war. In one or two of her fragmentary rehearsals upstairs she had supposed she would say something conventional to begin with. But the reality struck conventionality clean out of the realm of the possible. Her silent pause there was as significant as the crouch of a hound; and she perceived that it was recognised to be so by the other that was there. There was in him that quick, silent alertness she had expected: half defiant, half timid, as of a fierce beast that expects a blow.

Then she came a step forward and sideways to a chair, sat down in it with a swift, almost menacing motion, and remained there still looking.

This is what she saw:

There was the familiar background, the dark panelled wall, the engraving, and the shelf of books convenient to the hand; the fire was on her right, and the couch opposite. Upon the couch sat the figure of the boy she knew so well.

He was in the same suit in which he had travelled; he had not even changed his shoes; they were splashed a little with London mud. These things she noticed in the minutes that followed, though she kept her eyes upon his face.

The face itself was beyond her power of analysis. Line for line it was Laurie's features, mouth, eyes and hair; yet its signification was not Laurie's. One that was akin looked at her from out of those windows of the soul—scrutinised her cautiously, questioningly, and suspiciously. It was the face of an enemy who waits. And she sat and looked at it.

A full minute must have passed before she spoke. . . . The face had dropped its eyes after the first long look, as if in a kind of relaxation, and remained motionless, staring at the fire in a sort of dejection. Yet beneath, she perceived plainly, there was the same alert hostility; and when she spoke the eyes rose again with a quick furtive attentiveness. The semi-intelligent beast was soothed, but not yet reassured.

"Laurie?" she said.

The lips moved a little in answer; then again, the face glanced down sideways at the fire; the hands dangled almost helplessly between the knees.

There was an appearance of weakness about the attitude that astonished and encouraged her; it appeared as if matters were not yet consummated. Yet she had a sense of nausea at the sight. . . .

"Laurie?" she said again suddenly.

Again, the lips moved as if speaking rapidly, and the eyes looked up at her quick and suspicious.

"Well?" said the mouth; and still the hands dangled.

"Laurie," she said steadily, bending all her will at the words, "you're very unwell. Do you understand that?"

Again, the noiseless gabbling of the lips, and again a little commonplace sentence, "I'm all right."

His voice was unnatural—a little hoarse, and quite toneless. It was as a voice from behind a mask.

"No," said Maggie carefully, "you're not all right. Listen, Laurie. I tell you you're all wrong; and I've come to help you as well as I can. Will you do your best? I'm speaking to *you*, Laurie . . . to *you*."

Every time he answered, the lips flickered first as in rapid conversation—as of a man seen talking through a window; but this time he stammered a little over his vowels.

"I—I—I'm all right."

Maggie leaned forward, her hands clasped tightly, and her eyes fixed steadily on that baffling face.

"Laurie; it's you I'm speaking to—*you*. . . . Can you hear me? Do *you* understand?"

Again, the eyes rose quick and suspicious; and her hands knit yet more closely together as she fought down the rising nausea. She drew a long breath first; then she delivered a little speech which she had half rehearsed upstairs. As she spoke he looked at her again.

"Laurie," she said, "I want you to listen to me very carefully, and to trust me. I know what is the matter with you; and I think you know too. You can't fight—fight him by yourself. . . . Just hold on as tightly as you can to me—with your mind, I mean. Do you understand?"

For a moment she thought that he perceived something of what she meant: he looked at her so earnestly with those odd questioning eyes. Then he jerked ever so slightly, as if some string had been suddenly pulled, and glanced down again at the fire. . . .

"I . . . I . . . I'm all right," he said.

It was horrible to see that motionlessness of body. He sat there as he had probably sat since entering the room. His eyes moved, but scarcely his head; and his hands hung down helplessly.

"Laurie . . . attend . . . ." she began again. Then she broke off.

"Have you prayed, Laurie? . . . Do you understand what has happened to you? You aren't really ill—at least, not exactly; but—"

Again, those eyes lifted, looked, and dropped again.

It was piteous. For the instant the sense of nausea vanished, swallowed up in emotion. Why . . . why, he was there all the while—Laurie . . . dear Laurie. . . .

With one motion, swift and impetuous, she had thrown herself forward on to her knees, and clasped at the hanging hands.

"Laurie! Laurie!" she cried. "You haven't prayed . . . you've been playing, and the machinery has caught you. But it isn't too late! Oh, God! it's not too late. Pray with me! Say the Our Father. . . ."

Again, slowly the eyes moved round. He had started ever so little at her rush, and the seizing of his hands; and now she felt those hands moving weakly in her own, as of a sleeping child who tries to detach himself from his mother's arms.

"I . . I . . . I'm all—"

She grasped his hands more fiercely, staring straight up into those strange piteous eyes that revealed so little, except formless commotion and uneasiness.

"Say the Our Father with me. 'Our Father—'"

Then his hands tore loose, with a movement as fierce as her own, and the eyes blazed with an unreal light. She still clung to his wrists, looking up, struck with a paralysis of fear at the change, and the furious hostility that flamed up in the face. The lips writhed back, half snarling, half smiling. . . .

"Let go! let go!" he hissed at her. "What are you—"

"The Our Father, Laurie . . . the Our—"

He wrenched himself backwards, striking her under the chin with his knee. The couch slid backwards a foot against the wall, and he was on his feet. She remained terror-stricken, shocked, looking up at the dully flushed face that glared down on her.

"Laurie! Laurie! . . . Don't you understand? Say one prayer—"

"How dare you?" he whispered; "how dare you—"

She stood up suddenly—wrenching her will back to self-command. Her breath still came quick and panting; and she waited until once more she breathed naturally. And all the while he stood looking down at her with eyes of extraordinary malevolence.

"Well, will you sit quietly and listen?" she said. "Will you do that?"

Still he stared at her, with lips closed, breathing rapidly through his nostrils. With a sudden movement she turned and went to her chair, sat down and waited.

He still watched her; then, with his eyes on her, with movements as of a man in the act of self-defence, wheeled out the sofa to its place, and sat down. She waited till the tension of his figure seemed to relax again, till the quick glances at her from beneath drooping eyelids ceased, and once more he settled down with dangling hands to look at the fire. Then she began again, quietly and decisively.

"Your mother isn't well," she said. "No . . . just listen quietly. What is going to happen tomorrow? I'm speaking to *you*, Laurie . . . to *you*. Do you understand?"

"I'm all right," he said dully.

She disregarded it.

"I want to help you, Laurie. You know that, don't you? . . . I'm Maggie Deronnais. You remember?"

"Yes—Maggie Deronnais," said the boy, staring at the fire.

"Yes, I'm Maggie. You trust me, don't you, Laurie? You can believe what I say? Well, I want you to fight too. You and I together. Will you let me do what I can?"

Again, the eyes rose, with that odd questioning look. Maggie thought she perceived something else there too. She gathered her forces quietly in silence an instant or two, feeling her heart quicken like the pulse of a moving engine. Then she sprang to her feet.

"Listen, then—in the name of Jesus of Nazareth—"

He recoiled violently with a movement so fierce that the words died on her lips. For one moment she thought he was going to spring. And again, he was on his feet, snarling. There was silence for an interminable instant; then a stream of words, scorching and ferocious, snarled at her like the furious growling of a dog—a string of blasphemies and filth.

Just so much she understood. Yet she held her ground, unable to speak, conscious of the torrent of language that swirled against her from that suffused face opposite, yet not understanding a tenth part of what she heard.

. . . . . "In the name of . . ."

On the instant the words ceased; but so overpowering was the venom and malice of the silence that followed that again she was silent, perceiving that the utmost she could do was to hold her ground. So, the two stood. If the words were horrible to hear, the silence was more horrible a thousand times; it was as when a man faces the suddenly opened door of a furnace and sees the white cavern within.

He was the first to speak.

"You had better take care," he said.

★★★★★★

She scarcely knew how it was that she found herself again in her chair, with the figure seated opposite.

It seemed that the direct assault was useless.

And indeed, she was no longer capable of making it. The nausea had returned, and with it a sensation of weakness. Her knees still were lax and useless; and her hand, as she turned it on the chair-arm, shook violently. Yet she had a curious sense of irresponsibility: there was no longer any terror—nothing but an overpowering weakness of reaction.

She sat back in silence for some minutes, looking now at the fire too, now at the figure opposite, noticing, however, that the helplessness seemed gone. His hands dangled no longer; he sat upright, his hands clasped, yet with a curious look of stiffness and unnaturalness.

Once more she began deliberately to attempt to gather her forces; but the will, it appeared, had lost its nervous grasp of the faculties. It had no longer that quick grip and command with which she had begun. Passivity rather than activity seemed her strength. . . .

Then suddenly and, as it appeared, inevitably, without movement or sound, she began internally to pray, closing her eyes, careless, and indeed unfearing. It seemed her one hope. And behind the steady movement of her will—sufficient at least to elicit acts of petition— her intellect observed a thousand images and thoughts. She perceived the silence of the house and of the breathless spring night outside; she considered Mr. Cathcart in the inn across the road, Mrs. Baxter upstairs: she contemplated the future as it would be on the morrow— Easter Day, was it not?—the past, and scarcely at all the present. She relinquished all plans, all intentions and hopes: she leaned simply upon the supernatural, like a tired child, and looked at pictures.

In remembering it all afterwards, she recalled to herself the fact that this process of prayer seemed strangely tranquil; that there had been in her a consciousness of rest and recuperation as marked as that which a traveller feels who turns into a lighted house from a stormy night. The presence of that other in the room was not even an in-

301

terruption; the nervous force that the other had generated just now seemed harmless and ineffective.

For a time, at least, that was so. But there came a moment when it appeared as if her almost mechanical and rhythmical action of internal effort began to grip something. It was as when an engine after running free clenches itself again upon some wheel or cog.

The moment she was aware of this, she opened her eyes; and saw that the other was looking straight at her intently and questioningly. And in that moment, she perceived for the first time that her conflict lay, not externally, as she had thought, but in some interior region of which she was wholly ignorant. It was not by word or action, but by something else which she only half understood that she was to struggle. . . .

She closed her eyes again with quite a new kind of determination. It was not self-command that she needed, but a steady interior concentration of forces.

She began again that resolute wordless play of the will—dismissing with a series of efforts the intellectual images of thought—that play of the will which, it seemed, had affected the boy opposite in a new way. She had no idea of what the crisis would be, or how it would come. She only saw that she had struck upon a new path that led somewhere. She must follow it.

Some little sound roused her; she opened her eyes and looked up.

He had shifted his position, and for a moment her heart leapt with hope. For he sat now leaning forward, his elbows on his knees, and his head in his hands, and in the shaded lamplight it seemed that he was shaking.

She too moved, and the rustle of her dress seemed to reach him. He glanced up, and before he dropped his head again she caught a clear sight of his face. He was laughing, silently and overpoweringly, without a sound. . . .

For a moment the nausea seized her so fiercely that she gasped, catching at her throat; and she stared at that bowed head and shaking shoulders with a horror that she had not felt before. The laughter was worse than all: and it was a little while before she perceived its unreality. It was like a laughing machine. And the silence of it gave it a peculiar touch.

She wrestled with herself, driving down the despair that was on her. Courage and love.

Again, she leaned back without speaking, closing her eyes to shut out the terror, and began desperately and resolutely to bend her will again to the task.

Again, a little sound disturbed her.

Once more he had shifted his position, and was looking straight at her with a curious air of detached interest. His face looked almost natural, though it was still flushed with that forced laughter; but the mirth itself was gone. Then he spoke abruptly and sharply, in the tone of a man who speaks to a tiresome child; and a little conversation followed, in which she found herself taking a part, as in an unnatural dream.

"You had better take care," he said.

"I am not afraid."

"Well—I have warned you. It is at your own risk. What are you doing?"

"I am praying."

"I thought so. . . . Well; you had better take care."

She nodded at him; closed her eyes once more with new confidence, and set to work.

After that a series of little scenes followed, of which, a few days later, she could only give a disconnected account.

She had heard the locking of the front door a long while ago; and she knew that the household was gone to bed. It was then that she realised how long the struggle would be. But the next incident was marked in her memory by her hearing the tall clock in the silent hall outside beat one. It was immediately after this that he spoke once more.

"I have stood it long enough," he said, in that same abrupt manner.

She opened her eyes.

"You are still praying?" he said.

She nodded.

He got up without a word and came over to her, leaning forward with his hands on his knees to peer into her face. Again, to her astonishment, she was not terrified. She just waited, looking narrowly at the strange person who looked through Laurie's eyes and spoke through his mouth. It was all as unreal as a fantastic dream. It seemed like some abominable game or drama that had to be gone through.

"And you mean to go on praying?"

"Yes."

"Do you think it's the slightest use?"

"Yes."

He smiled unnaturally, as if the muscles of his mouth were not perfectly obedient.

"Well, I have warned you," he said.

Then he turned, went back to his couch, and this time lay down on it flat, turning over on his side, away from her, as if to sleep. He settled himself there like a dog. She looked at him a moment; then closed her eyes and began again.

Five minutes later she understood.

The first symptom of which she was aware was a powerlessness to formulate her prayers. Up to that point she had leaned, as has been said, on an enormous Power external to herself, yet approached by an interior way. Now it required an effort of the will to hold to that Power at all. In terms of space, let it be said that she had rested, like a child in the dark, upon Something that sustained her: now she was aware that it no longer sustained her; but that it needed a strong continuous effort to apprehend it at all. There was still the dark about her; but it was of a different quality—it cannot be expressed otherwise—it was as the darkness of an unknown gulf compared to the darkness of a familiar room. It was of such a nature that space and form seemed meaningless. . . .

The next symptom was a sense of terror, comparable only to that which she had succeeded in crushing down as she stood on the stairs four or five hours before. That, however, had been external to her; she had entered it. Now it had entered her, and lay, heavy as pitch, upon the very springs of her interior life. It was terror of something to come. That which it heralded was not yet come: but it was approaching.

The third symptom was the approach itself—swift and silent, like the running of a bear; so swift that it was upon her through the dark before she could stir or act. It came upon her, in a flash at the last; and she understood the whole secret.

It is possible only to describe it as, afterwards, she described it herself. The powerlessness and the terror were no more than the far-off effect of its approach; the Thing itself was the centre.

Of that realm of being from which it came she had no previous conception: she had known evil only in its effects—in sins of herself and others—known it as a man passing through a hospital ward sees flushed or pale faces, or bandaged wounds. Now she caught some glimpse of its essence, in the atmosphere of this bear-like thing that was upon her. As aches and pains are to Death, so were sins to this Personality—symptoms, premonitions, causes, but not Itself. And she was aware that the Thing had come from a spiritual distance so unthinkable and immeasurable, that the very word distance meant little.

Of the Presence itself and its mode she could use nothing better than metaphors. But those to whom she spoke were given to understand that it was not this or that faculty of her being that, so to speak, pushed against it; but that her entire being was saturated so entirely, that it was but just possible to distinguish her inmost self from it. The understanding no longer moved; the emotions no longer rebelled; memory simply ceased. Yet through the worst there remained one minute, infinitesimally small spark of identity that maintained "I am I; and I am not that." There was no analysis or consideration; scarcely even a sense of disgust. In fact for a while there was a period when to that tiny spot of identity it appeared that it would be an incalculable relief to cease from striving, and to let self itself be merged in that Personality so amazingly strong and compelling, that had precipitated itself upon the rest. . . . Relief? Certainly. For though emotion as most men know it was crushed out—that emotion stirred by human love or hatred—there remained an instinct which strove, which, by one long continuous tension, maintained itself in being.

For the malignity of the thing was overwhelming. It was not mere pressure; it had a character of its own for which the girl afterwards had no words. She could only say that, so far from being negation, or emptiness, or non-being, it had an air, hot as flame, black as pitch, and hard as iron.

That then was the situation for a time which she could only afterwards reckon by guesswork; there was no development or movement—no measurable incidents; there was but the state that remained poised; below all those comparatively superficial faculties with which men in general carry on their affairs—that state in which two Personalities faced one another, welded together in a grip that lay on the very brink of fusion. . . .

Chapter 18

The cocks were crowing from the yards behind the village when Maggie opened her eyes, clear shrill music, answered from the hill as by their echoes, and the yews outside were alive with the dawn-chirping of the sparrows.

She lay there quite quietly, watching under her tired eyelids, through the still unshuttered windows, the splendid glow, seen behind the twisted stems in front and the slender fairy forest of birches on the further side of the garden. Immediately outside the window lay the path, deep in yew-needles, the ground-ivy beyond, and the wet lawn glistening in the strange mystical light of morning.

She had no need to remember or consider. She knew every step and process of the night. That was Laurie who lay opposite in a deep sleep, his head on his arm, breathing deeply and regularly; and this was the little smoking-room where she had seen the cigarettes laid ready against his coming, last night.

There was still a log just alight on the hearth, she noticed. She got out of her chair, softly and stiffly, for she felt intolerably languid and tired. Besides, she must not disturb the boy. So, she went down on her knees, and, with infinite craft, picked out a coal or two from the fender and dropped them neatly into the core of red-heat that still smouldered. But a fragment of wood detached itself and fell with a sharp sound; and she knew, even without turning her head, that the boy had awakened. There was a faint inarticulate murmur, a rustle and a long sigh.

Then she turned round.

Laurie was lying on his back, his arms clasped behind his head, looking at her with a quiet meditative air. He appeared no more as-tonished or perplexed than herself. He was a little white-looking and tired in the light of dawn, but his eyes were bright and sure.

She rose from her knees again, still silent, and stood looking down on him, and he looked back at her. There was no need of speech. It was one of those moments in which one does not even say that there are no words to use; one just regards the thing, like a stretch of open country. It is contemplation, not comment, that is needed.

Her eyes wandered away presently, with the same tranquillity, to the brightening garden outside; and her slowly awakening mind, ex-panding within, sent up a little scrap of quotation to be answered.

"While it was yet early . . . there came to the sepulchre." How did it run?" Mary . . ." Then she spoke.

"It is Easter Day, Laurie."

The boy nodded gently; and she saw his eyes slowly closing once more; he was not yet half awake. So, she went past him on tiptoe to the window, turned the handle, and opened the white tall framework-like door. A gush of air, sweet as wine, laden with the smell of dew and spring flowers and wet lawns, stole in to meet her; and a blackbird, in the shrubbery across the garden, broke into song, interrupted himself, chattered melodiously, and scurried out to vanish in a long curve be-hind the yews. The very world itself of beast and bird was still but half awake, and from the hamlet outside the fence, beyond the trees, rose as yet no skein of smoke and no sound of feet upon the cobbles.

For the time no future presented itself to her. The minutes that passed were enough. She regarded indeed the fact of the old man asleep in the inn, of the old lady upstairs, but she rehearsed nothing of what should be said to them by and by. She did not even think of the hour, or whether she should go to bed presently for a while. She traced no sequence of thought; she scarcely gave a glance at what was past; it was the present only that absorbed her; and even of the present not more than a fraction lay before her attention—the wet lawn, the brightening east, the cool air—those with the joy that had come with the morning were enough.

Again, came the long sigh behind her; and a moment afterwards there was a step upon the floor, and Laurie himself stood by her. She glanced at him sideways, wondering for an instant whether his mood was as hers; and his grave, tired, boyish face was answer enough. He met her eyes, and then again let his own stray out to the garden.

He was the first to speak.

"Maggie," he said, "I think we had best never speak of this again to one another." She nodded, but he went on—

"I understand very little. I wish to understand no more. I shall ask no questions, and nothing need be said to anybody. You agree?"

"I agree perfectly," she said.

"And not a word to my mother, of course."

"Of course not."

The two were silent again.

And now reality—or rather, the faculties of memory and consideration by which reality is apprehended—were once more coming back to the girl and beginning to stir in her mind. She began, gently now, and without perturbation, to recall what had passed, the long *crescendo* of the previous months, the gathering mutter of the spiritual storm that had burst last night—even the roar and flare of the storm itself, and the mad instinctive fight for the conscious life and identity of herself through which she had struggled. And it seemed to her as if the storm, like others in the material plane, had washed things clean again, and discharged an oppression of which she had been but half conscious. Neither was it herself alone who had emerged into this "clear shining after rain"; but the boy that stood by her seemed to her to share in her joy. They stood here together now in a spiritual garden, of which this lovely morning was no more than a clumsy translation into another tongue. There stirred an air about them which was as wine to the soul, a coolness and clearness that was beyond thought, in a radiance that shone through all that was bathed within it, as sunlight that filtered through water.

She perceived then that the experience had been an initiation for them both, that here they stood, one by the other, each transparent to the other, or, at least, he transparent to her; and she wondered, not whether he would see it as she did, for of that she was confident, but when. For this space of silence, she perceived him through and through, and understood that perception was everything. She saw the flaws in him as plainly as in herself, the cracks in the crystal; yet these did not matter, for the crystal was crystal. . . .

So, she waited, confident, until he should understand it too.

"But that is only one fraction of what is in my mind—" He broke off.

Then for the first time since she had opened her eyes just now her heart began to beat. That which had lain hidden for so long— that which she had crushed down under stone and seal and bidden lie still—yet that which had held her resolute, all unknown to herself, through the night that was gone—once more asserted itself and waited for liberation.

"Yet how dare I—" began Laurie.

Again, she glanced at him, terrified lest that which was in her heart should declare itself too plainly by eyes and lips; and she saw how he still looked across the garden, yet seeing nothing but his own thought written there against the glory of sky and leaf and grass. His face caught the splendour from the east, and she saw in it the lines that would tell always of the anguish through which he was come; and again, the terror in her heart leapt to the other side, in spite of her confidence, and bade her fear lest through some mistake, some conventional shame, he should say no more.

Then he turned his troubled eyes and looked her in the face, and as he looked the trouble cleared.

"Why—Maggie!" he said.

Epilogue

The worst of it all is," said Maggie, four months later, to a very patient female friend who adored her, and was her *confidante* just then— "the worst of it is that I'm not in the least sure of what it is that I believe even now."

"Tell me, dear," said the girl.

The two were sitting out in a delightfully contrived retreat cut out at the lower end of the double hedge. Above them and on two sides rose masses of August greenery, hazel and beech, as close as the roof and walls of a summer-house: the long path ran in green gloom up to the old brick steps beneath the yews: and before the two girls rested the pleasant apparatus of tea—silver, china and damask, all the more delightful from its barbaric contrast with its surroundings.

Maggie looked marvellously well, considering the nervous strain that had come upon her about Eastertime. She had collapsed altogether, it seemed, in Easter week itself, and had been for a long rest—one at her own dear French convent until a week ago, being entirely forbidden by the nuns to speak of her experiences at all, so soon as they had heard the rough outline. Mrs. Baxter had spent the time in rather melancholy travel on the Continent, and was coming back this evening.

"It seems to me now exactly like a very bad dream," said Maggie pensively, beginning to measure in the tea with a small silver scoop. "Oh! Mabel; may I tell you exactly what is in my mind: and then we won't talk of it any more at all?"

"Oh! do," said the girl, with a little comfortable movement.

When the tea had been poured out and the plates set ready to hand, Maggie began.

"It seems perfectly dreadful of me to have any doubts at all, after all this; but . . . but you don't know how queer it seems. There's a kind of thick hedge—" she waved a hand illustratively to the hazels beside her— "a kind of thick hedge between me and Easter—I suppose it's the illness: the nuns tell me so. Well, it's like that. I can see myself, and Laurie, and Mr. Cathcart, and all the rest of them, like figures moving beyond; and they all seem to me to be behaving rather madly, as if they saw something that I can't see. . . . Oh! it's hopeless. . . .

"Well, the first theory I have is that these little figures, myself included, really see something that I can't now: that there really was something or somebody, which makes them dance about like that. (Yes: that's not grammar; but you understand, don't you?) Well, I'll come back to that presently.

"And my next theory is this . . . is this"—(Maggie sipped her tea meditatively)—"my next theory is that the whole thing was simple imagination, or, rather, imagination acting upon a few little facts and coincidences, and perhaps a little fraud too. Do you know the way, if you're jealous or irritable, the way in which everything seems to fit in? Every single word the person you're suspicious of utters all fits in and corroborates your idea. It isn't mere imagination: you have real facts, of a kind; but what's the matter is that you choose to take the facts in one way and not another. You select and arrange until the thing is perfectly convincing. And yet, you know, in nine cases out of ten it's simply a lie! . . . Oh! I can't explain all the things, certainly. I can't explain, for instance, the pencil affair—when it stood up on end before Laurie's eyes; that is, if it did really stand up at all. He says himself that the whole thing seems rather dim now, as if he had seen it in a very vivid dream. (Have one of these sugar things?)

"Then there are the appearances Laurie saw; and the extraordinary effect they finally had upon him. Oh! yes; at the time, on the night of Easter Eve, I mean, I was absolutely certain that the thing was real, that he was actually obsessed, that the thing—the Personality, I mean—came at me instead, and that somehow, I won. Mr. Cathcart tells me I'm right—Well; I'll come to that presently. But if it didn't happen, I certainly can't explain what did; but there are a good many things one can't explain; and yet one doesn't instantly rush to the conclusion that they're done by the devil. People say that we know very little indeed about the inner working of our own selves. There's instinct, for instance. We know nothing about that except that it is so. 'Inherited experience' is only rather a clumsy phrase—a piece of paper gummed up to cover a crack in the wall.

"And that brings me to my third theory."

(Maggie poured out for herself a second cup of tea.)

"My third theory I'm rather vague about, altogether. And yet I see quite well that it may be the true one. (Please don't interrupt till I've quite done.)

"We've got in us certain powers that we don't understand at all. For instance, there's thought-projection. There's not a shadow of doubt that that is so. I can sit here and send you a message of what I'm thinking about—oh! vaguely, of course. It's another form of what we mean by Sympathy and Intuition. Well, you know, some people think that haunted houses can be explained by this. When the murder is going on, the murderer and the murdered person are probably fearfully excited—anger, fear, and so on. That means that their whole being is stirred up right to the bottom, and that their hidden powers are frightfully active. Well, the idea is that these hidden powers are almost like acids, or gas—(Hudson tells us all about that)—and that they can actually stamp themselves upon the room to such a degree that when a sympathetic person comes in, years afterwards, perhaps, he sees the whole thing just as it happened. It acts upon his mind first, of course, and then outwards through the senses—just the reverse order to that in which we generally see things.

"Well—that's only an illustration. Now my idea is this: How do we know whether all the things that happened, from the pencil and the rappings and the automatic writing, right up to the appearances Laurie saw, were not just the result of these inner powers. . . . Look here. When one person projects his thought to another it arrives generally like a very faint phantom of the thing he's thinking about. If I'm thinking of the ace of hearts, you see a white rectangle with a red spot in the middle. See? Well, multiply all that a hundred times, and one can just see how it might be possible that the thought of . . . of Mr. Vincent and Laurie together might produce a kind of unreal phantom that could even be touched, perhaps. . . . Oh! I don't know."

Maggie paused. The girl at her side gave an encouraging murmur.

"Well—that's about all," said Maggie slowly.

"But you haven't——"

"Why, how stupid! Yes: the first theory. . . . Now that just shows how unreal it is to me now. I'd forgotten it.

"Well, the first theory, my dear brethren, divides itself into two heads—first the theory of the spiritualists, secondly the theory of Mr. Cathcart. (He's a dear, Mabel, even though I don't believe one word he says.)

"Well, the spiritualist theory seems to me simple R. O. T.—rot. Mr. Vincent, Mrs. Stapleton, and the rest, really think that the souls of people actually come back and do these things; that it was, really and truly, poor dear Amy Nugent who led Laurie such a dance. I'm quite, quite certain that that's not true whatever else is. . . . Yes, I'll come to the coincidences presently. But how can it possibly be that Amy should come back and do these things, and hurt Laurie so horribly? Why, she couldn't if she tried. My dear, to be quite frank, she was a very common little thing: and, besides, she wouldn't have hurt a hair of his head.

"Now for Mr. Cathcart."

There was a long pause. A small cat stepped out suddenly from the hazel tangle behind and eyed the two girls. Then, quite noiselessly, as it caught Maggie's eye, it opened its mouth in a pathetic curve intended to represent an appeal.

"You darling!" cried Maggie suddenly; seized a saucer, filled it with milk, and set it on the ground. The small cat stepped daintily down, and set to work.

"Yes?" said the other girl tentatively.

"Oh! Mr. Cathcart . . . Well, I must say that his theory fits in with what Father Mahon says. But, you know, theology doesn't say that this or that particular thing is the devil, or has actually happened in any given instance—only that, if it really does happen, it is the devil. Well, this is Mr. Cathcart's idea. It's a long story: you mustn't mind.

"First, he believes in the devil in quite an extraordinary way. . . . Oh! yes, I know we do too; but it's so very real indeed with him. He believes that the air is simply thick with them, all doing their very utmost to get hold of human beings. Yes, I suppose we do believe that too; but I expect that since there are such a quantity of things—like bad dreams—that we used to think were the devil, and now only turn out to be indigestion, that we're rather too sceptical. Well, Mr. Cathcart believes both in indigestion, so to speak, and the devil. He believes that those evil spirits are at us all the time, trying to get in at any crack they can find—that in one person they produce lunacy—(I must say it seems to me rather odd the way in which lunatics so very often become horribly blasphemous and things like that)—and in another just shattered nerves, and so on. They take advantage, he says, of any weak spot anywhere.

"Now one of the easiest ways of all is through spiritualism. Spiritualism is wrong—we know that well enough; it is wrong because it's trying to live a life and find out things that are beyond us at present. It's 'wrong' on the very lowest estimate, because it's outraging our human nature. (Yes, Mabel, that's his phrase.) Good intentions, therefore, don't protect us in the least. To go to *séances* with good intentions is like . . . like . . . holding a smoking-concert in a powder-magazine on behalf of an orphan asylum. It's not the least protection—(I'm not being profane, my dear)—it's not the least protection to open the concert with prayer. We've got no business there at all. So, we're blown up just the same.

"The danger? . . . Oh! the danger's this, Mr. Cathcart says. At *séances*, if they're genuine, and with automatic handwriting and all the rest, you deliberately approach those powers in a friendly way, and by the sort of passivity which you've got to get yourself into, you open yourself as widely as possible to their entrance. Very often they can't get in; and then you're only bothered. But sometimes they can, and then you're done. It's particularly hard to get them out again.

"Now, of course, no one in his senses—especially decent people—would dream of doing all this if he knew what it all meant. So, these creatures, whatever they may be, always pretend to be somebody else. They're very sharp: they can pick up all kinds of odds and ends, little tricks, and little facts; and so, with these, they impersonate someone whom the inquirer's very fond of; and they say all sorts of pious, happy little things at first in order to lead them on. So, they go on for a long time saying that religion's quite true. (By the way, it's rather too odd the way in which the Catholic Church seems the one thing they don't like! You can be almost anything else, if you're a spiritualist; but you can't be a Catholic.) Generally, though, they tell you to say your prayers and sing hymns. (Father Mahon the other day, when I was arguing with him about having some hymns in church, said that heretics always went in for hymns!) And so, you go on. Then they begin to hint that religion's not worth much; and then they attack morals. Mr. Cathcart wouldn't tell me about that; but he said it got just as bad as it could be, if you didn't take care."

Maggie paused again, looking rather serious. Her voice had risen a little, and a new colour had come to her face as she talked. She stooped to pick up the saucer.

"Dearest, had you better—"

"Oh! yes: I've just about done," said Maggie briskly. "There's hardly any more. Well, there's the idea. They want to get possession of human beings and move them, so they start like that.

"Well; that's what Mr. Cathcart says happened to Laurie. One of those Beasts came and impersonated poor Amy. He picked up certain things about her—her appearance, her trick of stammering, and of playing with her fingers, and about her grave and so on: and then, finally, made his appearance in her shape."

"I don't understand about that," murmured the girl.

"Oh! my dear, I can't bother about that now. There's a lot about astral substance, and so on. Besides, this is only what Mr. Cathcart says. As I told you, I'm not at all sure that I believe one word of it. But that's his idea."

Maggie stopped again suddenly, and leaned back, staring out at the luminous green roof of hazels above her. The small cat could be discerned halfway up the leafy tunnel swaying its body in preparation for a pounce, while overhead sounded an agitated twittering. Mabel seized a pebble, and threw it with such success that the swaying stopped, and a reproachful cat-face looked round at her.

"There!" said Mabel comfortably; and then, "Well, what do you really think?" Maggie smiled reflectively.

"That's exactly what I don't know myself in the very least. As I said, all this seems to me more like a dream—and a very bad one. I think it's the . . . the nastiest thing," she added vindictively, "that I've ever come across; I don't want to hear one word more about it as long as I live."

"But—"

"Oh, my dear, why can't we be all just sensible and normal? I love doing just ordinary little things—the garden, and the chickens, and the cat and dog and complaining to the butcher. I cannot imagine what anybody wants with anything else. Yes; I suppose I do, in a sort of way, believe Mr. Cathcart. It seems to me, granted the spiritual world at all—which, naturally, I do grant—far the most intelligent explanation. It seems to me, intellectually, far the most broad-minded explanation; because it really does take in all the facts—if they are facts— and accounts for them reasonably. Whereas the subjective-self business—oh, it's frightfully clever and ingenious—but it does assume such a very great deal. It seems to me rather like the people who say that electricity accounts for everything—electricity! And as for the imagination theory—well, that's what appeals to me now, emotionally—because I happen to be in the chickens and butcher mood; but it doesn't in the least convince me. Yes; I suppose Mr. Cathcart's theory is the one I ought to believe, and, in a way, the one I do believe; but that doesn't in the least prevent me from feeling it extraordinarily unreal and impossible. Anyhow, it doesn't matter much."

Again, she leaned back comfortably, smiling to herself, and there was a long silence.

It was a divinely beautiful August evening. From where they sat little could be seen except the long *vista* of the path, arched with hazels, whence the cat had now disappeared, ending in three old brick steps, wide and flat, lichened and mossed, set about with flower-pots and leading up to the yew walk. But the whole air was full of summer sound and life and scent, heavy and redolent, streaming in from the old box-lined kitchen-garden on their right beyond the hedge and from the orchard on the left. It was the kind of atmosphere suggesting Nature in her most sensible mood, full-blooded, normal, perfectly fulfilling her own vocation; utterly unmystical, except by very subtle interpretation; unsuggestive, since she was already saying all that could be said, and following out every principle by which she lived to the furthest confine of its contents. It presented the same kind of rounded-off completion and satisfactoriness as that suggested by an entirely sensuous and comfortable person. There were no corners in it, no vistas hinting at anything except at some perfectly normal lawn or set garden, no mystery, no implication of any other theory or glimpse of theory except that which itself proclaimed.

Something of its air seemed now to breathe in Maggie's expression of contentment, as she smiled softly and happily, clasping her arms behind her head. She looked perfectly charming, thought Mabel; and she laid a hand delicately on her friend's knee, as if to share in the satisfaction—to verify it by participation, so to speak.

"It doesn't seem to have done you much harm," she said.

"No, thank you; I'm extremely well and very content. I've looked through the door once, without in the least wishing to; and I don't in the least want to look again. It's not a nice view."

"But about—er—religion," said the younger girl rather awkwardly.

"Oh! religion's all right," said Maggie. "The Church gives me just as much of all that as is good for me; and, for the rest, just tells me to be quiet and not bother—above all, not to peep or pry. Listeners hear no good of themselves: and I suppose that's true of the other senses too. At any rate, I'm going to do my best to mind nothing except my own business."

"Isn't that rather unenterprising?"

"Certainly, it is; that's why I like it Oh! Mabel, I do want to be so absolutely ordinary all the rest of my life. It's so extremely rare and original, you know. Didn't somebody say that there was nothing so uncommon as common sense? Well, that's what I'm going to be. A genius! Don't you understand?—the kind that is an infinite capacity for taking pains, not the other sort."

"What is the other sort?"

"Why, an infinite capacity for doing without them. Like Wagner, you know. Well, I wish to be the Bach sort—the kind of thing that anyone ought to be able to do—only they can't."

Mabel smiled doubtfully.

"Lady Laura was saying—" she began presently.

Maggie's face turned suddenly severe.

"I don't wish to hear one word."

"But she's given it up," cried the girl. "She's given it up."

"I'm glad to hear it," said Maggie judicially. "And I hope now that she'll spend the rest of her days in sackcloth—with a scourge," she added. "Oh, did I tell you about Mrs. Nugent?"

"About the evening Laurie came home? Yes."

"Well, that's all right. The poor old dear got all sorts of things on her mind, when it leaked out. But I talked to her, and we went up together and put flowers on the grave, and I said I'd have a mass said for Amy, though I'm sure she doesn't require one. The poor darling! But . . . but . . . (don't think me brutal, please) *how* providential her death was! Just think!"

"Mrs. Baxter's coming home by the 6.10, isn't she?"

Maggie nodded.

"Yes; but you know you mustn't say a word to her about all this. In fact, she won't have it. She's perfectly convinced that Laurie overworked himself—Laurie, overworked!—and that that was just all that was the matter with him. Auntie's what's called a sensible woman, you know, and I must say it's rather restful. It's what I want to be; but it's a far-off aspiration, I'm afraid, though I'm nearer it than I was."

"You mean she doesn't think anything odd happened at all?"

"Just so. Nothing at all odd. All very natural. Oh, by the way, Laurie swears he never put his nose inside her room that night, but I'm absolutely certain he did, and didn't know it."

"Where is Mr. Lawrence?"

"Auntie made him go abroad."

"And when does he come back?"

There was a perceptible pause.

"Mr. Lawrence comes back on Saturday evening," said Maggie deliberately.

The Green Robe

The old priest was silent for a moment. The song of a great bee boomed up out of the distance and ceased as the white bell of a flower beside me drooped suddenly under his weight.

"I have not made myself clear," said the priest again. "Let me think a minute." And he leaned back.

We were sitting on a little red-tiled platform in his garden, in a sheltered angle of the wall. On one side of us rose the old irregular house, with its latticed windows, and its lichened roofs culminating in a bell-turret; on the other I looked across the pleasant garden where great scarlet poppies hung like motionless flames in the hot June sunshine, to the tall living wall of yew, beyond which rose the heavy green masses of an elm in which a pigeon lamented, and above all a tender blue sky. The priest was looking out steadily before him with great childlike eyes that shone strangely in his thin face under his white hair. He was dressed in an old cassock that showed worn and green in the high lights.

"No," he said presently, "it is not faith that I mean; it is only an intense form of the gift of spiritual perception that God has given me; which gift indeed is common to us all in our measure. It is the faculty by which we verify for ourselves what we have received on authority and hold by faith. Spiritual life consists partly in exercising this faculty. Well, then, this form of that faculty God has been pleased to bestow upon me, just as He has been pleased to bestow on you a keen power of seeing and enjoying beauty where others perhaps see none; this is called artistic perception. It is no sort of credit to you or to me, any more than is the colour of our eyes, or a faculty for mathematics, or an athletic body.

"Now in my case, in which you are pleased to be interested, the perception occasionally is so keen that the spiritual world appears to me as visible as what we call the natural world. In such moments, although I generally know the difference between the spiritual and the natural, yet they appear to me simultaneously, as if on the same plane.

317

It depends on my choice as to which of the two I see the more clearly.

"Let me explain a little. It is a question of focus. A few minutes ago, you were staring at the sky, but you did not see the sky. Your own thought lay before you instead. Then I spoke to you, and you started a little and looked at me; and you saw me, and your thought vanished. Now can you understand me if I say that these sudden glimpses that God has granted me, were as though when you looked at the sky, you saw both the sky and your thought at once, on the same plane, as I have said? Or think of it in another way. You know the sheet of plate-glass that is across the upper part of the fireplace in my study. Well, it depends on the focus of your eyes, and your intention, whether you see the glass and the fire-plate behind, or the room reflected in the glass. Now can you imagine what it would be to see them all at once? It is like that." And he made an outward gesture with his hands.

"Well," I said, "I scarcely understand. But please tell me, if you will, your first vision of that kind."

"I believe," he began, "that when I was a child the first clear vision came to me, but I only suppose it from my mother's diary. I have not the diary with me now, but there is an entry in it describing how I said I had seen a face look out of a wall and had run indoors from the garden; half frightened, but not terrified. But I remember nothing of it myself, and my mother seems to have thought it must have been a waking dream; and if it were not for what has happened to me since perhaps I should have thought it a dream too. But now the other explanation seems to me more likely. But the first clear vision that I remember for myself was as follows:

"When I was about fourteen years old I came home at the end of one July for my summer holidays. The pony-cart was at the station to meet me when I arrived about four o'clock in the afternoon; but as there was a short cut through the woods, I put my luggage into the cart, and started to walk the mile and a half by myself. The field path presently plunged into a pine wood, and I came over the slippery needles under the high arches of the pines with that intense ecstatic happiness of home-coming that some natures know so well. I hope sometimes that the first steps on the other side of death may be like that. The air was full of mellow sounds that seemed to emphasise the deep stillness of the woods, and of mellow lights that stirred among the shadowed greenness. I know this now, though I did not know it then. Until that day although the beauty and the colour and sound of the world certainly affected me, yet I was not conscious of them, any more than of the air I breathed, because I did not then know what they meant. Well, I went on in this glowing dimness, noticing only the trees that might be climbed, the squirrels and moths that might be caught, and the sticks that might be shaped into arrows or bows.

"I must tell you, too, something of my religion at that time. It was the religion of most well-taught boys. In the foreground, if I may put it so, was morality: I must not do certain things; I must do certain other things. In the middle distance was a perception of God. Let me say that I realised that I was present to Him, but not that He was present to me. Our Saviour dwelt in this middle distance, one whom I fancied ordinarily tender, sometimes stern. In the background there lay certain mysteries, sacramental and otherwise. These were chiefly the affairs of grown-up people.

"And infinitely far away, like clouds piled upon the horizon of a sea, was the invisible world of heaven whence God looked at me, golden gates and streets, now towering in their exclusiveness, now on Sunday evenings bright with a light of hope, now on wet mornings unutterably dreary. But all this was uninteresting to me. Here about me lay the tangible enjoyable world—this was reality: there in a misty picture lay religion, claiming, as I knew, my homage, but not my heart. Well; so, I walked through these woods, a tiny human creature, yet greater, if I had only known it, than these giants of ruddy bodies and arms, and garlanded heads that stirred above me.

"My path presently came over a rise in the ground; and on my left lay a long glade, bordered by pines, fringed with bracken, but itself a folded carpet of smooth rabbit-cropped grass, with a quiet oblong pool in the centre, some fifty yards below me.

"Now I cannot tell you how the vision began; but I found myself, without experiencing any conscious shock, standing perfectly still, my lips dry, my eyes smarting with the intensity with which I had been staring down the glade, and one foot aching with the pressure with which I had rested upon it. It must have come upon me and en-thralled me so swiftly that my brain had no time to reflect. It was no work, therefore, of the imagination, but a clear and sudden vision. This is what I remember to have seen.

"I stood on the border of a vast robe; its material was green. A great fold of it lay full in view, but I was conscious that it stretched for almost unlimited miles. This great green robe blazed with embroidery. There were straight lines of tawny work on either side which melted again into a darker green in high relief. Right in the centre lay a pale agate stitched delicately into the robe with fine dark stitches; overhead the blue lining of this silken robe arched out. I was conscious that this robe was vast beyond conception, and that I stood as it were in a fold of it, as it lay stretched out on some unseen floor. But, clearer than any other thought, stood out in my mind the certainty that this robe had not been flung down and left, but that it clothed a Person. And even as this thought showed itself a ripple ran along the high relief in dark green, as if the wearer of the robe had just stirred. And I felt on my face the breeze of His motion. And it was this I suppose that brought me to myself.

"And then I looked again, and all was as it had been the last time I had passed this way. There was the glade and the pool and the pines and the sky overhead, and the Presence was gone. I was a boy walking home from the station, with dear delights of the pony and the air-gun, and the wakings morning by morning in my own carpeted bedroom, before me.

"I tried, however, to see it again as I had seen it. No, it was not in the least like a robe; and above all where was the Person that wore it? There was no life about me, except my own, and the insect life that sang in the air, and the quiet meditative life of the growing things. But who was this Person I had suddenly perceived? And then it came upon me with a shock, and yet I was incredulous. It could not be the God of sermons and long prayers who demanded my presence Sunday by Sunday in His little church, that God Who watched me like a stern father. Why religion, I thought, told me that all was vanity and unreality, and that rabbits and pools and glades were nothing compared to Him who sits on the great white throne.

"I need not tell you that I never spoke of this at home. It seemed to me that I had stumbled upon a scene that was almost dreadful, that might be thought over in bed, or during an idle lonely morning in the garden, but must never be spoken of, and I can scarcely tell you when the time came that I understood that there was but one God after all."

The old man stopped talking. And I looked out again at the garden without answering him, and tried myself to see how the poppies were embroidered into a robe, and to hear how the chatter of the starlings was but the rustle of its movement, the clink of jewel against jewel, and the moan of the pigeon the creaking of the heavy silk, but I could not. The poppies flamed and the birds talked and sobbed, but that was all.

The Watcher

On the following day we went out soon after breakfast and walked up and down a grass path between two yew hedges; the dew was not yet off the grass that lay in shadow; and thin patches of gossamer still hung like torn cambric on the yew shoots on either side. As we passed for the second time up the path, the old man suddenly stooped and pushing aside a dock-leaf at the foot of the hedge lifted a dead mouse, and looked at it as it lay stiffly on the palm of his hand, and I saw that his eyes filled slowly with the ready tears of old age.

"He has chosen his own resting-place," he said. "Let him lie there. Why did I disturb him?"—and he laid him gently down again; and then gathering a fragment of wet earth he sprinkled it over the mouse. "Earth to earth, ashes to ashes," he said, "in sure and certain hope"— and then he stopped; and straightening himself with difficulty walked on, and I followed him.

"You seemed interested," he said, "in my story yesterday. Shall I tell you how I saw a very different sight when I was a little older?" And when I had told him how strange and attractive his story had been, he began.

"I told you how I found it impossible to see again what I had seen in the glade. For a few weeks, perhaps months, I tried now and then to force myself to feel that Presence, or at least to see that robe, but I could not, because it is the gift of God, and can no more be gained by effort than ordinary sight can be won by a sightless man; but I soon ceased to try.

"I reached eighteen years at last, that terrible age when the soul seems to have dwindled to a spark overlaid by a mountain of ashes— when blood and fire and death and loud noises seem the only things of interest, and all tender things shrink back and hide from the dreadful noonday of manhood. Someone gave me one of those shot-pistols that you may have seen, and I loved the sense of power that it gave me, for I had never had a gun. For a week or two in the summer holidays I was content with shooting at a mark, or at the level surface of water, and delighted to see the cardboard shattered, or the quiet pool torn to shreds along its mirror where the sky and green lay sleeping. Then that ceased to interest me, and I longed to see a living thing suddenly stop living at my will. Now," and he held up a deprecating hand, "I think sport is necessary for some natures. After all, the killing of creatures is necessary for man's food, and sport as you will tell me is a survival of man's delight in obtaining food, and it requires certain noble qualities of endurance and skill. I know all that, and I know further that for some natures it is a relief—an escape for humours that will otherwise find an evil vent. But I do know this—that for me it was not necessary.

"However, there was every excuse, and I went out in good faith one summer evening intending to shoot some rabbit as he ran to cover from the open field. I walked along the inside of a fence with a wood above me and on my left, and the green meadow on my right. Well, owing probably to my own lack of skill, though I could hear the patter and rush of the rabbits all round me, and could see them in the distance sitting up listening with cocked ears, as I stole along the fence, I could not get close enough to fire at them with any hope of what I fancied was success; and by the time that I had arrived at the end of the wood I was in an impatient mood.

"I stood for a moment or two leaning on the fence looking out of that pleasant coolness into the open meadow beyond; the sun had at that moment dipped behind the hill before me and all was in shadow except where there hung a glory about the topmost leaves of a beech that still caught the sun. The birds were beginning to come in from the fields, and were settling one by one in the wood behind me, staying here and there to sing one last line of melody. I could hear the quiet rush and then the sudden clap of a pigeon's wings as he came home, and as I listened I heard pealing out above all other sounds the long liquid song of a thrush somewhere above me. I looked up idly and tried to see the bird, and after a moment or two caught sight of him as the leaves of the beech parted in the breeze, his head lifted and his whole body vibrating with the joy of life and music. As someone has said, his body was one beating heart. The last radiance of the sun over the hill reached him and bathed him in golden warmth. Then the leaves closed again as the breeze dropped, but still his song rang out.

"Then there came on me a blinding desire to kill him. All the other creatures had mocked me and run home. Here at least was a victim, and I would pour out the sullen anger that had been gathering during my walk, and at least demand this one life as a substitute. Side by side with this I remembered clearly that I had come out to kill for food: that was my one justification. Side by side I saw both these things, and I had no excuse—no excuse.

"I turned my head every way and moved a step or two back to catch sight of him again, and, although, this may sound fantastic and overwrought, in my whole being was a struggle between light and darkness. Every fibre of my life told me that the thrush had a right to live. Ah! he had earned it, if labour were wanting, by this very song that was guiding death towards him, but black sullen anger had thrown my conscience, and was now struggling to hold it down till the shot had been fired. Still I waited for the breeze, and then it came, cool and sweet-smelling like the breath of a garden, and the leaves parted. There he sang in the sunshine, and in a moment I lifted the pistol and drew the trigger.

"With the crack of the cap came silence overhead, and after what seemed an interminable moment came the soft rush of something falling and the faint thud among last year's leaves. Then I stood half terrified, and stared among the dead leaves. All seemed dim and misty. My eyes were still a little dazzled by the bright background of sunlit air and rosy clouds on which I had looked with such intensity, and the space beneath the branches was a world of shadows. Still I looked a few yards away, trying to make out the body of the thrush, and fearing to hear a struggle of beating wings among the dry leaves.

"And then I lifted my eyes a little, vaguely. A yard or two beyond where the thrush lay was a rhododendron bush. The blossoms had fallen and the outline of dark, heavy leaves was unrelieved by the slightest touch of colour. As I looked at it, I saw a face looking down from the higher branches.

"It was a perfectly hairless head and face, the thin lips were parted in a wide smile of laughter, there were innumerable lines about the corners of the mouth, and the eyes were surrounded by creases of mer-riment. What was perhaps most terrible about it all was that the eyes were not looking at me, but down among the leaves; the heavy eyelids lay drooping, and the long, narrow, shining slits showed how the eyes laughed beneath them. The forehead sloped quickly back, like a cat's head. The face was the colour of earth, and the outlines of the head faded below the ears and chin into the gloom of the dark bush There was no throat, or body or limbs so far as I could see. The face just hung there like a downturned Eastern mask in an old curiosity shop. And it smiled with sheer delight, not at me, but at the thrush's body. There was no change of expression so long as I watched it, just a silent smile of pleasure petrified on the face. I could not move my eyes from it.

"After what I suppose was a minute or so, the face had gone. I did not see it go, but I became aware that I was looking only at leaves.

"No; there was no outline of leaf, or play of shadows that could possibly have taken the form of a face. You can guess how I tried to force myself to believe that that was all; how I turned my head this way and that to catch it again; but there was no hint of a face.

"Now, I cannot tell you how I did it; but although I was half beside myself with fright, I went forward towards the bush and searched furiously among the leaves for the body of the thrush; and at last I found it, and lifted it. It was still limp and warm to the touch. Its breast was a little ruffled, and one tiny drop of blood lay at the root of the beak below the eyes, like a tear of dismay and sorrow at such an unmerited, unexpected death.

"I carried it to the fence and climbed over, and then began to run in great steps, looking now and then awfully at the gathering gloom of the wood behind, where the laughing face had mocked the dead. I think, looking back as I do now, that my chief instinct was that I could not leave the thrush there to be laughed at, and that I must get it out into the clean, airy meadow. When I reached the middle of the meadow I came to a pond which never ran quite dry even in the hottest summer. On the bank I laid the thrush down, and then deliberately but with all my force dashed the pistol into the water; then emptied my pockets of the cartridges and threw them in too.

"Then I turned again to the piteous little body, feeling that at least I had tried to make amends. There was an old rabbit hole near, the grass growing down in its mouth, and a tangle of web and dead leaves behind. I scooped a little space out among the leaves, and then laid the thrush there; gathered a little of the sandy soil and poured it over the body, saying, I remember, half unconsciously, 'Earth to earth, ashes to ashes, in sure and certain hope'—and then I stopped, feeling I had been a little profane, though I do not think so now. And then I went home.

"As I dressed for dinner, looking out over the darkening meadow where the thrush lay, I remember feeling happy that no evil thing could mock the defenceless dead out there in the clean meadow where the wind blew and the stars shone down."

We reached in our going to and fro up the yew path a little seat at the end standing back from the path. Opposite us hung a crucifix, with a pent-house over it, that the old man had put up years before. As he did not speak I turned to him, and saw that he was looking steadily at the Figure on the Cross; and I thought how He who bore our griefs and carried our sorrows was one with the heavenly Father, without whom not even a sparrow falls to the ground.

The Blood-Eagle

One night when I went to my room I found in a little shelf near the window a book, whose title I now forget, describing the far-off days when the religion of Christ and of the gods of the north strove together in England. I read this for an hour or two before I went to sleep, and again as I was dressing on the following morning, and spoke of it at breakfast.

"Yes," said the old man, "that was one of my father's books. I remember reading it when I was a boy. I believe it is said to be very ill-informed and unscientific in these days. My parents used to think that all religions except Christianity were of the devil. But I think St. Paul teaches us a larger hope than that."

He said nothing more at the time; but in the course of the morning, as I was walking up and down the raised terrace that runs under the pines beside the drive, I saw the priest coming towards me with a book in his hand. He was a little dusty and flushed.

"I went to look for something that I thought might interest you, after what you said at breakfast," he began, "and I have found it at last in the loft."

We began to walk together up and down.

"A very curious thing happened to me," he said, "when I was a boy. I remember telling my father of it when I came home, and it remained in my mind. A few years afterwards an old professor was staying with us; and after dinner one night, when we had been talking about what you were speaking of at breakfast, my father made me tell it again, and when I had finished the professor asked me to write it down for him. So, I wrote it in this book first; and then made a copy and sent it to him. The book itself is a kind of irregular diary in which I used to write sometimes. Would you care to hear it?"

When I had told him I should like to hear the story, he began again.

"I must first tell you the circumstances. I was about sixteen years old. My parents had gone abroad for the holidays, and I went to stay with a school friend of mine at his home not far from Ascot. We used to take our lunch with us sometimes on bright days—for it was at Christmas time—and go off for the day over the heather. You must remember that I was only a schoolboy at the time, so I daresay I exaggerated or elaborated some of the details a little, but the main facts of the story you can rely upon. Shall we sit down while I read it?"

Then when we had seated ourselves on a bench that stood at the end of the terrace, with the old house basking before us in the hot sunshine, he began to read.

"About six o'clock in the evening of one of the days towards the end of January, Jack and I were still wandering on high, heathy ground near Ascot. We had walked all day and had lost ourselves; but we kept going in as straight a line as we could, knowing that in time we should strike across a road. We were rather tired and silent; but suddenly Jack uttered an exclamation, and then pointed out a light across the heath. We stood a moment to see if it moved, but it remained still.

"'What is it?' I asked. 'There can be no house near here.'

"'It's a broomsquire's cottage, I expect,' said Jack.

"I asked what that meant.

"'Oh! I don't know exactly,' said Jack; 'they're a kind of gipsies.'

"We stumbled on across the heather, while the light grew steadily nearer. The moon was beginning to rise, and it was a clear night, one of those windless, frosty nights that sometimes come after a wet autumn. Jack plunged at one place into a hidden ditch, and I heard the crackling of ice as he scrambled out.

"'Skating tomorrow, by Jove,' he said.

"As we got closer I began to see that we were approaching a copse of firs; the heather began to get shorter. Then, as I looked at the light, I saw there was a fixed outline of a kind of house out of which it shone. The window apparently was an irregular shape, and the house seemed to be leaning against a tall fir on the outskirts of the copse. As we got quite close, our feet noiseless on the soft heather, I saw that the house was built altogether round the fir, which served as a kind of central prop. The house was made of wattled boughs, and thatched heavily with heather.

"I felt more and more anxious about it, for I had never heard of 'broomsquires,' and also, I confess, a little timid; for the place was lonely, and we were only two boys. I was leading now, and presently reached the window and looked in.

"The walls inside were hung with blankets and clothes to keep the wind out; there was a long old settle in one corner, the floor was carpeted with branches and blankets apparently, and there was an opening opposite, partly closed by a wattled hurdle that leaned against it. Half sitting and half lying on the settle, was an old woman with her face hidden. An oil-lamp hung from one of the branches of the fir that helped to form the roof. There was no sign of any other living thing in the place. As I looked Jack came up behind and spoke over my shoulder.

"'Can you tell us the way to the nearest high-road?' he asked.

"The old woman sat up suddenly, with a look of fright on her face. She was extraordinarily dirty and ill-kempt. I could see in the dim light of the lamp that she had a wrinkled old face, with sunken dark eyes, white eyebrows, and white hair; and her mouth began to mumble as she looked at us. Presently she made a violent gesture to wave us from the window.

"Jack repeated the question, and the old woman got up and hobbled quietly and crookedly to the door, and in a moment, she had come round close to us. I then saw how very small she was. She could not have been five feet tall, and was very much bent. I must say again that I felt very uneasy and startled with this terrifying old creature close to me and peering up into my face. She took me by the coat and with her other hand beckoned quickly away in every direction. She seemed to be warning us away from the copse, but still she said nothing.

"Jack grew impatient.

"'Deaf old fool!' he said in an undertone, and then loudly and slowly, 'Can you tell us the way to the nearest highroad?'

"Then she seemed to understand, and pointed vigorously in the direction from which we had come.

"'Oh! nonsense,' said Jack, 'we've come from there. Come on this way,' he said, 'we can't spend all night here.' And then he turned the side of the little house and disappeared into the copse.

"The old woman dropped my coat in a moment, and began to run after Jack, and I went round the other side of the house and saw Jack moving in front, for the firs were sparse at the edge of the wood, and the moonlight filtered through them. The old woman, I saw as I turned into the wood, had stopped, knowing she could not catch us, and was standing with her hands stretched out, and a curious sound, half cry and half sob came from her. I was a little uneasy, because we had not treated her with courtesy, and stopped, but at that moment Jack called.

"'Come on,' he said, 'we're sure to find a road at the end of this.'

"So, I went on.

"Once I turned and saw the little old woman standing as before; and as I looked between the trees she lifted one hand to her mouth and sent a curious whistling cry after us, that somehow frightened me.

It seemed too loud for one so small.

"As we went on the wood grew darker. Here and there in an open patch there lay a white splash of moonlight on the fir needles, and great dim spaces lay round us. Although the wood stood on high ground, the trees grew so thickly about us that we could see nothing of the country round. Now and then we tripped on a root, or else caught in a bramble, but it seemed to me that we were following a narrow path that led deeper and deeper into the heart of the wood. Suddenly Jack stopped and lifted his hand.

"'Hush!' he said.

"I stopped too, and we listened breathlessly. Then in a moment more,——

"'Hush!' he said, 'something's coming,' and he jumped out of the path behind a tree, and I followed him.

"Then we heard a scuffling in front of us and a grunting, and some big creature came hurrying down the path. As it passed us I looked, almost terrified out of my mind, and saw that it was a huge pig; but the thing that held me breathless and sick was that there ran nearly the whole length of its back a deep wound, from which the blood dripped. The creature, grunting heavily, tore down the path towards the cottage, and presently the sound of it died away. As I leaned against Jack, I could feel his arm trembling as it held the tree.

"'Oh!' he said in a moment, 'we must get out of this. Which way, which way?'

"But I had been still listening, and held him quiet.

"'Wait,' I said, 'there is something else.'

"Out of the wood in front of us there came a panting, and the soft sounds of hobbling steps along the path. We crouched lower and watched. Presently the figure of a bent old man came in sight, making his way quickly along the path. He seemed startled and out of breath. His mouth was moving, and he was talking to himself in a low voice in a complaining tone, but his eyes searched the wood from side to side.

"As he came quite close to us, as we lay hardly daring to breathe, I saw one of his hands that hung in front of him, opening and shutting; and that it was stained with what looked black in the moonlight. He did not see us, as by now we were hidden by a great bramble bush, and he passed on down the path; and then all was silent again.

"When a few minutes had passed in perfect stillness, we got up and went on, but neither of us cared to walk in the path down which those two terrible dripping things had come; and we went stumbling over the broken ground, keeping a parallel course to the path for about another two hundred yards. Jack had begun to recover himself, and even began to talk and laugh at being frightened at a pig and an old man. He told me afterwards that he had not seen the old man's hand.

"Then the path began to lead uphill. At this point I suddenly stopped Jack.

"'Do you see nothing?' I asked.

"Now I scarcely remember what I said or did. But this is what my friend told me afterwards. Jack said there was nothing but a little rising ground in front, from which the trees stood back.

"'Do you see nothing on the top of the mound? Out in the open, where the moonlight falls on her?'

"Jack told me afterwards that he thought I had gone suddenly mad, and grew frightened himself.

"'Do you not see a woman standing there? She has long yellow hair in two braids; she has thick gold bracelets on her bare arms. She has a tunic, bound by a girdle, and it comes below her knees: and she has red jewels in her hair, on her belt, on her bracelets; and her eyes shine in the moonlight: and she is waiting,—waiting for that which has escaped.'

"Now Jack tells me that when I said this I fell flat on my face, with my hands stretched out, and began to talk: but he said he could not understand a word I said. He himself looked steadily at the rising ground, but there was nothing to be seen there: there were the fir-trees standing in a circle round it, and a bare space in the middle, from which the heather was gone, and that was all. This mound would be about fifteen yards from us.

"I lay there, said Jack, a few minutes, and then sat up and looked about me. Then I remembered for myself that I had seen the pig and the old man, but nothing more: but I was terrified at the remembrance, and insisted upon our striking out a new course through the wood, and leaving the mound to our left. I did not know myself why the mound frightened me, but I dared not go near it. Jack wisely did not say anything more about it until afterwards. We presently found our way out of the copse, struck across the heath for another half-mile or so, and then came across a road which Jack knew, and so we came home.

"When we told our story, and Jack, to my astonishment, had added the part of which I myself had no remembrance, Jack's father did not say very much; but he took us next day to identify the place. To our intense surprise the house of the broomsquire was gone; there were the trampled branches round the tree, and the smoked branch from which the oil lamp had hung, and the ashes of a wood-fire outside the house, but no sign of the old man or his wife. As we went along the path, now in the cheerful frosty sunshine, we found dark splashes here and there on the brambles, but they were dry and colourless. Then we came to the mound.

"I grew uneasy again as we came to it, but was ashamed to show my fear in the broad daylight.

"On the top we found a curious thing, which Jack's father told us was one of the old customs of the broomsquires, that no one was altogether able to explain. The ground was shovelled away, so as to form a kind of sloping passage downwards into the earth. The passage was not more than five yards long; and at the end of it, just where it was covered by the ground overhead, was a sort of altar, made of earth and stones beaten flat; and plastered into its surface were bits of old china and glass. But what startled us was to find a dark patch of something which had soaked deep into the ground before the altar. It was still damp."

When the old man had read so far, he laid down the book.

"When I told all this to the Professor," he said, "he seemed very deeply interested. He told us, I remember, that the wound on the pig identified the nature of the sacrifice that the old man had begun to offer. He called it a 'blood-eagle,' and added some details which I will not disgust you with. He said too that the broomsquire had confused two rites—that only human sacrifices should be offered as 'blood-eagles.' In fact, it all seemed perfectly familiar to him: and he said more than I can either remember or verify."

"And the woman on the rising ground?" I asked.

"Well," said the old man, smiling, "the Professor would not listen to my evidence about that. He accepted the early part of the story, and simply declined to pay any attention to the woman. He said I had been reading Norse tales, or was dreaming. He even hinted that I was romancing. Under other circumstances this method of treating evidence would be called 'Higher Criticism,' I believe."

"But it's all a brutal and disgusting worship," I said.

"Yes, yes," said the old man, "very brutal and disgusting; but is it not very much higher and better than the Professor's faith? He was only a skilled Ritualist after all, you see."

Over the Gateway

We were sitting together one morning in the common sitting-room in the centre of the house. There had been a fall of rain during the night, and it was thought better that the old man should not sit in the garden until the sun had dried the earth—so we sat indoors instead, but with the great door wide open, that looked on to a rectangle of lawn that lay before the house. Once a drive had led to this door through a gate with pedestals and stone balls, that stood exactly opposite, about fifteen yards away, but the drive had long been grassed over; although even now it showed faintly under two slight ridges in the grass that ran from the gate to the door. Otherwise the lawn was enclosed by a low old brick wall, almost hidden by a wealth of ivy, against which showed in rich masses of colour the heads of purple and yellow irises and tawny wallflowers.

The old man had been silent at breakfast. He had offered the Holy Sacrifice as usual that morning in the little chapel upstairs, and I had noticed at the time even that he seemed pre-occupied: and at breakfast he had talked very little, letting every subject drop as I suggested it; and I had understood at last that his thoughts were far away in the past; and I did not wish to trouble him.

We were sitting in two tall carved chairs at the doorway, his feet were wrapped in a rug, and his eyes were looking steadily and mournfully out across towards the ironwork gate in the wall. Tall grasses of the patch of uncut meadow outside leaned against it or pushed their feathery heads through it; and I saw presently that the priest was looking at the gate, letting his eyes rove over every detail of climbing plant, iron-work and the old brickwork—and not, as I had at first thought, merely gazing into the dim distances of the years behind him.

Suddenly he broke the long silence.

"Did I ever tell you," he asked, "about what I saw out there in the garden? It looks ordinary enough now: yet I saw there what I suppose I shall never see again on this side of death, or at least not until I am in the very gate of death itself."

I too looked out at the gate. The atmosphere was full of that "clear shining after rain" of which King David sang—it was air made visible and radiant by the union of light and water, those two most joyous creatures of God. A great chestnut tree blotted out all beyond the gate.

"Tell me if you can," I said. "You know how I love to hear those stories."

"Years ago, as perhaps you know, not long after my ordination I was working in London. My father lived here then, as his father before him. That coat of arms in the centre of that iron gate was put up by him soon after he succeeded to the property. I used to come down here now and then for a breath of country air. I hardly remember any pleasure so keen as the pleasure of coming into this glorious country air out of the smoke and noise of London—or of lying awake at night with the rustle of the pines outside my window instead of the ceaseless human tumult of the town.

"Well, I came down here once, suddenly, on a summer evening, bearing heavy news. I need not go into details; it would be useless to do that—but it will be enough to say that the news did not personally affect me or my family. It was a curious series of circumstances that led me to be the bearer of such news at all—but it was to a lady who happened by the merest chance to be staying with my family. I scarcely knew her at all—in fact I had only seen her once before. The news had come to my ears in London, and I had heard that the one whom it most concerned did not know it—and that they dared not write or telegraph. I volunteered of course to take the news myself.

"It was with a very heavy heart that I walked up from the station— the road seemed intolerably short. I may say that I knew that the news would be heart-breaking to her who had to hear it. I came in by the gate at the end of the avenue" (he waved his hand round to the right) "and passed right down to the back of the house, behind us. This door at which we are sitting had been the front door, but the drive had just been turfed over, and we used the door at the back instead, and this lawn here was very much as you see it now, only the drive still showed plainly like a long narrow grave across the grass.

"As I came in through the door at the back, she was coming out, with a book and a basket-chair to sit in the garden. My heart gave a terrible throb of pain—for I knew that by the time my business was done there would be no thought of a quiet evening in the garden, and that look of serene happiness would be wiped out of her face—and all through what I had to say. For a moment she did not recognise me in the dark entry and stood back as I came in, and then

"'Why it is you,' she said; 'you have come home. I did not know you were expected.'

"I breathed a moment steadily to recover myself.

"'I was not expected,' I said; and then, after a moment: 'May I speak to you?'

"'Speak to me? Why, certainly. In the garden or here?'

"'In here,' I answered, and went past her and pushed open the door into this room.

"She came past me, and stood here by the door still holding the book, with her finger between the leaves.

"Now you are wondering, I expect, why I did not get some other woman to break the news to her. Well, I had debated that ever since I had volunteered to be the bearer of these tidings: and partly because I was afraid of being cowardly—call it pride if you will—and partly for other reasons which I need not mention, I felt I was bound to fulfil my promise literally. It might be, I thought too, that she would prefer the news to be known by as few people as possible. At least, whether I judged rightly or wrongly, here was my task before me.

"She stood there," the old man went on, pointing to the doorpost on the right, "and I here," and he pointed a yard further back, "and the door was wide open as it is now, and the fragrant evening air poured past us into the room. Her face would be partly in shadow; but in her eyes there was just a dawning wonder at my abruptness, with perhaps the faintest tinge of anxiety, but no more.

"'I have come,' I said slowly, looking out into the garden, 'on a very hard errand.' I could not go on. I turned and looked at her. Ah! the anxiety had deepened a little. 'And—and it concerns you and your happiness.' I looked again, and I remember how her face had changed. Her lips were a little open, and her eyes shone wide open, half in shadow and half in light, and there were new and terrible little lines on her forehead. And then I told her.

"It was done in a sentence or two, and when I looked again her lips had closed and her hand had clenched itself into the moulding of the doorpost. I can see her rings now blazing in the light that poured over the chestnut tree (it was lower then) into the room. Then her lips moved once or twice—her hand unclenched itself hesitatingly—and she went steadily across the room. There was a great sofa there then, and when she reached it she threw herself face downwards across the arm and back.

"And I waited at the doorway, looking out at the iron gate. Sorrow was new to me then. I had not learnt to understand it then, or to be quiet under it. And as I looked I knew only that there was a terrible struggle going on in the room behind. There in front of me was a garden full of peace and sweetness and the soft glow of sunset light; and there behind me was something very like hell—and I stood between the living and the dead.

"Then I remembered that I was a priest, and ought to be able to say something—just a word of the Divine message that the Saviour brought—but I could not. I felt I was in deep waters. Even God seemed far away, intolerably serene and aloof; and I longed with all my power for a human person to pray and to bear a little of that strife behind me, from which I felt separated by so wide a gulf. And then God gave me the clear vision again.

"You see the iron gate," the old man went on, pointing. "Well, right between those posts, but a little above them, outlined clearly against the chestnut tree, beyond, was the figure of a man.

"Now I do not know how to explain myself, but I was conscious that across this material world of light and colour there cut a plane of the spiritual world, and that where the planes crossed I could look through and see what was beyond. It was like smoke cutting across a sunbeam. Each made the other visible.

"Well, this figure of a man, then, was kneeling in the air, that is the only way I can describe it—his face was turned towards me, but upwards. Now the most curious thing that struck me at the time was that he was, as it were, leaning at a sharp angle to one side; but it did not appear to be grotesque. Instead the world seemed tilted; the chestnut tree was out of the perpendicular; the wall out of the horizontal. The true level was that of the man.

"I know this sounds foolish, but it showed me how the world of spirits was the real world, and the world of sense comparatively unreal, just as the sorrow of the woman behind me was more real than the beams overhead.

"And again, compared with the kneeling figure, the chestnut tree and the gate seemed unsubstantial and shadowy. I know that men who see visions tell us that it is usually the other way. All I can say is that it was not so with me. This figure was kneeling, as I have said; his robe streamed away behind him—a great cloak—drawn tightly back from the shoulders, as if he were battling with a strong wind—the Wind of Grace, I suppose, that always blows from the Throne. His arms were stretched out in front of him, but opened sufficiently to let me see his face; and his face will be with me till I die, and please God afterwards. It was beardless, and bore the unmistakable character of a priest's face.

"Now you know how close the intensest pain and the intensest joy lie together. Their lines so nearly meet. In this man's face they did meet. Anguish and ecstasy were one. His eyes were open, his lips part-

334

ed. I could not tell whether he was old or young. His face was ageless, as the faces of all are who look upon Him who inhabits eternity. He was praying. I can say no more than that. He had opened his heart to this woman's sorrow. He had made it his own: and it met there, in petition if you wish to call it so, or in resignation if you prefer that name for it, or in adoration—you may call it what you will—all that is true, but each is inadequate—but that sorrow met there with his own purified will, which itself had become one with the eternal will of God. I tell you I know it.

"I looked at him, and in my ears was a sobbing from the room behind; but as I looked the glory of anguish deepened on his face, and the sobbing behind me slackened and ceased, and I heard a whispering and the name of God and of His Son, and then the sight before me had passed; and there stood the chestnut tree again as real and as beautiful as before; and when I turned the woman was standing up, and the light of conquest was in her eyes.

"She held out her hand to me, and I stooped and kissed it, but I dared not take it in my own, for she had been in heavenly places. I had seen her sorrow carried and laid before the throne of God by one greater than either of us, and something of his glory rested upon her."

The old man's voice ceased. When I turned to look at him he was looking steadily again at the iron gate in the wall, and his eyes were shining like the radiant air outside. "I do not know," he said in a moment, "whether she is alive or dead, but I offered the Holy Sacrifice this morning for her peace in either state."

Poena Damni

We were sitting at dinner one evening when the priest, who had been talkative, seemed to fall into a painful train of thought that silenced him. He grew more and more ill at ease, and was obviously relieved when I threw my cigarette away and he was able to propose a move to the next room. Presently his distress seemed to pass; and then, as we sat near the fireplace, he explained himself.

"I must ask your pardon," he said, "but somehow I fell into a very dreadful train of thought. It was suggested to me, I think, by the red lamp on the table and the evening light through the windows, and the silver and glass. (You know the power of association!) I went through one of the most fearful moments of my life under just those circumstances."

I was silent, as the priest seemed to have more to say.

335

"It has affected my nerves," he said, "and it would be rather a relief to tell you. Would you mind if I did so?"

On my assurance that it would greatly interest me, he began.

"It is a fashion among those who do not really accept Revelation as revelation to believe in a kind of Universalism. Quite apart from authority, this doctrine contravenes, as you of course know, the reality of man's free will. The incident of which I wish to tell you concerns the way in which I first caught a glimpse of that for myself.

"A good many years ago I made the acquaintance of a man in the West of England, under circumstances that I need not describe further than saying that he seemed to have confidence in me. He asked me to stay with him in his country house, and I went down from London for the inside of a week. I found him living the usual country life, fishing and so forth; for it was summer when I visited him. It was a fine old house that he lived in, surrounded by coverts. He had a charming wife and two or three children, and at first, I thought him extremely happy and contented.

"Then I thought that I noticed that things were not so well with him. The cottages on his estate were ill-cared for, and that is always a bad sign. From one or two small signs, such as you can guess, I found that the tone among his servants was not what it should be; and one or two horrid pieces of cruelty came under my notice. I know this sounds as if I were a sort of spy, greedy for information; but all that I can say is, that these signs were unmistakable and obvious, and came to me, of course, unsought and unexpected. Then I saw that his domestic relations were not right. I do not know how else to describe all this than by saying that there seemed a kind of blight upon his surroundings. Nothing was absolutely wrong, and yet all was just wrong.

"At first, I thought that I myself was depressed or jaundiced in some way; but at last I could not continue to believe that; and on the Friday of my stay, the last day, I became finally certain that something was horribly wrong with the man himself. Then that evening he opened his heart to me, so far as it was possible for him to do so.

"His wife, with the two daughters, had left us after dessert and gone into the garden, and we remained in the dining-room. The windows looked to the west, across a smooth sloping lawn, with the lake at the end; beyond that rose up a delicate birch wood, and beyond that again a soft green sky, where the sun had set, deepening into a liquid evening blue overhead, in which a star or two glimmered. I could see, as I looked out, the white figures of his wife and daughters against the shining surface of the lake at the end of the lawn.

"After he had lit his cigarette, and had a glass or two of wine, suddenly he opened his heart to me, and told me an appalling story that I could not tell you. I sat and watched his strong sinewy hand rise and fall with the cigarette, under the red lamplight; I glanced at his quiet well-bred face with the downcast eyes and the long moustache, and I wondered whether it was possible really for such a tale to be true; but he spoke with a restrained conviction that left no room for doubt. What I gathered from the story was this;—that he had identified himself, his whole will, his whole life practically, with the cause of Satan. I could not detect as he talked that he had ever seriously attempted to detach himself from that cause. It has been said that a saint is one who always chooses the better of the two courses open to him at every step; so far as I could see this man had always chosen the worse of the two courses. When he had done things that you and I would think right, he had always done them for some bad reason. He had been continuously aware, too, of what was happening. I do not think that I have ever heard such a skilful self-analysis. Now and then, as I saw the gulf of despair towards which his talk was leading, I interrupted him, suggesting alleviations of the horror—suggesting that he was pessimistic—that he had acted often under misconceptions—and the like; but he always met me with a quiet answer that silenced me. In fact," said the priest, who was beginning to tremble a little, "I have never thought it possible that a heart could be so corrupt and yet retain so much knowledge and feeling.

"When he had finished his story, he looked at me for a moment, and then said:

"'Lately I have seen what I have lost, and what I shall lose; and I have told you this to ask if the Christian Gospel has any hope for such as I am.'

"Of course, I answered as a Christian priest must answer, for I honestly thought that here was the greatest miracle of God's grace that I had ever seen. When I had finished I lifted my eyes from the cloth and looked up. His fingers, while I was speaking, had been playing with an apostle spoon, but as I looked up he looked up too, and our eyes met."

As the priest said this, he got up, and leaned his head against the high oak mantelpiece, and was silent a moment. Then he went on:

"God forgive me if I was wrong—if I am wrong now—but this is what I think I saw.

"Out of his eyes looked a lost soul. As a symbol, or a sign, too, his

337

eyes shone suddenly with that dull red light that you may see some-times in a dog's eyes. It was the *poena damni* of which I had read, which shone there. It was true, as he had said, that he was seeing clearly what he had lost and would lose; it was the gate of heaven opening to one who could not enter in. It was the chink of light under the door to one who cried, 'Lord, Lord, open to me,' but through the door there came that answer, 'I know you not.' Ah! it was not that he had never known before what God was, and His service and love; it was just his condemnation that he had known: that he had seen, not once or twice but again and again, the two ways, and had, not once nor twice but again and again, chosen the worse of those two; and now he was powerless.

"I tell you I saw this for a moment. There was this human face, so well-bred, with its delicate lines, looking almost ethereal in the soft red light of the lamp: behind him, between the windows hung a portrait of an ancestor, some old Caroline divine in ruff and bands. Through the windows was that sweet glory of evening—with the three figures by the lake. Here, between us, was the delicate sooth-ing luxury of cleanliness and coolness and refreshment, such as glass and silver and fruit suggest: and there for one second in this frame of beauty and peace looked the eyes of one who desired even a drop of living water to cool his tongue, for he was tormented in a flame.

"And I saw all this; and then the room began to swim and whirl, and the table to tilt and sway, and I fell, I suppose, forward, and sank down on to the floor. When I recovered there were the men in the room, and the anxious face of my host looking down on me.

"I had to return to town the next morning. I wrote to him a long letter the following week, saying that I had been ill on the evening on which he had given me his confidence: and that I had not said all that I could say: and I went on, giving the lie to what I had thought I had seen, speaking to him as I should speak to any soul who was weary of sin and desired God.

"Indeed, I thought it most possible, as I wrote the letter, that I had had a horrible delusion; and that all could be well with him. I got an answer of a few lines, saying that he must apologise for having trou-bled me with such a story; adding that he had greatly exaggerated his own sin; that he too had been over-excited and unwell: and that he too trusted in a God of Love—and begging me not to refer to the conversation again."

The priest sat down again.

"Now you may of course accept this version of it, if you will. I only would to God that I could too."

"Consolatrix Afflictorum"

The following letter will explain itself. The original was read to me by my friend on one of those days during my stay with him; and he allowed me, at my request, to make a copy. The sermon referred to in the first sentence of the letter was preached in a foreign watering-place on Christmas Day.

******

Villa ——
December 29 , 18—

Reverend and Dear Sir,

I listened with great attention to your sermon on Christmas Day; I am getting on in years, and I am an invalid; so you will understand that I have few friends—and I think none who would not think me mad if I told them the story that I am proposing to tell you. For many years I have been silent on this subject; since it always used to be received with incredulity. But I fancy that you will not be incredulous. As I watched you and listened to you on Christmas Day, I thought I saw in you one to whom the supernatural was more than a beautiful and symbolical fairy-story, and one who held it not impossible that this unseen should sometimes manifest itself.

As you reminded us, the Religion of the Incarnation rests on the fact that the Infinite and the Eternal expresses Himself in terms of space and time; and that it is in this that the greatness of the Love of God consists. Since then, as you said, the Creation, the Incarnation, and the Sacramental System alike, in various degree, are the manifestation of God under these conditions, surely it cannot be 'materialistic' (whatever that exactly means), to believe that the 'spiritual' world and the personages that inhabit it sometimes express themselves in the same manner as their Maker. However, will you have patience with me while I tell you this story? I cannot believe that such a grace should be kept in darkness.

I was about seven years old when my mother died, and my father left me chiefly to the care of servants. Either I must have been a difficult child, or my nurse must have been a hard woman: but I never gave her my confidence. I had clung to my mother as a saint clings to God: and when I lost her, it nearly broke my heart. Night after night

I used to lie awake, with the firelight in the room, remembering how she would look in on her way to bed; when at last I slept it seems to me now as if I never did anything but dream of her; and it was only to wake again to that desolate emptiness. I would torture myself by closing my eyes, and fancying she was there; and then opening them and seeing the room empty. I would turn and toss and sob without a sound. I suppose that I was as near the limit that divides sanity from madness as it is possible to be. During the day I would sit on the stairs when I could get away from my nurse, and pretend that my mother's footsteps were moving overhead, that her door opened, that I heard her dress on the carpet: again, I would open my eyes, and in self-cruelty compel myself to understand that she was gone.

Then again, I would tell myself that it was all right: that she was away for the day, but would come back at night. In the evenings I would be happier, as the time for her return drew nearer; even when I said my prayers I would look forward to the moment, into which I had cheated myself in believing, when the door would open, after I was in bed, and my mother look in. Then as the time passed, my false faith would break down, and I would sob myself to sleep, dream of her, and sob myself awake again. As I look back it appears to me as if this went on for months: I suppose, however, in reality, it could not have been more than a very few weeks, or my reason would have given way. And at last I was caught on the edge of the precipice, and drawn lovingly back to safety and peace.

I used to sleep alone in the night-nursery at this time, and my nurse occupied a room opening out of it. The night-nursery had two doors, one at the foot of my bed, and one at the further end of the room, in the corner diagonally opposite to that in which the head of my bed stood. The first opened upon the landing, and the second into my nurse's room, and this latter was generally kept a few inches open. There was no light in my room, but a night-light was kept burning in the nurse's room, so that even without the firelight my room was not in total darkness.

I was lying awake one night (I suppose it would be about eleven o'clock), having gone through a dreadful hour or two of misery, half-waking and half-sleeping. I had been crying quietly, for fear my nurse should hear through the partly opened door, burying my hot face in the pillow. I was feeling really exhausted, listening to my own heart, and cheating myself into the half-faith that its throbs were the footsteps of my mother coming towards my room; I had raised my face and was staring at the door at the foot of my bed, when it opened suddenly without a sound; and there, as I thought, my mother stood, with the light from the oil-lamp outside shining upon her. She was dressed, it seemed, as once before I had seen her in London, when she came into my room to bid me goodnight before she went out to an evening party. Her head shone with jewels that flashed as the firelight rose and sank in the room, a dark cloak shrouded her neck and shoulders, one hand held the edge of the door, and a great jewel gleamed on one of her fingers. She seemed to be looking at me.

I sat up in bed in a moment, amazed but not frightened, for was it not what I had so often fancied? and I called out to her:

'Mother, mother!"

At the word she turned and looked on to the landing, and gave a slight movement with her head, as if to someone waiting there, either of assent or dismissal, and then turned to me again. The door closed silently, and I could see in the firelight, and in the faint glimmer that came through the other door, that she held out her arms to me. I threw off the bed-clothes in a moment, and scrambled down to the end of the bed, and she lifted me gently in her arms, but said no word. I too said nothing, but she raised the cloak a little and wrapped it round me, and I lay there in bliss, my head on her shoulder, and my arm round her neck. She walked smoothly and noiselessly to a rocking-chair that stood beside the fire and sat down, and then began to rock gently to and fro. Now it may be difficult to believe, but I tell you that I neither said anything, nor desired to say anything. It was enough that she was there. After a little while I suppose I fell asleep, for I found myself in an agony of tears and trembling again, but those arms held me firmly, and I was soon at peace; still she spoke no word, and I did not see her face.

When I woke again she was gone, and it was morning, and I was in bed, and the nurse was drawing up the blind, and the winter sunshine lay on the wall. That day was the happiest I had known since my mother's death; for I knew she would come again.

After I was in bed that evening I lay awake waiting, so full of happy content and certainty that I fell asleep. When I awoke the fire was out, and there was no light but a narrow streak that came through the door from my nurse's room. I lay there a minute or two waiting, expecting every moment to see the door open at the foot of my bed; but the minutes passed, and then the clock in the hall below beat three. Then I fell into a passion of tears; the night was nearly gone, and she had not come to me. Then, as I tossed to and fro, trying to stifle my crying, through my tears there came the misty flash of light as the door opened, and there she stood again. Once again, I was in her arms, and my face on her shoulder. And again, I fell asleep there.

Now this went on night after night, but not every night, and never unless I awoke and cried. It seemed that if I needed her desperately she came, but only then.

But there were two curious incidents that occurred in the order in which I will write them down. The second I understand now, at any rate; the first I have never altogether understood, or rather there are several possible explanations.

One night as I lay in her arms by the fire, a large coal suddenly slipped from the grate and fell with a crash, awaking the nurse in the other room. I suppose she thought something was wrong, for she appeared at the door with a shawl over her shoulders, holding the night-light in one hand and shading it with the other. I was going to speak, when my mother laid her hand across my mouth. The nurse advanced into the room, passed close beside us, apparently without seeing us, went straight to the empty bed, looked down on the tumbled clothes, and then turned away as if satisfied, and went back to her room. The next day I managed to elicit from her, by questioning, the fact that she had been disturbed in the night, and had come into my room, but had seen me sleeping quietly in bed.

The other incident was as follows. One night I was lying half dozing against my mother's breast, my head against her heart, and not, as I usually lay, with my head on her shoulder. As I lay there it seemed to me as if I heard a strange sound like the noise of the sea in a shell, but more melodious. It is difficult to describe it, but it was like the murmuring of a far-off crowd, overlaid with musical pulsations. I nestled closer to her and listened; and then I could distinguish, I thought, innumerable ripples of church bells pealing, as if from another world. Then I listened more intently to the other sound; there were words, but I could not distinguish them. Again, and again a voice seemed to rise above the others, but I could hear no intelligible words. The voices cried in every sort of tone—passion, content, despair, monotony. And then as I listened I fell asleep. As I look back now, I have no doubt what voices those were that I heard.

And now comes the end of the story. My health began to improve so remarkably that those about me noticed it. I never gave way, during the day at any rate, to those old piteous imaginings; and at night, when, I suppose, the will partly relaxes its control, whenever my distress reached a certain point, she was there to comfort me. But her visits grew more and more rare, as I needed her less, and at last ceased. But it is of her last visit, which took place in the spring of the following year, that I wish to speak.

I had slept well all night, but had awakened in the dark just before the dawn from some dream which I forget, but which left my nerves shaken. When in my terror I cried out, again the door opened, and she was there. She stood with the jewels in her hair, and the cloak across her shoulders, and the light from the landing lay partly on her face. I scrambled at once down the bed, and was lifted and carried to the chair, and presently fell asleep. When I awoke the dawn had come, and the birds were stirring and chirping, and a pleasant green light was in the room; and I was still in her arms. It was the first time, except in the instance I have mentioned, that I had awakened except in bed, and it was a great joy to find her there.

As I turned a little I saw the cloak which sheltered us both—of a deep blue, with an intricate pattern of flowers and leaves and birds among branches. Then I turned still more to see her face, which was so near me, but it was turned away; and even as I moved she rose and carried me towards the bed. Still holding me on her left arm she lifted and smoothed the bedclothes, and then laid me gently in bed, with my head on the pillow. And then for the first time I saw her face plainly. She bent over me, with one hand on my breast as if to prevent me from rising, and looked straight into my eyes; and it was not my mother.

There was one moment of blinding shock and sorrow, and I gave a great sob, and would have risen in bed, but her hand held me down, and I seized it with both my own, and still looked in her eyes. It was not my mother, and yet was there ever such a mother's face as that? I seemed to be looking into depths of indescribable tenderness and strength, and I leaned on that strength in those moments of misery. I gave another sob or two as I looked, but I was quieter, and at last peace came to me, and I had learnt my lesson.

I did not at the time know who she was, but my little soul dimly saw that my own mother for some reason could not at that time come to me who needed her so sorely, and that another great Mother had taken her place; yet, after the first moment or so, I felt no anger or jealousy, for one who had looked into that kindly face could have no such unworthy thought.

Then I lifted my head a little, I remember, and kissed the hand that I held in my own, reverently and slowly. I do not know why I did it, except that it was the natural thing to do. The hand was strong and white, and delicately fragrant. Then it was withdrawn, and she was standing by the door, and the door was open; and then she was gone, and the door was closed.

I have never seen her since, but I have never needed to see her, for I know who she is; and, please God, I shall see her again; and next time I hope my mother and I will be together; and perhaps it will not be very long; and perhaps she will allow me to kiss her hand again.

Now, my dear sir, I do not know how all this will appear to you; it may seem to you, though I do not think it will, merely childish. Yet, in a sense, I desire nothing more than that, for our Saviour Himself told us to be like children, and our Saviour too once lay on His Mother's breast. I know that I am getting an old man, and that old men are sometimes very foolish; but it more and more seems to me that experience, as well as His words, tells me that the great Kingdom of Heaven has a low and narrow door that only little children can enter, and that we must become little again, and drop all our bundles, if we would go through.

That, dear and Reverend Sir, is my story. And may I ask you to remember me sometimes at the altar and in your prayers? for surely God will ask much from one to whom He has given so much, and as yet I have nothing to show for it; and my time must be nearly at an end, even if His infinite patience is not.

Believe me,
Yours faithfully,

——— ———

The Bridge over the Stream

We were at tea one afternoon on the little low, tiled platform that marked the site of an old summer-house. Tall hurdles covered with briar-roses on the further side of the path fenced off the rest of the garden from us, and the sun had just sunk below the level of the house, throwing both ourselves and the garden into cool shadow. The servant had brought out the tea-things, but he presently returned with something of horror on his face. The old man looked up and saw him.

"What is it, Parker?" he asked.

"There's been an accident, sir. Tom Awcock at the home farm has been drawn into some machine, and they say he must lose both arms, and maybe his life."

The old man turned quite white, and his eyes grew larger and brighter.

"Is the doctor with him?" he asked, in a perfectly steady voice.

"Yes, sir, and they've sent a message, would you be good enough to step down? The rector's away, and Tom's mother's crying terrible. But not yet, sir. About seven o'clock, they say. It won't be over till then, and there's no immediate danger."

"Tell them I will be there at seven," said the clergyman.

Parker went back to the house, and presently we heard the footsteps of a child running down the drive towards the farm.

"How shocking it is!" I said in a moment or two.

"Ah!" said the old man, smiling, "I have learnt my lesson. It is not really so shocking as you think. Does that sound very hard?"

I said nothing, for it seemed to me that all the consolations of religion could not soften the horror of such things. If such agonies are necessary as remedies or atonements, at least they are terrible.

"I learnt my lesson," the old man went on, "down the road there outside the hedge—down by the bridge. Would you like to hear it? Or are you tired of an old dreamer's stories?" and he smiled at me.

"Now I know you think that I am hard—that I am a little apart maybe from human life—that I cannot understand the blind misery of those who suffer in ignorance; yet you would be the first, I believe, to think that Mrs. Awcock's consolations are unreal, and that when she tells me that she knows there is a wise purpose behind, she is only repeating what is proper to say to a clergyman. But that is not so; that old threadbare sentence is intensely real to these people, and, I hope, to myself too. For there is nothing that I desire more than to be a child like them. It is the apparent purposelessness that distresses you: it is the certainty of a deliberate purpose that comforts me. Well, shall I tell you what I saw?"

I was a little distressed at what looked like callousness, but I told him I would like to hear the story.

"I was standing one evening—it would be about five years ago—in the field down there near the stream. You remember the bridge there, over which the road goes, just outside the hedge. I love running water, and I went slowly up and down by the side of the beck. There were children on the road, coming back from school, and they stopped on the bridge to look at the water, as children and old men will. They did not see me, as the field is a little below the road, and besides their backs were turned to me. I could see a pink frock or two, and a pair of stout bare legs. Two girls were taking their brother home—he was between them, a hand clasped by each of the sisters. I suppose the eldest girl would be about nine, and the boy five. They were talking solemnly, and I could hear every word.

"Why are children always supposed to be gay? There is no solemnity in the world to be compared to the solemnity of a little boy, or of his sister who has charge of him.

"One of the girls said, 'Look, Johnny, there are little fishes down there.'

"'When I am a man'—Johnny began very slowly.

"'Look, Johnny,' said the other girl, 'there's a blue flower.'

"Up to this I remember every word. But then I began to watch Johnny.

"The girls went on talking, but they leaned over more, and I could not hear them plainly. Johnny stealthily withdrew a hand from each of his sisters, and began to look for a stone to throw at the fishes or the blue flower, I suppose; for man is lord of Creation. I could see him presently through the hedge digging patiently with his fingers and loosening a stone that was firm in the road. And at that moment I heard a far-away shout and the distant bark of a dog.

"The evening was wonderfully still: every leaf hung quiet: and there were far-off clouds heaping themselves up in the west, tower over tower. We had a thunderstorm that night, I remember. The brook was quiet, just slipping noiselessly from pool to pool.

"Still Johnny was digging and the girls were talking. Then out of the village above us came again far-off noises. I could hear a rumble, and the clatter of hoofs, then a cry or two more, and the nearer terrified yelp of a dog. But the girls were intent on the brook—and Johnny on the stone.

"Even now I did not understand what was happening: but I grew uneasy—and with great difficulty, for I was an old man even then, tried to scramble up the high bank by the bridge. As I reached the top I saw that one of the girls had gone. She had run, I suppose, off the bridge down by the side of the road. The other girl was still standing—but looking in a frightened way up the hill. Down the hill came the loud rumble of a cart and the clatter of hoofs, terribly near.

"The girl by the side of the road began to scream to her sister, who darted off, and then remembered Johnny and turned. Johnny got up too and ran to the parapet and stood against it.

"I was shouting too by now, through the hedge: but I could do nothing more, nothing more, because the hedge was high and thick, and I was an old man. Then in a moment I remembered that shouting would only distract them, and I stopped. It was useless. I could do absolutely nothing. But it was very hard.

"Then I saw the galloping body of a horse through the branches, with a butcher's cart that rocked behind him. There was no one on the cart.

"Now there was room for the cart to pass the boy safely. By the wheel-marks, which I looked at afterwards, there were three clear feet—if only the boy had stood still.

"The girls seemed petrified as they stood, one in act to run, the other crouching and hiding her face against the hedge. The cart was now within ten yards, as I could see, though I was still staring at Johnny. Then this is what I saw.

"Somewhere behind him over the parapet of the bridge there was a figure. I remember nothing about it except the face and the hands. The face was, I think, the tenderest I have ever seen. The eyes were downcast, looking upon the boy's head with indescribable love, the lips were smiling. One hand was over the boy's eyes, the other against his shoulder behind. In a moment the memory of other stories I had heard came to mind—and I gave a sob of relief that the boy was safe in such care.

"But as the iron hoofs and rocking wheels came up, the hand on the boy's shoulder suddenly pushed him to meet them; and yet those tender eyes and mouth never flinched, and the child took a step forward in front of the horse, and was beaten down without a cry: and the cart lurched heavily, righted itself; and dashed on out of sight.

"When the cloud of dust had passed, the little body lay quiet on the road, and the two girls were clinging to one another, screaming and sobbing, but there was nothing else.

"I was as angry at first as an old man could be. I nearly (may He forgive me for it now!) cursed God and died. But the memory of that tender face did its work. It was as the face of a mother who nurses her first-born child, as the face of a child who kisses a wounded creature, it was as I think the Father's Face itself must have been, which those angels always behold, as He looked down upon the Sacrifice of His only Son.

"Will you forgive me now if I seemed hard a few minutes ago? Perhaps you still think it was hardness that made me speak as I did.

347

But, for myself, I hope I may call it by a better name than that."

In the Convent Chapel

One evening about this time, on coming indoors for tea, I found the old man seated at the open door that looked on to the lawn, with a book on his knees, and his finger between the pages. He held the book towards me as I came near him, and showed me the title, *The Interior Castle*. "I have just been reading," he said, "Saint Teresa's description of the difference between the intellectual and the imaginative vision. It is curious how she fails really to express it, except to anyone who happens to have had a glimpse already for himself of what she means. I suppose it is one of the signs of reality in the spiritual world that no one can ever describe so much as he knows."

I sat down.

"I am afraid I don't understand a word you are saying," I answered smiling.

For answer he opened the book and read Saint Teresa's curious gasping incoherent sentences—at least so I thought them.

"Still," I said, "I am afraid—"

"Oh," he said almost impatiently, "surely you know now; indeed, you know it, but do not recognise it."

"Can you give me any sort of instance?" I asked.

He thought for a moment or two in silence; and then

"I think I can," he said, "if you are sure it will not bore you."

He poured out tea for us both, and then began:

"Most of the tales I have told you are of the imaginative vision, by which I do not mean that the vision is in any way unreal or untrue, which is what most people mean by 'imaginative,' but only that it presents itself in the form of a visible picture. It seems chiefly the function of the imagination to visualise facts, and it is an abuse of that faculty to employ it chiefly in visualising fancies. But it is possible for spiritual facts to represent themselves vividly and clearly to the intellect instead, so that the person to whom the intellectual vision is given does not, so to speak, 'see' anything, but only 'apprehends' something to be true. However, this will become more clear presently.

"Some years ago, I took my annual holiday in the form of a solitary walking tour. I will not tell you where I went, as there are others concerned in this story who would dislike intensely to be publicly spoken of in the way that I shall have to speak of them; but it is enough to say that I came at last to a little town towards sunset. My object in coming to this place was to visit a convent of enclosed nuns whose reputation for holiness was very great. I carried with me a letter of introduction to the Reverend Mother, which I knew would admit me to the chapel. I left my bag at the inn, and then walked down to the convent, which stood a little way out of the town.

"The lay sister who opened the door to me asked me to come into the parlour while she told the Reverend Mother; and after waiting a few minutes in the prim room with its bees-waxed floor and its religious engravings and objects, a wonderfully dignified little old lady, with a quiet wrinkled face, came in with my letter open in her hand. We talked a few minutes about various things, and I had a glass of cowslip wine in a thick-lipped wineglass.

"She told me that the convent was a very ancient foundation, that it had been a country house ever since the Dissolution of the Religious Houses, until about twenty years ago, when it had been acquired for the community. There still remained of the old buildings part of the cloisters, with the south transept of the old church, which was now the chapel; the whole, with a wall or two, forming the courtyard through which I had come. Behind the house lay the garden, on to which the window of the parlour looked; and as I sat I could see a black cross or two marking the nuns' graveyard. I made inquiries as to the way the time of the community was spent.

"'Our object,' said the old lady, 'is perpetual intercession for sinners. We have the great joy of the Blessed Sacrament amongst us in the chapel, and, except during the choir offices and Mass, there is always a nun kneeling before It. We look after one or two ladies incurably ill, who have come to end their days with us, and we make our living by embroidery.'

"I asked how it was that she could receive strangers if the order was an enclosed one.

"'The lay sisters and myself alone can receive strangers. We find that necessary.'

"After a little more talk I asked whether I might see the chapel, and she took me out into the courtyard immediately.

"As we walked across the grass she pointed out to me the cloisters, now built up into a corridor, and the long ruined wall of the old nave which formed one side of the quadrangle. A grave-faced and stout collie dog had joined us at the door, and we three went together slowly towards the door in the centre of the west wall of the restored transept. The evening sun lay golden on the wall before us and on the ruined base of the central tower of the old church, round which jackdaws wheeled and croaked."

The old priest broke off and turned to me, with his eyes burning:

"What a marvellous thing the Religious Life is," he said, "and above all the Contemplative Life! Here were these nuns as no doubt they and their younger sisters are still, without one single thing that in the world's opinion makes life worth living. There is practically perpetual silence, there are hours to be spent in the chapel, no luxuries, no amusements, no power of choice, they are always rather hungry and rather tired, at the very least. And yet they are not sacrificing present happiness to future happiness, as the world always supposes, but they are intensely and radiantly happy 'now in this present time.' I don't know what further proof any one wants of Who our Lord is than that men and women find the keenest, and in fact their only joy, in serving Him and belonging to Him.

"Well, I remember that something of this sort was in my mind as I went across the courtyard beside this motherly old lady with her happy quiet face. She had been over fifty years in Religion, my friend had told me.

"At the door she stopped.

"'I will not come in,' she said, 'but you will find me in the parlour when you come out.'

"And she turned and went back, with the collie walking slowly beside her, his golden plumed tail raised high against her black habit.

"The door was partly open, but a thick curtain hung beyond. I pushed it quietly aside and stepped in. It seemed very dark at first, in contrast to the brilliant sunshine outside; but I presently saw that I was kneeling before a high iron-barred screen, in which was no door. On the left, in the further corner of the chapel, glimmered a blue light in a silver lamp before a statue of our Lady.

"Opposite me rose up the steps before the high altar; but not far away, because, as you remember, the chapel had once been the transept of a church, and the east wall, in the centre of which the high altar stood, was longer than both the south wall where a second altar stood, and the modern brick wall that closed it on the north. A slender crucifix in black and white and six thin tapers rose above the altar, and high above stood the Tabernacle closed by a white silk curtain, before which flickered a tiny red spark.

"I said a prayer or two, and then I noticed for the first time a dark outline rising in the centre of the space before the altar. For a moment I was perplexed, and then I saw that it was the nun whose hour it was for intercession. Her back was turned to me as she knelt at the faldstool, and her black veil fell in rigid lines on to her shoulders, and mingled with her black serge habit below. There she knelt perfectly motionless, praying. I had not, and have not, a notion as to her age. She might have been twenty-five or seventy.

"As I knelt there I thought deeply, wondering as to the nun's age, how long she had been professed, when she would die, whether she was happy; and, I am afraid, I thought more of her than of Him Who was so near. Then a kind of anger seized me, as I compared in my mind the life of a happy good woman in the world with that of this poor creature. I pictured the life, as one so often sees it in homes, of a mother with her children growing up about her, her hands busy with healthy home work, her life glorified by a good man's love; as she grows older, passing from happy stage to happy stage, comforting, helping, sweetening every soul she meets. Was it not for this that women—and men too, I thought, rebuking myself—were made? Then think of the sour life of the cloister—as loveless and desolate as the cold walls themselves! And even, I thought, even if there is a strange peculiar joy in the Religious Life—even if there is an absence of sorrows and anxieties such as spoil the happiness of many lives in the world—yet, after all, surely the Contemplative Life is useless and barren. The Active Life may be well enough, if the prayers and the discipline issue in greater efficiency, it the priest is more fervent when he ministers outside, and the sister of charity more charitable. Yes, I thought, the active Religious Life is reasonable enough; but the Contemplative——! After all it is essentially selfish, it is a sin against society. Possibly it was necessary when the wickedness of the world was more fierce, to protest against it by this retirement; but not now, not now! How can the lump be leavened if the leaven be withdrawn? How can a soul serve God by forsaking the world which He made and loves?"...

"And so," said the priest, turning to me again, "I went on—poor ignorant fool!—thinking that the woman who knelt in front of me was less useful than myself, and that my words and actions and sermons and life did more to advance God's kingdom than her prayers! And then—then—at the moment when I reached that climax of folly and pride, God was good to me and gave me a little light.

"Now, I do not know how to put it—I have never put it into words before, except to myself—but I became aware, in my intellect alone, of one or two clear facts. In order to tell you what those facts were I must use picture language; but remember they are only translations or paraphrases of what I perceived.

"First I became aware suddenly that there ran a vital connection from the Tabernacle to the woman. You may think of it as one of those bands you see in machinery connecting two wheels, so that when either wheel moves the other moves too. Or you may think of it as an electric wire, joining the instrument the telegraph operator uses with the pointer at the other end. At any rate there was this vital band or wire of life.

Now in the Tabernacle I became aware that there was a mighty stirring and movement. Something within it beat like a vast Heart, and the vibrations of each pulse seemed to quiver through all the ground. Or you may picture it as the movement of a clear deep pool when the basin that contains it is jarred—it seemed like the movement of circular ripples crossing and recrossing in swift thrills. Or you may think of it as that faint movement of light and shade that may be seen in the heart of a white-hot furnace. Or again you may picture it as sound—as the sound of a high ship-mast with the rigging, in a steady wind; or the sound of deep woods in a July noon."

The priest's face was working, and his hands moved nervously.

"How hopeless it is," he said, "to express all this! Remember that all these pictures are not in the least what I perceived. They are only grotesque paraphrases of a spiritual fact that was shown me.

"Now I was aware that there was something of the same activity in the heart of the woman, but I did not know which was the controlling power. I did not know whether the initiative sprang from the Tabernacle and communicated itself to the nun's will; or whether she, by bending herself upon the Tabernacle, set in motion a huge dormant power. It appeared to me possible that the solution lay in the fact that two wills co-operated, each reacting upon the other. This, in a kind of way, appears to me now true as regards the whole mystery of free-will and prayer and grace.

"At any rate the union of these two represented itself to me, as I have said, as forming a kind of engine that radiated an immense light or sound or movement. And then I perceived something else too.

"I once fell asleep in one of those fast trains from the north, and did not awake until we had reached the terminus. The last thing I had seen before falling asleep had been the quiet darkening woods and fields through which we were sliding, and it was a shock to awake in the bright humming terminus and to drive through the crowded streets, under the electric glare from the lamps and windows. Now I felt something of that sort now. A moment ago, I had fancied myself apart from movement and activity in this quiet convent; but I seemed somehow to have stepped into a centre of busy, rushing life. I can scarcely put the sensation more clearly than that. I was aware that the atmosphere was charged with energy; great powers seemed to be astir, and I to be close to the whirling centre of it all.

"Or think of it like this. Have you ever had to wait in a city office? If you have done that you will know how intense quiet can coexist with intense activity. There are quiet figures here and there round the room. Or it may be there is only one such figure—a great financier— and he sitting there almost motionless. Yet you know that every movement tingles, as it were, out from that still room all over the world. You can picture to yourself how people leap to obey or to resist—how lives rise and fall, and fortunes are made and lost, at the gentle movements of this lonely quiet man in his office. Well, so it was here. I perceived that this black figure knelt at the centre of reality and force, and with the movements of her will and lips controlled spiritual destinies for eternity. There ran out from this peaceful chapel lines of spiritual power that lost themselves in the distance, bewildering in their profusion and terrible in the intensity of their hidden fire. Souls leaped up and renewed the conflict as this tense will strove for them. Souls even at that moment leaving the body struggled from death into spiritual life, and fell panting and saved at the feet of the Redeemer on the other side of death. Others, acquiescent and swooning in sin, woke and snarled at the merciful stab of this poor nun's prayers."

The priest was trembling now with excitement.

"Yes," he said; "yes, and I in my stupid arrogance had thought that my life was more active in God's world than hers. So a small provincial shopkeeper, bustling to and fro behind the counter, might think, if only he were mad enough, that his life was more active and alive than the life of a director who sits at his table in the city. Yes, that is a vulgar simile; but the only one that I can think of which in the least expresses what I knew to be true. There lay my little foolish narrow life behind me, made up of spiritless prayers and efforts and feeble dealings with souls; and how complacent I had been with it all, how self-centred, how out of the real tide of spiritual movement! And meanwhile, for years probably, this nun had toiled behind these walls in the silence of grace, with the hum of the world coming faintly to her ears, and the cries of peoples and nations, and of persons whom the world accounts important, sounding like the voices of children at play in the muddy street outside; and indeed that is all that they are, compared to her—children making mud-pies or playing at shop outside the financier's office."

The priest was silent, and his face became quieter again. Then in a moment he spoke again.

"Well," he said, "that is what I believe to have been an intellectual vision. There was no form or appearance or sound; but I can only express what was shown to me to be true, under those images. It almost seems to me as I look back now as if the air in the chapel were full of a murmurous sound and a luminous mist as the currents of need and grace went to and fro. But I know really that the silence was deep and the air dim."

Then I made a foolish remark.

"If you feel like that about the Contemplative Life, I wonder you did not try to enter it yourself."

The priest looked at me for a moment.

"It would be rash, surely, for a little shopkeeper of no particular ability to compete with Rothschild."

Under Which King?

Within a day or two of our conversation on St. Teresa, I asked the old priest about what is called "Quietism." A friend had given me an old copy of Molinos' *Spiritual Guide*, and I knew that the writer had been condemned and imprisoned for life, and yet I could not understand in what lay his crime.

"It is difficult to put into words," said the priest, "or even to understand, why certain sentences are condemned, since it is probably possible to parallel them from other Catholic mystics whose names are honoured. Yet the fact remains that the result of Molinos' teaching was neglect of the Sacraments and of external means of grace, which was not so in the case of the schools of other mystics."

"But I will tell you a story," he went on, "to illustrate the effect of certain kinds of mysticism; and I must leave you to judge whether my friend was right or wrong in what he decided, for I must tell you first that the incident did not happen to me. On the whole I may say that I have my own opinion on the subject, but I will not tell you what it is, as sometimes I am strongly inclined to change it. However, you shall hear the story. Shall we take a stroll on the terrace?" And when we had reached it, he began:

"My friend was a priest of about thirty years of age (this happened some forty years ago). He was working in the country at the time, and had a great deal of leisure for reading, and this he chiefly occupied in the study of various mystics, and most of them of the Quietistic school. You know, too, that one of their characteristic lines of thought lies in the abandonment of all effort save that of adhering to God, and even that is to be a passive rather than an active effort. The soul must lie still, says one of them, and be drawn as if by a rope up the Mount of Perfection. The slightest movement will check or divert that swift and steady approach towards God.

"But my friend not only studied writers of this school intellectually, but he put himself more or less under their spiritual direction. He told me afterwards that it seemed to him that if he used the Sacraments faithfully, and if he found that his devotion towards them did not cool, he would be sufficiently protected against possible extravagances or heresies in his spiritual reading. His daily meditation, too, he told me, began to mean more to him than ever in his lifetime: the presence of God seemed more real and accessible, and, above all, the guidance of God in his daily life more apparent. The time that really matters, as he said to me once, is the time between our religious exercises; and in this time, too, God manifested Himself. In fact, from all that he said to me, I have very little doubt that his character and spiritual life were both deepened and purified, at any rate at first, by his devotional study of these mystics.

"One word more before I begin the actual story.

"I said just now that the guidance of God began to be more apparent in his daily life. There are two main ways of settling questions that come up for decision, and both ways are possible to a religious man. One way is to lay stress on the intellectual side, to weigh the arguments carefully, and decide, as it were, by reasoning alone: the other is to lay comparatively little stress on the arguments and the intellectual side generally, and to make the main effort lie in the aspiration of the will towards God for guidance. We may call them, roughly, the intellectual and the intuitive. Now of course my friend's mystical studies inclined him more and more towards the latter. He told me, in fact, that in the most ordinary questions—in his visiting his people—in his preaching—in his dealings with souls—he began more and more to refuse intellectual light, and to trust instead to the immediate interior guidance of the Holy Ghost. More than once, for example, he laid aside the sermon he

355

had prepared, as he entered the pulpit, and preached from a text that had seemed to be suggested to him. Of course, it was not so good from the literary point of view; but that, as he very justly said, is not the most important question in judging of a sermon. He seemed to find, he told me, that his spiritual power in every way developed, both in his interior life and in his dealings with others.

"In his conversations, too, he would allow long silences to come, if it did not seem to him that God moved him to speak; at other times he would drop conventional modes of speech and say things that, humanly judged, were calculated to do the very opposite of what he personally desired. Sometimes in such a case his wish was attained, and sometimes not; but in both cases he forced himself to regard it as if he had succeeded. In short, he acted and spoke in obedience to this interior drawing, and disregarded consequences entirely. And this, I need hardly say, is one road to interior peace.

"And then at last a startling thing happened.

"There had been some crime committed: I have not an idea what it was. Two men were involved in the consequences. One, whom we will call A., had committed the crime: but he could only be prosecuted if B., whom he had seriously injured, consented to take action. Now my friend was deeply interested in A., and he thought he knew that the one chance of A.'s salvation lay in his being allowed to go unpunished. But Lord B., who, by the way, was an Irish peer, of no importance himself, though his father had been well known, was a hard, vindictive man, and had publicly announced his intention of ruining A. In this state of affairs my friend was asked to intercede by A. and his friends.

"Lord B. lived in a large country-house some four or five miles from my friend's house. He was an unmarried man, but generally had his house fairly full of his friends, who did not bear the best possible reputation.

"My friend arrived at the house by appointment with B., whom he did not personally know, towards the close of a rainy autumn afternoon. In spite of his anxiety he had resolved to be guided as usual by the interior monitor whom he had learnt to trust, and he had hardly thought of a single argument which he could use. Yet he felt confident that he was right in coming, and equally confident that he would know what to say when the time came. As he got near the house this confident sense of guidance increased to an extent that almost terrified him. It seemed to him, as he walked under the dripping yellow branches, that a strong, almost physical, oppression carried him forward. As if in a dream he saw the manservant appear in answer to his ring, and heard, as from a great distance, the man tell him that Lord B. had come in a little while before, and was now expecting him in the smoking-room.

"On entering the house these curious sensations, which he hardly attempted to describe to me, seemed to diminish a little, and he felt cool and confident. He told me that the sense of oppression resting on him was dispelled, as if by a breeze, as he passed along the corridor on the ground floor on his way to the smoking-room in the west wing of the house.

"The servant threw open the door and announced him, and my friend went through, and the door closed behind him: but the moment he had crossed the threshold he felt that something was wrong.

"There was a circle of men, some in shooting costume, and some as if they had not been out all day, sitting in easy chairs round the fire, which was to the right of the door. My friend could see most of their faces, and Lord B.'s face among them, as he paused at the door; but not one offered to move, though all looked curiously at him.

"There was silence for a moment, and then Lord B. said suddenly and loudly:

"'Well, here's the parson at last, sermon and all.'

"And then two or three of the men laughed.

"My friend saw of course that Lord B. had arranged the interview in this way simply in order to insult him, and that he would not be able to speak to him in private at all, as he had hoped. There was, he told me, just one great heave of anger in his heart at this offensive behaviour; but he did his best to crush it down, and still stood without speaking. He had not, he said, an idea what to say or do, so he stood and waited.

"Lord B. got up in a moment and lit a cigarette with his back to my friend; and then turned and faced him, leaning against the mantelpiece.

"'Well,' he said, 'we're all waiting.'

"Still there was silence. One of the men beyond the fire suddenly laughed.

"'Now then,' said Lord B. impatiently, 'for God's sake say what you came to say, and go.'

"As this sentence ended my friend felt a curious sensation run over him, like those he had experienced in the park, but far stronger.

He could never give me any description of it, except by saying that it seemed as if a force were laying hold of him in every remote fibre of his bodily and spiritual being. His own will seemed to give up the control into some stronger hand, and he felt a sense of being steadied and quieted.

"Then he was aware that his own voice said a single sentence of some half-dozen words; but though he heard each word, it was instantly obliterated from his mind. In his description of it all to me afterwards, he said it was like words that we hear immediately before we fall asleep in a lecture-room or a railway carriage: each word is English and intelligible, but the sentence conveys no impression.

"While his voice spoke for perhaps two or three seconds, his eyes were fixed on Lord B.'s face, and in that momentary interval he saw a terrible fear and astonishment suddenly stamped upon it. The mouth opened in loose lines and the cigarette fell out, and B.'s hands rose instinctively as if to keep my friend off". One of the men, too, at the further end of the circle suddenly sprang erect, with the same kind of imploring horror on his face.

"That was all that my friend had time to see; for the same power that had laid hold of him turned him immediately to the door, and he opened it and went out and down the corridor. As he went the strange sensation passed, but he felt the sweat prick to his skin and then pour down his face. He heard, too, as he reached the end of the corridor, a bell peal violently somewhere. He passed out into the hall, and even as he opened the front door a servant dashed past him through the hall and down the corridor, up which he had just come.

"He went straight home, feeling terribly tired and overwrought, and had to go to bed on reaching his house, tortured by neuralgia.

"Two hours later a note was brought by a groom from Lord B., written in a shaking hand, with an abject apology for his reception in the afternoon; an entreaty to him not to mention the subject again which he had spoken of in the sitting-room, with a scarcely veiled offer of a bribe, and an emphatic promise to withdraw all proceedings against A.

"On the following day he was told that Lord B. was supposed to be unwell, and that the house-party had been hurriedly broken up the night before.

"From that day to this he has never had an idea of what the sentence was that his voice spoke that worked such a miracle."

"That is a most curious story," I said. "What do you make of it?"

The priest smiled.

"I will tell you what my friend made of it. He gave up his study of mysticism, yet without in any sense condemning that line of thought of which I have spoken. His reasons, which he explained to me after coming to a decision, were that such a visitation might or might not be from God. If it were not from God, then that proved that he had been meddling with high things, and had somehow slipped under some other control. If it were from God, it might be that it was just for that very purpose that he had been brought so far, but that he dared not pursue that path without some distinct further sign. 'In any case,' he said, 'no soul can be lost by following the simple and well-beaten path of ordinary devotion and prayer.' And so he returned to intellectual forms of meditation, such as most Christians use. He died a few years ago, full of holiness and good works.

"But for you there are several opinions open. Either that it was an intensely strong case of hypnotic thought-transference from Lord B. to my friend, and that the latter only spoke mechanically of something that lay in the former's mind; or you may decide that the whole affair was of the Evil One, and that A. would have been all the better for prosecution, and that an evil being somehow found entrance into the strained nature of my friend, and used it for his own purposes; or that the prophetic gift was bestowed on him. but that the ordeal was too fierce and he too cowardly to claim it. And there are other solutions as well, no doubt possible.

"For myself I think I have formed my opinion; but I would prefer, as Herodotus says, to keep it to myself."

With Dyed Garments

When the second post came in one morning I saw a letter addressed to the priest, in the trembling large characters of an old man's hand, lying upon the slab in the hall. When I came in to lunch I found the old clergyman with an open letter in his hand, and his face full of almost childish happiness.

"I have heard from my oldest friend," he said, making a little movement with the letter. "It is months since he has written. I have known him ever since we were boys."

We sat down to lunch, but he kept on referring to his friend, and to the pleasure the letter gave him.

"We are always planning to meet," he said to me presently. "But we never can manage it. We are both so old. He is much more active than

I am, however. He is full of good works, while I, as you know, lead an idle life. I could not take charge of a church. It is all I can do now to serve my own little chapel upstairs."

"Where is he working?" I asked.

"I think perhaps you fancy he is in Holy Orders, but he is not. He has been on the Stock Exchange till a few years ago, and now he is living in the country, getting ready to die, as he tells me. But he is full of good works; his letter here has news about the village, and of a man whose acquaintance he has made in the reading-room there, which he himself built a year ago; but he is full of plans too, and asks my advice."

"It is not often you come across a business man like that," I said.

"No, he is wonderful, but he has been like that for years. He has done a great deal all his life among poor people in London. For years he never missed his two or three nights a week in some club, or on some committee, or visiting sick people."

I began to think that it might have been through the friendship of the priest that this man had been such a worker. But presently he began again.

"Perhaps the most wonderful thing was the way he first began to do such work. Let me see, have I mentioned his name? No? Then I can tell you, otherwise it would not be discreet; that is—" he added, "if you would care to hear."

I told him I should be very much interested.

"Then after lunch we will have coffee in the garden, and I will tell you."

When we had sat down under the shade of a wall, with the tall avenue of pines opposite us making a dark tangled frieze against the delicate sky, he began.

"What I am going to tell you now has been gathered partly from conversations with my friend: and partly from letters he has written to me. Years ago, I jotted down the order of events, with names and dates, but that, of course, I fear I cannot show even to you. However, I know the story well, and you may rely on the main facts.

"I must tell you first that many years ago now, my friend, who was about forty years old, had lately become a partner in his father's firm: and of course, was greatly occupied with all the details of business. It was a broker's firm, well established and did a good steady business. My friend at that time had no idea of doing any work outside his occupation. I heard him say in fact, about this time, that his work seemed to absorb all his energies and capacity. Then the first event of the series took place.

"He was coming home one frosty afternoon in December, between three and four o'clock, on the top of an omnibus. He was sitting in front and looking about him. He noticed a poorly-dressed man standing on the pavement on the right-hand side, as if he wished to cross. Then he began to cross, and came at last right up to the omnibus on which my friend was sitting, and paused a moment to let it pass. As he stood there, my friend watching him with that listless interest with which a tired man will observe details, a hansom cab moving quickly came in the opposite direction. It seemed as if the horse would run the man down.

"It was too sudden to warn him, but the man saw it, and to avoid the horse sprang quickly forward, his head half turned away, and his feet came between the front and back wheels of the omnibus. There was a jolt and a terrible scream, and my friend horrified leant far over the side to see. When the omnibus had passed the man stood for a moment on his crushed feet, and then swayed forward and fell on his face. My friend started up and made a movement to go to him, but several others had seen the accident and ran to the man, and a policeman was crossing quickly from the other side, so he sat down again and the omnibus carried him on.

"Now this horrible thing remained in my friend's mind, haunted him, shocked him profoundly. He could not forget the terrible face of pain that he had seen upturned for an instant, and his imagination carried him on in spite of himself to dwell on the details of those crushed feet. He wrote me a long letter a week or two afterwards, minutely describing all that I have told you.

"The following summer he was going down to the Kennington Oval one Saturday afternoon to see the close of some famous cricket match. He travelled by the Underground Railway as far as Westminster, and from there determined to walk at least across the Bridge. He walked on the right-hand side, and had reached the steps of St. Thomas' Hospital. He waited here a moment undecided whether to walk on or drive.

"As he waited, he half turned and saw a beggar sitting in the angle between the steps and the wall. There was a white dog beside him. The beggar's face was partly bandaged; but what caught my friend's attention most were his two hands. They were lying palms downwards on the beggar's knees, bandaged like his face, but in the centre of each was a dark spot, showing through the wrapping, as if there were a festering wound that soaked through from underneath. My friend looked at him in disgust for a moment: but terribly fascinated by those quiet suffering hands; and then he passed on. But during all that afternoon he could not forget those hands. I daresay he was overwrought and nervous. But his memory too went back to the accident by the Marble Arch. That night too, as he told me in a conversation afterwards, as he tossed about, his windows wide open to catch the night air, half waking visions kept moving before him of a man with crushed feet and bandaged hands, who moaned and lifted a drawn face to the sky,

"Early that autumn he was alone, except for the servants, in his father's house in London. A maid was taken ill. I forget the nature of the illness, but perhaps you will be able to identify it when I have finished. At any rate the girl grew quickly worse. One morning just before he started to the City the doctor, who had called early that morning, asked to have a word with him, and told him he thought he ought to operate immediately, and asked for his sanction.

"'Well,' said my friend, 'of course I must speak to the girl about it. Have you told her yet?'

"'No,' said the doctor, 'I thought I should mention it to you first. I understand that the girl has no relations in the world.'

"'Can you tell me the nature of the operation?' asked my friend.

"'It is not really serious. It is an incision in the right side,' and he added a few details explaining the case.

"'Well,' said my friend, 'we had better go upstairs together.'

"They went up and found the girl perfectly conscious and reasonable. She consented to the operation, which was fixed for that evening.

"But all that day the picture floated before his eyes of the quiet room at the top of the house, and the girl lying there waiting. And then the scene would shift a little. And he would see the girl after it was over, with a bandage against her side, and the knowledge of the little wound beneath. When he reached home, late in the evening, the doctor was waiting for him.

"'It has been perfectly successful,' he said, 'and I think she will recover.'

"Now, that evening, as my friend sat at the dinner-table alone, smoking and thinking, his old experiences came to his mind again. In less than a year he had seen three things, none of which seemed to have any very close relation to him, but each of which had deeply affected him. He told me afterwards that he began to suspect a design underlying them; but he had not a glimmer of light, strange as it may seem to you and me, as to the nature of that design. Within a month, however, I received a letter from him, from some place in the country where he was staying, describing the following incident.

"He had gone down from a Saturday to Monday to a friend's house in Surrey. On the Sunday afternoon he and his friend went for a walk through some woods. Autumn was in full glory, and the trees were blazing in red and gold: and the bramble branches were weighed down with purple fruit. As they walked together along a grass ride they heard shouts and laughter of children in the woods on one side. They could hear footsteps pattering through dry leaves, and the tearing and trampling of brushwood; and in a moment more a boy burst out of the thin hedge, tripped in a bramble, and rolled into the grass walk. He was up again in a moment laughing and flushed, but my friend saw across his forehead a little thin red dotted line where a thorn had scratched him. As the boy laughed up into their faces, he lifted his hand to his forehead.

"'Why it's wet,' he said, and then, looking at his fingers: 'Why, it's blood! I've scratched myself.'

"Other footsteps came running through the undergrowth, and the boy himself ran off down the road, and the footsteps in the wood stopped, retraced themselves and died away in faint rustlings up the hill. But as my friend had looked he had seen in his memory those other experiences of the last year. And all seemed to concentrate themselves on one Figure—with wounded feet and hands and side—and a torn forehead.

"My friend stood quiet so long that his companion spoke to him and touched his arm.

"'Yes, I am ready,' he said; 'let us go home.'

"The end of the letter I cannot quote to you. It is too intimate and personal. But it ended with a request to myself to give him an introduction to some friend who would give him work to do in some poor district. And work of that kind he has carried on ever since."

The old priest's voice ceased.

"There is one thing my friend did not know," he said after a moment. "When that particular operation on the side is performed, of which I have spoken, there comes out blood and water. A doctor will tell you so."

And then:

"That is my friend's story," he said. "Do you not think it remarkable?"

Unto Babes

A few days after the conversation I have described my visit to the old man came to an end, and my work drew me back to London; but I left behind me a promise to return and spend Christmas at his house. He in the meantime would, he promised me, try to put together some other stories for me against the time that I should return. There were many others, he said, that he had come across in his life which he hoped would interest me, besides a few more personal experiences of his own.

And so I left him smiling and waving to me from his bedroom window that overlooked the drive (for I had to go by an early train), with the clean-shaven face of his old servant looking at me discreetly and gravely from the clear-glass chapel window next to the priest s room, where he had been setting things ready before his master was dressed.

It was a dark winter afternoon when I returned, a week or so before Christmas.

The coachman told me on my inquiry that his master seemed very much aged during the autumn and winter, that he had scarcely left the house since the leaves had fallen, except to sit for an hour or two in sunshiny weather in the sheltered angle of the wall where was the tiled platform that I have spoken of; and that he was afraid he had been suffering from depression. There had been days of almost complete silence, at least so Parker had told him, when the master had sat all day turning over letters and books and old drawers.

I reproached myself with having troubled the old man with demands for more stories; and feared that it had been in the attempt to please me that he had fallen brooding over the past, perhaps dwelling too much on sorrows of which I knew nothing.

As we passed under the pines that tossed their sombre plumes in the wind, the sun, breaking through clouds in an angry glory on my right, blazed on the little square-paned windows of the house on my left. The chapel-window on the top story seemed especially full of red light streaming from within, but the flame swept across the upper story as we drove past, and left the windows blank and colourless just before we turned the corner at the back of the house.

The old man met me in the hall, and I was startled to see the change that had come to him. His eyes seemed larger than ever, and there was a sorrow in them that I had not seen before. They had been the eyes of a stainless child, wide and smiling; now they were the eyes of one who was under some burden almost too heavy to be borne. In the stronger light of the sitting-room as the candles shone on his face, I saw that my impression had only been caused by a drooping of the eyelids, that now hung down a little further. But it looked a tired face.

He welcomed me, and said several charming things to me that I should be ashamed to quote, but he made me feel that he was glad that I had come; and so, I was glad too. But he said among other things this:

"I am glad you have come now, because I think I shall have something further to tell you. I have had indications during this autumn that the end is coming, and I think that if I have to pass through a dark valley—and I feel that I am at its entrance even now—I think that He will give me His staff as well as His rod. But I am an old man and full of fancies, so please do not question me. But I am very glad," and he took my hand and stroked it for a moment, "very glad that you are here, because I do not think that you will be afraid."

During the following days he told me many stories, bringing out the old books and letters of which the coachman had spoken, and spelling out notes through his tortoiseshell glass, as he sat by the open fireplace in the central sitting-room, with the logs crackling and over-run with swift sparks as they rested on their bed of ashes. The door into the garden where the old drive had once been was now kept closed, and a heavy curtain hung over it.

We did not go out very much together—only in the early after-noons we would walk for an hour or so, he leaning on my arm and on a stick, up and down the terraced walk that lay next the drive under the pines, as the sunset burned across the hills like a far-away judgment. Someday perhaps I will write out some of the stories that he told me, although not all. I have the notes by me.

Here is one of them.

We were walking on one of these dark winter afternoons very slowly uphill towards the village that the priest might get a change from the garden. The morning had been gusty and wet, with sleet showers and even a sprinkle of pure snow as the sky cleared after lunch-time; and now the weather was settling down for a frost, and the snow lay thinly here and there on the rapidly hardening ground.

"It is remarkable," the old man was saying to me, "how in spite of our Lord's words people still think that faith is a matter more or less of intellect. Such a phrase as 'intelligent faith' is, of course, strictly most incorrect."

He stopped and looked at me as he said this, as if prepared for dispute. I did not disappoint him.

"You are very puzzling;" I said. "I cannot believe that you do not value intellect. Surely it is a gift of God, and therefore may adorn faith, as any other gift may do."

"Yes," he said, walking on, "it may adorn it; but it has nothing more to do with it really than jewels have to do with a beautiful woman. In fact, sometimes faith is far more beautiful unadorned, and it is quite possible to crush a delicate and growing faith with a weight of learned arguments intended to adorn and perfect it. Christian apologetics, it seems to me, are only really useful in the mouth of one who realises their entire inadequacy. You can demonstrate nothing of God. You can, by arguments, draw a number of lines that converge towards God, and render His existence and His attributes probable; but you cannot reach Him along those lines. Faith depends not on intellectual but on moral conditions. 'Blessed are the pure in heart,' said our Saviour, not 'Blessed are the profound or acute of intellect'—'for they shall see God.' It is certainly true of intellectual as of all other riches that they who possess them shall find difficulty in entering into the kingdom of God."

"And so," I said, "you think that intellectual powers are not things to covet, and that education is not a very important question after all?"

"No more than wealth," he answered, "at least so far as you mean by education instruction in demonstrable facts or exact sciences. The point of our existence here is to know God. Well, you know for yourself how the race for wealth is ruining millions of souls today. No less surely is keen intellectual competition ruining souls.

Mr. ——, for instance," he said, naming a well-known critic and poet; "was there ever a man of keener and finer intellect, or of more unerring instinct in matters of literary taste? Well, once I talked with that man most of a day on all his own subjects; in fact, he did nearly all the talking, and I was astonished, I must confess, at the perfection of the training of his already brilliant powers. So much I could perceive, though of course I could not follow him. And of course, there were many delicate shades of beauty, if not much more, invisible to me in his talk and criticism. His scale of intellectual beauty ran up out of my sight altogether. But what astonished me more was the coarseness and dullness of his spiritual instinct. I will not call him a child in matters of faith, because that would be high praise; but he was just an ill-bred boor. I have known many a Sussex villager of far purer and finer spiritual fibre. No, no; faith can and does exist quite apart from intellect; and to increase or develop the one often means the decrease and incoherence of the other. *Seigneur, donnez-moi la foi du charbonnier!*" (Lord, give me the faith of the coalman!)

I must confess that this was a new point of view for me; and I am not sure now whether I do not still think it exaggerated and dangerous; but I said nothing, because it did seem to open up difficult questions, and also to throw light on other difficult questions. The priest turned to me again as he walked.

"Why, it must be so," he said; "if it were not, clever people would have a better hope of salvation than stupid people; and that is absurd—as absurd as if rich people should be nearer God than poor people. No, no; talents are distributed unevenly, it is true: to one ten and to another five; but each has one pound, all alike."

We had reached the top of the slope, and the towering hedges had gradually fallen away, so that we could now see far and wide over the country. Away behind us, as we paused for breath, we could see the misty Brighton downs, while in the middle distance lay tumbled wooded hills, with smoke beginning to curl up here and there from the evening fires of hidden villages. The sky was clear overhead, but in the west, where the sunset was beginning to smoulder, a few heavy clouds still lingered.

"And God sees all:" said the priest. "Can you put up with another story as we walk home again? I think I ought to be turning now."

We turned and began to retrace our steps downhill.

"This is not an experience of my own," he said. "It was told me by a friend of mine in Cornwall. He was the squire of a little village a few miles out of Truro, and lived there most of the year except a few weeks in the spring, when he would go abroad. He was a man of great learning and taste, but had the faith of a little child. It was like a spring of clear water to hear him speak of God and heavenly things.

"There was a boy in the village who was an idiot. His parents were dead, and he lived alone with his old grandmother, who was a strict Calvinist, and who regarded her grandson as hopelessly damned because his faith and his expression of it were not as hers. There were evident signs, she said, that God's inscrutable decrees were against him. The local preachers there would have nothing to do with the boy; and the clergyman of the parish, after an attempt or two, had given the child up as hopeless. I think my friend told me that the clergyman had tried to teach him Old Testament history.

"Well, the boy was a terrible and disgusting case. I will not go into details beyond saying that the boy's head had the look of a mule about it; his mother, I think, had had a fright shortly before his birth, and the boy used to think sometimes that he was a horse or mule, and the village children used to encourage him in it, and ride and drive him on the green, for he was quite harmless. And so, he grew up, neglected and untaught, spending much of his time out of doors, and creeping home on all fours in the evening, snorting and stamping and neighing when he was much excited; and he would stable himself in a corner of the wide dark kitchen, and munch grass; while his grandmother sat in her high chair by the fire reading in her Bible, or looking over her spectacles at the poor misshapen body in the corner that held a damned soul.

"Now my friend hated to see this child. It was the one thing that troubled his faith. Those who have the faith of children have also the troubles of children; and this living example before his eyes of what looked like the carelessness of God, or worse, was a greater offence to my friend's faith than all *infidel* arguments, or the mere knowledge that such things happened.

"On a certain Christmas Eve my friend had been a long tramp over the hills with a guest who was staying with him for the shooting. They were returning through his own property towards evening, and were just dropping down from the hill. Their path lay along the upper edge of an old disused stone-quarry, whose entrance lay perhaps a hundred yards away from the valley-road that led into the village—so it was a lonely and unfrequented place. The evening was closing in; and my friend, as he led the way along the path, was trying to make out the outlines of stones and bushes on the floor of the quarry, which lay perhaps seventy feet below them. All at once his eye was caught by the steady glimmer of light somewhere in the dimness beneath, and the sound of a voice.

"He guessed at once that there were tramps below, and was angry at the thought that they must have wilfully disregarded the notice he had put up about making a fire so close to the wood: and he determined to turn them out, and, if need be, to give them shelter for the night in one of his own outhouses. So, he stopped and explained to his friend which path would take him home, while that he himself intended to make his way along the lip of the quarry to the entrance, and then to go on into its interior where the tramps had made their camp; and he promised to be at the house five minutes after his friend.

"So, they separated, and he himself soon found his way down a narrow overgrown path that brought him to the opening of the quarry.

"It was a good deal darker here, as the hill shadowed it from the west, and high trees rose on one side; but he was able to stumble along the stony path which led to the interior, though it grew darker still as he went. Presently he turned the corner of a tall boulder, and emerged into the kind of semi-circus that formed the heart of the quarry: before him, about a third way up the slope, burned the glimmer of light he had noticed from above, but even as he saw it it went out: my friend stood in the path and called out, explaining who he was, not threatening at all, but offering, if it was any one who wanted shelter, to provide it for the night.

"There was no answer, only the sound of scuffling in the dimness in front, and then the confused sound of footsteps scrambling: my friend ran forward, calling, and made out presently an oddly shaped thing scrambling over the silt and stone towards a shoulder of rock that stood out against the sky on his left (I think he said). He tried to follow, but it was too dark, and after he had stumbled once or twice, he gave up the pursuit. In a moment more the climbing figure stood out clear against the sky for an instant, and then disappeared: and the squire saw with a shock of disgust the mule-like head and tangled hair rising from the high shoulders of the village idiot, and his hands dangling on each side of him; and he heard a high-screaming neighing. But at least, he thought to himself, he would go and see what the boy had been doing.

"He made his way up the slope of silted gravel and mud that lay against the face of the rock, and at last reached a little platform apparently stamped and cut out at the top of the scree just where it touched the quarry-side. It was too dark for him to distinguish anything clearly, so he struck a match and held it in the still sheltered air while he looked about him. This is what he saw.

"There was a short halter, with a kind of rude head-stall, fastened to a rusty iron staple driven into the rock. There was a little pile of cut grass below it. There was a kind of mud trough constructed against the stone, with a little straw sprinkled in it and holly berries and leaves in front of it; but this showed signs of having been hastily trampled down, though parts of it survived: there were marks of hob-nailed boots in it here and there. So much my friend had noticed when the match burned his fingers: but just before he dropped it he noticed something else which made him open his box and light another match: and then he saw the end of a farthing taper sticking out of the ground into which it had been pushed, and another crushed into a ball. He drew out the first and lighted it, and then noticed this last thing. Quite plainly marked on the soft edge of the mud-trough, in a place which the hob-nailed boots had not touched, was the mark of a tiny child's naked foot, as if a baby had stood in the trough or manger, with one foot on the floor and another on the edge.

"Now I do not know what you think of this, but I know what my friend thought of it, and what I myself think of it. But before he went home he went first to the cottage where the boy lived and found him as usual tethered in the corner, with his grandmother nodding before the fire. The boy would do nothing but snort and stamp: and the grandmother could only say that ten minutes ago the boy had run in and gone straight to his corner as usual. The squire asked whether the boy had been trusted with a child by anyone; but the grandmother said it was impossible. Nor indeed did he ever after hear a word of a child having been missed on that afternoon.

"Then, before he went home, he went to the little church, already decorated for the festival, and there with the fragrance of the holly and yew in the air about him, and the glimmer of a candle near the altar where the church-cleaner was sweeping, he praised the Holy Child whose Birth-night it was, and who had not disdained to lie in a manger and be adored by the beasts of the stall.

"The following morning on his way back from church he went to the quarry again with his friend to show him what he had seen; but the manger and the holly-berries and crumpled taper were all gone, and there was nothing to see but the iron staple and the platform beaten hard and flat."

We had reached the avenue of pines by now that led to the house, and turned in by the little garden-gate.

"The story seems to show," the priest added, "that intellect has not much to do with the knowledge of God; and that the things which He hides from the wise and prudent He reveals to babes."

The Traveller

On one of these evenings as we sat together after dinner in front of the wide open fireplace in the central room of the house, we began to talk on that old subject—the relation of Science to Faith.

"It is no wonder," said the priest, "if their conclusions appear to differ, to shallow minds who think that the last words are being said on both sides; because their standpoints are so different. The scientific view is that you are not justified in committing yourself one inch ahead of your intellectual evidence: the religious view is that in order to find out anything worth knowing your faith must always be a little in advance of your evidence; you must advance *en échelon*. There is the principle of our Lord's promises. 'Act as if it were true, and light will be given.' The scientist on the other hand says, 'Do not presume to commit yourself until light is given.' The difference between the methods lies, of course, in the fact that Religion admits the heart and the whole man to the witness-box, while Science only admits the head—scarcely even the senses. Yet surely the evidence of experience is on the side of Religion. Every really great achievement is inspired by motives of the heart, and not of the head; by feeling and passion, not by a calculation of probabilities. And so are the mysteries of God unveiled by those who carry them first by assault; 'The Kingdom of Heaven suffereth violence; and the violent take it by force.'

"For example," he continued after a moment, "the scientific view of haunted houses is that there is no evidence for them beyond that which may be accounted for by telepathy, a kind of thought-reading. Yet if you can penetrate that veneer of scientific thought that is so common now, you find that by far the larger part of mankind still believes in them. Practically not one of us really accepts the scientific view as an adequate one."

"Have you ever had an experience of that kind yourself?" I asked.

"Well," said the priest, smiling, "you are sure you will not laugh at it? There is nothing commoner than to think such things a subject for humour; and that I cannot bear. Each such story is sacred to one person at the very least, and therefore should be to all reverent people."

I assured him that I would not treat his story with disrespect.

"Well," he answered, "I do not think you will, and I will tell you. It only happened a very few years ago. This was how it began:

"A friend of mine was, and is still, in charge of a church in Kent, which I will not name; but it is within twenty miles of Canterbury. The district fell into Catholic hands a good many years ago. I received a telegram, in this house, a day or two before Christmas, from my friend, saying that he had been suddenly seized with a very bad attack of influenza, which was devastating Kent at that time; and asking me to come down, if possible at once, and take his place over Christmas. I had only lately given up active work, owing to growing infirmity, but it was impossible to resist this appeal; so, Parker packed my things and we went together by the next train.

"I found my friend really ill, and quite incapable of doing anything; so, I assured him that I could manage perfectly, and that he need not be anxious.

"On the next day, a Wednesday, and Christmas Eve, I went down to the little church to hear confessions. It was a beautiful old church, though tiny, and full of interesting things: the old altar had been set up again; there was a rood-loft with a staircase leading on to it; and an ambry on the north of the sanctuary had been fitted up as a receptacle for the Most Holy Sacrament, instead of the old hanging pyx. One of the most interesting discoveries made in the church was that of the old confessional. In the lower half of the rood-screen, on the south side, a square hole had been found, filled up with an insertion of oak; but an antiquarian of the Alcuin Club, whom my friend had asked to examine the church, declared that this without doubt was the place where in the pre-Reformation times confessions were heard. So, it had been restored, and put to its ancient use; and now on this Christmas Eve I sat within the chancel in the dim fragrant light, while penitents came and knelt outside the screen on the single step, and made their confessions through the old opening.

"I know this is a great platitude, but I never can look at a piece of old furniture without a curious thrill at a thing that has been so much saturated with human emotion; but, above all that I have ever seen, I think that this old confessional moved me. Through that little opening had come so many thousands of sins, great and little, weighted with sorrow; and back again, in Divine exchange for those burdens, had returned the balm of the Saviour's blood. 'Behold! a door opened in heaven,' through which that strange commerce of sin and grace may be carried on—grace pressed down and running over, given into the bosom in exchange for sin! O bonum commercium!"

The priest was silent for a moment, his eyes glowing. Then he went on,

"Well, Christmas Day and the three following festivals passed away very happily. On the Sunday night after service, as I came out of the vestry, I saw a child waiting. She told me, when I asked her if she wanted me, that her father and others of her family wished to make their confessions on the following evening about six o'clock. They had had influenza in the house, and had not been able to come out before; but the father was going to work next day, as he was so much better, and would come, if it pleased me, and some of his children to make their confessions in the evening and their communions the following morning.

"Monday dawned, and I offered the Holy Sacrifice as usual, and spent the morning chiefly with my friend, who was now able to sit up and talk a good deal, though he was not yet allowed to leave his bed.

"In the afternoon I went for a walk.

"All the morning there had rested a depression on my soul such as I have not often felt; it was of a peculiar quality. Every soul that tries, however poorly, to serve God, knows by experience those heavinesses by which our Lord tests and confirms His own: but it was not like that. An element of terror mingled with it, as of impending evil.

"As I started for my walk along the high road this depression deepened. There seemed no physical reason for it that I could perceive. I was well myself, and the weather was fair; yet air and exercise did not affect it. I turned at last, about half-past three o'clock, at a milestone that marked sixteen miles to Canterbury.

"I rested there for a moment, looking to the south-east, and saw that far on the horizon heavy clouds were gathering; and then I started homewards. As I went I heard a far-away boom, as of distant guns, and I thought at first that there was some sea-fort to the south where artillery practice was being held; but presently I noticed that it was too irregular and prolonged for the report of a gun; and then it was with a sense of relief that I came to the conclusion it was a far-away thunderstorm, for I felt that the state of the atmosphere might explain away this depression that so troubled me. The thunder seemed to come nearer, pealed more loudly three or four times and ceased.

"But I felt no relief. When I reached home a little after four Parker brought me in some tea, and I fell asleep afterwards in a chair before the fire. I was wakened after a troubled and unhappy dream by Parker bringing in my coat and telling me it was time to keep my appointment at the church. I could not remember what my dream was, but it was sinister and suggestive of evil, and, with the shreds of it still clinging to me, I looked at Parker with something of fear as he stood silently by my chair holding the coat.

"The church stood only a few steps away, for the garden and churchyard adjoined one another. As I went down carrying the lantern that Parker had lighted for me, I remember hearing far away to the south, beyond the village, the beat of a horse's hoofs. The horse seemed to be in a gallop, but presently the noise died away behind a ridge.

"When I entered the church, I found that the sacristan had lighted a candle or two as I had asked him, and I could just make out the kneeling figures of three or four people in the north aisle.

"When I was ready I took my seat in the chair set beyond the screen, at the place I have described; and then, one by one, the labourer and his children came up and made their confessions. I remember feeling again, as on Christmas Eve, the strange charm of this old place of penitence, so redolent of God and man, each in his tenderest character of Saviour and penitent; with the red light burning like a luminous flower in the dark before me, to remind me how God was indeed tabernacling with men, and was their God.

"Now I do not know how long I had been there, when again I heard the beat of a horse's hoofs, but this time in the village just below the churchyard; then again there fell a sudden silence. Then presently a gust of wind flung the door wide, and the candles began to gutter and flare in the draught. One of the girls went and closed the door.

"Presently the boy who was kneeling by me at that time finished his confession, received absolution and went down the church, and I waited for the next, not knowing how many there were.

"After waiting a minute or two I turned in my seat, and was about to get up, thinking there was no one else, when a voice whispered sharply through the hole a single sentence. I could not catch the words, but I supposed they were the usual formula for asking a blessing, so I gave the blessing and waited, a little astonished at not having heard the penitent come up.

"Then the voice began again."

The priest stopped a moment and looked round, and I could see that he was trembling a little "Would you rather not go on?" I said. "I think it disturbs you to tell me."

"No, no," he said; "it is all right, but it was very dreadful—very dreadful.

"Well, the voice began again in a loud quick whisper, but the odd thing was that I could hardly understand a word; there were just phrases here and there, like the name of God and of our Lady, that I could catch. Then there were a few old French words that I knew; 'le roy' came over and over again. Just at first, I thought it must be some extreme form of dialect unknown to me; then I thought it must be a very old man who was deaf, because when I tried, after a few sentences, to explain that I could not understand, the penitent paid no attention, but whispered on quickly without a pause. Presently I could perceive that he was in a terrible state of mind; the voice broke and sobbed, and then almost cried out, but still in this loud whisper; then on the other side of the screen I could hear fingers working and moving uneasily, as if entreating admittance at some barred door. Then at last there was silence for a moment, and then plainly some closing formula was repeated, which gradually grew lower and ceased. Then, as I rose, meaning to come round and explain that I had not been able to hear, a loud moan or two came from the penitent. I stood up quickly and looked through the upper part of the screen, and there was no one there.

"I can give you no idea of what a shock that was to me. I stood there glaring, I suppose, through the screen down at the empty step for a moment or two, and perhaps I said something aloud, for I heard a voice from the end of the church.

"'Did you call, sir?'" And there stood the sacristan, with his keys and lantern, ready to lock up.

"I still stood without answering for a moment, and then I spoke; my voice sounded oddly in my ears.

"'Is there anyone else, Williams? Are they all gone?' or something like that.

"Williams lifted his lantern and looked round the dusky church.

"'No, sir; there is no one.'

"I crossed the chancel to go to the vestry, but as I was half-way, suddenly again in the quiet village there broke out the desperate gallop of a horse.

"'There! there!' I cried, 'do you hear that?'

"Williams came up the church towards me.

"'Are you ill, sir?' he said. 'Shall I fetch your servant?'

"I made an effort and told him it was nothing; but he insisted on seeing me home: I did not like to ask him whether he had heard the gallop of the horse; for, after all, I thought, perhaps there was no connection between that and the voice that whispered.

"I felt very much shaken and disturbed; and after dinner, which I took alone of course, I thought I would go to bed very soon. On my way up, however, I looked into my friend's room for a few minutes. He seemed very bright and eager to talk, and I stayed very much longer than I had intended. I said nothing of what had happened in the church; but listened to him while he talked about the village and the neighbourhood. Finally, as I was on the point of bidding him goodnight, he said something like this:

"'Well, I mustn't keep you, but I've been thinking while you've been in church of an old story that is told by antiquarians about this place. They say that one of St. Thomas à Becket's murderers came here on the very evening of the murder. It is his day, today, you know, and that is what put me in mind of it, I suppose."

"While my friend said this, my old heart began to beat furiously; but, with a strong effort of self-control, I told him I should like to hear the story.

"'Oh! there's nothing much to tell,' said my friend; 'and they don't know who it's supposed to have been; but it is said to have been either one of the four knights, or one of the men-at-arms.'

"'But how did he come here?' I asked, 'and what for?'

"'Oh! he's supposed to have been in terror for his soul, and that he rushed here to get absolution, which, of course, was impossible.'

"'But tell me,' I said. 'Did he come here alone, or how?'

"'Well, you know, after the murder they ransacked the Archbishop's house and stables: and it is said that this man got one of the fastest horses and rode like a madman, not knowing where he was going and that he dashed into the village, and into the church where the priest was: and then afterwards, mounted again and rode off. The priest, too, is buried in the chancel, somewhere, I believe. You see it's a very vague and improbable story. At the Gatehouse at Mailing, too, you know, they say that one of the knights slept there the night after the murder.'

"I said nothing more; but I suppose I looked strange, because my friend began to look at me with some anxiety, and then ordered me off to bed: so, I took my candle and went.

"Now," said the priest, turning to me, "that is the story. I need not say that I have thought about it a great deal ever since: and there are only two theories which appear to me credible, and two others, which would no doubt be suggested, which appear to me incredible.

"First, you may say that I was obviously unwell: my previous depression and dreaming showed that, and therefore that I dreamt the whole thing. If you wish to think that—well, you must think it.

"Secondly, you may say, with the Psychical Research Society, that the whole thing was transmitted from my friend's brain to mine; that his was in an energetic, and mine in a passive state, or something of the kind.

"These two theories would be called 'scientific,' which term means that they are not a hair's-breadth in advance of the facts with which the intellect, a poor instrument at the best, is capable of dealing. And these two 'scientific' theories create in their turn a new brood of insoluble difficulties.

"Or you may take your stand upon the spiritual world, and use the faculties which God has given you for dealing with it, and then you will no longer be helplessly puzzled, and your intellect will no longer overstrain itself at a task for which it was never made. And you may say, I think, that you prefer one of two theories.

"First, that human emotion has a power of influencing or saturating inanimate nature. Of course, this is only the old familiar sacramental principle of all creation. The expressions of your face, for instance, caused by the shifting of the chemical particles of which it is composed, vary with your varying emotions. Thus, we might say that the violent passions of hatred, anger, terror, remorse, of this poor murderer, seven hundred years ago, combined to make a potent spiritual fluid that bit so deep into the very place where it was all poured out, that under certain circumstances it is reproduced. A phonograph, for example, is a very coarse parallel, in which the vibrations of sound translate themselves first into terms of wax, and then re-emerge again as vibrations when certain conditions are fulfilled.

"Or, secondly, you may be old-fashioned and simple, and say that by some law, vast and inexorable, beyond our perception, the personal spirit of the very man is chained to the place, and forced to expiate his sin again and again, year by year, by attempting to express his grief and to seek forgiveness, without the possibility of receiving it. Of course, we do not know who he was; whether one of the knights who afterwards did receive absolution, which possibly was not ratified by God; or one of the men-at-arms who assisted, and who, as an anonymous chronicle says, 'sine confessione et viatico subito rapti sunt.'

"There is nothing materialistic, I think, in believing that spiritual beings may be bound to express themselves within limits of time and space; and that inanimate nature, as well as animate, may be the vehicles of the unseen.

"Arguments against such possibilities have surely, once for all, been silenced, for Christians at any rate, by the Incarnation and the Sacramental system, of which the whole principle is that the Infinite and Eternal did once, and does still, express Itself under forms of inanimate nature, in terms of time and space.

"With regard to another point, perhaps I need not remind you that a thunderstorm broke over Canterbury on the day and hour of the actual murder of the Archbishop."

The Sorrows of the World

As the days went on I became more reassured about my friend. Parker told me there was an improvement since I had come: and the shadow in his eyes seemed a little lightened. On Christmas Eve the Rector called, and they were shut up together in the chapel for an hour after tea; and the old man, I suppose, made his confession. He seemed brighter than ever that evening, and told me story after story after dinner, old tales of when he was a child.

On Christmas morning he celebrated the Holy Mysteries as usual in the chapel, and I received the Communion at his hands. We went to church in the brougham, and that was the last time the old priest was seen in public. There was intense curiosity about him in the village, as well as the greatest reverence and love for him, and I noticed a ripple of interest along the benches as we passed up to the Hall pew.

On the evening of Christmas Day he had provided a Christmas tree in the servants' hall; but we only looked in for a moment when the shouting was at its loudest, and he nodded at a child or two who caught sight of him, and I saw his whole face kindle with joy and tenderness, and then we went back to the fire in the sitting-room.

The morning of St. John's Day broke dark and heavy. We had to have candles at breakfast, and the old man seemed curiously changed and depressed again. He hardly spoke at all, and looked at me almost resentfully, like an overwrought child, when I failed to blow out the spirit lamp at the first attempt.

All day long the gloom outside seemed to gather, the sun went down in a pale sky barred with indigo, and the wind began to rise.

The old man, after a word or two, went to his room soon after dinner, and I understood from Parker, who presently came in, that the master was exceedingly sorry for his discourtesy, but that he did not feel equal to conversation, and intended to go to bed early, and that he would be obliged if I could manage to amuse myself alone that evening. But I too went upstairs early, feeling a little uneasy.

On the top landing of the north end of the house there are three doors: the central one is the chapel door; that on the right, approached by two little steep steps of its own, was the priest's room; that on the left opposite was my own room. As I went in, I noticed that a light shone from under the chapel door, and that his own door was wide open, showing the flickering light of the fire within. As I paused I saw Parker pass across the doorway, and called to him in a low voice.

"Yes, sir; he's fairly well, I think," he answered to my inquiry. "He is in the chapel just now, and is coming to bed directly. He told me just now, sir, too, to ask whether you would serve him tomorrow morning."

"Certainly," I said; "but are you sure he ought to get up? He has not been well all day."

"Well, sir," said Parker; "I will do my best to persuade him to stay in bed, and will let you know if I succeed, but I doubt whether the master will be persuaded."

As I crossed outside the chapel door to go to my own room I heard a murmur from within, with a word or two which I cannot write down.

Before I was in bed I heard the chapel door open, and footsteps go up the little steps opposite, and the door close Presently it opened again; and then a tap at my door.

"It's only me, sir," said Parker's voice. "May I speak to you a moment?" and then he came in with a candle in his hand.

"I'm not easy about him, sir," he said. "But he won't let me sleep in his room, as I asked. I've come to ask you whether you will let me lie down on your sofa. I don't like to leave him. My own room is at the other end of the house. Excuse me, sir, if I've asked what I shouldn't. But I don't like to sleep on the landing for fear he should look out and see me, and be displeased."

Of course, I assented, almost eagerly, for I felt a strange discomfort and loneliness myself.

Parker went noiselessly downstairs and got a rug or two and a pillow, and then, with many apologies, lay down on the sofa near the window. My bed stood at the other end of the long narrow room under the sloping side of the roof. I blew the candles out presently, and the room was in darkness.

I could not sleep at first. I was anxious for my friend, and I lay listened for the slightest sound from the landing. But Parker's face, as I had seen it as he had stood with the candle in his hand, reassured me that he too would be on the watch. The wind had half died down again. Only there came gusts from time to time that shook the leaded windows. Gradually I began to doze, then I suppose I dropped off to sleep, and I dreamed.

In my dream I knew that I was still in my room, lying on my bed, but the room seemed illuminated with a light whose source I could not imagine. The curtains, I thought, were no longer drawn over the

379

windows, but looped back, and the light from my room fell distinctly upon the panes. I thought I was sitting up in bed watching for something at the window, something which would terrify me when it came. And then as I watched there came a gust of wind, and lashed, to judge by the sound, a big spray of ivy across the outside. Then again it came, and again, but the sound grew more distinct. I could see nothing at the window, but there came that ceaseless patter and tap, like a thousand fingers. Then a dead leaf or two was whirled up, stuck for a moment on the glass, and whirled away again. It seemed to me that the ivy-spray and the leaves were clamouring to be admitted into shelter from that wild wind outside. I grew terrified at their insistence, and tried in my dream to call to Parker, whom I fancied to be still in the room, and in the struggle awoke, and the room was dark.

No; as I looked about me it was not quite dark. There lay across the floor an oblong patch of light from the door. I gradually realised that the door was open; there came a draught round the corner at the foot of my bed. I sat up and called gently to Parker. But there was no answer. I got out of bed noiselessly, and went across the floor to where I saw the dim outlines of the sofa. As I drew near I stumbled over a rug, and then felt the pillow, also on the floor. I put my hands almost instinctively down, and felt that the sofa was still warm, but Parker was gone. Then I looked out of the door. The landing was lit by an oil-lamp, and its light fell upon the priest's door. It was almost closed, but I could hear a faint murmur of voices.

I put on my dressing-gown and slippers and went out. Almost simultaneously the door opposite opened a little wider, and Parker's face looked out, white and scared. When he saw me, he came swiftly out and down the stairs, beckoning to me; but as we met, a loud high voice came from the priest's room.

"Parker, Parker! tell him to come in—at once—at once. Don't leave me."

"Go in, sir: go in," Parker said, in a loud whisper to me, pushing me towards the door. I went quickly up the two steep steps and entered, Parker close behind me, and I heard him close the door softly.

There was a tall screen on my left, and behind it was the bed, with the head in the corner of the room: a fire was burning near the bed. I came round the screen quickly, and saw the priest sitting up in bed. He wore a tippet over his shoulders and a small skull-cap on his head. His eyes were large and bright, and looked at me almost unintelligently. His hands were hidden by the bedclothes. There was a little round table by the head of the bed, on which stood two burning candles in silver candlesticks. I drew up a chair by the table and sat down.

"My old friend," I said, "what is it? Cannot you sleep?"

He made no answer to me directly, but stared past me round the room, and then fixed his eyes at the foot of the bed.

"The sorrows of the world," he said, "and the sorrows under the earth. They come to me now, because I have not understood them, nor wept for them."

And then he drew out his old, thin, knotted hands, and clasped them outside the rug that lay on the outside of the bed. I laid my own hand upon them.

"You have had a greater gift than that," I said. "You have known instead the joys of the world."

He paid no attention to me, but stared mournfully before him, but he did not withdraw his hands.

There came a sudden gust of wind outside; and even in that corner away from the window the candle flames leant over to one side, and then the chimney behind me sighed suddenly.

The priest unclasped his hands, and my own hand fell suddenly on the coverlet. He stretched out his left hand to the window as it still shook, and pointed at it in silence, glaring over my head as he did so.

Almost instinctively I turned to the long low window and looked. But the curtains were drawn over it: they were just stirring and heaving in the draught, but there was nothing to be seen. I could hear the pines tossing and sighing like a troubled sea outside.

Then he broke out into a long wild talk, now in a whisper, and now breaking into something like a scream.

Parker came quickly round from the doorway, where he had been waiting out of sight, and stood behind me, anxious and scared. Sometimes I could not hear what the priest said: he muttered to himself: much of it I could not understand: and some of it I cannot bring myself to write down—so sacred was it—so revealing of his soul's inner life hidden with Christ in God.

"The sorrows of the world," he cried again; "they are crying at my window, at the window of a hard old man and a traitorous priest . . . betrayed them with a kiss. . . . Ah! the Holy Innocents who have suffered! Innocents of man and bird and beast and flower; and I went my way or sat at home in the sunshine; and now they come crying to me to pray for them. How little I have prayed!" Then he broke into a torrent of tender prayer for all suffering things. It seemed to me as he prayed as if the wind and the pines were silent. Then he began again:

"Their pale faces look through the glass; no curtains can shut them out. Their thin fingers tap and entreat. . . . And I have closed my heart at that door and cannot open it to let them in. . . . There is the face of a dog who has suffered—his teeth are white, but his eyes are glazed and his tongue hangs out. . . . There is a rose with drenched petals—a rose whom I forgot. See how the wind has battered it. . . . The sorrows of the world! . . . There come the souls from under the earth, crying for one to release them and let them go—souls that all men have forgotten, and I, the chief of sinners. . . . I have lived too much in the sweetness of God and forgotten His sorrows."

Then he turned to a crucifix of ebony and silver that hung on the wall at his side, and looked on it silently. And then again, he broke into compassionate prayer to the Saviour of the world, entreating Him by His Agony and Bloody Sweat, by His Cross and Passion, to remember all suffering things. That prayer that I heard gave me a glimpse into mysteries of which I had not dreamed; mysteries of the unity of Christ and His members, a unity of pain. These great facts, which I thank God I know more of now, stood out in fiery lines against the dark sorrow that seemed to have filled the room from this old man's heart.

Then suddenly he turned to me, and his eyes so searched my own that I looked down, while his words lashed me.

"You, my son," he said, "what have you done to help our Lord and His children? Have you watched or slept? Couldst thou not watch with me one hour? What share have you borne in the Incarnation? Have you believed for those who could not believe, hoped for the despairing, loved and adored for the cold? And if you could not understand nor do this, have you at least welcomed pain that would have made you one with them? Have you even pitied them? Or have you hidden your face for fear you should grieve too much? But what am I that I should find fault?" Then he broke off again into self-reproach.

At this point Parker bent over me and whispered:

"He will die, sir, I think, unless you can get him to be quiet."

The old man overheard, and turned almost fiercely.

"Quiet?" he cried, "when the world is so unquiet! Can I rest, do you think, with those at my window?" Then, with a loud cry, "Ah! they are in the room! They look at me from the air! I cannot bear it." And he covered his face with his old thin hands, and shrank back against the wall.

I got up from my seat, and looked round as I did so. It seemed to my fancy as if there were some strange Presence filling the room. It seemed as I turned as if crowding faces swiftly withdrew themselves over and behind the screen. A picture on the wall overhead lifted and dropped again like a door as if to let something escape. The coverlet, which was a little disarranged by the old man's movement, rippled gently as if someone who had been seated on the bed had risen. I heard Parker, too, behind me draw his breath quickly through his teeth. All this I noticed in a moment; the next I had bent over the bed towards the priest and put my hand on his shoulder. Either he or I was trembling, I felt as I touched him.

"My dear old friend," I said, "cannot you lie down quietly a little? You cannot think how you are distressing us both."

Then I added a word or two, presumptuously, I felt, in the presence of this old man, who knew so much about the Love of God and the Compassion of our Saviour.

Presently he withdrew his hands and looked at me.

"Yes, yes," he said; "but you do not understand. I am a priest."

I sat down again. I tried hard to control a great trembling that had seized me. Still he watched me. Then he said more quietly:

"Is it nearly morning?"

"It is not yet twelve o'clock, sir," said Parker's voice steadily behind me.

"Then I must watch and pray a little longer," said the old man. "Joy cometh in the morning."

Then quite quietly he turned and lifted the crucifix from its nail, kissed it and replaced it. Then he put his hands over his face again and remained still.

The wind outside seemed quieter. But whenever it sighed in the chimney or at the window the priest winced a little, as it a sudden pain had touched him.

He was supported by pillows behind his back and head, against which he leaned easily. After a few minutes of silence his hands dropped and clasped themselves on his lap. His eyes were closed, and he seemed breathing steadily. I hoped that he would fall asleep so. But as I turned to whisper to Parker, I suppose I must have made a slight noise, for when I looked at the servant he paid no attention to me, but was looking at his master. I turned back again, and saw the old man's eyes gazing straight at me.

"Yes," he said; "go and sleep; why are you here? Parker, why did you allow him to come?"

"I woke up and came myself," I said. "Parker did not disturb me."

"Well, go back to bed now. You will serve me in the morning?"

I tried to say something about his not being fit to get up, but he waved it aside.

"You cannot understand," he said quietly. "That is my one hope and escape. Joy cometh in the morning. There are many souls here and elsewhere that are waiting for that joy, and I must not disappoint them. And I too," he added softly, "I too look for that joy. Go now, and we will meet in the morning." And he smiled at me so gently that I got up and went, feeling comforted.

After I had been in bed a little while, I heard the priest's door open and close again, and then Parker tapped at my open door and came in.

"I have left him quiet, sir. I do not think he will sleep, but he would not let me stay."

"Have you ever seen him like this before?" I asked.

"Never quite like this, sir," he said; and as I looked at the old servant I saw that his eyes were bright with tears, and his lips twitching.

"Well," I said, "we have both heard strange things tonight. Your master whom you love is in the hands of God."

The old servant's face broke into lines of sorrow; and then the tears ran down his face.

"Excuse me, sir," he said, "I am not quite myself. Shall I put the candle out, sir?" Then he lay down on the sofa.

"One word more, Parker. You will wake me if you hear anything more. And anyhow you will call me at seven if I should be asleep."

"Certainly, sir," answered Parker's voice from the darkness.

I slept and woke often that night. Each time I woke I went quietly to the door and looked across the landing and listened. Each time I was not so quiet but that Parker heard me and was by me as I looked, and each time there was a line of light under the priest's door; and once or twice a murmur of one voice at least from the room.

Towards morning I fell into a sound sleep, and awoke to find Parker arranging my clothes and setting ready my bath. The rugs and the pillow were gone from the sofa, and there was no sign on the servant's face that anything unusual had happened during the night.

"How is he?" I asked quickly. "Have you seen him?"

"Yes, sir," said Parker; "he is dressing now, and will be ready at half-past seven. It is a little before seven now, sir."

"But, how is he?" I asked again.

"I scarcely know, sir," answered Parker. "He does not seem ill, but he is very silent again this morning, sir."

Then, after a pause, "Is there anything I can do for you, sir?"

"There is nothing more, thank you," I said, and he left the room.

I got up presently and dressed. The morning was still dark, and I dressed by candlelight. When I drew the curtains back the sky had just begun to glimmer in the reflected dawn from the other side of the house; but it was too dark to see to read except by artificial light.

I went out on to the landing, paused a moment, and heard a footstep in the priest's room. Then I opened the door of the oratory and went in.

In the Morning

The oratory is a little room, white-washed, crossed by oaken beams on the walls. The window is opposite the door; and the altar stands to the left. There is a bench or two on the right.

When I entered on this morning the tapers were lighted, the vestments laid out upon the altar, and all prepared. I went across and knelt by the window. Presently I heard the priest's door open, and in a moment more he came in, followed by Parker, who closed the door behind him and came and knelt at the bench. I looked eagerly at the old man's face; it was white and tired-looking, and the eyebrows seemed to droop more than ever, but it was a quiet face. It was only for an instant that I saw it, for he turned to the altar and began to vest: and then when he was ready he began.

It was strange to hear that voice, which had rung with such intensity of pain so few hours before, now subdued and controlled; and to watch the orderly movements of those hands that had twisted and gesticulated with such terrible appeal. I felt that Parker too was watching with a close and awful interest what we both half feared would be a shocking climax to the scenes of the night before, but which we half hoped too would recall and quiet that troubled spirit.

Dawn was now beginning to shine on the western sky. There was a tall holly tree that rose nearly to the level of the window. As I looked out for a moment my eye was caught by the outline of a bird, faintly seen, sitting among the upper branches.

Now I will only mention one incident that took place. I was in such a strange and disordered state of mind that I scarcely now can remember certainly anything but this. As the Priest's Communion drew near there came a sudden soft blow against the window panes. . . .

When the priest began to unvest, I left the chapel and went downstairs to await him in the breakfast room. But as he did not come, I went outside the house for a few minutes, and presently found myself below the chapel window. It seemed to me that I was in a dream—the very earth I trod on seemed unreal. I was unable to think connectedly. The scene in the chapel seemed to stand out vividly. It seemed to me as if in some sense it were a climax, but of what nature, whether triumphant or full of doom, I could not tell.

As I stood there, perplexed, downcast, in the growing glimmer of the day, my eyes fell upon a small rumpled heap at my feet, and looking closer I saw it was the body of a thrush; it was still limp and warm, and as I lifted it I remembered the sudden blow against the window panes. But as I still stood, utterly distracted, the chapel window was thrown open, and Parker's face looked out as I gazed up. He beckoned to me furiously and withdrew, leaving the window swinging.

I laid the thrush under a bush at the corner of the house as I ran round, and came in quickly and up the stairs. Parker met me on the landing.

"He just reeled and fell, sir," he said, "up the stairs into his room. I've laid him on the bed, and must get down to the stables to send for the doctor. Will you stay with him, sir, till I come back?" And without waiting for an answer he was gone.

That evening I was still sitting by my friend's side. I had food brought up to my room during the day, but except for those short intervals was with him continually. The doctor had come and gone. All that he could tell us was that the old man had had a seizure of some kind, and he had looked grave when I told him of the events of the night before.

"His age is against him, too," the doctor had said; "I cannot say what will happen."

And then he had given directions, and had left, promising to return again, any rate the next morning.

I had been trying to read with a shaded lamp, looking from time to time at the figure of the old man on the bed, as he lay white and quiet, with his eyes closed, as he had lain all day.

At about six o'clock, I had just glanced at my watch, when a slight movement made me turn to the bed again, and I could see in the dim light that his eyes were open and fixed upon me, but all the pain was gone out of them, and they were a child's eyes again. I rose and went to his side, and sat down in the same chair that I had occupied the night before. Immediately I had sat down he put out his hand, and

I took it and held it. His eyes smiled at me, and then he spoke, very slowly, with long pauses.

"Well," he said, "you have been with me and have seen and heard, last night and this morning; but it is all ended, and the valley is lightening again at its eastern end where the sun rises. So it was not all dreams and fancies—those old stories that you bore with so patiently to please me. Now tell me what you heard and saw. Did you see them all in the room last night? and—and"—his eyes grew wide and insistent—"what did you see this morning?"

Now the doctor had told me that he must not be over-excited, but soothed; and honestly enough, though some who may read this may not agree with me, I thought it was better to speak plainly of those things so strange to you and me, but so dear and familiar to him. And so, I told him all I had heard and seen.

"Ah!" he said when I had finished, "then we were not quite as one. But still you saw and heard more than most men. Now will you hear one more story? I will not tell you all I saw last night, because the Lord has been gracious to me, and is rising with healing in His wings on me and on many other poor creatures. But the wounds are aching still, and if you will spare me, I will not speak much of the shadows of last night, but only of the joys that came in the morning. Will you hear it?"

"My dear old friend," I said, "are you sure it will not be too much for you?"

He shook his head; and then, still holding my hand in his, his fingers tightening and relaxing as he told his tale, with many pauses and efforts, he began:

"Last night the sorrows of death came to me," he said, "and all the blood and agony and desolation of the whole world seemed to be round me. And I have had so little sorrow in my life that I was ill prepared to meet them. Our Lord has always shown me such grace and given me so much joy. But He warned me again and again this autumn. That was why I spoke to you as I did when you came before Christmas.

"Well, last night, all this came to me. And it seemed as if I were partly responsible. Years ago, I was set apart as a priest to stand between the dead and the living. It was meant that I should be the meeting-place, as every priest must be, of creation's need and God's grace—as every Christian must be in his station. That is what intercession and the Holy Sacrifice both signify and effect. The two tides of need and fulfilment must meet in a priest's heart. But all my life I have known

387

much of fulfilment and little of need. Last night the first was almost withdrawn, and the second deepened almost beyond bearing. But I knew, as I told you last night, that with the morning would come peace—that I should be able to carry up the burden laid on me, and make it one with Him on Whom the iniquities of us all are laid. But I need not say more of that now. This morning when I went to the altar a lull had come in the storm. But it was all in my heart still. I felt sure that I should have the clear vision once more: and as I lifted up the Body of our Lord, it came.

"As I lifted It up It disappeared; as those tell us who look in crystals. And this is what I saw. I do not know how long I saw it, it seemed as if time stood still, but you told me there was no perceptible pause. Well"—and the old man raised himself slightly in the bed—"between my hands I saw a long slope running as it seemed from me downhill. On the nearer higher end of the slope were men going to and fro, and I knew they needed something—and yet many of them did not seem to know it themselves—but they were all in need. One there was who walked quickly, clenching and unclenching his hands, and I knew he fought with sin. And there was a woman with a dead child across her knees; and there was a blind child crying in a corner.

"Then further down the slope were wounded creatures of all kinds, and lonely beasts seeking a place to die, and the very grass of the field seemed to be in sorrow, and there were blind sea-creatures gasping. They were not small, as you might think, but I saw them as if I looked through a hole in a wall.

"And they stretched down, rank on rank, heaving and striving, men and beasts warring and trampling down the flowers. There was a thrush I saw, too, shivering in a tree; and the thought of the story I have told you came to my mind, and there were a thousand things that I forget.

"Now when I saw all this my hands trembled, but what I saw did not tremble, so I knew that it was real. And then very far away and faint at the foot of the slope was a level silvery mist, like a sea-fog, with delicate currents and lines, now swift and piercing, now slow; and in the mist moved faces; but I could not distinguish the features. And these were the souls that waited until their sins should be done away.

"And then with something like terror I remembered that I held in my hands the Body of the Lord. And I was puzzled and distracted, but I knelt to adore, and as I lowered the Holy Thing, the clouds closed and the light died out. And it may be that I was cowardly—and I think

God will pardon an old man for whom the light was too strong—but when I consecrated the chalice, I dared not look at it. At the Communion, too, I closed my eyes again." The old man paused a moment and then continued. "I heard no sound such as you describe. As I unvested and went to my room I was still perplexed at what I had seen, and could not understand it, and then on a sudden I understood it, and it was then I suppose that I fell down."

There was a silence for a moment: then I answered.

"I cannot understand even now."

The priest smiled at me, and his hand closed again on mine.

"I think there is no need for me to tell you that. It will be plain to you soon. Remember what it was that I saw, and where I saw it, and all will be easy.

"You can leave me now for a little," he went on. "I am perfectly free from pain, and I wish to think. Would you send Parker to me in about an hour's time?" And then, as I went towards the door, he added:

"One word more. I had forgotten something. I have yet one more clear vision to see before I die. I have seen, you remember, what you too have seen, how all things need God; but there is yet one more thing to see which will make all plain, and I think you can guess what that is. And I pray that you will be with me when I see it."

Then I turned and went quietly out.

The Expected Guest

As day after day went by and the old man seemed no worse, I began to have hopes that he might recover, but the doctor discouraged me.

"At the best," he said, "he may just linger on. But I do not think the end is far off. You must remember he is an old man." And so, at last the end came.

During these days, since Parker was of course too much occupied with his master, a boy waited on me. On the last evening, as the boy came in for the second time at dinner, he looked white and frightened.

"What is it?" I asked.

"We don't like it, sir, in the servants' hall. Two children ran in just now and said they had seen something, and we are all upset, sir. The maids are crying."

"What was it the children thought they saw?" I asked. The boy hesitated.

"Tell me," I repeated.

The boy put down the dish he held and came closer to me.

"They say they saw the master himself, sir, on the front lawn, at the gate."

"Where were the children?" I asked.

"Passing round from the house, sir, in front, under the chestnut. They had been sent by the rector to inquire."

I got up from the table.

"Where are they?" I asked.

"In the servants' hall, sir."

"Bring them into the sitting-room." And I followed him out and waited. Presently the swing-door opened and the children looked in. Behind them were the pale faces of the servants, whispering and staring.

"Come in," I said to the children, "and sit down. Don't be afraid."

They came timidly in, evidently very much frightened. The door closed behind them.

This was their story.

They had been to the house to inquire how the old man was, and were returning to the rectory. But they had hardly started, in fact had only just reached the chestnut-tree in front of the house, when both of them, who were looking towards the lighted windows, had seen quite plainly the figure of the old priest standing just inside the gate. He was bareheaded, they said, dressed in black, but they could only see his head and shoulders over the bank, as the road is a little lower than the grass which borders on it and runs up to the gate. He seemed, they said, to be looking out for someone. When I asked them how they could possibly see anyone at that distance on such a dark night, they had no sort of explanation; they could only repeat that they did see him quite plainly.

At last I took them out myself, and made them point out to me the place where they had seen it; but, as I expected, all was dark, and we could not even make out the white balls on the pedestals. I took them on to the end of the drive, as they still seemed upset; and they told me there that they would not be frightened to go the rest of the way alone. Fortunately, however, as we waited a man passed in the direction of the village, and he consented to see them as far as the rectory gate.

When I entered the house again the maids with the boy were standing in the hall. They looked eagerly towards the door as I opened it, and one of them cried out.

"What is it now?" I asked. One of the elder servants answered:

"Oh sir, the master's worse. Parker's afraid he's going. He's just run downstairs for you, sir; and now he's gone back."

I did not wait to hear any more, but pushed past them, through the sitting-room, and ran upstairs.

The door of the old man's room was open, and I heard faint sounds from within. I went straight in without knocking, and turned the corner of the screen.

Parker, who was kneeling by the bed, supporting his master in his arms, turned his head as I came in sight, and made a gesture with it. I came close up.

"He's going fast, sir, I'm afraid," he whispered.

The old man was sitting up in bed looking quite straight before him. His lips were slightly parted; and his eyes were full of expectancy. He kept lifting his hands gently, half opening them with a welcoming movement, and then letting them fall. Now he leaned gently forward, as if to meet something with his hands extended, then sinking a little back upon Parker's arm. He paid no attention to me, and it seemed as if his eyes were focused to an almost infinite distance.

I too knelt down by the bed and waited watching him. Then there came soft footsteps at the door, but it was not for that he waited. Then a whispering and a sobbing: and I knew that the servants were gathering outside.

Still he waited for that which he knew would come before he died. And the expectancy deepened in his eyes to an almost terrible intensity; and it was the expectancy that feared no disappointment. It was perfectly still outside, the servants were quiet now, and the old man's breathing was inaudible. Once I heard the far-off bark of a dog away somewhere in the village.

As I watched his face I saw how wrinkles covered it, the corners of his eyes and his forehead were deeply furrowed, and the lines deepened and shifted as his face worked. And then suddenly he cried out: "He is coming, my son, He is coming far away." And then silence.

I heard a sudden movement outside and then stillness again. Then a maid broke out into sobbing: and I heard footsteps, and then the door of my room across the landing open and shut: and the sobbing ceased. But the old man paid no heed. Then suddenly he cried out again:

"Behold He stands at the door and knocks."

He made an indescribable gesture with his hands. Then I was startled, for there came a loud pealing at the bell downstairs.

Parker whispered to me to send one of the servants downstairs: and I went to the door for an instant and told the boy to go: then I came back. The boy's footsteps died away down the staircase. I knelt down again by the bed.

Then once more the old man cried out:

"He is coming, my son. He is here and then, "Look!"

As he said this across his face there came an extraordinary smile; for one moment, as I started up and looked, his face was that of a child, the wrinkles seemed suddenly erased, and a great rosy flush swept from forehead to mouth, and his eyes shone like stars. I noticed too, even at this moment, for I was almost facing him as I sprang up, that the focus of his eyes was contracted to a point at the foot of his bed where the screen stood.

Then he fell back; and Parker laid him gently down.

A moment after footsteps came up the stairs: and the boy whispered from the doorway that the rector had come.

LEONAUR

ALSO FROM LEONAUR

AVAILABLE IN SOFTCOVER OR HARDCOVER WITH DUST JACKET

MR MUKERJI'S GHOSTS *by S. Mukerji*—Supernatural tales from the British Raj period by India's Ghost story collector.

KIPLINGS GHOSTS *by Rudyard Kipling*—Twelve stories of Ghosts, Hauntings, Curses, Werewolves & Magic.

THE COLLECTED SUPERNATURAL AND WEIRD FICTION OF WASH-INGTON IRVING: VOLUME 1 *by Washington Irving*—Including one novel 'A History of New York', and nine short stories of the Strange and Unusual.

THE COLLECTED SUPERNATURAL AND WEIRD FICTION OF WASH-INGTON IRVING: VOLUME 2 *by Washington Irving*—Including three novelettes 'The Legend of the Sleepy Hollow', 'Dolph Heyliger', 'The Adventure of the Black Fisherman' and thirty-two short stories of the Strange and Unusual.

THE COLLECTED SUPERNATURAL AND WEIRD FICTION OF JOHN KENDRICK BANGS: VOLUME 1 *by John Kendrick Bangs*—Including one novel 'Toppleton's Client or A Spirit in Exile', and ten short stories of the Strange and Unusual.

THE COLLECTED SUPERNATURAL AND WEIRD FICTION OF JOHN KENDRICK BANGS: VOLUME 2 *by John Kendrick Bangs*—Including four novellas 'A House-Boat on the Styx', 'The Pursuit of the House-Boat', 'The Enchanted Typewriter' and 'Mr. Munchausen' of the Strange and Unusual.

THE COLLECTED SUPERNATURAL AND WEIRD FICTION OF JOHN KENDRICK BANGS: VOLUME 3 *by John Kendrick Bangs*—Including twor novellas 'Olympian Nights', 'Roger Camerden: A Strange Story', and ten short stories of the Strange and Unusual.

THE COLLECTED SUPERNATURAL AND WEIRD FICTION OF MARY SHELLEY: VOLUME 1 *by Mary Shelley*—Including one novel 'Frankenstein or the Modern Prometheus', and fourteen short stories of the Strange and Unusual.

THE COLLECTED SUPERNATURAL AND WEIRD FICTION OF MARY SHELLEY: VOLUME 2 *by Mary Shelley*—Including one novel 'The Last Man', and three short stories of the Strange and Unusual.

THE COLLECTED SUPERNATURAL AND WEIRD FICTION OF AME-LIA B. EDWARDS *by Amelia B. Edwards*—Contains two novelettes 'Monsieur Maurice', and 'The Discovery of the Treasure Isles', one ballad 'A Legend of Boisguilbert' and seventeen short stories to cill the blood.